As Toreen slumped to the dirt of the alley the killer stood over him, stepped back, and then kicked him, hard against the side of the head, just behind the ear. Once, twice, then again, the booted foot smashed the head with a heavy solid sound.

The killer stopped, and stood there breathing easily while his bright eyes surveyed the alley. Satisfied, he knelt beside the motionless body, pulled something from the palm of his left glove, and curled it slightly before pushing it down into Toreen's bloody, ruined mouth. Then he stood, looked down at his victim, turned, and walked slowly out of the alley . . .

The symbol of retribution the city will never forget

THE PATCH

Cherokee Paul
McDonald

CORGI BOOKS
A Bernard Geis Associates Book

THE PATCH

A CORGI BOOK   0 552 13245 4

First publication in Great Britain

PRINTING HISTORY
Corgi edition published 1987

Copyright © 1986 by Cherokee Paul McDonald

This book is set in Baskerville 10/11 pt

HKY8 1995 MRKT

Corgi Books are published by Transworld Publishers Ltd.,
61–63 Uxbridge Road, Ealing, London W5 5SA,
in Australia by Transworld Publishers (Aust.) Pty. Ltd.,
15–23 Helles Avenue, Moorebank, NSW 2170, and in New
Zealand by Transworld Publishers (N.Z.) Ltd., Cnr. Moselle
and Waipareira Avenues, Henderson, Auckland.

Printed and bound in Great Britain by
Hazell Watson & Viney Limited,
Member of the BPCC Group,
Aylesbury, Bucks

For Christine,
and Pepper too.

For he is the minister of God to thee for good. But if thou do that which is evil, be afraid; for he beareth not the sword in vain: for he is the minister of God, a revenger to *execute* wrath upon him that doeth evil.

—Romans 13:4

Blessed are those
who help the meek
to inherit the earth
by thwarting those
who would inherit the meek,
for they shall be called
  Policemen.

—Anonymous

Prologue

The jungle, like the men hidden in it, waited tense and silent for the dawn. It was the eerie, mystic, lethal time between the night's secrets and the day's confessions. It was as if after another long, black night of stalking terror and trembling hiding and sudden screaming death, the jungle needed a little dew-wet misty time to compose itself for the coming sigh that was the rising of the sun.

The lieutenant was one of six men embracing the jungle in practiced stillness. He watched with detached fascination as a drop of water ran hesitantly along the ridge of a large green leaf inches from his eyes. When it reached the tapered, drooping end of the leaf, it paused, then fell slowly through the heavy hot-wet air until it hit and spread and scattered into many sparkling droplets against the lieutenant's hand and the soot-black stock of his M16 automatic rifle.

The lieutenant was twenty years old and had known war all his life, which had somehow become compressed into the eight months he had been in Vietnam. He realized he had been holding his breath and now released it quietly, his body relaxed even though his mind and senses were alert with a predator's tuned awareness of everything around him. He moved his eyes slowly over the broken black track that was the thin trail through this part of the jungle. He again checked the location of each of his men waiting silently in ambush, knowing he could find them only because he knew where they were. He breathed again and watched as the mist seemed to lose some of its ethereal denseness, rising slowly from the trail and becoming more opaque as it reached the first hanging branches that formed a hollow arch overhead. The solid wet-black night had already gone through the few minutes of darker time, and now, strangely, almost imperceptibly, the gray gauze shadows of dawn let his eyes see an edge here, a curve there. He waited, his body melting into the contours of the soft ground, his jungle fatigues warm-wet beneath him and cool-damp on his back. His body stayed relaxed but warm . . . idling, humming. Waiting.

They came. They were not there, and then they were. Five of them, all armed with AK-47s and SKS rifles, all with packs on their backs and hammock rolls and web belts over their olive-drab pants and pea-green long-sleeved shirts. Each wore some type of headgear, though each was different, and all wore soft leather and rubber-tyre-soled sandals. The one in front had small red tabs on his collar. He carried his AK-47 in a ready position across his chest, one hand on the upper stock and the other resting near the trigger. His face was tense, and his black, glittering eyes never stopped flicking and darting from side to side along the trail. The others came behind him, hurrying to keep up, their eyes on the ground. They had left the perimeter of their main unit only moments before, and they knew they only had to follow the trail for a short distance before they came to the guarded river, crossing that was the first stop on their two-day tour of the many small and large units in the area. The third man behind the leader had the extra pouch. In it were messages, orders, intelligence summaries, trail maps, and supply locations for the various units and teams in the area that had gathered for the upcoming attack on the American base camp at Dak To, in the Central Highlands of South Vietnam.

The leader of the five brushed past a large wet frond and began to slow his pace. He had walked this trail several times this week – he knew he was in a staging area full of friendly troops – and there were no American units reported nearby. But something was wrong. The jungle

8

whispered to him that it held a secret; it whispered danger. The leader stopped and turned to spread his men off the trail.

The lieutenant gathered himself, felt his muscles coil, and threw himself forward and upward with a grunt. His teeth were clenched and his eyes bulged as he lunged powerfully at the leading North Vietnamese Army soldier. He brought his M16 up in a swinging arc, crashing it against the AK-47 and tearing it up and out of the other man's hands. He heard and felt the plastic forestock on the M16 break as it impacted the other weapon, but he ignored it and prepared to bring the barrel of the rifle down across the fear-stretched face of the NVA. He felt rather than saw his men pouncing on the other NVA soldiers at the same time. He knew they were all using their K-bar knives to kill as quickly and silently as possible. Their lives depended on how quietly they could ambush this courier unit; his men, all veterans, loved their knives for this type of situation. He had killed before with his knife, but it was, to him, sloppy and filthy and he had been sickened by it. He chose now to put the NVA leader down with the weight of his rifle. Then he would finish him with his hands.

The NVA leader felt his AK-47 pulling out of his grasp and instinctively lunged to the right to follow it. He gasped as the American's rifle cut savagely downward across his left ear and crashed against his shoulder. He stopped following his rifle downward, brought his left forearm up to deflect the M16 outward, and swung his body and right leg around wickedly, hissing air out between his teeth and grunting as his foot dug into the American's rib cage. The American winced and faltered, and the NVA leapt for the bigger man, getting his hands onto his throat and pushing him backward as he brought his left knee up into the American's groin. The American started to gag as they fell together off the trail, through the thick foliage, and into a small muddy ditch along-side.

The lieutenant felt his fear rising as he fell backward, the steellike fingers digging into his throat. He felt no pain from

9

the kick in the ribs or the knee in the groin; he just knew that they had happened. He was aware only of the fingers in his throat, digging, squeezing, hurting him. He felt the other man's weight on him and stared into the savage, frightened face only inches from his. He tried to bring his rifle up again to hit the man, but his swing was blocked by the NVA's elbow. He thought he could turn the barrel of the M16 enough to fire it point-blank into his side or lower body, but he knew the noise of the weapon could get them all killed. He felt a roaring in his ears and the hot breath of the other man on his face, and he let his fear become his strength as he arched his back, put his weight on his shoulders, dug in with his boots, and threw himself backward, farther into the jungle, the NVA tumbling with him. He came up on top of the NVA leader, whose hands were still at his throat, but whose eyes were now even wider with surprise and fear.

The NVA leader had not been ready for the enormous surge of strength that had carried the American up and over him. Now he was on his back, staring up into the grim face that hung over his. He tried to squeeze the man's throat harder, but the American kept forcing his chin down against his chest, arching his back at the same time. The NVA leader felt his grip loosening at the same time he heard the American grunt, and then the evil, black M16 was across his own throat, the American was leaning on it with both strong arms, the NVA leader felt himself gagging and choking, and he kicked his feet and tore at the other man's throat with his fingers, but the M16 became heavier and he felt his head being pushed down into the mud. And then he couldn't tell if he still gripped the American's throat or not, and then he couldn't remember why he was there, and the terrible face of the American faded away, and then . . .

The lieutenant sucked his breath into his lungs in shuddering gasps, the sweat from his face mixing with the blood from his torn throat and falling in heavy pink drops against the horribly grinning face of the NVA leader. The roar in his ears gradually subsided, and he heard the silence of the jungle enveloping him. He kept the pressure on the throat of

10

the NVA as he took slow, deep breaths and calmed himself. Suddenly there was a rustling behind him, and the sweaty, tight face of one of his men pushed through the foliage and stared at him. He stared back and nodded his head when the man whispered, 'You all right, Lieutenant?' Shakily he got to his knees beside the body of the NVA leader. Then he lurched up and climbed back onto the trail to join his men.

The NVA soldiers were sprawled dead along the trail, throats gaping, eyes staring sightlessly at the jungle canopy. The squad sergeant had quickly searched them all until he found the pouch full of papers and maps that they had come for. He stood in the hush of a shocked jungle, in the body-littered trail, and nodded triumphantly at the lieutenant. He put the pouch into his own pack, saw that the men had collected their gear and were ready, and reached into his pocket and brought out a couple of pieces of cloth. He looked at the lieutenant questioningly.

The lieutenant looked into the sergeant's young-but-oh-so-old eyes and nodded. The sergeant kneeled beside one of the NVA bodies and stuffed something into the unresisting mouth. He then moved quickly to another body and did the same. Some of the other men took pieces of the cloth from the sergeant and went to the other bodies and knelt beside them until they were finished.

The lieutenant watched. He knew his men would not pull out their knives now, they would not cut parts off the dead enemy as others sometimes did. His men did not take ears, but still they left a sign. The lieutenant looked at the body of the NVA soldier nearest him on the trail. He looked into the glazed eyes and into the slack mouth. He stared at the unit patch stuck between the teeth. The small cloth patch was not one of those camouflage black-on-green patches, either. No, it was a stateside PX patch with the colors and the white border and, in the middle, the sword. It was the insignia patch of the unit that sent him and his squad out to intercept these NVA couriers. The patch of *his* unit.

They had hidden, waiting in the darkness, and then they had killed, and now they left a sign for their enemy. They

11

left a sign so the brothers of these NVA dead would know who had done the killing. As the boys they used to be, they left the sign as a challenge, as a proud symbol of who they were. As the old men they had become, they left the sign as a warning and, in some abstract way, as a symbol of the reasoning behind the quiet, violent deaths in the awakening jungle.

The sergeant moved back along the trail to stand beside the lieutenant. The lieutenant held out his hand, and the sergeant gave him one of the small colorful pieces of cloth. The lieutenant turned and climbed down off the trail and into the jungle where the NVA leader lay. He stood over him briefly, looking into the dead face. Then he jammed the unit patch into the grinning mouth and turned away to join his men.

Chapter One

Patrolperson Roxanne 'Rocky' Springfield sat in the darkness and tried not to fidget. She and her partner had been sitting in their patrol car for almost ten minutes now, and she was not very good at waiting. She had been told by older cops that stakeouts were a big part of the job, that it was important to learn how to relax, to be patient, and still be ready when it was time. But she hated it, always had, and sitting in the dark, in a beat-up patrol car, in a smelly alley, waiting for the hastily thrown together trap to be sprung, was driving her crazy. She glanced at her partner, saw that he still slumped down behind the wheel with his head back and his eyes closed, and wondered again about the deal they were part of.

Normally they would have ended their shift at midnight, but tonight, as they headed for the station, they were told to meet a Tactical Squad sergeant and some TAC officers behind a Mormon church in the south end of the city. Fort Lauderdale had been quiet that night, and their shift had gone by with no real problems. Still, her partner had been annoyed, bitching as he swung the car around and crossed back over the Third Avenue Bridge.

Springfield had been excited but kept quiet after seeing how her partner had reacted. The TAC Squad was a special felony squad that handled all the 'heavy' stuff: stakeouts, robbery surveillance, in-progress crimes, and big narcotics deals, and it was rare for them to call for assistance from the patrol units.

The meeting behind the church had been brief and tense.

13

There were only two TAC officers there and a sergeant. When her partner parked the cruiser and they climbed out, she saw one of the TAC guys look at her and then at his partner and roll his eyes. She stood five-four and weighed one hundred and twelve, and she was a relatively new police officer, just nearing the end of her first-year probation period. As they walked over to an unmarked TAC unit to be briefed, she heard one of the TAC officers, a ten-year cop who stood six-two and weighed two hundred and twenty pounds, made up mostly of muscle, teeth, and knuckles, mumble to the sergeant, 'Well, we got half a patrol unit, anyway.'

The sergeant had shrugged and briefed them. 'Look, McShaun . . . uh, Springfield . . . here it is . . .' The sergeant rubbed his eys. 'This is a fluke, we think, but I got a feeling it's gonna go down. I don't have even half of my people tonight, and I need a marked unit. A little earlier a citizen spotted a couple of guys we been watchin' on and off for a while. Real badasses. They go into houses at night, ski masks and guns, pistol-whip the people in the house, usually old ladies, take what they can, and get out. We haven't been able to make them on any yet, but we're pretty sure they're good for one homicide from a couple of days ago. Anyway, citizen sees these guys snoopin' around a house in the dark – two old ladies live there. Then the two guys leave, slow. I got a feelin' they're comin' back tonight, so I put a couple of my guys inside the house with the old ladies. I've got these guys here to cover the front and move in when the inside guys give the word. And what I need is for you guys, uh, officers, to wait in the alley behind the place and move in to cover the rear when it goes down. I'll be floating around trying to cover what's left. I got no description, 'cept they're white guys and they got an old beat-up car.'

The sergeant waved the two TAC officers toward their car and turned toward his. He looked back at McShaun and said, 'Badasses, McShaun. Both carry guns and probably won't hesitate to use 'em. Be careful.'

Timothy McShaun felt his partner glance at him as she fidgeted around. He kept his eyes closed and stayed slumped against the seat as he thought of her sitting in the patrol car with him, excited and vibrating with anticipation about this trap they were part of. Oh, boy, real police work. I mean a real stakeout – and with the TAC squad! He sighed and thought, Shit. He had been trying to get into the station early tonight because he was supposed to meet a girl from the Records division at her apartment when he got off duty. It would have been the first time they had spent any time together under the right circumstances, and he had been ready for it. Then the lieutenant had called the sergeant, and the sergeant had called him and his little split-tailed partner, and here they were, sitting in an alley in the dark because TAC squad couldn't keep their shit together. What a pain in the ass.

He shifted slightly in his seat and again felt his partner glance over at him. Springfield, Rocky Springfield. The first time he heard some of the other guys talking about her, he told them her name sounded like either a prizefighter or a rock and roll star. Roxanne, that was her name, but he suspected she billed herself as Rocky to better fit into this man's world of police work.

Typical.

He thought about how he came to be riding with her in the first place. He and his regular partner, Chick Hummel, had been broken up by the sergeant so that two officers coming off probation, Springfield and a young black cop named Greg Hammer, could have a final check-over by older guys in the squad. Hammer went with Hummel, and McShaun got Springfield. The sergeant let him know that she was sharp, her ratings were good, and she was probably ready to make it on her own. The couple of weeks with him was just a formality, but that didn't make him feel any better.

McShaun sat up and ran his fingers through his short light brown hair. He looked at his watch; twelve thirty-four in the A and M. Damn. He looked at Springfield and saw her gray-green eyes watching him. Nice eyes, he thought, most of the time gray, but once in a while a surprise of intense green. He looked away, out of the windshield and into the dark alley. She had dark brown curly hair cut fairly short. He liked the way it was shaped around her head and remembered her telling one of the dispatchers that it wasn't permed. Nope, it was naturally curly. The dispatcher and all the other women in the room had made noises of envy and approval, and he turned away and rolled his eyes at the old communications sergeant, who just shook his head. But still, her hair did look cute, and it stayed neat no matter what kind of shift they were having.

Yeah, neat, that's another thing he liked about her. McShaun had a reputation for being neat and staying neat. His uniform was always sharp and clean, and his brass was always shined. He had had more than one partner laugh with the other guys in telling how they had been in some knock-down drag-out brawl in the back room of some smelly bar, and when it was all over and the entire world had been arrested and they were all standing up and brushing themselves off, there was old McShaun, looking like he had just stepped out of a recruiting poster even though he had been in the thick of the kicking and biting as usual.

He slumped down again, his ear still tuned to the quiet radio, and thought about the way she looked, trim and tight and fit in her uniform. A lot of new cops looked like kids trying to wear their daddy's clothes, awkward and floppy. She wore her uniform as if she knew what she was doing. It always looked neat and sharp. She looked right too. Good legs, smooth-firm arms, a flat stomach, nice shape to her breasts, a tight little ass. Hell, as far as he could tell, she looked very fine. But, he reminded himself, partners are not made of ass alone. No, there has to be more.

The radio bubbled with one of the TAC men checking in negative with the sergeant. McShaun saw Springfield's head hunch to the left as she tried to hear what was coming from the speaker clipped to her uniform shirt. He thought, Let's see, she had a degree in the social sciences but had never really come on to him with it – none of that holier-than-thou crap. In fact, he remembered her laughing once when he asked her about it. She had said she had worked through the degree with the intent of 'saving the world'. And she was pretty much on the ball, he had to give her that. Her paperwork was good and she wasn't lazy; didn't mind doing a little extra if it was necessary. Not a bad working partner really, he thought, except for that one thing.

She was a girl.

He had been a street cop for eight years. He was smart, tough, and aggressive. He had been in the military before becoming a cop, and he knew how to take care of himself. He believed, like most police officers who were trying to survive, that while it was best to get the job done without getting physical, once in a while, no matter what kind of a cop you were, you would find yourself in a situation that required a physical solution. He knew this, and he had been in enough scrapes to bear it out. In fact, he thought grudgingly, that was one of his 'problems,' according to the brass: just a little too quick with his hands sometimes. Well, maybe, but he knew for sure that even though he was tough and experienced, he still came across those situations where being five-eight and one hundred and fifty-five pounds was barely enough. What about this sharp, educated, dedicated, well-trained little girl sitting here? How would she act when the shit *really* hit the fan? He grunted and thought about what it would be like to have her for a partner in the northwest section on Saturday night when things turned into a head-busting contest between the bricklayers and the stevedores at Bradley's Bar on Fifth Street. He looked at Springfield and thought, Riiight.

Springfield saw her partner look at her and looked down and straightened an already straight crease in her uniform blouse. She heard him grunt and look away. She thought about him. At thirty, four years older than her, and not a bad-looking man. He had a nice tight body – she smiled a little in the dark – and nice buns and a good face, although

17

she thought he looked too serious most of the time. She was sure there was a softness behind those hard brown eyes. He was hard, all right, and he almost vibrated with an energy level that seemed to envelop him and anyone near him.

She thought of how he had treated her as a field training officer. At first she had secretly resented having to ride with another training officer. She had been on the job almost a year and felt pretty self-confident. She felt she knew the job and could take care of herself. When her sergeant had called her in a week ago, she thought he was going to tell her she could hit the road solo. She had had trouble hiding her disappointment when he told her she had one more training officer to work with.

At first McShaun had acted as if he resented having her for a partner. She knew he watched her very closely while they were out on the street. She had to admit, though, that he hadn't pulled any of that 'male' crap. He hadn't made the cute comments or treated her with a condescending, big-brother kindness. He hadn't praised her for no reason, and he hadn't put her down for no reason either. He had been fair with her, had played it straight. He hadn't asked her about boyfriends or affairs or steered the conversation toward the latest sex crimes.

In fact, McShaun had almost made it a point of keeping it business only. He would work with her with his usual intensity through the shift, guiding her, teaching her, critiquing her, and when the shift was over, he'd say, 'See you tomorrow,' and that would be that. She admitted to herself that she wanted to see him off duty, as a person, maybe as a friend, to learn about him as a man. She wanted to see him in a nonpolice mode, although she suspected he probably never was in a nonpolice mode.

Rocky looked out the window into the shadows in the alley and made a face. *Watch it*, she thought, *that's just what you've been working so hard to avoid since you came to this department. Remember? You made yourself a promise: no cops for boyfriends, no interdepartmental relationships. That's what they're looking for.* She knew she wasn't bad-looking, and she knew she attracted men, and she knew she was attracted to men, and she knew that as a female officer in a male department she would really have to watch it, even if she was tempted. Boys will be boys will be boys, and she kept her relationships, fewer and fewer though they might be, out in the world of civilian men. She just didn't need the hassle.

She sighed and yawned, getting tired. The original nervous excitement about being on this stakeout was fading. She felt worn and dirty and wished she could take a long shower and have a nice cup of hot tea. She closed her eyes, listened for a few seconds to the silent radio, and thought of him. Timothy Stephen McShaun. She'd heard some of the older guys call him 'TS', or 'Tough Shit', but most people called him Tim. Tim seemed like such a gentle name to her, but then she thought about how he moved on the street, how he worked with the people, how he always seemed locked and loaded, ready to pounce. He was intelligent and well read. He wasn't one of those noncerebral dinosaur cops that she had pictured as the enemy while she was in college . . . but still. He had that underlying core of potential violence in him – she could feel it – and he used physical means as often and as competently as he used the other, more mental tools of his trade. She looked at him slumped behind the wheel, relaxed, with his eyes closed, and thought, A complex man for sure. Complex, maybe dangerous, and very, very interesting.

The night paused, suddenly silent in anticipation, and although nothing had been said on the radio and there had been no visible movement or furtive sound, McShaun tensed and sat up. He reached over and quietly pulled the 12-gauge Remington 870 pump shotgun out of the bracket and said evenly, with a sureness that was eerie, 'Get ready.'

Springfield had heard and seen nothing, and she knew the TAC officers in the house had been silent, but she saw how McShaun was coiling, and she heard his voice, and she sat up and felt herself tightening in anticipation of the unknown.

19

The soft hiss of static on the radio was broken by the voice of the TAC officer in the rear hallway of the house. 'They're here . . . at the back door. I can hear 'em working on the lock. . . . Wait. Okay, get ready . . .'

McShaun silently opened his door and climbed out with the shotgun, motioning for Springfield to follow. The two outside TAC officers would try to cover the front of the house and be ready to charge inside to help their partners. McShaun and Springfield were to leave their unit and walk through the rear alley to the back of the house. There they were to hide and wait and come in when needed.

Springfield ran behind her partner, hurrying to keep up, running awkwardly, trying to keep her equipment from jiggling and creaking and bouncing all over the place. She carried her three-cell flashlight in her left hand. Her right hand rested lightly on the wooden grips of her Smith and Wesson Model 19 .357 Magnum in the holster on her right hip. Her eyes were open wide, and she felt the morning air cool the line of perspiration on her upper lip. As she ran behind McShaun she could see him move through the night shadows with a fluid certainty. He looked back at her only once, the nearby hedges and bushes throwing splotched shadows across his face, making his bright eyes seem more intense than usual. Suddenly he stopped, crouched, and pointed to a corner of the alley and a wooden fence. He made hand motions, and she nodded and duck-walked to her position. She crouched down and leaned her left shoulder against a telephone pole. She was completely hidden in the dark clutter of the pole, the bushes, the fence, and a couple of garbage cans. McShaun checked her position from where he was and was satisfied to hear the muted click of her holster snap as she drew her weapon.

They were ready.

The night split with hoarse yells, two loud explosions, and then screams. The back door of the house suddenly crashed open, and out they came, two figures wearing ski masks and carrying guns. One was limping slightly as he broke to his left and ran across the backyard toward the alley. Springfield was frozen in her crouch as she saw McShaun spin with incredible speed with the shotgun held across his chest. She knew he had moved to his right in the dark, but then he was gone. She looked at the yard again and saw the other ski-masked figure running right at her but looking to his left.

McShaun slid to a stop at the edge of the alley and the yard, came up from his crouch, and lunged forward, bringing the shotgun up to his left shoulder and pointing it at the limping thief running right at him. He saw the eyes widen behind the holes in the ski mask, and he saw the .45 automatic in the man's right hand start to come up in an arc. McShaun planted his feet and fired the 12 gauge. As the buckshot slashed into the man's chest and stomach he started screaming and his pistol went off. The knowledge that even a dying man can kill you flashed through McShaun's mind as he pumped the shotgun and fired again. The first blast had straightened the man up as he ran; the second caught him in the face. The ski mask ballooned, and the thief flew backward with his arms swinging out to his sides. He hit the wet grass like a rumpled doll and was still. McShaun stood motionless, pointing the warm shotgun at the figure lying in the grass. Then he whirled to his left and started running hard when he heard the yells, followed by two shots, back where he had positioned his partner.

Springfield had leapt up and pointed her revolver at the man running across the yard toward her and had started to shout, 'Halt, police!' when the terrible roar of McShaun's shotgun crashed through the darkness. She heard the screams, and then the man she was pointing her gun at lifted his pistol and fired at her. Bam! Bam! And she saw the red-orange globs sail past her head. Then the man wheeled to his right and jumped the fence at the edge of the yard. As his feet hit the ground she had the barrel of her revolver pointed right at the small of his back. He started running, and she again yelled, 'Halt! Halt! Police!' But he didn't even slow down. He was quickly cutting out of her line of vision in the darkness as she sighted along the barrel and lined up her sights in his back. She hesitated.

Doubt.

Should she?

Could she?

Was it . . . right?

And the man as gone, and she was staring into an empty yard with nothing to shoot at. She stood there, braced, and noticed that her hands held her weapon steady; they did not shake and her breathing was even.

She was startled by McShaun, who came running out of the darkness with his shotgun tight in his hands. His eyes were glowing and his face was stretched tight as he hissed, 'You all right, Springfield?' She nodded, and he yelled at one of the TAC officers, who came running around from the front of the house. 'I wasted one! The other one's running south through the yards!'

The officer waved and yelled, 'Okay, we're on the radio now. Other patrol units are moving in and they're trying to get a K-9 unit over here too! You guys okay?' Then he was gone.

One of the other TAC officers came out of the house and walked slowly over to the far corner of the yard where the body lay. McShaun turned his head and stared quietly at Springfield.

She held steady under his gaze.

He pointed silently, and she turned around and saw two cruel gouges cut out of the black wood of the telephone pole where the bullets from the thief's gun had impacted. She stood still while he slowly reached out with one hand and gently brushed a twig from the fringe curls of her hair on the left side of her face. Then he turned away and walked back across the yard.

Chapter Two

McShaun walked across the yard to where the TAC officer was standing by the body. The officer said, 'We waited until they were into the living room and then braced 'em. They just turned and ran. My partner got a couple of quick shots off and hit this one in the upper leg somewhere. He must have been limping when he came across the yard.'

McShaun nodded, and the TAC officer went on. 'Took a shot at you with his .45, huh? Well, you sure enough ruined his whole night with that 12 gauge.'

McShaun nodded again and looked down at the body laying spread out on its back. The .45 automatic lay in the grass a few inches from the fingers of the right hand. He looked at the wet, distorted mass covered with the cloth of the ski mask and gently prodded the dead man's right leg with the toe of his shoe. He didn't hear Springfield walk up behind him as he said quietly, 'Oh, by the way, halt. Police.'

The activity in the rear yard of the house increased rapidly. The TAC sergeant got there quickly after it went down and started coordinating things. The K-9 team arrived, and the dog immediately started dragging the handler through the dark yards. The handler was gone only a few seconds when he came on the radio and advised the other units that he had found a ski mask and a pair of gloves and, a few minutes later, the gun. A couple of homicide detectives showed up, as did the shift lieutenant and the captain. To add to the general confusion, in the yard were the other TAC officers. Patrol officers came and went, and the brass and detectives stood around the body, staring. The two elderly women who lived in the house were being interviewed in their living room. Things were slowly coming under control. During all of this McShaun and Springfield stood waiting a few feet away from the crowd.

Springfield listened to the reports from the patrol units on the radio as they continued to search for the suspect who had fled. She was filled with doubt, nervous about what would be said, afraid she would be criticized for letting the suspect get away from her. The cold silence of McShaun standing beside her did not help.

Finally, when all the brass and detectives had assembled around the body, they were called over by the sergeant, who said, 'Hey, McShaun, give us a quick rundown on what happened, okay?'

In a steady voice McShaun told them about the alert call from the TAC officer, and the moving in, and the shots in the house, and the suspects breaking out the back, and the confrontation in the yard. He spoke very clearly when he told of how the suspect had fired at him and of how he had killed him.

There was a silence when he finished. Then the captain said, 'This isn't the first one for you is it, Tim? You shot one last year in a robbery, didn't you?'

McShaun nodded. He knew the captain knew damn well he had killed a robbery suspect last year. He had shot him in the back and killed him, and he had been found justified by the Grand Jury even though he had been crucified by the local media. He looked at the captain now and thought, No, this isn't the first one. The sergeant looked at the captain as he said, 'Well, this looks like a righteous shooting to me. I'd say you did a good job here, Tim.'

Others spoke up then.

'Yeah, TS, you done good, man.'

'Nice shooting if you ask me . . . took him clean out.'

'Way to go, Tim.'

Then they looked at Springfield.

'McShaun, what about the other suspect? How did he get

away?' the captain asked as he stared at Rocky.

Springfield started to say something but was cut off by some of the men. 'Shit. That other asshole shoulda been wasted too.'

'Yeah. He came out shooting too. Shoulda blown him away.'

'Pretty hard to see how he managed to jump that fence and split like that if you ask me.'

Before Springfield could answer the captain, the radio crackled and one of the patrol units came on and said they were pretty sure they had the suspect in custody. They'd found him cutting through some yards near one of the main roads in the area. He was unarmed, of course, but was sweating heavily and not sure of his answers. When the K-9 unit was brought to him, the dog had to be restrained by its handler.

The lieutenant looked at Springfield and said, 'I know you can't ID his face because of the ski mask, but you remember what he was wearing, right? Color of his shirt and pants, right?'

Springfield nodded and tried to think of the colors. Light? Or dark? She looked at the ground and nodded.

McShaun said, 'Look, Lieutenant, she'll ID him as best she can. We'll do our report and it will be right. We can put him at the scene and we've got enough to charge him with all the felonies in the world, including attempted murder of a police officer.'

The lieutenant started to reply but was interrupted by the captain, who said, 'Fine, fine. It will be done right. What I still want to know is, why did the other suspect get away in the first place? Springfield, you were fired on by that guy. Was it a shooting situation or not?'

Again came the chorus of voices.

'Hell, if it had been me, I'da blown his shit away.'

'You better believe it . . . could have given him all six with no problem.'

'Yeah . . . she just got scared, that's all.'

Springfield felt her face redden as she said, 'I yelled for

him to halt. He shot at me and then ran. I saw his back . . . I
. . . yelled at him . . . I—'

Everyone started to speak at once, then stopped when
McShaun said savagely, *'Hold it!* Just hold it for a minute.'
He looked slowly around at the group of faces, men he
worked with, some he respected more than others, and he
looked into the tired face of the lieutenant and the accusing
face of the captain and said, 'None of you swinging dicks
was here. *We were.* When it went down, there was just me
and her, and I had my hands full with this crud here. How
many of you guys been shot at from close range, huh? She
was shot at and she recovered and she had a fleeting target
and she had a target that was running through a residential
backyard with an occupied house behind him and she had
two TAC guys who she knew were coming from the front of
the house and who might be in her line of fire without her
knowing it.' He glared at them. There was silence except for
the sound of breathing.

Rocky was staring at him as he went on. 'She sized it up
and made a decision and there it is. The guy is in custody,
none of the wrong people got hurt, and *there it is.* She did
what she thought she should do, and she was in a position
that her partner, *me,* put her in. So *leave it.* Sometimes you
shoot and sometimes you don't.'

There was awkward silence for a moment. Then the captain cleared his throat and said, 'Yes, okay. Well, let's let
the crime-scene boys do their thing and we can all get out of
here before the sun rises maybe.' He and the lieutenant
turned and walked off, talking together in low tones.

Later, when the crime-scene team had almost finished,
they were ready to take a couple of photos of the dead suspect without the ski mask. All of the officers who were still
there stood by curiously, and a couple called to McShaun,
who stood quietly in the alley. He shook his head and waited
with his back turned. Springfield, drawn somehow to the
scene, left him and stood with the small crowd around the
body. She felt revulsion mixed with a macabre fascination
and wonder. She didn't want to watch but she had to. When

they slowly pulled the soggy ski mask off the destroyed face and misshapen skull, several of the officers turned away. But she didn't – she watched – and she would not be sick in front of the others. She would not be sick until later, when she was alone.

Timothy McShaun walked out the back door of the Fort Lauderdale police station on Broward Boulevard at nine that morning. After he and Springfield had driven into the station from the scene of the shooting and had turned in their unit, they went to work with the Detective Division, compiling the official paperwork. Since a homicide was involved, the Detective Division would do most of the work in this case, coordinating the reports from TAC squad with the reports and statements from McShaun and Springfield. McShaun and Springfield had to do their supplements to TAC squad's original report, they had to do use-of-force forms, and they had to give statements to a homicide detective. Before it was all over, McShaun would be investigated and tried in the shooting death of the armed burglar by a departmental firearms review board, the chief's office, the Broward County Grand Jury, and all the local newspapers and television news shows.

McShaun drove to his apartment, squinting in the sunlight, tired and gritty. Once at his apartment he fed his loudly protesting cat, Radar, took a shower, made a quick breakfast of eggs and tea, and was in bed by ten o'clock. He was sinking into a fitful sleep by a quarter after ten when the phone rang.

'Huh . . . hello?'

'Yes, Officer McShaun?'

'Yeah . . . yes, what . . . ?'

'Officer McShaun, this is Ben Seever at the State Attorney's office. I got your number from the liaison office, told them I needed to talk to you directly about the Simmons case.'

'What?'

'The Simmons case, Officer. Remember the Simmons case? It might go to trial today.'

'Uh . . . Simmons . . . I thought you guys worked a deal with his lawyer.'

'Yes, well, apparently they've now decided to push it to the limit. It may very well go to trial today, and I've got to be sure you're available if it does. Without you putting Simmons at the scene, we've got no case.'

'Put him at the scene? For chrissake, I took him outta the fuckin' building, didn't I? Shit.'

'Yes, Officer McShaun. Yes, you did. It's a good case, no problem. Anyway, I'll call you later one way or the other.'

'Yeah, All right, I'll be here tryin' to get some sleep.'

'Still sleeping, Officer? My, you must have had a hell of a night.'

Seever hung up, chuckling, and McShaun dropped the phone into its cradle and rolled over in the bed. He went back to sleep. At eleven o'clock the phone rang again. It rang twelve times, although McShaun thought he answered it on the third ring.

'Hello?'

'Mister . . . um, Officer McShaun? This is Phyllis Green from the *Fort Lauderdale Herald*. I'd like to ask you a couple of quick questions on that killing last night.'

Who? *The Herald?* Listen, how did you get my home number? It's an unpublished number.'

'Yes. Can you tell me if the gun the suspect allegedly had was registered to him? Can you tell me what the police officers were arguing about while they stood over the body of the murdered man? Can you tell me why he was shot *twice* with a 12-gauge shotgun. Wouldn't one shot have been enough? Do you feel it was easier to kill this suspect because you had done it already last year and were cleared on that one by the Grand Jury . . . ?'

All Phyllis Green heard was the buzzing of the line. McShaun had already hung up.

Then again, a little after noon, the phone rang and rang. Finally he fumbled for it and spoke hoarsely. 'Yeah?'

'Officer McShaun? This is Mr. Seever's secretary. He's gone to lunch, but he wanted me to call and tell you that the, um, Simmons case is *not* going today. He says you can forget about it. All right? Have a nice day. Bye.'

'Right.'

McShaun slowly climbed out of his disheveled bed, went to the bathroom, came back and unplugged the phone, and fell back into the sweaty sheets, observed only by a disapproving Radar.

He dozed and rolled around until just after two o'clock in the afternoon, then sat up with a curse and threw the sheets away from him. He stared at Radar for a moment, then slowly got up and padded out to the small living-kitchen-dining room of the one-bedroom apartment. He let Radar out and stood naked in front of the open refrigerator for a few minutes. Then he reached in, grabbed a quart of orange juice, and drank in several large gulps of the cold liquid. He put it back, closed the door, looked out the window at the beautiful sun-shiny day, and said, 'Hello, world.'

McShaun took a long shower, made his bed, put on a pair of shorts, made a cup of tea with sugar and milk, and sat down on the floor in his living room with his back against the couch. His mind felt fogged and unclear, and he struggled to make the pictures sharp as he tried to think of the night before, and then of the days and weeks and months and years before that. He settled back with his tea and let his mind wander.

He had come home from Vietnam in 1969. He had come home in the face of his country's disapproval, but it hadn't bothered him. He did not resent the protestors or the draft dodgers or the kids who had fled to Canada. He felt it was their right; he felt that his country was made up of just those kinds of rights and he had no problem with it. He also felt that what he and the others in the military had tried to do there was just. They had done the right thing but had gone about it the wrong way.

The only bitterness he held was toward those who initiated and directed the war. Once the decision was made to have a war, they should have had a *war,* not the silly, restricted, deadly charade they had had. McShaun's bitterness stemmed from the feeling of being hamstrung by his own brass and government, who did not really comprehend what was going on out in the field. They wanted McShaun and the other young soldiers to do a job, but then they kept them from doing the job with an unbelievably complicated set of 'rules'. Rules? In a *war*?

McShaun had done the best he could do, and he'd come home and tried to get back into a normal life. He resented those Vietnam veterans who were always on the news crying about this and that. It embarrassed him. Oh, he knew there were guys with legitimate problems; trauma cases; breakdowns; cripples, both mental and physical. What bothered him were the more and more publicized cases of some poor Vietnam veteran who had finally 'lost it' and hurt or killed someone and then threw himself in front of the cameras crying about how it was all the fault of that 'terrible war'. Agent orange, nightmares, combat fatigue . . . Shit, he had been there, in the bush, as a grunt, and he had come home – even if some good friends had not. It had been a bad war and he had fought it, and now he was home and that's all there was.

After almost a year of bumping around doing nothing, wandering, he had decided it was time to get into the mainstream again. He married a girl he had dated before he went into the army, and he joined the Fort Lauderdale Police Department. The girl had been his first serious girlfriend before he had gone off to the war. He was pretty sure he loved her, and they were very comfortable with each other. They had an excellent physical relationship and did a lot of sports activities together and laughed a lot. He married her because he felt it was time, time to settle down with a woman, to get a good job, to make a life. His wife had been working as a cocktail waitress for a while and now wanted to go to college so that she could eventually be a teacher. He married her and promised to put her through college. He would work and she could go to school.

He was attracted to the police department for various

reasons. He had tried many different jobs while wandering and had found all of them dull, with no real challenge, no real charge. He wanted something that gave him a reason for being there, something that counted, something that would test him as a man and as a person. The thought of wearing a gun to work every day and the thought of having the power to make controlling decisions and the courage to take responsibility intrigued him. He had lived in Fort Lauderdale all of his life and knew the city well. The police department was a civil service job; it had benefits, it paid reasonably well, and it was a respected position in the community. He would be a participant, not an observer. He could do things that had an affirmative effect on people's lives. He could help.

McShaun's mind came back to the present as he stared at the small clock on the bookshelf. He stood up and stretched and said, 'Right'. He thought, Yeah, help. That's what I was trying to do, and I guess that's what I'm still trying to do. Help. Only now I'm divorced because she thought that everything that had to do with being a cop was 'stupid', all of my cop friends were stupid, and I was stupid for being a cop who tried so hard. Yeah, the more she went to school and became more and more immersed in the academic womb and more and more liberal, the more stupid I was and the more stupid was the job I did. She never tried to see it my way, wouldn't let herself see it from a different perspective. So, okay, we're divorced and good-bye and good luck. A good clean break.

And not only that – the job. I'm still on the job and I'm still trying to believe in it after all the bullshit and unfairness and apathy and deceit I've seen. I'm still trying to do the job like I know in my heart it should be done, even though I know that my bosses see me as a danger to their image, my peers see me as a cop who should be old enough to know better, and the people of this lovely town see me as an aloof, inconsiderate, brutal, racist pig – until they need me.

He looked at the clock again and walked into the bedroom to put on his uniform. He had to go to work in time for the late-evening shift briefing. If he hurried, he could make it. As he dressed he looked at himself in the mirror. He saw more gray around his temples, and his eyes looked hard and old, even to him. His body looked fit, and his uniform looked good on him still. He reached for his car keys and looked at the reflection of his scarred, battered hands in the mirror. He stared into his own eyes again, and before he turned to go, he said, 'You're all right, Tim. You're still a cop – and at least *you* know what needs to be done.'

Rocky Springfield sat on the balcony of her second-floor apartment looking out at the beautiful green grass of the surrounding eighteen-hole golf course. As she watched, two old men went by in a cart and smiled and waved at her. She still felt a little funny going in and out of her apartment building. She was barely half the age of most of the tenants and had only taken the apartment because the building was owned by friends of her parents who had given her a good deal. She liked the quiet, though, and the people were nice to her, calling her 'that pretty young lady policeman' and shaking their gray heads in wonder and concern.

She took another section of tangerine and thought about the past night and morning.

She had ridden into the rear parking lot of the station with a silent McShaun. She felt uncomfortable and disturbed by the whole incident, still full of doubt about her own actions, or lack of them, and slightly sickened by the memory of the body. She had looked at McShaun as he turned off the engine and started collecting his gear. She wondered how he felt about it, wondered how it felt to kill another human being. She looked at his face but could read nothing there, just the same hard intensity as always. She had been wondering if they were going to go the rest of their lives without speaking when he looked at her and said evenly, 'This is a pretty big city, Lauderdale, but this police department, even if it does have almost five hundred employees, is still pretty smalltown in a lot of ways. Out of all the working cops in this department only a handful have ever actually been in a fatal shooting situation. The rest only talk about it, and they're all quick to Monday-morning quarterback on somebody else.'

He stood there by the unit, in the soft glow of the parking lot lights in the early-morning darkness. He looked down and scuffed one foot on the ground as he went on. 'Also, you're a female police officer, and even though this is 1978 and LAPD and NYPD and all those big progressive PDs have had female cops for a long time, it's a relatively new thing here, especially in the patrolman role. Most of the male cops here think the street is no place for a woman—' He held up his hand as she started to protest. 'Hey, I know. It's all been said and you've been through the academy and female cops have proven themselves capable of doing the job. Fine. I'm just trying to tell you to get ready for the reaction you might get from some of the troops over this deal. Believe me, every time a heavy situation goes down, every guy here thinks he could have handled it better. They run up and down the hallways and hang out in the locker room telling anyone who'll listen how they would have captured the bad guy, killed the dragon, made incredible, mad passionate love to the helpless but eternally thankful maiden, and basically saved the world.' He smiled at her then, and she wondered at how his eyes changed.

He swung the trap on the shotgun over his shoulder and started to turn away as he said, 'So, just look at your actions tonight from the standpoint of *being* there. As far as I'm concerned, you did exactly what you could have done tonight. You covered my flank and you kept from getting your head blown off . . . and, even more important, you didn't shoot when you weren't sure. You'll know – you'll know in your heart and know immediately – when the time comes to shoot. And then you will. As far as I'm concerned, what you did showed good self-discipline and control. Sometimes it's harder *not* to shoot, believe me. Anyway, I don't think you have anything to be ashamed of. So c'mon. Let's go throw ourselves with professional zeal into the six tons of paperwork we have to do before we go home.' Then

33

he had turned and walked off, across the parking lot and into the back door of the station. She had had to hurry to catch up.

She stood up on the balcony, stretched her tired body, and went inside her apartment. She felt as if she could sleep for another week or so, but she had to get ready to go back into the station for another shift. It was as if she had never left there, and she wondered again about all the talk she had heard in the academy about how the administration was vitally concerned about the emotional and mental well-being of its officers. There had been talk of 'stress days', and even counseling for any officer who had been involved in a potentially upsetting experience. She thought about the night before and felt that the events she had gone through in the last twelve hours were pretty extraordinary. Oh, well. She sighed and started to clean up her breakfast dishes and thought again about how it had gone.

After they had worked together on their supplemental reports, she and McShaun had been separated. He had gone with a couple of homicide detectives, and she went with the TAC sergeant to the booking desk in the jail. They had the suspect there, and they wanted her to take a look at him. When they walked into the booking area, all the officers and booking personnel, along with the old booking sergeant and the suspect, stared at her and it was quiet for a few seconds. She stood still as the sergeant handed the booking sheet to her and she read: 'Bobby Nails, Cau/Male, 27 yrs.' She looked up into the eyes of the suspect, who stood close against the bars on the other side of the booking desk. She saw a thin, pale, pockmarked face with yellow, watery eyes staring back at her with disinterest. The man had wet lips and bad teeth, and his thinning pale hair was plastered against his head. He was wearing a black T-shirt and jeans, and he had old tennis shoes on his feet. She looked at him again and tried to see the eyes behind the ski mask in the dark yard, tried to see that open mouth as the gun went off, pointed at her head.

As Rocky stood there Nails started to turn his head, but

the big officer behind him grabbed him by the neck and smashed his face back against the bars. His forehead made a hollow sound as it hit the steel, and the officer hissed, 'No, motherfucker. Don't look away now. That's the cop you tried to kill, asshole. That's the cop you shot at. And because of that, we're gonna *fry* your ass.'

Nails swallowed hard, and the old booking sergeant said easily, 'Hey, Al, be cool. Don't be smashin' up my prisoner now. I'll have to clean up the mess, if you know what I mean.'

The officer let Nails go and grinned.

Springfield had turned to the sergeant and whispered, 'Was that what he was wearing when they got him? I remember dark clothes – a jacket or something.' The sergeant smiled triumphantly, walked over to the booking desk, and held up a navy-blue windbreaker. 'How's this?' he asked, and, seeing her nod, turned to his officers and said, 'Besides all the other info we've got, and the trail from the K-9, Springfield here can ID him good enough. Book him, and then you guys c'mon down to the office so we can put this thing together.' He motioned for Rocky to follow him.

Rocky had been told to go on home a little after eight-thirty in the morning. She had wanted to say something – she didn't know exactly what – to McShaun, but he was busy with the detectives, so she left. She had driven home, squinting into the harsh sunlight, feeling the fine sandpaper behind her eyelids. When she got to her apartment, she had taken a long bath and then a shower, closed all the shades, and slid into bed. Though she was exhausted, she found herself staring at the ceiling for a long time before she finally drifted off.

Now she stretched again, still tired, then hurried into her uniform. As she strapped on her gun belt she wondered to herself again, Where was all the emotion? Was she scared? Guilty? Did she feel remorse? A loss? No, she just felt tired and a little empty. She slowly lifted the steel-blue revolver off the night table beside the bed and slid it into the holster, sensing its hardness and its weight. She sighed, grabbed her car keys, and headed out the door. She fluffed her hair after she locked the door and thought, *Well, maybe I just need to be held for a little while.*

McShaun saw Chick Hummel pull into the rear parking lot of the station in his MGB sportscar as he climbed out of his own old Firebird.

'Hey, T.S. How ya doin' guy?'

'Still making it, Chick. Still making it.'

'Yeah, listen, Tim. I heard about last night after I got home. I wanted to call you today but thought I'd wait so you could get some sleep.'

McShaun shook his head irritably and said, 'Shit, you wouldn't have been able to get through, anyhow. The line was busy all day with the usual bullshit – including that bitch from *The Lauderdale Herald*.' He looked at the concerned face of his friend and shook his head again. 'She wanted to know if it was easier for me to shoot this asshole than it was to shoot the last one.'

Hummel didn't say anything; he just took the big cigar out of his mouth and spat off to the side. They walked past the gas pumps, their hands in their pockets and their shoulders hunched forward as if walking into a driving rain. Finally Hummel said, 'Actually, I didn't think you'd be coming in tonight, Tim.'

'Hell, where else am I gonna go?'

'Well, you do look a little tired, my man. You look like you could do with a couple of days off. You know, kick back a little.'

McShaun changed the subject. 'How's that new kid you got working with you doing? That Hammer kid. I heard you guys got into a little scuffle with some ridge runners out on Davie Boulevard. Was he shy, or did he participate with vigor and enthusiasm?'

Hummel grinned and started pointing rapidly into the air with the cigar. 'Oh, man! I'll tell ya what, Timmy, that kid is all right! I mean, we go in and it's broken-beer-bottle time, and I'm trying to talk the whole thing down when a couple of buddies of the original combatants decide we're ruining a good thing and decide to jump *us*. Of course, when they do, then the first two guys join in again. It could have gotten real bad, real fast.' He took a couple of quick puffs on the cigar and then smiled. 'Well, you know I don't mind dancin' if the music has to play, so I responded with my usual ungainly roundhouse attack.' McShaun nodded and grinned, knowing full well the effectiveness of Hummel's sloppy form of combat. 'Anyway, Hammer just *unloaded* on that place. Fists and feet and flashlight and forehead, and the next thing you know, there's only the sound of my ragged breathing and the tinkle of broken glass falling around the edges. Fast . . . real fast. Everybody is on the floor, and Hammer turns to me and wants to know if *I'm* all right!'

They were walking past the motorcycle shed, heading for the back door. Hummel's eyes crinkled up as he smiled and said, 'Couple of the backups got there just as the last skulls were bouncing off the bar. After we got it all sorted out and got ready to go home – you were on your magic assignment with the TAC squad by then – well, a couple of the guys came over and kidded around with us and told us they weren't going to call us Hummel and Hammer anymore. From now on it will be Hummel and Pummel.'

They were both laughing quietly as they walked into the back door of the station, headed for evening shift briefing.

Rocky Springfield saw McShaun and Hummel walk in the back door, and she hurried across the parking lot, afraid she would be late for briefing. She hated to be late because, like most other police departments, Lauderdale had an unwritten rule that the more senior officers sat in the rear of the room while the newer people took the chairs to the front. Cops have a funny thing about their backs, anyway, but more than that, she hated to open that door, walk into the room, fumble for a hotsheet, and try to fall into a chair without her holster getting hung up or something while everybody just stared. She ran up the steps and reached for the door as it was pulled open by Detective Lieutenant James Track.

'Officer Springfield.'

'Sir?'

He smiled and she looked at him. He was in his early forties, fit and trim. He wore a beautiful charcoal-gray three-piece suit and a pearl-colored shirt. Sharp. His almost white hair was styled, and his tanned face had a Hollywood-rugged look. He reached out with what looked like a manicured hand, and she took it and they shook, him straight and appraising and somehow making the handshake seem man-to-man.

He still held her hand as he said, 'Just wanted to congratulate you, um . . . Rocky isn't it? Just wanted to tell you I've read over what happened last night, and I think you did a fine job. A fine job. Yes, it was a difficult situation and you handled yourself admirably.'

Rocky pulled her hand away and stood there awkwardly, not knowing what to say.

He went on, 'Anyway . . . Rocky . . . I know this may be a bit premature, but I've been watching you through your probation period, and I like what I've seen. I've been telling some of the higher brass up there' – he pointed up with a stiff thumb – 'that we need some new blood, some new perspective, some new professionals in the Detective Division. Just wanted you to know that I'm pulling for you . . . hard. When you get off probation, I'm hoping to be able to get you an assignment up there where the *real* police work takes place.'

Springfield knew she was late now but wasn't as worried about it as she normally would be. Detective Division! Plainclothes work! She tried not to grin as the smooth lieutenant said, 'Of course, you would be jumping over a lot of officers who are senior to you and waiting for that assignment, but don't worry about it. I'll be watching over you.' He took her hand again and shook it and nodded toward the briefing room. 'Guess you'd better get in there. Mustn't be late, right?'

She nodded and said, 'Thanks, Lieutenant,' and hurried away.

She *was* late and tried not to notice the patrol lieutenant's cocked eyebrow as she struggled into her seat in the front row.

Lieutenant Detective James Track stood in the doorway as Springfield hurried off, watching the way she moved in her uniform. Then he turned and walked out into the parking lot, heading for his new Corvette. *Yes,* he thought, *we do need some new blood up there.* He chuckled to himself. He hadn't checked her records, he had checked her legs. The way he saw it, the faster she was assigned to the Detective Division, the faster he would be able to investigate the inside of her pants.

Chapter Three

The video camera zoomed in on a young redheaded girl's crotch as her bikini was ripped off her by the muscular man with the tattoos on his arms. Then the camera pulled back to take in the whole scene as the girl squirmed around and pretended to struggle. The muscular man pulled off his pants and played with his large penis until it was erect. He knelt over the girl and entered her roughly. The girl turned her head to the side, and a voice from behind the camera said, 'Turn your face this way, kid. Yeah, that's right. And move a little, will ya? C'mon, let's see some action, kid. Move those hips. Smile.'

The girl turned her head, and the camera purred on.

'Harv, squeeze her tits. Yeah, that's good. Okay, now a close-up on his face. Now hers. All right, back to get the whole thing. Good. How's it going, Harv? Let us know, right?'

The muscular man with the tattoos started to grunt, his hips pounding the girl harder and harder. A couple of minutes went by and he clenched his teeth and said, 'Okay, here it comes.'

The voice behind the lights and the camera said, 'So soon? All right, zoom in on her face and chest, good, okay, there he goes . . . out of her, follow him up . . . fine, kid, look what he's got for you in his hand, now look into his face and smile, and—'

The man with the tattoos grunted and bucked and jerked his hand back and forth rapidly, then arched his back and stiffened. The young redheaded girl watched, fascinated, as he ejaculated his wet warmth onto her breasts and her face. She instinctively tried to pull her head back, but he was ready for her and held her tight with his other hand dug into her hair.

'Good. Now pull back a little. Fine, Harv . . . Harv, rub it against her face and then put it all the way into her mouth. Good. Good. All right, kid, now lick it and then turn toward the camera and smile. Okay, turn toward the camera now . . . good. End it.'

The man named Harv squeezed one last drop onto the girl's small breasts and laughed. Then he scratched and stretched and jumped off the bed. He stood there grinning as Tom Odom, the voice behind the camera, threw him a pack of cigarettes.

Over the last year Tom Odom had made a bundle smuggling cocaine into the south Florida area. Now he was using some of the money to operate a sweet little pornography shop in his home. He had set it up with the blessings and business cooperation of the local syndicate. Odom didn't need the money from the porno films, he just liked it. He liked watching the films, and now that he had money to burn, he liked making them, actually being there as they happened. He chuckled and looked over at the young redheaded girl as she slowly climbed out of the bed and walked unsteadily toward the bathroom. He thought maybe he'd have her give him a little head before they threatened the shit out of her and dropped her off where they had picked her up, out on Fort Lauderdale's 'strip'.

The redheaded girl was fifteen years old, a runaway from Upstate New York. She had been in Lauderdale less than a week. She had met the guy named Harv on the beach, and he had been friendly and sympathetic. They had done a couple of joints in the sunshine the first day she met him, yesterday, and she had slept with him last night in a motel on Federal Highway. He had talked to her about the 'modeling job' he could get for her, and about the money, and maybe a little cocaine they could do. He had told her that he knew that if she was just a kid, she could never handle the

41

job, but since she was a woman, in every sense of the word, it would be easy for her. She was intrigued and high and infatuated with Harv, so she said yes.

First it had been just some fun Polaroids – a little tit, a little ass. Some grass, some coke, and then the other guys were there with the movie camera. They were all talking big money, and it was like a challenge or something. Now she stood shaking in the cold bathroom and looked at herself in the mirror. It had been awful. She wanted to go home.

She looked closer and saw that her face was shiny-slick wet, her tears mixing with his semen.

Chapter Four

Rocky Springfield leaned against the fender of her patrol car and read the newspaper under the lights in the high school parking lot. It had been a quiet evening, and there was only an hour or so left of the shift. She knew she shouldn't be standing in the lot reading the paper, but it had been a bad day for her and she just didn't care.

She had been off probation and out on her own for a week. Tim McShaun had written only good things on her final evaluation, and she heard later that a couple of the patrol sergeants had actually requested her on their squads. She had been assigned to evening shift, south end, and she was still trying to get to know the men she worked with. She knew McShaun and Hummel were back together in the northwest part of the city, since the young black cop, Hammer, had made his probation also and was now working midnights up in the northeast section. Rocky hadn't seen much of McShaun other than in briefing, where he would give her a polite nod and occasionally ask her how it was going, but she had kept up with how things were going with him by listening to the gossip during coffee breaks. She had been called in to testify in front of the Departmental Firearms Review Board and then the Broward County Grand Jury about McShaun's shooting. In both cases, when she was finished, she was excused and that was that. Finally she heard that the Firearms Review Board had found that McShaun had not violated any departmental procedures. Then the grand jury published its decision that the homicide was 'justified'.

McShaun hadn't come out so clean in his trial by the media, she reflected.

The shooting he had been involved in a year ago was repeatedly dredged up and somehow linked to the current shooting. The media also had a field day with the fact that McShaun shot the already wounded suspect twice with the shotgun, when everyone knew the power of the weapon made it unnecessary to fire twice. Very little was mentioned about the background of the suspects or the series of crimes they had committed. Most of the articles questioned the need for the shooting and inferred that if the police had set the scene up correctly in the first place, it never would have happened. Springfield had bought the paper this evening to see the final articles now that the grand jury's decision was out.

Earlier in the day she had been sent by the dispatcher to the courthouse where she was to meet with the prosecutor handling the case against Bobby Nails, the one who had shot at her. She was met there by her sergeant and the department's legal adviser. She went into the meeting thinking it was just more paperwork and came out of it stunned, trying to make sense out of what she had heard. The prosecutor and the legal adviser had nodded their heads together and talked softly for a few minutes before agreeing to whatever it was they were agreeing to. Then they turned and advised Springfield that the case against Nails was 'weak'. It seemed that none of the TAC officers could honestly identify Nails as the person they saw under the ski mask in the house, and, of course, she couldn't.

The prosecutor told her that with Nails's partner dead, and Nails not being caught inside the house or being facially ID'd as the one who shot at her, and there being no link made between Nails and the gun found or the car used, it was . . . 'weak'. The prosecutor assured Rocky that he would love to hang the guy for trying to shoot her, but he couldn't waste the time and money needed to go to trial on a 'maybe' case. Nails's bond would be immediately lowered to almost nothing while they tried to come up with something

44

realistic with which to charge him. Her sergeant had looked at her and sighed and shook his head. She had said, 'Thank you' and walked out. She left the courthouse trying to determine if she felt angry or confused or just frustrated. She settled on angry.

Now she folded the paper irritably and began to read the front page of the local section. The story about the grand jury was headlined: COP NOT INDICTED BY GRAND JURY IN DEATH. It was made to sound as if McShaun had gotten away with something. She finished the article in disgust to see that next to it was a companion article by Phyllis Green about the charges being all but dropped against Nails. Green made it sound like this heightened the suspicion against the action taken by McShaun the night of the shooting. Rocky's hands trembled as she read how young Officer Springfield incompetently let the *real* suspect get away, and then mistakenly, or erroneously, ID'd poor Nails as the bad guy. The article questioned the fact that a 'young, inexperienced probationary officer' was even on the scene of such a potentially dangerous situation.

Rocky threw the paper into the backseat of the car. She stood looking up into the night sky and said, 'Jesus'. She was still standing there thinking about it all when the shift ended and she was called to return to the station.

There was always a lot of activity in the rear parking lot of the Fort Lauderdale Police Station as one shift ended and another started. Cars pulled in and out, and police officers walked back and forth, carrying their gear and calling to one another. Springfield stopped at the gas pumps and filled the unit's tank, then she pulled around and parked in a numbered slot and started to collect her gear. She got everything together, got out, reached into the back and got the newspaper, and turned to head for the back door. She took three steps, and the entire pile of things in her arms – briefcase, traffic books, hat, flashlight, raincoat, newspaper – started to slide toward the pavement. She muttered 'Shit' and tried hopelessly to catch it before it all went.

'Is that a comment on life in general or just tonight's activities?' Tim McShaun said quietly as he stepped beside her and caught the avalanche, steadying it.

She gave him an exasperated smile and said, 'Oh, I guess it could apply where needed. Thanks for the help. You'd think that by now I'd be able to manage my gear, huh?'

He laughed quietly and shook his head. He folded the paper and looked at it and her. 'I thought you'd mentioned once that you were into reading fiction.'

She made a face and said, 'Fiction, yes, garbage, no. What a bunch of—'

'Shit,' he said, and they laughed, looking at each other.

They started walking toward the back door, then he stopped. He looked at her, hesitated, then said, 'Listen, some of the guys are gonna get together for a drink in a little while at the bar out near Plantation that stays open late. I know you don't usually drink with the guys, but . . . well, I thought tonight maybe you'd let me buy you a drink.' He smiled and shrugged and pointed at the paper again. 'It's the least I can do after getting your good name tangled up with mine here on the front page of this bird-cage liner.'

She nodded and said, 'I could *use* a drink after today. You heard about Nails? A drink sounds damn good.'

He grinned. 'All right. I'll meet you out there. Know where it is? I'll see you there in about a half hour.'

He held the door for her and then walked off toward the locker room while she made her burdened way to the write-up room. She didn't have that much to do, but she hurried anyway.

The inside of the bar was dark and comfortable. The sound system was turned down low enough so as not to interfere with conversation. Although it wasn't a 'police' bar, the small club attached to the motel on State Road 7 was frequented by police officers from all over the county. It was just outside the city limits of Fort Lauderdale and had a closing time of four A.M.

McShaun and Springfield sat at a table in the rear corner,

46

out of the crush, and talked with their faces close together, hunched over their drinks. McShaun had been waiting, and when Springfield walked in, moved toward her, and escorted her to their table, there was more than one raised eyebrow and speculative grin. People swirled and swayed around them to the accompaniment of the tinkle of ice, the clinking of glasses, the sound of quiet laughter and teasing, and the inevitable, 'So this guy gets out of his car, right? And he starts comin' toward me, so I take my . . .'

McShaun allowed himself really to look at her. She was wearing a pair of tight jeans, a violet pastel polo shirt with the back of the collar turned up, and soft leather boat shoes. He deliberately and completely devoured her with his eyes, slowly, carefully, with an intensity that should have made her turn away but didn't. She held his gaze with her gray eyes, and he knew he was being devoured also. He looked into her eyes and felt a dangerous warmth. He couldn't pull himself away. She was beautiful and he was comfortable with it. Finally someone across the room shouted, and it pulled them out of it.

McShaun took a taste of his Bushmill's and said, 'How's your drink? What was that again, Black Jack and ginger?'

Springfield swirled her drink with her finger, then tasted it. She smiled and crinkled up her face, 'I think it's the same thing my grandmother used to call a highball. Anyway, I really appreciate the invitation out here, Tim. I really needed to relax. What a day.'

'I know. It can get to you sometimes. I've gone through periods when I never went straight home, always stopped at a bar first. Now I try to stay away from that as much as possible. Oh, I'll go out once in a while, like tonight, but most of the time I go home and then go for a walk around the neighborhood for an hour or so.'

'C'mon . . .'

'No, I really do. Hell, it's cheaper than buying booze, and I feel better about the whole thing the next day.'

She laughed. 'You've got a point there. Some of those next days can be pretty rough.'

They were quiet for a minute, playing with their thoughts, then he looked up and said, 'Nice, the way they handled that Nails thing, huh?' He knew she was still stewing about it; the drink would probably only nurture it, and she would carry it home with her like a little thermite grenade in her stomach if the pressure wasn't released.

He sat up quickly and grabbed his drink off the table as Rocky slapped her hand down hard and said, 'Oh! Oh . . . it was just swell. Very polite and all. They *so* wanted to make sure I understood. If they had started talking baby talk, I wouldn't have been surprised.'

He nodded.

'Well, at least they had the professional decency to talk it over with me before they did anything,' she said, taking a long sip of her drink. 'At least I was part of what was going on.'

He looked at her and sighed. He said, 'Think about that for a minute.'

She cocked her head to the side and looked at him. He went on, 'This all happened this afternoon, right? In the prosecutor's office, right? And then you were reading about it in this evening's paper – I mean, about the charges against Nails being changed and his bond being lowered and all—'

'Dammit! Dammit . . . those . . . those . . . Of course, Tim, you're right. They had already made their decision, and they had already made their moves, and that Green woman already knew about it before they called me in or there would have been no way it could have made it into this evening's edition.' She ran her fingers through her hair, then banged her fist down onto the table, again making her drink bounce. 'Boy, that makes me angry!'

He watched her, knowing exactly how she felt, knowing, in fact, that she was only beginning to feel, to hurt. He watched her and felt his own similar frustrations rise to the surface to parallel hers.

She took another sip of her drink and said, 'But, Tim, dammit, aren't they supposed to be working on our side?

Aren't we a *team* and all that? I mean, I'm aware that as the cop on the street I'm the low guy on the totem pole, but still, what I do on the street is supposed to be complemented and reinforced by the rest of the system, isn't it?'

McShaun shook his head slowly and said, 'You'll find as you go along that sometimes it appears that what you do is actually supported by no one. You're doing something out on the street that's not aligned with anything or any system. Once the paperwork is generated, you begin to lose control, the situation is taken out of your hands, and you cease to be an active part of what takes place after that. Forget thinking that the different parts of the judicial system work together. Those people in that courthouse' – he took a long drink and looked at the ceiling – 'well, don't look at them as part of your team. They're not.'

'Oh, Tim, I don't know. This is just one incident. It doesn't make the whole courthouse the enemy.'

McShaun looked at her for a few seconds and then said, 'Want another drink?' He was off to the bar before she could answer.

When he came back, they were both quiet for a moment, hoping to slip back into their earlier mood, but it didn't happen. Finally he shrugged and started speaking. As he talked and heard himself he knew what was happening but couldn't stop it.

'Look, Rocky, thinking of the inhabitants of the courthouse as "the enemy" can be a help to your sanity. Maybe *enemy* is the wrong word, but what label would you put on a group of people who don't understand your work but have total control of your final product? Hell, you've heard all the horror stories about good cases being messed with and bad guys skating on technicalities – it's old news. I could sit here for hours and tell you about my own cases, where I've walked out of that courthouse feeling as if the whole world has just shit on my head. I mean, I've felt like running for cover, and I'm the *good* guy!'

Springfield turned her head away and looked at the floor. 'You're still new, and you're trying to believe in the system and do the good work and be a part of the team and all that shit. All I'm saying is that as you go along you'll find that it isn't quite that way.'

Springfield put her elbows on the small table and leaned closer to him. She looked into his eyes and tried to understand why she felt the need to argue with him about this. They were supposed to be relaxing, having a good time, getting to know each other. She could feel his intensity; she could see how the skin had tightened around his eyes. She felt herself fighting his influence. She said, 'Bullshit. The problem is, most of you guys don't want to use your heads and your knowledge of the law to work *with* the system. Your cases fall apart and you look for someone to blame – other than yourself, of course. You ever hear a cop talking about a crappy case that he threw together and tried to push through the system? No. It's always some *perfect* case that the system rejected.' She straightened up a little, buoyed by the drinks. 'What I'm getting at is this: I really feel that a new attitude, a professional attitude is necessary today for a police officer.' She looked into his dark eyes. 'We can't be effective as cops if we're fighting with our own judicial system. We have to contribute our small part of the action and then let the other members of the team carry it from there. And we have to trust the system and have faith in its ability to get the job done.' She sat back, suddenly feeling a little pompous.

McShaun was quiet for a few seconds, nodding as if in agreement. Then, playing with his drink, without looking up, he said, 'And what about Mr Nails?'

She hesitated, then straightened. 'You know as well as I do that none of us could really ID him, or put him at the scene, or link him to the gun that was found. Listen to me – he shot at me. Don't you think I'd like to see him go down the tubes? But here it is: We had a shitty case on Nails, so he walks. You know what they say about his type. We'll see him again.'

'You're missing the point, Rocky,' McShaun said quietly. He looked up and stared into her eyes. 'You're missing the point. We, you and I, we *know* that scumbag is the one. The question is, what are we gonna do about it? In our world, as the rules are laid out, there's only one system we can use to get him, a system based on the honorable premise that we should let a thousand guilty men go free rather than hang the one innocent, a system rendered impotent by its own paranoia. And when that system lets us down, all we can do is feel frustrated. What I'm saying to you is that the frustration will be there, burning inside you, smoldering there while you go along trying so hard to believe in the system – and that frustration will hurt you, more than you can believe, unless you take on a realistic attitude.'

He leaned forward and pointed at her. 'We *know* – and you're part of that "we" now, Rocky, don't kid yourself – that most of the assholes in the courthouse and most of the living anachronisms that allegedly run this police department are working *against* us. They don't know what we're trying to do out there, and they don't care. And if you're not aware of it, it can hurt you even worse than facing the truth.'

She pushed her drink away and looked for her handbag, obviously getting ready to leave. She sat up straight in her chair and said, 'This is all very interesting, Tim, but why are we talking about it? It's pretty obvious that we have different views on this whole thing, so why yell at each other? Why did you start this whole thing, anyway? Why are you telling me all this?'

He stood up as she did, and followed her out of the bar and into the parking lot. He saw some of the guys gesturing toward them and grinning as they walked out.

He was quiet as they reached the car, and she unlocked it and opened the door. He held it open as she sat behind the wheel. He said, 'I really didn't mean to ruin what started out as a nice time.'

'Yeah.'

'Rocky, listen. I started the conversation about Nails to let you blow off a little steam, but I guess the steam just heated up on my own totally fried brain and I launched off into my own thing. I didn't want to make you angry, I just wanted to help you survive this idiocy, that's all.'

She sat in her car and looked up into his tight, concerned face. She found herself wishing she could tell him how surprised she was at her reaction to the conversation, wishing she could tell him that she knew she had overreacted and was mystified as to the reason. She looked into his eyes and could see the intensity and the torment. She started the car and said, 'Good night, Tim, thanks for the drinks, and for . . . for . . .' She shrugged and drove off.

McShaun stood in the parking lot watching her go.

Chapter Five

Sam Beachwood sat back in the soft chair and watched the movie screen on the far wall through half-closed eyes. His hands rested lightly on either side of the young girl's head as she knelt in front of him, between his legs, her pretty face buried in his crotch. He heard soft laughter from across the dark room and knew that either Tom Odom or Alan Giles was also doing more than just watching Odom's newest film.

They were at Odom's big house on the water off Bayview Drive. They had all gotten together a little after midnight for some fun and games. Sam Beachwood was Tom Odom's attorney and had been for a couple of years, ever since Odom had started making it big in the cocaine business and could afford Beachwood. Sam Beachwood was known locally as a top criminal lawyer, a man to be reckoned with in the judicial arena. He was a respected fighter for the rights of his clients and was known professionally as an attorney who might lose a case in the courtroom, only to win it later in the appeals court. He was a known cop-hater and would encourage his clients to sue any police department at any time for any alleged violation of rights. He was flamboyant and controversial and aggressive and confident. New police officers feared him in court. Older, experienced officers respected his prowess but hated his guts and his methods, which usually included harassing and ridiculing the officer in court if possible.

Beachwood liked the company of young good-looking women. With his trim body, good clothes, and manicured appearance, and with his money and the cocaine he got from Odom, he usually had no trouble finding female company, even though most police officers said that with his sandy blond hair, thick lips, puffy cheeks, and pasty complexion, he looked like a cross between Howdy Doody and Alfred E. Newman.

The girl moved her fingers on him and he stiffened, then relaxed again. He watched the redheaded girl on the screen, then looked across the room to where he could see Alan Giles's profile in the dim light. He couldn't tell what he was doing, but he knew there was another girl over there with Giles.

Beachwood leaned back and closed his eyes and smiled. These girls that Odom came up with for the films, and for the fun, they were just . . . toys, silly, meaningless, slutty little toys. And so easy. He opened his eyes again and watched the redheaded girl on the screen moving her hips and smiling. He closed his eyes again, thinking; Alan Giles was part of the City Manager's Office of Fort Lauderdale. One of the biggies. And the City Manager's Office was, in effect, the police department's boss. They practically *ran* the police department. And here was Giles, snorting Odom's cocaine, watching Odom's porn flicks, and enjoying one of Odom's stable of stupid young girls before heading home to his plump, oh-so-correct wife.

Beachwood played with the long blond hair of the girl kneeling in front of him and watched the screen again. No wonder Tom Odom wasn't too worried about his operations here in the 'Venice of America.' He watched as the tattooed man on the screen suddenly pulled out of the redheaded girl and moved up toward the face. At the same time the blond between his legs moved faster and harder. Then, as it happened to the man on the screen, it happened to Sam Beachwood in Tom Odom's living room.

Chapter Six

Rocky Springfield stood amid the pieces of broken glass and
bent chrome strewn in the street. Traffic flowed slowly and
awkwardly around the two smashed and mangled cars, here
a horn blaring, there a hoarse voice raised in frustration.
She ignored it all and concentrated on the information she
would need to file her report. The injured people, two from
each car, had already been taken away by the ambulances,
and motorcycle officers were trying to keep the traffic moving. All Springfield had to do now was wait for the wreckers
to remove the battered cars from the street. Normally the
motorcycle officers would handle an accident report, but
since she had been the first on the scene, and because she felt
she needed more experience at doing more than just fender-
bender accident reports, Springfield had told the motor
guys she would handle it.

They hadn't argued with her.

As the first wrecker backed up against one of the cars, she
walked off the street and leaned against her patrol car,
parked in a service station lot. She was there, making more
notes for her report, when another patrol unit pulled into
the lot and stopped. Springfield looked up and grinned as
Bell Peoples, a gangly black female police officer with flat
hips, a puffy Afro, and an always ready smile, surveyed the
mess in the street and rolled her eyes. She walked over to
Springfield's unit with an exaggerated strut and said,
'Why, Officer Springfield, I hope you can give this here
curious black police officer a good reason why *you* is doin'
this sig-an-al four when I can plainly see a coupla dose

simply *macho* skintight paddy motorcycle po-leeses just standin' in the street, wavin' their traffic-oriented arms and shakin' their cute little asses at the world. What's the matter with you, girl, you tryin' to make sergeant or somethin'?'

Springfield looked at Bell's smiling face and wondered again about the way she played with her street-black character. Peoples had been on the job only a month longer than Springfield, but she had the air of a veteran, and despite the fact that she could sound like the street when she wanted to, Springfield knew Bell had at least one degree in communications, with a minor in English.

Rocky said, 'It's like this, Bell: The sergeant will have heard me advising the dispatcher that I'm taking this accident and he'll think I'm doing my usual fine job on being the bright new kid on the block. But just between you and me, the truth is that one of those oh-so-masculine and virile motor cops told me that if I handled this little accident for them, he would actually let me sit on his beautiful Harley-Davidson macho machine while he told me real stories about the incredibly brave and wonderful things he had done as an older and more experienced po-leese officer. Why, it almost makes me wet just to *think* of it!'

They collapsed against the side of the unit laughing. Then Peoples helped Springfield finish her report, and they made plans to meet for coffee later. As Rocky drove away from the cleared scene and headed toward a nearby fire station to do her paperwork she thought of Bell and the other female cops who were on the force. She knew there had been a couple of women detectives on the FLPD for years, but they had been kept either in the juvenile unit or helping out with rape victims. They had been good investigators and good workers, but they were 'women' and had done only those jobs the administration thought they should do. Then, in the early seventies, the FLPD, like other departments around the country, started taking offered federal monies to augment its budget. After doing so they became more and more subject to the federal governments rules of hiring on an equal-opportunity basis. This not only included blacks and Hispanics but also females – and not just for 'women's work,' either. No, now it was time to put uniformed female patrol officers out on the street with the big boys.

Springfield parked her unit in the small fire station lot and sat for a moment thinking of the women she had met on the job so far. On the whole they reflected any gaggle of people – some sharp, some not so sharp, and some that had no business being there at all. She admitted to herself that any woman who went into the police business had to be a *little* different from the average woman, in the sense that, obviously, being a female street cop was a greater challenge than almost any other job she could think of. Oh, she knew most people thought a woman interested in police work must have been a 'tomboy' in the first place, and they probably just wanted to keep playing with the boys. But this was belied by the fact that so many of the women on the job were cream-puff feminine, did their nails, always looked nice, and had a trail of guys following them around.

Springfield gathered her papers and smiled ruefully to herself. And then there were the others. One of the girls she worked with, Peggy Shepard, could curse so long and so intricately purple that she frequently caused hardened old street cops to turn away in embarrassment. Another, the first girl to make sergeant on the department, was one of those people who put personal hygiene far down on her list of priorities. Sergeant Donna Baggett was a good cop, a hard worker, a street dancer, and when she and Springfield worked in the same area, Baggett always took the younger cop under her wing. Springfield shook her head and laughed to herself, remembering the time in a dark alley when Sergeant Baggett had shown young Officer Springfield how to urinate without having to take off all that leather gear. 'Yep, just sort of get into a sumo-type squat, pull things this way and that, and there you go, without even removing your culottes, panty hose, and all.' There was a story that once, Baggett had challenged some of the guys in her squad to a pissing contest and won, but Springfield doubted the validity of that one.

She got out of the petrol car and headed for the typewriter, thinking, *Oh, well, we females are here, and we seem to be doing the job, and so far none of us has been seriously hurt or really let a partner down. And, hell, we like it.*

Lorenzo Walker sat on his bed and stared at the gray wall. His usually placid mind had been shaken into a small turmoil, and he was trying to calm it down. Normally he didn't think or, more correctly, he went through each day only thinking those thoughts that were required to make it through the routine. He had spent his life responding to simple basic animal urges: those he understood and those he sought to satisfy. Any other thinking was a waste, except when he was being chased, and then he trusted his survival instincts.

He scratched his bristly head and thought about the last time he had been chased.

He had taken over a dozen girls – he couldn't remember exactly how many, but it was over a dozen. The lawyers liked to say he had 'raped' them, but he knew he had just taken them. He had used them and then set them free. There had been that one he had made dance for him there in the darkness and quiet of the park, and *then* he had taken her. When he was finished, he thanked her and let her go. All he wanted to do after he let one go was to go to sleep and rest. He always felt so right afterward.

His brow wrinkled, and he thought of *that* night. No, no rest that night. That policeman with the bright eyes that kept staring, staring. The policeman had 'invited' him to the station to talk. He remembered how his mind wouldn't think, wouldn't work. He went, and then later he stood in a courtroom with a jury, and he remembered that he knew it would be all right because half the jury was black people, like him.

But no. They had been like the others and they said he was guilty. Guilty of taking the girl.

He reached out with one big hand and bunched his pillow up before he slowly rolled to his side and lay down on the bed. He stared at the ceiling and tried to think of the sentence – eight-five years? That was a lot, he knew. And just for taking that girl. Well, the judge did say some stuff about the other times he had been to jail for that same thing. He had come up to the big Raiford prison, and here he was, expecting to be here for a long time, relaxed here, comfortable here, and then – today.

He had been called in from the gym and told to meet with some people from the parole board in an office. The meeting was short and he didn't say much, but all the lawyers there – he thought they were lawyers, they had suits – they smiled and nodded their heads and said it was fine that he hadn't been into any trouble in Raiford and he had been going to woodworking class all the time (a dude he knew there always had some reefer) and he had been going to the church meetings (he liked the music) and they thought he might be paroled soon. They couldn't say how soon, but for sure he wouldn't be spending no eighty-five years there.

Lorenzo Walker lay there and stared at the gray ceiling and thought about leaving Raiford and going back out into the world. He wondered why they didn't know that once he got out, he would have to find a nice girl and would have to take her. He would take her, and then take another and then another.

He *liked* it.

McShaun lay on his side and watched the young woman sleeping beside him. It was late afternoon, and the bronze-gold of the sun made the inside of his apartment glow. He let his fingers gently trace the smooth path from just below her neck, down her back, up across her soft hip, and down along her firm leg muscles. She was a beauty, no doubt about it. He leaned up and looked at her sleeping face, the small fist of her right hand bunched up against her pouting lips. Her breathing was deep and regular. He smiled. He had been seeing her for a while now, and their lovemaking only got better and better. They had been to the beach earlier where they had had a picnic and talked for a while. Then she looked at him in that way and it was time to go. Once back at his apartment she had let herself be swept into his bed and loved with an intensity she had come to know but still wondered at. There was no place on her body he hadn't kissed; there was no inch of skin that hadn't felt his rough but gentle fingers. She gave herself to him in trust and anticipation, and he took her with a consuming strength and selfless desire to please.

He gently rubbed the back of her arm with his fingers while he lay back and thought about them.

It was almost time, he knew, to make it end. She was getting closer every day. Soon she would want all of him: his time, his dreams, his energy, his secrets. His fingers stopped as her breathing caught, then started again. She had a right to want more, he thought. She had given herself to him, had let him see her past, her fears and her triumphs. She had given him her trust, and soon she would want to give him herself.

Too close. She was getting too close.

He felt a knot forming in his stomach as he thought of the hurt she would feel. It was inevitable. He would hurt her, and he would hurt while doing it. How could he explain it? How could he tell her that there was something unfinished inside him? How could he explain it to her when he wasn't sure he could explain it to himself? He just knew there was unfinished business in him – hard, cold, hot, intense, unforgiving, unsharing, unfinished business. He heard her make a small sound like a kitten and looked at her lying there, looking like the quality woman that she was. She deserved a man who could commit. A man who could promise. A man who was finished with his own business and ready to share his life with her.

He was not that man.

He eased himself out of the rumpled bed, pulled the sheet gently over the sleeping girl, and tiptoed out into the kitchen. He quietly made himself a cup of tea and, while waiting for the water to boil, was surprised to find himself thinking of Rocky Springfield. It seemed to him that it had been happening a lot lately. He rubbed his eyes, thinking, wondering. Because he knew he would soon be breaking up with the girl in his bed? Because Rocky was a cop and he felt he could talk to her as he could talk to no other woman? Because he felt she *had* to be an important part of his life somehow?

He listened to the sleeping sounds of the beautiful girl in his bed, and he stared out the window at the setting sun while he thought of Rocky Springfield.

The next day McShaun sat groggily in a Juvenile Division judge's office, waiting for a hearing involving a fifteen-year-old he had arrested for breaking into a car. The kid sat across the room now, between his parents, and next to them sat his lawyer, Peter Schuller, who used to be a biggie with the Public Defender's Office but had recently gone into private practice.

McShaun was tired and emotionally spent. He had been up most of the night with the girl. He hadn't intended it that way, he hadn't really been ready for it, but after their dinner she said she knew he was getting ready to end it and she wanted to talk about it. He had fumbled at first, had tried to let it lay, but she said she knew, and they had to work it out. They had gotten into it, and the more intricate and involved the conversation had become, the more filled with resolve he'd become, until, in the early morning hours, he'd told her that he no longer wanted her as part of his life. He had looked into her eyes and told her he needed to be without her, he needed to let her go. She had seen the decision in his eyes and heard the finality in his voice, and she had cried and argued and cried – and finally had run from his apartment and down the street into the night.

She came back an hour later and cried herself to sleep in his arms. He had held her, but he did not sleep. And then he had slipped out quietly to make it to the courthouse on time.

The bailiff motioned them into the judge's chambers, and things got under way. The judge asked McShaun to present his case, which he did, feeling it was cut-and-dried. He had been talking with a citizen near the beach about a CB radio being taken out of a car when he had heard the sound of glass breaking in a parking lot separated from him by a line of hedges. He had gone through the hedges and found a parked car with the passenger-side window smashed out and had seen the kid pedaling away on a bicycle. He had cut through a yard and intercepted the kid, and the kid had fought with him before he managed to get him cuffed. In a bag on the bike had been the CB from the first car and a couple of other items that were later found to belong to the owner of the second car. McShaun couldn't say it in open court – it would be 'prejudicial' – but he was more concerned with the resisting arrest charges against the kid because the kid had been arrested in the past for the same thing: fighting a cop.

When McShaun finished his presentation, Peter Schuller proceeded to tear it apart – at least in the judge's eyes. Did McShaun actually *see* his young client smash the window of the car? Did McShaun get fingerprints that matched those of his client from the car? Wasn't it a fact that the defendant stated that he had found the 'stolen' objects lying in the parking lot and that he intended to take them home so his parents could tell him what to do with them? Wasn't it a fact that his young client 'resisted' this officer only after being rudely pulled off his bicycle? Wasn't it a fact that Officer McShaun used excessive force against this young teenager? And wasn't it also true that Officer McShaun had a known reputation for being a little too rough a lot of the time?

The judge not only dismissed the charges against the kid, but also he reprimanded McShaun for not making a better case and for roughing up the kid. The kid sat there uninterested, the parents sat there firing reproachful glances at McShaun, and Peter Schuller puffed himself up and positively beamed.

As they filed out McShaun pulled the bailiff aside and quietly asked if he could see the judge privately for one minute. The bailiff clearly didn't approve but said he would ask. He came back and nodded his head and McShaun went back into the judge's chambers.

The judge looked up from a desk full of paperwork and said, 'Yes?'

'Your Honor, because of the rules I know I'm only allowed to give you structured testimony in any case, but in this case I want you to have a little more info so you will better understand my actions with that kid.'

'That won't be necessary, Officer—'

'I couldn't present it to you, although Schuller could present it about me, but if you'll have your bailiff pull that kid's sheet, you'll learn that he has been arrested nine times in the last year, and in seven of those arrests he has fought with the arresting officer, two times actually injuring the officer to a minor degree.'

'That has no bearing—'

'Oh, I know, Your Honor, I know you can't take any of that into account when you're hearing the case. I just wanted you to know about it on the off chance that the kid might be brought before you again. Or, on the off chance that the next time he fights some cop trying to arrest him, he ends up getting his young ass beaten right into the emergency room – and you wind up reading about it one morning while you're sitting there eating your curds and whey.'

McShaun walked out.

Peter Schuller was waiting for him out in the hallway. The kid and his parents were gone. Schuller stepped beside McShaun as he came out of the office and said, 'What's the matter, T.S., couldn't let it lay? Had to go back and tell the judge he was wrong?'

McShaun started walking down the hallway, looking straight ahead.

Schuller followed along. 'C'mon, T.S., admit it. I beat you. You did your thing out there on the street, played with the law until it fit what you wanted it to do, and then you brought it in here – where the *real* law works – and I kicked your ass. Is that it, huh? Is that it?'

McShaun stopped and turned to face the lawyer.

'Yeah, that's it, Schuller. You kicked my ass and I'm so sore about it that I had to go whine to the judge.' He stepped closer to the other man, reached down with his left hand, and grabbed the front of Schuller's pants and belt buckle. McShaun pulled up hard and pushed back, and as Schuller's crotch was caught in the tightening cloth, Schuller let out a squeal and backed against the hallway wall. His eyes were wide, and he licked his lips as he said, 'You can't do—'

McShaun put his face close to Schuller's and in a quiet voice said, 'Look, Pete, you got your three-piece suit. You got your briefcase. You got your Rolex. You got your thousand dollars from that kid's parents. So why don't you just leave it at that? Why try to turn it into something else? What the fuck, you think you *beat* me, man? You think you *kicked my ass*?' McShaun pushed the fingers of his right hand lightly against Schuller's throat, ignoring the bailiff, who had stepped into the hallway and was standing there gawking. 'Hear this, motherfucker. You played your little game here in the court-house. You puffed yourself up and danced around tough, using the rules here to get your way. But let me give you a hint: Out in the street, in my world, you ain't shit. Out where I apply the law – the real law, the *people's* law – I'd have you for fucking breakfast. Hear me?'

Schuller was sweating heavily, trying to swallow, shaking his head up and down, and staring into McShaun's burning eyes. McShaun released the pressure on Schuller, put his face against Schuller's ear, and said, 'Come see me, Pete. Come see me where I live, where I work. Come see me and challenge me there.'

The bailiff had ducked back inside the office, either to call for help or pretend he had seen nothing. Schuller slumped against the wall and stared at McShaun as McShaun took one more long look at him and then walked slowly and easily down the hallway and out the door.

McShaun drove back to his apartment seeing nothing. He pulled into his spot, checked his mail – you are eligible to win fifty-six billion dollars in this super sweepstakes if you'll only subscribe to – patted Radar on the top of the head absently, and stepped inside.

64

In a small pile on the floor were the cork and label from a bottle of Pouilly-Fuissé, a program from a Gordon Lightfoot concert, a small cross made of wood from South America, a book of poetry, an old football jersey with his name across the back, and a note. He read the note, then looked through the jumble of things, then read the note again.

He felt sad and tired and alone.

He was standing there, staring off into the distance, when the piercing cry of a hungry Radar brought him out of it. He looked in the refrigerator and the cupboard only to find that he was out of cat food. No orange juice, either, and the milk was low. He locked up, got into his car, and headed for the grocery store.

McShaun turned his car into the alley behind the supermarket to cut through to the side parking lot where he knew there was usually more room. He eased past a big green garbage dumpster and saw a beige rental car coming slowly toward him, the driver waving one arm out the window. Probably from Toronto, looking for Ocean World, thought McShaun as he slowed and stopped alongside the other car.

But the man in the other car didn't look as if he were from the north; he looked as if he were from Cuba, and when he spoke, this was confirmed by a heavy Latin accent.

'Hey, señor, how you doing? You have a minute? I'm having many troubles lately and I am needing some money, so I'm selling some things. You know?'

McShaun looked at the man. He was tired and in no mood to hear about someone else's problems. And he was irritated to feel little alarms going off in his rather fuzzy brain.

'Listen, señor. I can see you're doing okay, so you understand why I stop you here and see if maybe you want to buy something I have to sell . . . yes? Look, do you like guns?'

Now the alarms going off in McShaun's skull were insistent enough to make him sit up and really pay attention.

He was beginning to know what, or who, he had bumped into here. McShaun the magnet does it again, he thought. Always attracting trouble, even off duty. He looked at the man in the rental car. He was in his late twenties, and although it was hard to tell since he was sitting, he looked like he went five-ten, maybe six feet. He had black curly hair and was kind of pudgy, probably two hundred pounds. McShaun couldn't see the man's hands but guessed there would be a tattoo on the right one, on the skin between the thumb and index finger.

The man was staring at him, and McShaun's mind raced over the telexes and lookout notices that had been read at the briefings over the last couple of weeks, information on a Cuban male who offered to sell his victim a gun at a low price and then stuck the gun in the victim's face and took the fool's money and anything else that was worth taking. So far he had shot two people, both in the legs. He had been hitting from West Palm Beach all the way down the coast to South Miami.

McShaun looked around nervously and said, 'Well, sure, I mean, if you have something that I might want. Actually, I know very little about guns – they scare me – but I've been thinking about buying one to have around the house. Well, you know how things are getting to be. I, uh, I only have a couple of hundred dollars on me . . . what kind of gun did you say it was?'

The Cuban's eyes lit up and he smiled a big smile, which was accentuated by a shiny gold tooth just off center. 'It's a .45 automatic, a Colt.' He smiled again. 'It's only been fired a couple of times. Why don't you pull over there and take a look at it? Maybe we can save you some money.'

McShaun parked his car and got out. His Smith and Wesson Model Ten .38 Special was tucked into his waist, under his sport jacket. The gun was his service revolver that he carried in his holster when on duty, and although most of the officers preferred to carry short-barreled guns when not in uniform, he felt more comfortable with his good old four-inch. He watched as the Cuban got out of the rental car and walked toward him, smiling. McShaun noticed that the rental car was still running, and he wasn't yet sure of how he was going to handle the situation.

The Cuban didn't give him time really to think about it.

They came together face-to-face just to the side of the green dumpster that blocked half the alley. The Cuban's smile got wider, and then he reached down into his waistband, under the crisp white starched shirt, and pulled out the .45. McShaun had time to notice, before the Cuban stuck the barrel of the piece into his chest, that it was a Colt Commander with a brushed nickel finish, and that the hammer was back, indicating that there was a round in the chamber.

The Cuban said, 'Tell you what. I think I better keep this gun and take your money, anyway – okay? Or would you rather make me kill you here in this poor alley?'

McShaun took a breath and slowly raised his hands, palms out, up to the level of his shoulders. He spread his legs slightly and considered the situation. If McShaun wanted to push the gun out of his chest, he would have to use his left hand to move the gun down and away. That would make it difficult for him to get to his own gun, which was tucked into his left side. His eyes flicked around the alley. Even though it was behind the stores, it connected with the streets and the parking lot. McShaun knew that other cars could come driving through and people could come walking through at any time. There could be no shooting without taking a chance of hitting someone.

'C'mon, señor. Give me the money. *Pronto*!'

The Cuban held out his left hand, still holding the .45 about four inches from McShaun's chest. McShaun licked his lips and said, 'Okay. All right . . . please, I'll get the money . . . just be careful with that . . . .' Then he twisted to his right as he brought his left hand down hard onto the Cuban's right wrist, pushing the .45 down and away. At the same time he whipped his right hand across in a claw and raked the other man's eyes. The Cuban yelled, 'Bastard!' and tried to bring the gun up toward McShaun's groin.

McShaun turned away, still holding on to the Cuban's wrist, and punched him in the face, hard. The Cuban grunted and swung his left arm around, hitting McShaun in the side of the head. McShaun started to reach for the gun with his right hand, still pushing it away with his left, when the Cuban started screaming in Spanish and squeezed the trigger twice.

The two explosions boomed and echoed through the alley. The bullets hit the metal sides of the dumpster and splintered and whined away. The force and noise of the gun going off so close enraged McShaun. He managed to grab the gun with both hands and pull it up toward the Cuban's face. The Cuban's eyes widened with fear. McShaun let his weight fall onto his left leg as he started kicking the Cuban in the groin and stomach with his right leg.

Again and again McShaun's right foot and knee impacted the other man's groin and belly with vicious power. The Cuban tried to struggle free, but McShaun pulled his face closer to the other man's head and hissed, 'No . . . no, motherfucker . . . now you're *mine*!'

Locked into the struggle, McShaun felt himself turning to steel; he was strong, he was on fire, and he was going to hurt the Cuban. He felt all of the hurt and frustration and fatigue and loss and injustice of the last few days and nights coming back to him – and he almost went berserk. He sank his teeth into the Cuban's right ear and bit as hard as he could. The Cuban screamed and tried to pull away, causing McShaun to rip out a piece of flesh, which he then spit against the other man's head.

The gun went off one more time before slipping out of the Cuban's hands, the round going straight into the air as the gun clattered to the pavement. McShaun ignored it as he held the man's arm up with two hands and kicked him in the groin again. He felt the man go limp and heard him crying and pleading. Finally the Cuban slumped down against the steel wall of the dumpster. As he did, McShaun let go and stepped back to kick him in the face. But he didn't kick him. He reached down for the man's throat to choke him, but he didn't choke him, either.

Instead he knelt over the Cuban, who was gagging and choking and crying, and, with his fingers poised like talons over the Cuban's throat, he let out a low growl and in a grating whisper said, 'I should . . . kill . . . you.' He stared with wonder at his hands, so close to the sweaty throat, and he felt himself torn by conflict.

'McShaun!'

'Tim . . . Tim.'

'Enough . . . that's enough!'

McShaun heard the voice coming to him from far away. It kept calling him, and it bothered him. He felt strong hands grab his arms to lift him up.

'Tim! Let it go, man. Let it go! That's enough!'

McShaun sat up and pulled his arms down slowly and turned to look into the frightened face of one of the day-shift sergeants. It was Chris Dryesdale, a young sergeant who looked like the Pillsbury Dough Boy with a black Dutch-boy haircut. McShaun had worked with Dryesdale, and he knew that under the soft exterior was steel. He blinked his eyes and said, 'Chris . . . I'm okay, I'm all right.'

McShaun got up slowly and stood beside the sergeant as two other day-shift cruisers slid into the alley, lights flashing.

Dryesdale looked down at the bloody body of the Cuban and said, 'Guy has the flower store a couple of doors down saw the Cuban pull the gun. He called. We got here as fast as we could.' He turned and looked at McShaun closely, his concerned eyes seeking something in McShaun's tight face. He told one of the patrolmen to call for an ambulance for the Cuban and told the other one to collect the .45 and the shell casings. He gently took McShaun's arm and led him over to his unit.

McShaun leaned against the fender, rubbed his bloody hands against his face. He said, 'He's the guy that's been hitting all over the place . . . He . . . tried to shoot me. He tried . . .'

Dryesdale nodded and said evenly, 'Tim, Tim, listen. You're all right. Calm down now and get your mind running smoothly. You're gonna have to come down to the station to give a statement to the dicks and make out a report.' He stopped, then went on. 'Tim, look at me, man. Calm down, get your act together. The report will have to be right. The statement will have to be right. You hurt that Cuban bad. Real bad. So your paper is gonna have to be right, yes?'

McShaun looked at the sergeant, his friend, and knew he was right.

'I'm all right now, Chris. I'll make it technically correct. No problem.'

Dryesdale looked at McShaun closely for a moment and then turned away as the ambulance came purring into the alley. McShaun leaned against the sergeant's car and took a deep breath and looked up into the clear blue sky.

He was all right.

The next day Springfield waited for McShaun by the back door of the station. She had heard all about McShaun and the Cuban; that's all anyone had talked about the evening before during her shift. She was worried about him and hoped to see him for a moment, if only to give him some encouragement and support.

She tapped one foot as she thought, *And now there's something else I might want to speak with him about, although it definitely is none of my business.* When she had first entered the station, Rocky had gone to the second-floor locker room, which was for the female officers, to check her gear and use the bathroom. She had been there only a moment when two girls burst into the room, one crying and the other apparently trying to comfort her friend. Rocky had recognized the one who was crying as the girl who worked in the Records Division on the evening shift. She also recognized her as the girl that everyone said McShaun was involved with.

She couldn't help listening to the conversation.

The crying girl covered her face with her hands and sobbed, 'I don't think I can stay here now. He made it so clear . . . so *final.*'

Her friend held her lightly and patted her arm. The girl went on, 'He's always been so nice, so *good* to me. I thought we were getting closer and closer.' She wiped her eyes with the back of her hands. 'Maybe that was the problem, maybe he won't let *anyone* get really close to him. He has a . . . remoteness, a scary kind of remoteness that makes him seem far away sometimes.'

Rocky had stood there listening, knowing it was impolite but finding herself drawn to the conversation. The crying girl blew her nose and looked at her friend with a small smile as she went on. 'I love him and I want him . . . but he's gone. He made up his mind that he would give me so much of himself and then he would leave me. And he did.' The girl had stopped talking, and the room grew very quiet. Rocky had slowly turned to go, and as she eased the door open she heard the girl say, 'I don't know what I'm going to do now. It's going to be . . . hard. I swear, sometimes when you're with him, you feel like you're standing too close to the sun. Know what I mean? I mean, his *intensity* is enough to make you tired or scared – or both.'

Rocky had walked away from the locker room and down-stairs to the back door where she now waited for McShaun, her thoughts in conflict. Even though she was not friendly with the girl from Records, she felt a kind of sisterhood. She was surprised to find herself angry that McShaun had hurt the girl. It was irrational, but she felt it, anyway.

She turned now as she heard the day-shift sergeant, Dryesdale, call out McShaun's name and walk across to him in the parking lot. He spoke with Tim for a moment, and then they both turned and walked toward Springfield. As they approached, Rocky could see that McShaun looked tired, drawn, and angry. She bit her lip and said, 'Hi, Sarge. Um . . . Tim, do you think I could talk with you for a minute?'

Sergeant Dryesdale nodded and pushed past her into the hallway, then turned and waited. McShaun stopped in front of her and said, 'Sure, Rocky. But it will have to wait until later on in the shift.' His eyes tightened and he looked up, as

71

into the heavens, and said, 'Seems like I have to go talk with the *chief* right now, though. Yep, the actual living *chief* wants to see me about a certain Cuban gentleman that I did some molecular rearrangement on.' Sergeant Dryesdale cleared his throat and said, 'Tim, easy. Right? Let's just go talk with him and see what the program is. Okay?'

McShaun nodded at the sergeant and turned to face Springfield again. He smiled a little and looked into her eyes, and she could feel the fire there as he said, 'I would like to talk to you, too, Rocky. Maybe later, okay?' Then he turned and walked down the hallway with the sergeant.

Springfield stood by the open back door, watching him go, not knowing what to think.

Chapter Seven

McShaun sat tensely in the comfortable leather chair in front of the chief's large polished desk. Sergeant Dryesdale sat to his right and a little behind him. The chief had nodded them into the chairs while he spoke on the phone quietly. As he sat there McShaun looked around the office. It was large, airy – an executive's office, except that most of the photos on the walls showed people in some kind of uniform, and most of the plaques bore some kind of badge or star.

McShaun looked at the chief, who was turned sideways to him with the phone tucked against his shoulder and ear as he lit a cigarette. He was a professional man, a man who had that slick look of the politician and the assured look of success and confidence. He tried to maintain an easy manner, but close inspection showed that it was fabricated. He was taut and had a hardness about him. His eyes, though watery and pale, were constant in their searching, always searching. He was not a big man physically and so carried himself very erect with his shoulders back. His quick, aggressive mannerisms and his politician's voice gave one the impression that he was bigger than he was.

The chief had made his way up through the ranks and had been a detective captain when the old chief suddenly died and he had been selected by the city management as the new chief. He had come into office on a wave of optimism – the sixties were gone, here come the seventies and a new chief, a chief who was a cop, a chief who knows the guys, and a chief who wants to get the job done with no bullshit. Everyone wanted to like him and respect him.

The first positive thing he did as chief was to order the termination of the rule that forced all the patrolmen and sergeants in uniform to wear a tie at all times. The decision was applauded and there were smiles all around.

That had been the last positive thing the chief had done for the working cop on the department. Once in office, he shed his cop skin and gratefully and knowingly slid into his political skin. He became more concerned with appearances than with real police work. He became obsessed with public relations, which he allowed to become paramount over effectiveness. As the years went by and the working officers on the street saw how he responded to conflicts concerning his officers, the confidence and respect he once enjoyed dwindled. By the time McShaun sat in his office, he was a chief who headed a department made up of cops who saw that he had long ago forgotten what it meant to be a cop.

The chief hung up the phone and put down his cigarette. He stood up and leaned over his desk to reach out and shake McShaun's hand. 'Tim . . . good to see you, guy. You're looking fine, as always. Yes, sir, never a wrinkle, never in need of a haircut, always one of my better-looking officers, Tim.' McShaun released his hand from the chief's strong grip and sat down as the chief nodded at Dryesdale and said, 'And you, Chris. Good to see you too.' The sergeant nodded back and settled himself into the chair.

The chief picked up his cigarette and waved his hand. 'Smoke if you want, guys. Oh, wait a minute, you don't, do you, Tim? And Chris? No? Hell, I keep telling myself I'm going to quit one of these days too.' He took a long drag, turned in his chair, looked up at the ceiling, and said, 'Broken right wrist. Three broken ribs left side. Broken nose. Two broken front teeth. Contusions and abrasions. Some throat injuries.' He turned his head and looked at McShaun, then turned back. 'I'm told he'll probably come out of intensive care today. They had him in there because of the head injuries. Oh, did I forget to mention the chunk of ear that appears to have been bitten off?' He turned again in his chair and put his elbows on his big desk while his eyes looked into McShaun's face. 'Don't you think that's just a little much, McShaun, even for you?'

Before McShaun could answer, Sergeant Dryesdale said quietly, 'Chief, I guess you know that the guy was one of those bad Cubans, had one of those tattoos on his hand that means he'd been an enforcer back in Cuba. And you know the .45 had been stolen in a burglary down in Miami and that the car was an overdue rental and that every jurisdiction from here to Palm Beach has been able to ID him on their robberies. And I'm sure you know he pulled his .45 on—'

'Yes, yes, I know all that, Sergeant,' said the chief tersely. 'I know the guy's bad news. I know it was an arrest that will clear crimes. I know . . . I know. But I also know that the *Herald* will be doing a big thing on it this evening. One of their reporters, Green, was at the ER when the ambulance brought the guy in.' He looked at McShaun again. 'And I also know that McShaun here beat the guy to a *pulp*. I mean, the poor bastard wasn't just subdued and arrested. McShaun here damn near killed the guy! Jesus!'

The chief suddenly stood up, knocking his chair away from him as he stepped to the window that looked down over the parking lot. He stood there with his hands on his hips, his legs spread, his back to McShaun. He said, 'Tell you what, Chris, and you, McShaun – it was an armed robbery. McShaun is a cop. If deadly force had to be used, fine.' He lowered his voice. 'Fine. But it would have been better if McShaun had just pulled out his piece and blown the guy's fucking head off! Yes?' He turned and looked down at McShaun. 'You've already blown a couple away – fatal shootings – and the department stayed with you all the way through the grand jury. And you were commended and all the rest of it. Nice clean shootings. Oh, I know you took some flack on that last one, but shit, *twice* with a twelve-gauge?' He put his hands on the small of his back and stretched before he went on. 'But now . . . now we have Officer Tim McShaun in a deadly force situation. And instead of shooting the bad guy, for *whatever* reason, instead

75

of shooting him our boy McShaun fucking nearly beats the guy to death with his bare hands!'

The chief turned his back again and stared out the window, his heavy breathing the only sound in the office. McShaun sat looking down at his legs, thinking of the Cuban's grin as he put the .45 against his chest. On the other side of the chief's closed door the steady hammering of the secretary's typewriter seemed to go on, muted, forever.

Sergeant Dryesdale cleared his throat and said, 'Uh, Chief, McShaun indicated in his report why he didn't try to draw and fire his weapon, and our Public Information Officer should be able to go to the media with the angle that our officer went up against an armed man with his hands in order to protect any citizen—'

The chief waved his arms as he interrupted Dryesdale again. 'Yeah, yeah. Three shots *were* wildly fired during the struggle. PIO knows how to cover for us, and they will. But that's not the point.' He looked at McShaun coldly for a few seconds, then continued, 'Let's talk about another little matter, one that you're not familiar with, Sergeant. I get a call – actually, it turned out to be two calls – one from a Juvenile Division judge. The judge tells me that McShaun here gets unhappy about a ruling the judge made, waits until the room clears, and then climbs into the judge's face about it. The judge told me he would describe McShaun's comments as "threatening." He also tells me his bailiff saw something going on in the hallway between McShaun and Peter Schuller, the attorney. The bailiff told the judge he couldn't swear to what he saw, but it wasn't too cool.' The chief kept looking at McShaun as he sat down at his desk and said, 'With me so far, Sergeant? Then I get a call from Schuller, Attorney at Law and well-known local up-and-coming politico. He tells me about McShaun here *assaulting* him in the hallway of the courthouse. Tells me McShaun actually roughed him up because of some comments he made to McShaun.'

The room fell silent again, comforted by the continuous gentle patter of the secretary's typewriter.

McShaun sat tensely, looking at the chief. Sergeant Dryesdale sat looking at his fingernails. The chief sat staring at the cigarette that had found its way into his hands.

Finally the chief said, 'Schuller is no dummy, and like I said, he's a politico. He tells me he would like nothing better than to take this all the way. He says he really wants to jam McShaun's shiny badge right up his aggressive ass. And he says he would, except. Except. Except for the fact that he has always had the utmost respect for this police department and all the fine officers that work here and he knows how hard it is and blah, blah, blah. And also, except for the fact that even though he knows the bailiff saw the whole thing, the bailiff told him that he didn't know anything and would not give him any statement.'

The chief lit the cigarette and leaned back in his chair. 'So what we have basically is McShaun's word against Schuller's – and Schuller won't go to war unless his chances are better. But he did call me and he did tell me. And I think I should believe him. Should I, McShaun?'

McShaun sat very still for a moment, then said quietly, 'Believe him, only believe there was more to it.' He rubbed his eyes hard in frustration at not being able to explain to the chief how he had been right in what he had done. He said, 'Believe I only acted as I did after being provoked, after being . . . taunted.'

'Oh, were you provoked, McShaun? Were you taunted?' The chief blew a column of smoke at the ceiling. He sighed. 'Tim . . . c'mon, Tim, is it getting worse or what? First four or five years on the job here and you filled your personnel file with attaboys and letters of commendation – always good work, always right. Then . . . well, a guy gets punched out by you after a foot chase, or another guy in the jail resists you and gets fifteen stitches, or how 'bout the guy that spit on you and they had to pull you off him in the middle of Broward Boulevard?' The chief rubbed the bridge of his nose. 'Sure, McShaun, you're good with your paperwork, and you know the damn system and police officers' rights and all that crap as well as anybody around here. So you've managed to avoid really getting in a jam over any of this stuff so far, but – *shit*!' He leaned across his desk and stared at McShaun, his fingers digging into the blotter on his desk. 'You ever heard of "negligent retention" Tim? Huh? It means I can be found negligent if it's proved that I've retained a cop who's fucked up. Know what I mean? I, me . . . me and the city . . . we're *negligent* if we *retain* you when there's solid evidence that you're losing control of yourself. Are you losing control, Tim? Can't you handle it anymore? Or are you still the good cop we all know – hope – you are?'

The room was silent.

The chief looked suddenly tired. He sighed again and said, 'Look. Here it is, Tim . . . Chris . . . there will be no official record or action on the Schuller thing. It's dead. On the Cuban thing we'll weather the coming storm with our Public Information Officer, and we'll keep falling back verbally until it's time to take some placating action say three or four days.' He looked at McShaun. 'McShaun should take a couple of days vacation time – starting now. That way we can honestly say it isn't suspension. And when he comes back, he's transferred off the road and into the Communications Division.'

The sergeant looked sad but nodded his head. McShaun sat ramrod straight and said, 'But, Chief—'

The chief shot back, 'But *shit*, McShaun! But *nothin'*! You're coming in off the road. The media will be told, if it goes that far, that it's a routine transfer to fill a slot in the Comm Center. I'm taking you off the road . . . I am . . . *me* . . . because I think you need to settle down, McShaun.'

The chief stood up and looked at his watch. Dryesdale stood, and then, slowly, so did McShaun. The chief said to the sergeant, 'I'll get the word to the shift captain and he'll get the paperwork started. You put Tim out on a couple of days vacation and coordinate with the Comm lieutenant as far as when he's supposed to report and all that.' Dryesdale nodded.

The chief turned to McShaun, who stared back with cold

eyes. 'Look, Tim, you're hurting us and you're hurting yourself, so I'm taking this action. I'm doing it for all of us.'

McShaun sat morosely in the sergeant's office while Dryesdale spoke on the phone and filled out forms. The door crashed open, and Chick Hummel pushed into the room, his cigar leaving a thick trail of smoke. He looked at the sergeant and then at McShaun before he asked, 'Is it true?' The sergeant made a face, and McShaun just looked at his friend and shrugged his shoulders. Hummel took the cigar out of his mouth and said, 'Shit.'

Sergeant Dryesdale hung up the phone and said, 'Hey, Hummel, how about closing the damn door? And put that cigar out, would ya? This place stinks bad enough already, what with all the bullshit that gets slung around.'

Hummel nodded and stubbed out the cigar in an ashtray while he kicked the door closed. He looked at his partner and said, 'Tim, you did a hell of a job with that Cuban, and don't even start to think otherwise. I just talked with one of the day-shift guys who works out on West Davie Boulevard where that little Cuban business community has sprung up over the last couple of years. He said he was having a coffee with the owner of the gas station there, who's a Cuban, and some of the guy's friends were there, and they were talking about your deal from yesterday. Seems the word is already out on the street that you did a complete job on that bean-belly.' Hummel ignored Dryesdale, who sighed audibly, shook his head, and went on. 'Anyway, this day-shift guy said that all of those Cubans thought you did the right thing. They're people who had to flee Castro, and since coming here they've been working their asses off trying to make it in this country. They know there's some bad ones that have come across, and they resent these criminal-type Cubans giving them all a bad name. The whole conversation was in your favor according to the day-shift guy. He said the Cubans all thought you shoulda kicked the crud's ass all the way back to Havana.'

McShaun stretched his arms over his head, spreading his fingers, but he said nothing.

Hummel looked at the sergeant and said, 'So who the hell am I gonna ride with, huh? Some new kid? Some split-tail?'

Dryesdale looked at him, knowing how close Hummel and McShaun were and knowing how long they had worked together in the northwest part of town. He said, 'I don't know, Chick. I can only tell you right now that this whole thing is bigger than all of us, and we just have to live with it for now.'

McShaun grabbed his partner above the elbow and said quietly, 'Chick, maybe this is the time to put that letter in for Vice-Narc-OCB, like you've been talking about. You know that lieutenant over there has told you he wants you. And you've told me a bunch of times you'd like to try it. I know you've held off because I'm the only one who'll let you eat at McDonald's every friggin' night of the week, so maybe now's a good time to make the move. Hell, who knows how long I'll be in the Comm Center? Figure six months at least.' McShaun saw Dryesdale nod in agreement. 'So what the hell? Try it.'

Hummel stood quietly for a moment. Then he said, 'Maybe I will, Tim. But I still think this sucks real bad, and I'd rather work with you on the street for the rest of my time here than do anything else.' Then, embarrassed, he shook his head and walked out. He did not slam the door as he left.

Dryesdale sat watching Hummel go, then said to McShaun, 'He's a good one – and you're right about a transfer for him. He'd be good at it, and they do want him over there. Don't worry about him, Tim, I'll find somebody for him to work with until he transfers.'

McShaun shook his head.

'And listen, I've talked to the Comm lieutenant. He says, without sarcasm, that he'd be thrilled to have you up there. Went into the thing about how none of the street cops really appreciate what the Comm Center is all about, said that it would be great to have a working cop up there so they could learn from him. Anyway, how about going up there now and talking with the head dispatcher before you start your . . . uh . . . vacation? You know Janie, right? Okay. And then just give me a call in a couple of days and I'll fill you in on the new schedule and Hummel's partner and all that. Right?'

Janie Majors had been the head dispatcher at FLPD for as long as anyone could remember. She was a small woman with a raspy voice, a cigarette always dangling from her lips, a bouffant hairdo held fixed in place with hair spray, and a drill-sergeant demeanor. She was a legend for her talent in commanding the action on the radio. Through the radio she gave orders, gave help, gave instructions, and gave hell to patrolmen and captains alike. Sometimes she was called 'Major Janie,' but she was very much respected for her mastery of everything that was going on on her radio channel at all times. Many were the cops that had stories to tell about how little Major Janie had saved their ass by having her act together. She was gruff and tough and sometimes loud and always aggressive, but she loved 'her boys', the street cops, with a passion.

She looked at McShaun with one eye squinted from the cigarette smoke, her hips cocked, one fist resting on the high side. McShaun stood unhappily before her, like a schoolboy who has been bad, standing in front of a substitute teacher. He didn't know what to say but was spared when Janie put her head back and said, 'Timothy McShaun. Off the street, huh? Well, no matter, you'll find some work here. You could answer the phones, you know, and talk to the citizens.' She gave him a knowing look. 'Or you could help out by dispatching. You could learn it easy enough, and it's important and we *need* dispatchers. But before I get on to that subject, let me just say this: I'm your immediate supervisor up here, okay? You work for *me* and I'll take care of you.'

McShaun looked at her. Immediate supervisor? Her? He was her *aide*?

She pulled the cigarette from her mouth and eyed him up and down before she said, 'And also – what size culottes do you wear?'

McShaun stood looking at her, then down at his legs, then over beyond the glass partition at the girls sitting at the radio consoles. His face tightened and he felt his lips go dry. He started to speak, but Janie patted him on the arm and said softly, kindly, 'Hey, kid, I'm just bustin' your balls a little. We need you up here, and we'll take care of you, no problem. And . . . and, it will be all right. You'll see.'

Chapter Eight

Harvey Jensen was feeling pretty smug as he eased his black
Porsche 911 through the heavy beach traffic and west over
the Oakland Park Bridge. He had been out along the strip,
cruising and looking for some new 'talent' for Odom's
films. He changed lanes, adjusted his Ferrari sunglasses,
and laughed out loud, thinking of the never-ending supply
of young 'starlets' out there on Fort Lauderdale's famous
strip. He down-shifted through the gears and made the turn
northbound onto Bayview Drive, in the northeastern part of
the city. A nice neighborhood. Nice houses. Nice people.
Most of the homes started in the quarter-million-dollar
range, and most were on the water, actually just a couple of
hundred yards from the Intracoastal Waterway.

Jensen pushed it now, feeling the Porsche wanting to take
off. He checked his Piaget watch and frowned. He might be
a couple of minutes late, and Odom wouldn't like that, not
with the visitor they were going to entertain today. He
tapped his fingers on the leather-covered steering wheel as
he coasted along behind a large Olds with Pennsylvania tags
full of older types who were craning their necks and gawking
at the outrageous displays of wealth. He saw that he could
not pass, so he sighed and sat back and thought about his
situation with Odom.

Odom had started a couple of years back smuggling grass
by boat from Bimini to Lauderdale. It had been good, but
when it got big, it got complicated, with too many people
and too much equipment required. Odom had been smart
enough to see that a change was needed, so he had switched

from the large amounts of grass to small amounts of cocaine. Jensen had worked for Odom the whole time, first as a captain of one of the yachts loaded with grass and then as the captain of a boat bringing in cocaine. Things had gone well for them; Odom was too smart to go crazy, he didn't get tempted by the hundred-kilo deals, and he only dealt with those corrupt Bahamian officials he knew. Through the years, although there had been some losses to the competition and a couple of busts in the lower ranks, it had been profitable.

Jensen slowed as he made the turn onto Odom's street and smiled. Profitable, yes. Odom's cocaine scam with small boats had gone so well that now Odom wanted to try it with airplanes. That's why they were entertaining a guest today. And things had gone so well for Odom that recently Jensen – without Odom's knowledge, of course – had been able to put together his own group to bring in medium-size loads of marijuana. He also shrugged his shoulders as he thought, Oh, well, it may not be as glamorous as coke, but the market is still there.

Jensen pulled into the circular drive of Odom's house just as a taxi pulled out at the other end. He parked and jumped out and hurried toward the front steps of the house where Odom was standing by the door. Odom was waiting for a man dressed in a tennis outfit with one of those shapeless terry-cloth hats pulled down on his head and large dark sunglasses. The man carried a briefcase and seemed to be in a hurry to get inside the house.

Odom hung back and said to Jensen, 'Nice to see you could make it, Harv.'

Jensen looked hurt and said softly, 'Hey, boss, I hung back a little and watched the cab on Bayview – to see if he was cool.'

Odom looked at him hard for a few seconds, shook his head, and led him into the house.

Sam Beachwood was sitting on a sofa in the living room, looking out past the swimming pool at the dock where his slick twenty-seven-foot Magnum racing boat sat. She was a

84

clean boat with twin 350s and Volvo outdrives. The highly polished hull was dark blue with white highlights, and the teak gleamed. He had avoided having some kind of outrageous name painted in large letters on the side of the hull, as many owners did. This way she was clean, and she blended nicely with all the other hundreds of boats out on the waterways of Fort Lauderdale on a sunny weekend day.

Beachwood had made his way to Odom's house by water at his leisure, not having to fight the traffic or worry about his car being spotted at Odom's house. Careful, careful. Beachwood was always careful. Besides, later he would slide over to Shooter's on the Waterway and meet that sweet young thing from one of his competitor's firms who would be waiting, tanned and firm and warm, to go for a little boat ride.

Beachwood heard Odom bringing in their guest. He stood and turned as Odom said, 'Sam, you know Larry. I was just telling him how good it is of him to come by today. Harv, how about some drinks? You know what Sam and I take. And Larry . . .?'

Congressman Larry Lavon put his briefcase down awkwardly beside his left foot and said, 'Uh . . . just some Diet Pepsi or something like that will be fine.' He sat in the chair that Odom motioned to, nodded at Beachwood, and looked around the room. Beachwood and Odom both sat also. They moved their chairs around so they formed a little circle around a small coffee table. Lavon asked quietly, 'Uh, Tom, are we alone? I mean, is there anyone else here in the house?'

Odom smiled and said, 'Not a soul. I almost invited a friend we have over in the City Manager's office, but Sam suggested that even though we trust the man completely and he is a part of what we've got going here – well, Sam suggested that to better protect *you* we'd best keep this nice and small. Of course, Harv here has been with me for years. He'll be around the house to make sure we have what we need and all . . . okay?'

Congressman Larry Lavon nodded his head and took a

sip of his drink. He was surprised at how nervous he was. He had known both Odom and Beachwood for years. In fact, both had contributed heavily to his early campaigns, and he was normally comfortable with them. He looked down at the briefcase beside his leg and felt his stomach tighten. The moisture from his glass dripped onto his pant leg, and as he reached out to put the drink on the coffee table he noticed that his hand was shaking slightly.

Lavon was in his early thirties, neat and trim. His light brown hair was styled nicely, and his attire was always modern conservative. He had a friendly smile and boyish good looks that made him a favorite at the polls. He was only a junior congressman, but he was an up-and-comer. He sat on several important committees in Tallahessee. One was the Anti-Drug-Trafficking Committee.

Odom put down his drink and said, 'Okay, here's what this is all about – just for the record, as they say.' No one smiled. 'We've been moving our stuff by boat with not too many problems, and now we're thinking of moving by air. With the Air Defense Zone Radar along the coast, that can be a tricky proposition . . . and now with these Custom Task Forces and Drug Enforcement Agency things being started, the radar coverage is better and better. Which of course, makes it harder and harder for us to slide through unnoticed. What Larry has been able to get for us . . . and maybe has an example to show today? Yes? Good. What he can get for us is a chart of Florida showing not only the permanent Air Defense Zone Radar coverage but also the flexible DEA and Task Force coverage. He'll know in advance, say a week at a time, where the Task Force will be concentrating their coverage. And naturally, when we know that, we can either take another route or abort and wait until things move to another part of the state.'

Beachwood, slumped in his chair, his eyes closed, said, 'Why does the Committee have that information?'

Lavon, opening his briefcase, spoke as if he were addressing the actual committee as he said, 'There's great public interest in all of this, and the congressmen on the committee want to be able to show their constituents that they're working closely with the feds to get the job done. DEA and Customs were *very* reluctant to do this, but finally their public relations people – and some other pressures – convinced them that it was the right move. They'll be giving us weekly copies of projected areas of coverage, and, of course, they'll be telling us what and how many planes and boats are seized each week. They should be able to, uh, to catch a lot of smugglers this way. Except, of course, for those that, uh, those that know—'

'Exactly, Larry, exactly,' said Odom as he motioned to Jensen for another drink. 'That's why what you're doing for Sam and me here is so valuable. And don't think we don't realize it. Let's take a look at what you've got there.'

The three of them huddled over the charts showing the state of Florida, with certain areas tinted in pink and blue.

Jensen put Odom's drink down on the table and looked out the back sliding glass doors as two small boys, barefoot and in shorts, moved along the seawall, fishing. They cast their lines around the bow of Beachwood's boat, then walked to the stern where they fooled around just long enough for Jensen to consider chasing them. Then they moved on, and he turned back into the living room. He heard Odom say, '. . . fifty thousand today to show you we're pleased with what you have for us. And, of course, there'll be more every time you can help us.'

Odom motioned to Jensen and said, 'Harv, Larry is about ready to take off. Why don't you go ahead and call him a cab?'

Beachwood was sipping his drink through a grin as Odom said to the congressman, 'Larry, listen, sure you don't have time to take in a quick movie before the cab gets here?'

Chapter Nine

The next day, in the late afternoon, Springfield pulled her patrol car into the small parking lot in front of McShaun's apartment building, got out, and walked to the door of number three. After briefing, Sergeant Dryesdale had stopped her and asked if she wanted to go by McShaun's place and let him know the changes, because he had promised he would let Tim know. Dryesdale had explained that he didn't want to call Tim on the phone. It seemed so impersonal. And while he knew that Hummel would go over there after the shift, he wanted to let McShaun know as soon as possible . . . so would she mind?

She stood outside the door of McShaun's apartment for a moment, could hear the intricate and delicate sounds of a classical flute. She knocked. The sound of the flute grew louder as McShaun opened the door and looked at her. He was wearing old jeans and a faded yellow T-shirt. His hair was messed up and he needed a shave. He looked at her hard for a moment, then smiled and said, 'C'mon in.'

Springfield followed him into the apartment and watched him as he went to the stereo on the bookshelf and turned the volume down. She felt awkward and bulky standing there in her uniform with the radio on her hip. He turned and motioned toward one of the small dinette chairs near the front window.

As she sat down she asked, 'Who's the flute?'

He put the book he was holding on a wooden coffee table and said, 'James Galway. He does some really nice stuff.'

She nodded, 'And the book? What were you reading when I so rudely interrupted?'

He looked at the book, then back at her before he said, 'Uh
. . . *Dispatches*. you probably haven't heard of it. It's about
Vietnam.' He started to pull out the other chair and sit down,
but then straightened and asked, 'Hey, something cold to
drink? Iced tea? Juice?'

She shook her head and said, 'No thanks, I can only stay a
minute.' She bit her lip and realized that she really could stay
for a while and wondered why she hadn't said yes. She saw
him shrug his shoulders and sit down and wondered if there
was some way she could get him to ask again.

He looked at her with those intense eyes and said, 'So, is
this official, or did you want to try to finish the last conversation we got into?'

'No, I mean, yes. I mean, Sergeant Dryesdale asked me to
come by and let you know about the schedule. And, yes, I
would like to get back into that conversation someday, but
that will have to wait until we have more time.'

He nodded his head and said, 'Time. I've got plenty of
time.'

She told him what Dryesdale had told her; McShaun
would be working the same evening shift schedule as before,
only he would be up in the Comm Centre. She would be
Hummel's new partner in the northwest. McShaun raised
his eyebrows at that, and she hurried to explain that she had
requested the northwest because she felt that it was a good
area of the town not only to see more action but also to see how
the other parts of the community lived.

She told him that Hummel had laughed at first but then
had agreed, and how she felt comfortable with Chick and
respected him. She did not tell him that part of the reason she
wanted to ride with Hummel was so she could learn more
about McShaun; she didn't even have that settled in her own
mind yet.

She told him that it would only be for a while, anyway,
because Hummel had submitted his letter to be transferred to
the Narcotics Unit. She did not tell him that Lieutenant
James Track had talked to her again and told her it was only a
matter of time before he got her up to the Detective Division.

She added that Dryesdale felt strongly that McShaun wouldn't be upstairs too long. He felt that, when the media noise died down, the need for men on the street would force the chief to put McShaun back out.

McShaun listened. He said nothing. As Springfield finished, her radio crackled and the dispatcher advised that she was holding a call for her.

Springfield got up to leave, and McShaun thanked her for coming. He held the door for her as she left. As she walked down the sidewalk toward her unit she could hear the lilting song of the flute.

The evening paper carried headlines about the Cuban who had been beaten into the intensive care unit by an off-duty cop who, rather than draw his weapon and apprehend the alleged 'robbery suspect,' chose to disarm the suspect and then beat him unmercifully until he was finally dragged off him by other police officers. Phyllis Green's article went on to tell how the cop was the same one who had been involved in two fatal shootings in the last year. She detailed both incidents and hinted that the chief had suspended the officer pending a transfer off the road.

The article listed in detail all of the Cuban's injuries, but it failed to mention his past criminal history or his tattoo.

Chick Hummel's face was forced into a look of consternation and disbelief. His cigar was not lit but was still clenched tightly in the corner of his mouth as he held the plastic bag of marijuana in the air and let it dangle in front of the kid's face. Rocky Springfield stood a few feet away on the sidewalk, watching Hummel and the other three kids still in the car. Their patrol car was parked behind the kid's Camaro, lights flashing. They were a few blocks from one of the larger high schools in the area. Springfield waited with her ticket book to see what Hummel would do.

Hummel pulled the cigar out of his mouth, looked down at the ground, scuffed his shoe, looked at the kid, and said, 'You gotta be kidding me. You must have smoked another bag of this shit even before you left the parking lot to go to lunch.'

The kid looked perplexed but said nothing.

'So here I am with my partner there in our little poleese car, minding our own business, thinking about our lunch, and here you come in your hot Camaro, smoking up the streets, squealing your tyres, and doing a lot more than the posted twenty-five-mile-an-hour limit. Huh?' He shook his head and stared at the kid. The kid looked at Hummel and then at the ground.

'So I gotta pull you over, right? Right. I gotta pull you over and look at your driver's license and maybe write you a ticket for speeding or reckless driving or somethin'. Okay, so it's no big deal . . .' Hummel threw a quick glance at Springfield, who could see the smile behind his eyes before he continued.

'So I do pull you over, and I walk up to your car like one-Adam-twelve, all ready to go into my act about your less than pristine driving, and what do I see? I mean, what do I see sitting there glaring at me, saying, "Look at me, Mister Poleese, look at me"? Why, I see this fat little baggie of grass.' He held the bag in front of the kid's eyes. 'Right on the dashboard, kid? When you know you've been pulled over by the poleese? Geesh, kid, so what am I supposed to do? Just issue you a citation and smile and say have a nice day while this illicit bag of the dreaded poison weed lounges on your dash? Huh?'

The kid, wishing he was back in his Camaro with his girl on his way to the beach, or back to school, or to the dentist, or *anywhere*, still didn't know what to say. He was doomed. He knew it. The big cop with the cigar had him; there was no way out. He was . . . doomed. He looked up at the cop and said, 'Uh, the grass is mine. I mean, the others didn't know it was there . . . uh, and about the way I was driving . . . I, uh . . .'

Hummel put his hands on his hips and rocked back on his heels. He looked at the kid, he looked at Springfield, he looked at the Camaro, he looked at he marijuana, he looked

91

up into the sunlight. 'Very honorable. Yes, the grass is yours and none of your friends had anything to do with it. I shouldn't go ahead and pat you down and cuff you and stuff you into my car right now. I shouldn't get your friends out of your car, one at a time, and search them . . . girls too.' The kid's eyes widened at the thought of this. 'And I shouldn't rip your car to shreds in my search for more of this evil weed. Right? All because you've confessed to being the sole owner of this narcotic substance. Right?'

'Uh . . . yes, sir . . . I mean . . . no, sir . . . I mean . . .'

Hummel put his cigar back into his mouth, opened the plastic bag with his fingers, held it up and away from him, and let its leafy contents fall out and flutter gently to the ground, spread slightly by the breeze. He said nothing as he shook the bag to make sure it was all out, then he used one of his feet to scatter the bigger clumps of the marijuana into the dirt beside the sidewalk.

The kid's eyes were wide with wonder and controlled hope as he watched the big cop fold the bag neatly and hand it to him, along with his driver's license. The kid didn't want to, but he looked into the big cop's eyes as the cop got ready to speak again. When he did, the kid saw, surprisingly, honest concern.

In a gentle voice Hummel said to the kid, 'Look, guy, do yourself a favor. About the driving, this is a residential area with lots of kids, little kids, riding their bikes all over the place. Suppose you hit one with your car while you're acting like an asshole out here? You'd live with it the rest of your life. So take it easy in the hot car, right? About the grass: Hey, I know it's cool, and I'll stand here for an hour and listen to your argument that it's less harmful than booze and all that. Okay. But it's still trouble. Not for me, for you. You have grass in your car, I can tow your car away. And even though your parents could pay some attorney to beat my charges in court, you'd still have to spend some time in the big gray hotel over on Broward Boulevard, and believe me, it sucks.' He looked at the other kids, still sitting in the car staring at him, then back at the kid standing with him on the sidewalk. 'So look, today you skate. I'm not gonna write you for your driving and the grass is gone. You get a free ride. But, kid, there ain't many free rides in this life, so watch your ass from now on, okay? Now get outta here.'

He turned and walked back to the driver's side of the unit and settled in behind the wheel as Springfield slid into the passenger side. They watched as the kid hesitated for a moment, then got into the Camaro and slowly drove away.

As Hummel started the car Springfield looked at him and said, 'Mister Nice Guy, huh? Thought you were pretty strong against dope, Chick. And I know one of the children in the neighborhood you were telling that kid about is your own daughter. So how come?'

Hummel drove a while, thinking. Then he said, 'Yeah, I *am* against dope, I think it's stupid, and I think it hurts ya. But, shit, I wanna get the big guys, the ones that bring it in and sell it, not some high-school kid who will probably grow out of it in a while, anyway.' He laughed. 'Just using some of my police discretion, Your Honor. Oh, hell, Rocky, you'd have done the same thing.'

Springfield laughed too. 'Probably. Not always, but sometimes . . . maybe . . .'

Hummel drove slowly past a cabdriver sitting by a pay phone, waved at the man, and said, 'Listen, since we were talking about our boy McShaun before we stopped that Camaro, let me tell you, he was one of the first cops I ever worked with that would do what I just did. Believe me, there was a time back in the early seventies when a baggie of grass was a big deal, real serious stuff. He and I even got a commendation once for nailing this fool with about a half pound of the stuff, broken down into a whole bunch of one-ounce bags for sale. I mean, that was heavy narcotics, ya know? But I've seen him do what I just did plenty of times. Some damn kid with barely enough shit on him to get him in trouble. So ya dump it. If it's done right, I think it has a better effect on the kid than runnin' him right into the slammer – and then through our wonderful and all-knowing judicial system.'

Springfield nodded her head and said, 'What is it with Tim and "the system"? He's pretty intense about it. I've been a cop for a while now, and I've seen some things, and been to court, and seen the lies and the injustice, and all of it – but I still feel as if I'm a part of a system that works. Even you – yes, even you, Chick – you're a veteran and a hard-charger and a butt-kicker, and you've been around for almost as long as Tim has, but you see it differently than he does.'

Hummel started to say something, but she hurried on. 'Oh, I know you're cynical, and I know you've been burned, but you're not fighting it the way Tim is.'

Hummel was quiet as they waited through a red light and then turned left off Broward Boulevard and headed into the black area of Lauderdale. Finally he said, 'You gotta know Tim a little better.' He glanced at her. 'When I was new here, they put me with McShaun. I was a bachelor living with a couple of other single cops. Holy shit, it was unreal. Party-hearty and all that. Tim took care of me. I was sorta disorganized a lot of the time, would forget to put my collar brass on my uniform, no money for dinner, late for briefings all the time, real screwed up.' He shifted a little on the seat and glanced at Springfield. 'This is gonna sound soapy, but hell, when I met Dee, my lady, well, she turned me right around. Tim was still my street partner, and he still took care of me here on the job, but she helped me get squared away. Tell ya somethin', Springfield, maintaining a relationship with a working street cop has to be one of the hardest things in the world. And the irony of it is that a working street cop really needs somebody. Anyway, Tim always jokes with Dee about it, tellin' her how she relieved him of one of his biggest daily problems – keepin' Hummel's act together.'

He was quiet for a few minutes, and Springfield thought about Hummel's wife. She had met her once, briefly, and remembered her as a smart dark-haired girl with bright eyes and a shy smile. She remembered that she was a nurse and that she looked very comfortable and relaxed standing arm in arm with her guy.

The dispatcher came over the radio and issued a call to one

94

of the other units. A house had been broken into sometime during the morning. The owner had just returned home from her half-day job, and all the things she was working to pay for had been stolen. Would the police come? Could the police take the report? Could the police *do* something? Springfield and Hummel both unconsciously noted where the burglary was and listened as the other unit responded.

Hummel waited at a stop sign while an old black wino scurried in front of their car, head held high, wine bottle hidden under his worn coat. When he was clear, Hummel drove through the intersection and on down the street lined with small houses and apartment buildings.

'You used the word *intense*,' he said as they cruised. 'That's a good word to use when you're talking about McShaun. He is a very intense person, so naturally it carried over into his police work. He sees things in absolutes. It's hard for him to work in the gray. He's out here, they've given him a mission, and he intends to do the job – no ifs, ands, or buts.'

Rocky said, 'But,' and then smiled and went on. 'But what about his taking the law and using it the way he wants? You said he'd go hard after a dope dealer but turn right around and dump out some kid's marijuana, even though the same law applied to both.'

Hummel nodded and said, 'When I mention black and white and gray when I talk about Tim, I mean the way *he* sees it. He'll tell you the law is the law, and at the same time he'll tell you that discretion is one of his favorite working tools. He sees what his job is out here as black and white, clear-cut. He sees anyone else's interpretation of it as gray.'

'So when he rails against the system, it's because it doesn't parallel *his* system?'

Hummel shook his head. 'What bothers Tim most is that his bosses, his leaders – city admin guys, police brass, judges – in *his* eyes have lost touch with the reality of the law and its applications. He feels like he sees it very clearly while the guys that control him, or try to, see it in a diluted form.'

They both tried to talk at once, but the alert tone came

piercing through their radio receivers and they were dispatched code three to a cutting in an alley behind one of the small food stalls off Sistrunk Boulevard.

As Hummel moved the unit deftly through the afternoon traffic, lights and siren going, he glanced once at Springfield and yelled, 'Hey, remember that Tim started like we all did. Tim started by believing in the system and the whole shootin' match completely and without a doubt. He . . . *believed*.'

Springfield felt the hot sun on her shoulders as she tried to keep it out of the eyes of the teenage black girl who lay in the dirt of the alley. She knelt over the girl and held two four-inch compresses together over the deep cut that started at the girl's left shoulder and sliced its way cleanly down across the top of her left breast and then fishhooked back up to her throat. The blood, which was everywhere at once, was an incredible bright red. The inner flesh of the girl's chest was a hot pink that contrasted wickedly against her dark cocoa skin. Springfield looked up to see that Hummel was still standing beside the unit, bending down to talk with the handcuffed girl sitting in the backseat. The handcuffed girl was shaking her head and scowling as Hummel said something to her.

Rocky knelt there in the dirt feeling her hands grow wet and sticky as she waited for the ambulance. The girl groaned once and put both of her hands, fingers spread, across her belly. It wasn't until then that Springfield noticed that the girl would have a baby in a month or so.

If she lived.

McShaun walked out of the Comm Center, down the stairs to the back door, and out into the parking lot. It was his day off, but he had picked up some doughnuts for the dispatchers who were on duty and had brought them by while he was out running errands. They loved it. On the way out he had been yelled at a couple of times and said hello to by some of the guys. He squinted up at the sun and walked to his car.

He had been working in the Comm Center for a couple of weeks now and felt comfortable with it. It was, for sure, not even close to being on the street, but he was surprised to find that what went on there related to the street in an important way. Janie Majors had managed to talk him into dispatching, and once he got the hang of it, he found it to be a challenging and difficult job. He quickly acquired a new respect for the women who did the job full-time. It was a double handful. It was not uncommon for him to go home at the end of a normal day with a sizable headache, and on the busy days he felt as if someone had set his stomach on fire with a blowtorch. His biggest problem was the frustration he felt when some action situation was in progress and he was merely the dispatching voice, sending units, relaying messages, making sure the backups were there . . . all the while sitting glued to his chair with his headset on, instead of being out there on the street helping.

He decided that being a dispatcher on a working police department was one of the hardest jobs on the payroll, and he felt that all the people working in the Comm Center should immediately be paid twice what they were getting, which wasn't that much. He would never criticize a dispatcher again, he would never bitch at that faceless voice that ordered him here and there out on the road. He would do what he could to make their life easier. And he would be a good boy in the meantime, waiting until they let him get back out onto the street.

At the end of the day McShaun got into his old Firebird and drove out of the lot, making sure his take-home radio was on the seat beside him. He always listened while he drove through the city. He remembered arguing with his wife about it while they were still married, 'Always the radio, even to dinner or the movies. And always the gun. For what? The big grab? To get into some caper while your wife is with you? Can't you leave it for even a little while?'

McShaun had tried to explain to her that he wasn't just a cop when he was on duty, that tired old line about being a cop twenty-four hours a day. He tried to explain to her that he carried the gun and took the radio because of the chance – the off chance – that someday, while they were out and going about their business, they would be nearby when a cop needed help. If that time came, he wanted to be ready. Ready with his radio and ready with his gun, if that's what it came to.

He shook his head and remembered how when things got bad between him and his wife she had made a reference to the gun, the always-gun, being used as a symbol of virility, as a .38-caliber penis that never got soft.

McShaun waited for the traffic to clear on Broward Boulevard before he eased out into it and headed east, and then north. As he drove, he thought of the gun and of himself as a sexual man, and of the idea of using the gun as a penis, and he said out loud, 'No way. It would ruin the blueing.'

Two hours later McShaun was headed back to his apartment from the north end of the city. His mind was in a jumble, thoughts racing around and bumping into emotions, and he had a slight headache. He had gone from the station after dropping off the doughnuts to visit a friend, a cop – a cop who had been hurt on the job and was home recuperating. He had been friends with Scott Kelly since working with him a few years back. They had been together in a double unit before Scott went undercover with the Narcotics Unit. Sometime after that Scott had been shot in the legs during a cocaine buy that went bad. He had been in and out of the hospital, and it had been an uphill struggle all the way. McShaun knew that Scott Kelly had been a hardworking cop and a dynamite narc agent, and he knew that all Scott wanted in this world was to get himself back in shape so he could come back and do the job. Now, on the way home, McShaun thought about the conversation he had had with Scott at the wounded cop's apartment.

Scott's wife had served them Kool-Aid while they sat on the front porch. What Scott told him bordered on the unbelievable. He told McShaun of the complex and almost imcomprehensible workings of the Pension Board and the Workman's Compensation office of the City Administration. He told McShaun how he was supposed to get sixty-five percent of his full pay while he was out on injury and how the city was supposed to help him get therapy and medical attention until he was ready to get back to work. He told McShaun that it sounded simple, right? He knew McShaun was like he had been, was like most working cops who go out into the streets every day, wearing the badge and the patch of the city that hired them; cops who went out to work never worrying about what would happen if they were injured or killed. They never worried because they knew that if something happened, then the city that hired them and put them out there would do all it needed to do to care for that cop and his family.

McShaun sat there feeling the drink cold against his hands as Scott told him, '*Wrong*'.

Since Scott had been injured, he and his wife had had to fight for every penny they got from the city. They had had to beg and plead for someone from one of the offices to approve of anything that was needed before they got it, *if* they got it. Scott told of how his wife had had to care for him alone, with no help at all, and of how she, in desperation, had called the City and asked for help – assistance with a laundry service, a part-time nurse, or something . . . anything. She had been told no.

McShaun listened, bewildered, as Scott told him of how he needed physical therapy so he could get back into shape and go back to work. He told how his requests had been turned down by the City even after one of his doctors had prescribed it. He recalled a conversation he had had with one of the city officials when the man on the phone reminded him of all the police 'back injuries' and of all the years of police 'abuses' of help, and he advised Scott that compensation for injury on the job was 'no free ride' anymore, no way. Scott recalled his frustration at not being able to make the man hear him when he tried to explain what he saw as a simple situation: Help me now, help me get back on my feet, and I'll come back to work full-time as a working cop. I won't have to sit here like a liability, like a drain on the compensation and pension funds. The man from the City would not hear him.

McShaun listened as Scott told him of how the meager checks that kept them barely getting by would suddenly stop coming without explanation and of how he would have to make nine phone calls and send out three letters to City Admin people and his own former bosses before finally, grudgingly, the checks would begin to trickle in again, with no explanation of what had happened in the first place. He told McShaun of how, through family and friends, he had raised enough money to buy a membership at a health spa where he could work out and swim to get back into shape. All he wanted to do, he said, was go back to work on the street. He had been a narc when he was shot, and he had been promised by the chief that if he got better and was able to come back, his old job would be waiting for him.

When McShaun stood to leave, Scott had held his arm for a moment and said, 'Hey, Tim, thanks for comin' by, really. Sorry I kinda dumped on you. It's just that sometimes we, uh . . . we feel like we've been abandoned. Like nobody really cares whether we make it or not. Anyway, listen, I hear that your crazy partner Hummel is trying to slide over into the Narc Unit.' McShaun could see the pain in Scott's eyes. 'You tell Chick I said to be careful when he goes over there, okay? Tell him I said to watch his back – always – not just out on the street. Tell him to watch his back.'

As McShaun drove along, thinking about his visit with Scott Kelly, he heard the tone of the voices on the radio change, heard and felt the sudden tension. He listened more closely. TAC squad had been watching a neighborhood for some burglars. They had arrived. They had hit a house. TAC squad had moved in and there was a chase. The chase had just ended with a car crash. Shots had been fired and the burglars were fleeing on foot.

It was all going down two blocks from where McShaun was.

As McShaun headed toward the action he heard one of the TAC men come on and say that they had two of the burglars in custody and one was still at large. They thought he was armed and heading south through the yards and houses in the area.

As he drove, McShaun thought of the area; he saw it clearly, he saw where the car had crashed, and in his mind he knew where the burglar was heading. A block from where the getaway car had crashed there was a small, dirty canal, and on the other side was a large, overgrown field that used to be watermelon and squash and peppers but was now neglected, waiting to be a new housing development. South of the field was a large residential area with many small apartment complexes. McShaun passed by where the getaway car had crashed. He glanced at all the activity: TAC officers running around yelling at one another, citizens standing gawking. He eased on by and headed south. He drove a couple of blocks while he heard one of the TAC sergeants tell the dispatcher to remind all units that the suspect was armed.

McShaun parked his car, locked it, grabbed the radio, turned the volume way down, and walked out into the field. He headed north and a little east until he was in heavy brush that was higher than his head. He didn't hurry. He was relaxed, comfortable. He found a spot in the shade near a clearing, crouched, and waited.

Two minutes passed. The radio murmured. Bugs hummed around him. A bird flew off squawking. Then the bushes rustled and rattled, and McShaun heard the sound of heavy breathing. Then the soaking wet and dirty burglar came crawling through the clearing on his belly.

McShaun sat on his haunches, watching. As the burglar got closer he pulled his revolver out from under his shirt, pushed it through the brush, and said quietly, 'Halt, asshole, it's me, the police.' He smacked the end of the barrel solidly between the wide, frightened eyes of the sweaty burglar.

The man froze, and they contemplated each other for a few seconds before McShaun said, still very quietly, 'They said on the radio that you have a gun. If you have a gun,

I will have to blow your head off. Do you have a gun?'

The burglar did not take his crossed eyes off the barrel of McShaun's revolver as he shook his head slowly from one side to the other.

McShaun could see the man's hands. They were scratched and dirty but empty. 'I'll tell you what, guy,' he said. 'I'll bet you threw the gun in the canal as you swam across. I'm gonna pat you down real good, though, while you lay there like a good boy. If you move, I'll kill you. After I check you out you're gonna stand up nice and easy. I'm gonna grab you from behind by your belt, and we're gonna walk out of this field and to my car. If you as much as hiccup while we are doing so, I will fire my gun into your back until there are no bullets left. Do you hear me? Understand?'

The burglar nodded, and McShaun checked him and walked him to his car, all the while listening to the radio as more and more supervisors told more and more troops what to do and where to go and how far to extend the perimeter.

McShaun had the burglar lie down in the shade beside the front wheel of his car as he tried several times to break through all the chatter on the radio. Finally there was enough of a pause for him to break in with his off-duty call number. The dispatcher advised him that he would have to go to another channel with whatever his business was. They were working a *chase* on this channel. There were a few seconds of silence after he advised her that, yes, he knew about the chase, and he was calling her to tell her that he had the chasee in custody.

The next thing McShaun heard was a lieutenant asking, 'Well, where the hell *is* he, anyway?'

McShaun stood with the shift captain while the burglar was taken away in one of the TAC squad cars. The TAC sergeant, Yorrman, patted McShaun lightly on the arm, winked, and said quietly, 'You did good, Tim.' Then he drove off with some of the other officers and the field got quiet again.

The captain stood with his arms folded and crossed in

front of him looking out across the field. Finally he spoke. 'Well, Tim. Nice grab. Really. You made a nice grab.'

McShaun said nothing; he just stood beside his car, looking up at the tall older man in the dark three-piece suit.

The captain went on. 'Actually, you did such a nice job that the TAC lieutenant and sergeant both came to me and said you should get an ''attaboy'' from one of us. One of us should write you a letter of commendation.' He looked down at the shiny toes of his Florsheims. 'And you know, Tim, they're right. You did a nice job here. You apprehended the bad guy nice and clean, no fuss, no muss. Real good, and you should be commended.'

McShaun waited.

'But it won't happen. You know you did a good job, and so do we. But there won't be any letter in it for you. Not on this one.' He sighed and turned to walk away. 'You did the right thing, Tim. You did a nice job. But you weren't supposed to be here.'

Chapter Ten

One of the problems with Harv Jensen's grass-running operation was the quality of personnel he had been able to hire. Since he was trying to put his scam together while he still worked for Odom, he had to be very quiet about it. He couldn't really go off on a talent hunt around the area. So you get what you pay for, and in this case what Jensen got was a girl named Lydia Taylor.

Tom Odom would never have had Lydia involved in any of his drug-running operations. Of course, being used in a porno film was another thing, and that's how Lydia first came into Jensen's life. She had been with a younger girl once when Harv had made his pitch at the beach. The younger girl liked Harv's grass, but she didn't think she wanted to have her picture taken while she played with herself. Lydia jumped at the chance. She thought it would be a real kick to get it on in front of the camera, then be able to watch herself doing it later.

Lydia also liked to do cocaine, lots and lots of cocaine. And good ol' Harv Jensen had enough cocaine to party almost all of the time.

After Lydia did her first film with Harv, she kept in touch. She was always available, and as far as Harv could see, she kept her mouth shut most of the time. When he asked her if she would like to make some money riding on a boat full of grass – well, actually a couple of hundred pounds of grass – she had said, 'Yes, yes, yes, yes.'

Lydia had gone on two rides so far. They had been exciting, she had made money, and she had partied her little heart out with the other crew members.

Today Lydia had promised Harv she would stop at one of the marine stores and pick up a guidebook to the Bahamas. It was a nice sunny day, and she was wearing almost nothing, as usual – very short shorts and a lace-fringed cotton sleeveless T-shirt – and she was enjoying the stares she was getting. It was hot, so she decided to drop in at a convenience store to get a Slurpee. She found one, got out of her Austin-Healey, and went inside. She told the clerk what she wanted, and while he was getting it she wandered over to the candy rack to get some gum.

She was busy trying to make up her mind between regular gum and the kind that 'squirted sweet juice into your mouth,' so she didn't notice the man hovering behind her.

Lydia couldn't know it, of course, but most cops working in the area would have tiny lights flashing way back in the recesses of their brains if they heard the man's name: Ronald Toreen. Some of the cops wouldn't exactly remember what it was, but they would know that they had heard the name before, and it had something to do with . . . with some kind of sex crime. Wait! A little over a year ago they had nailed Toreen up in Oakland Park for molesting a little girl. Yeah, that was it. They made a case on him for that one, but there had been others, scattered all along the Gold Coast. He hadn't killed any, but he had hurt more than one. In fact, the one they finally made him on had been beaten pretty badly. Ronald Toreen – back out on the streets already. Wonder how?

Ronald Toreen had been declared mentally incompetent at the time of his trial and sent to a hospital for testing and rehabilitation. It had been bad for him because there were no little girls, and he needed them. Actually, no little boys, either. He had seen this immediately and had worked very hard to get himself back out on the street. He had some help from the 'system', which passed responsibility for him from one agency to another, farther away from the criminal system each time, until finally he was controlled by overworked doctors who were interested in him as a 'case,' not as a 'criminal'.

Toreen talked with a lot of nice men and women who seemed genuinely concerned about him. He smiled and spoke quietly and told them about how he wanted to be good and go through life minding his own business. They listened and nodded, and one day people smiled at him and told him he could go home. He wasn't sure of his status as far as the court went, or even if the original judge on his case was aware of what was happening; he just knew he could go home, which meant Lauderdale, and which meant a place where little boys and girls lived.

Ronald had been home a week, back with his old mother. He was thirty-eight years old, but he had always lived with his mother. He got back to Lauderdale and found her there, still in the same old house. He settled in and had spent the week getting to know the area again. It was too soon to look for little boys and girls.

Now Ronald Toreen stood behind Lydia at the candy rack. Actually, he had been there, hanging back, trying to decide on what candy to buy when Lydia Taylor came swaying through. Ronald wasn't ordinarily interested in regular girls, grown-up girls. He knew they looked at his toadlike fat little body, his thick wet lips, his hooded eyes, his greasy hair, his fat stubby fingers, and his blotched and puffy complexion with disgust. For a while he thought he should hurt them for it, but since he was only five feet four inches tall, most of them seemed intimidating to him when he was close, so he contented himself with the little people.

However, he looked at Lydia's bare, tanned back, at the creamy smooth cheek that showed under her shorts as she bent over, at the perfect nipples jutting out against the soft fabric of her shirt, and he knew he had to touch her.

Lydia made up her mind to go for the gum that squirted in her mouth, and Ronald stuck three stubby fingers of his left hand up inside her shorts while he cupped her right breast with his right and pinched her nipple, hard.

Lydia said, 'Oh!' and then. 'Why, you little shit . . .' before she stomped her high heels down hard on top of Ronald's foot, swung both her elbows back, one-two, into

Ronald's flabby chest, and then turned and slapped him hard, one-two, across the face.

Ronald Toreen squealed in dismay, backed away from Lydia, and ran out the door of the store and down the sidewalk. Lydia watched him go, threw her hair back, and said, 'Creep.' She paid for her gum and the Slurpee and went off about her business.

The clerk, who had witnessed the incident, just shook his head and went back to reading his horoscope.

Tim McShaun was on his way back to his place. It was on his day off, and his car was full of clean laundry. He used a Laundromat a few blocks from his apartment, found the time of doing his laundry a relaxing one, and did it usually once every two weeks. Today he was in a hurry because Rocky Springfield was going to come over, and they were going to go on a picnic.

A half hour later McShaun heard the knock on his door and opened it to find Rocky standing there looking fine. She was wearing a pair of shorts and a long-sleeved cotton blouse with the sleeves pushed up. She looked clean and fresh and alive. He smiled and let her in, and their day began.

Rocky had stopped at a delicatessen on Las Olas Boulevard on the way over, and the basket in her car was filled with a selection of cheeses, breads, vegetables, and a couple of pieces of chocolate. McShaun had the wine, white and chilled, a small stereo cassette player, and an old blanket. They took her car.

It was in the middle of the week, and the small park off Las Olas, across from the big old church, was almost empty. They spread the blanket on the grass, in the shade, near the bend in the New River, and sat down.

'No work-related discussions today . . . yes?' he said.

She smiled and nodded.

He watched her. Casually, relaxingly. He wanted to really see her, to take his time, to enjoy her, and he did.

He poured some wine into the heavy glasses he had brought, gave Rocky hers, touched them together with a pleasing ring, and said, 'Here's to you, Rocky – you are beautiful.'

She nodded again, accepting his compliment, and tilted her head. She looked into his deep brown eyes, wondering at the depth and the richness she saw there.

He snapped his fingers and fumbled with the cassette player, mumbling about how he hadn't thought of turning it on because, when he looked into her eyes, he heard an angel's choir, anyway. She laughed and hit him in the face with a paper napkin.

They listened to Jim Croce tell them about his name, they watched the squirrels sizing up their basket, they listened to the breeze in the Spanish moss, they felt the sunshine on their faces through the leaves, they watched the sparkling dark water of the river flow by, and they enjoyed each other.

He listened as she told him of her growing up, her high-school days, her first love. She told him of how hard she worked in college to find something that had meaning. Her generation, the 'me' generation, had nothing really for them to go after but their own personal success. She said that maybe that was why she finally came on the job as a cop. She came out of high school, she went to college, she became a woman, full of desire to actually participate in things, and despite all the new, modern you've-come-a-long-way-baby propaganda, there wasn't anything open to her that had . . . bite. She looked at him as if he might not understand, but he nodded his head and told her that he did.

He told her he felt it would be hard to go through life without actually being in the thick of things, in the action, in the *cause*. He had been lucky in that way. There had always been a mission for him. All he had to do was choose sides.

They went for a walk and were surprised to find that the cassette player was still there when they got back. They ate. He told her stories as he held her hand. They sat on the seawall and threw acorns into the river, waving at the people that went by in boats.

She sat cross-legged on the blanket while he lay with his head in her lap. She rubbed his forehead and he could feel her warmth. He told her of his growing up, of high school and surfing and motorcycles. She listened closely while he brushed quickly over the Army and Vietnam, and laughed at his stories of being a rookie cop.

He found himself talking to her with an ease he hadn't known before. He wanted to tell her little things. He wanted her to feel the importance of things he felt were important. He wanted to share things with her, tell her things, teach her things. He wanted to make her laugh, and she did, and he could see that even as she laughed, she really understood what he was telling her.

The day passed in quiet ease. It was good for both of them.

The sun was going down as they got back to his apartment. He talked her into staying for diner – one of his famous omelettes. She cleaned up a little, then got into deep and meaningful eye contact and conversation, though one-sided, with Radar, who for her part treated McShaun's guests with wary aloofness.

While they ate, and Rocky had to admit that the omelette was terrific, she said to him, 'Tim . . . earlier today you said you have a lot of photos of when you were a kid – motorcycles – and all that – and of your Army time.' She ran her fork around the edge of her plate. 'If you wouldn't mind, sometime, I'd like to see them, to look through them with you.' She looked at him and smiled, 'And if you do let me see them, I'll show you my pictures, including the time I was ten years old and decided to cut my own hair.'

McShaun looked at her and cocked his head. He seemed unsure.

She said, 'Tim, I have a couple of reasons. I'd like to learn more about you, of course, but also . . . that whole Vietnam thing. I was born later than you and I kind of missed it. And now, even though there are a lot of movies and books and articles about it, well, I've never really known anyone who was there, who could tell me what it was *really* like.'

McShaun finished his dinner and got up to boil water for tea. Finally he said quietly, 'I get caught up sometimes when I talk about Nam – I don't want to let that happen tonight, not when it's the first time we've really been together as people. You know?' He saw her nod, and he saw her conflict between understanding and disappointment. He said, 'Tell you what. We'll have some tea, I'll drag out the old photos, we'll look through them, and I'll even answer questions. But if I start to get fired up, or if I think I'm wasting my time telling war stories instead of looking into your eyes, then the pictures go back in the closet and we'll find something else to do.'

She agreed.

They sat side by side on his small couch. Their legs and arms touched, and she rubbed the back of his neck lightly. The photos were kept in cheap albums, some in order, some just thrown in. She couldn't believe how young he looked in most of them. The school pictures were fun: McShaun grins from behind a surfboard; grins while sitting on a Harley-Davidson; grins between the legs of a bikini-ed girl sitting on his shoulders.

When they got to the Army pictures, she saw the same grin, but there was something different in his carriage, something different in the way he stood. He still looked young but somehow more hard.

Then the pictures of Vietnam.

He explained to her that most of the pictures were of his early months there. He had photographed everything when he first got in-country, and then, as time went on he became less interested in taking pictures and more interested in making it through the day. He turned the pages of the album slowly. She looked closely at a photo of McShaun being hugged by a Vietnamese soldier. He said, 'A lot of them were pretty good, but a lot of them were cowards, or at least acted like it because they really had no belief in what they were fighting for. They weren't like the ones from the north, or even the VC. Those guys *knew* what their war was all about. 'Course, like this guy hugging me here, he was just a common soldier, and he was aware that the big guys, the guys in Saigon, mostly were corrupt, that most of them would leave the country as rich men when it finally fell. And he was right.'

She ran her finger across a picture of a young McShaun

with a tight grin, swaying in a hammock in the green of a jungle clearing. McShaun holds up a captured weapon; McShaun shoots the finger at the camera as he stands naked in a river, his white bottom contrasting sharply with the rest of his sun-browned body; McShaun in the middle of a group of men, all yelling at the camera and holding cans of beer. McShaun standing stiffly at attention while a three-star general pins a medal to his chest. 'Bronze Star with *V*. Vietnamese Cross of Gallantry with Silver Star.'

'Big deal. Did you ever see the picture of those wounded vets throwing their medals over the White House fence? No? Well, a bunch of them did.' He saw the question in her eyes. 'I don't know if I'd throw my medals away, Rocky. They mean something to *me*, a private thing.'

She nodded and looked at more pictures of McShaun: asleep in the mud, wrapped in a poncho; McShaun looking very tired and dirty, 'coming in from patrol'; McShaun talking to a door gunner on a Huey helicopter.

'Even now, if I hear the *wop, wop, wop* of a Huey, I'll run outside to watch it go over. If you ask me, they're the greatest – and so were those guys that flew 'em. And also, I don't have any pictures, but there's this fighter jet called the F–4 Phantom. What an ass-kicker *that* thing was. I was in the shit a couple of times and had to call 'em down to help out . . . it was outrageous . . . napalm, para frags, the whole thing. Just kicked ass.'

The next picture showed McShaun standing, looking into the camera, two poncho-wrapped bodies on the road beside him, two pairs of jungle boots sticking out. Rocky felt him tense on the couch. She waited. He looked at the floor and said, 'You can read volumes now about that war. Books and books about how and why and what-all. It was a mistake, we know that now, but it was a shame too. A shame because the guys who were there fighting, like me, we were *good*. We were good enough to make the whole thing turn out differently. I'm not saying there was a definite military solution; I'm saying that the guys in the bushes, like me, we had a job, and we knew what it was, and we did it. But our bosses, our leaders,

111

didn't know what the job was. We were out there doing it, and the people that gave us our orders didn't understand what we were doing. They had lost touch with the mission.'

Springfield sat there, remembering her conversation with Hummel about McShaun's feelings about the police brass.

McShaun became agitated, turning the pages of the album faster, saying less. He stopped once, and Springfield looked on pages of bodies – North Vietnamese and VC soldiers in various postures of death. She noticed that many looked like little boys, and then she saw something else, something about the bodies that bothered her, something about the bodies that was unnatural. She bent closer to look, and he closed the book.

They sat there for a couple of minutes in silence. She rubbed the back of his neck, then she said, 'Take a lady for a walk around the neighborhood, guy?'

He looked at her and nodded his head. He got up and put the albums away, and they went out into the night.

McShaun lived in a fairly quiet residential neighborhood with a lot of trees and nice sidewalks. The night was clean and fresh, and the breeze felt good against their faces. They were quiet for several blocks, until she said, 'Thank you, Tim . . . I mean that.'

He stopped, took her other hand, turned her, and kissed her softly, leaving his lips brushing against hers for a long time. Then he pulled back and smiled. They walked on.

When they got back, he helped her put her things into her car. She held him for a moment, kissed him again, and went home.

Before she drove off, he made her promise to call him when she got to her apartment so he would know she made it all right. She thought of her off-duty .38 in her purse and laughed to herself. But she did call him when she was safely home and said good night.

It made her feel good.

A week later Springfield was standing under a large tree between her patrol unit and that of Bell Peoples. Chick Hummel had been transferred to the Narc Unit, and the shift

112

lieutenant was trying to decide on a partner for Springfield. In the meantime she was riding solo in the downtown area. She chafed at the delay in getting back into the northwest full-time but was mollified by the chance to work in the same area as Bell.

It was early in the shift, and quiet. Rocky was telling Bell about herself and McShaun.

'You and ol' Timmy McShaun, huh?' said Bell with a big grin. 'Why, lady, you must be *lookin'* for trouble.'

'C'mon, Bell. He's not so bad, really. He just has a reputation around the department, that's all.'

'Reputation. You got that right, uh-uh.'

'No . . . really, Bell. He's . . . he's nice.' Rocky looked at her friend closely for a minute, then said, 'Tell you something, Bell. We've been together several times now. I mean, on real dates where we got out, and then we go back to his place or my place . . . you know?'

Bell's big brown eyes sparkled as she smiled and said, 'I know.'

'And, Bell, I'm comfortable with him. We're relaxed with each other physically. And I'm . . . I've accepted . . . I wouldn't think it was too soon if we, if he . . . ' Rocky saw Bell's look and hurried on, 'Well we haven't – and it's not because of me, either.'

Bell, rubbed one long finger absently across her lips and said, 'Well, well. You have to know that ol' McShaun has a hell of a reputation around here. It's common knowledge that he's a swordsman, if you know what I mean. Likes his ladies . . . for sure.'

Springfield frowned.

Peoples laughed, punched Rocky on the arm, and said, 'Hey girl. I think he's doin' right. I think you ain't just some new leg that he wants to rub up against, dig? Did you think of that, maybe? Huh? That he might see you as different? As special, maybe? Hell, girl, if he don't want to rush it, then let him be. It will happen when it's time.' She grinned a big grin and stuck out a very pink tongue. 'You little white girls are just like rabbits sometimes!'

Springfield laughed and tried to kick Bell, but she jumped out of the way, still grinning. Then the dispatcher called both of their numbers; they were told to respond to a residential area east of Federal Highway, on the fringes of the downtown area, to help search for a missing five-year-old boy. They got into their units and headed that way.

One of the sergeants was on the scene, directing things when Springfield and Peoples got there. They saw that four other units were already there. They were given a description of the little boy and told to search, on foot, a certain area. They stood in front of the house with the sergeant while he gave them what info he had.

The boy was part of a family that had come down from the north to visit relatives. He was supposed to come in from playing at lunchtime, and after lunch his uncle was going to take him out to Castle Park where he could play putter golf and ride the water slide. The family advised that they were sure the boy would not have forgotten about it. Lunchtime had come and gone and the boy hadn't shown. Some time went by, and the family started to worry and search. Finally, in desperation, the police were called. The sergeant told them that, of course, the first thing they had to do was to check inside the house, under the beds, in the closets, where many 'runaways' turned up, hiding from worried or angry parents. The search proved negative all around the house, so now it was expanding. The boy had been missing for over four hours.

Springfield looked at the house, at the several cars and one camper-truck sitting on the side, and shook her head. Then she and Peoples walked off to begin their search. They went through hedges, through yards, under clotheslines, around swimming pools, over fences, and into carports. They were barked at by several dogs, they were stared at by old women, and they surprised two naked men covering each other with suntan oil on an open back porch.

They did not find the boy.

Almost an hour later they were told to clear the scene and respond to some other minor calls that had backed up while the search went on. They were told the search would stay active; it would go on from the mobile units and from the air. The parents and relatives were still checking with friends and neighbors.

Two hours later, as it was starting to turn into night, Springfield cleared a stolen bicycle report and was told by dispatch to meet Peoples back at the house where the little boy was reported missing. She thought it was curious but headed that way, anyway.

When she arrived, she found Bell standing out front, leaning against her patrol car with her arms folded across her chest. There were no other police units there, but Springfield could see lights on in the house and thought some of the family must be home. She got out of her car and walked up to Peoples, who looked at her sheepishly and shrugged. Then her eyes clouded over and she bit her lip as she said, 'Thanks for comin' over. I asked for you because I didn't want to be alone.'

Springfield looked at her friend and saw that she was very nervous or scared. 'What is it, Bell? What's wrong?'

The black girl shrugged again, looked down at her feet, and made a half circle in the sand with the toe of one shoe. 'I got a feelin', Rocky. It's been with me since we left here. Maybe it was with me while we were still here, I don't know. I just got a feelin'.'

Springfield looked around her and said, 'Bell, we were told what area to search, and we did, and then we were cleared. This area was searched. Hell, the kid's probably spending all his money at some video arcade around here.'

Peoples did not smile; she only shook her head and said, 'I have a feeling, Rocky. Look over there by the side of the house. What do you see?'

Rocky looked. 'An old Chevy, two bicycles, and that big pickup truck with the camper on the back.'

'That's a *big* camper sittin' there on that truck, Rocky, and I'll bet you it's got a refrigerator or icebox of some kind in it.'

115

Rocky's eyes went wide. She understood what Bell was saying. Old refrigerators were dangerous things when lying around where a kid could get inside; it happened all the time. Rocky couldn't know it, but a long time ago, when Bell Peoples was a little girl living on Northwest Twelfth Terrace in a dirty apartment building she had stood by one day when some men opened up an old lime-green refrigerator that had been lying in the alley for months. When they did, they found her cousin Bobby, sleeping so peacefully, sleeping forever. Rocky couldn't know this, but she could see the fear and concern in her friend's eyes. She said, 'Hey, look, Bell. I'll go take a look. Damn camper's probably locked, anyway. I'll go look and then we'll leave here and get some coffee. Okay?'

Peoples stood very still for a moment and then said softly, 'We'll both go look.'

They walked through the brown grass until they reached the back of the camper. Springfield grabbed the door handle and pulled. It swung open smoothly. They shined their lights inside and saw the refrigerator sitting there. It was not more than four feet high. They hesitated, then both reached for the handle at the same time. They stopped. They looked at each other, and then Bell reached out again, grabbed the handle, and pulled.

The little boy's eyes were closed, and he had one thumb in his mouth. He was curled as he had been in the womb. He was very dead.

Springfield felt Peoples trembling against her, felt her slump down as she sighed. She put her arm around Bell's waist, and they stayed like that for a few minutes. The only sound was that of the black girl's tears as they hit the linoleum floor of the camper.

When she could, Rocky advised the dispatcher to have the sergeant return to the house. They waited quietly until he got there, not saying anything to the family. When he arrived and was shown what they found, he swore for a long time under his breath, then got on the radio and mobilized everyone from the shift captain to the on-call priest. He told Springfield to close the door of the camper, hesitated, and then walked across the yard, knocked on the door of the house, and went inside. He didn't come out for a long time.

Rocky stood with Bell in the dark while men moved back and forth through the yard and cars came and went. Rocky had already talked to the sergeant, so she wasn't surprised when he walked over to them and said, 'Listen Bell, why don't you go ahead to the station, call it a night? Okay?' He saw her look and said, hard, 'Look Bell, we were all here, we all tried. You and Rocky looked where I told you to look. If the boy was in there before noon, he would've been – he would have died before we were even called, anyway. Look at me, Bell. It's not your fault! It's not my fault, either . . . it's just . . . just . . .'

Rocky touched Peoples on the arm and said, 'Hey, the sarge is right. Why not knock off for the night? Go home to that big ugly old man of yours and get some rest.'

Bell stood there for a minute, looking at the sergeant. She said, 'Thanks, Sarge. Thanks for saying it.' She got into her car and drove away slowly.

Ten minutes later Rocky was heading for another call when she heard Bell's voice, strained, coming over the radio, asking for help. She needed a backup – now. She advised that she was at Seventh Avenue and Broward Boulevard.

As she accelerated, Rocky heard pieces of info between Peoples and the dispatcher. She learned that on the way to the station Bell had come across a car that earlier in the shift had been reported stolen. There were two white guys in the car, and when she pulled them over, they got out and jumped her. One was running away, and Bell was apparently fighting with the other one.

Rocky came down Seventh Avenue touching seventy, lights and siren going. She slid to a smoking stop beside Bell's unit, which was right up against the back of a new Monte Carlo. At first Rocky couldn't see them, but then she heard grunting and ran around to the left front end of the Monte Carlo. She found Bell on the ground with a very big man with long brown hair and a beard on top of her. The man was punching Bell with one fist while he reached and pulled at her service revolver with the other, trying to pull it out of the holster.

Rocky ran up and grabbed the man's hand and pulled it away from Bell's side, but the man was strong, and when he pulled his arm back, he pulled Rocky down on top of both of them.

The man was cursing and grunting, and Bell was crying and spitting, and all three of them were punching and kicking for all they were worth.

Finally Rocky managed to get to her knees and hold on to the man's right arm while Bell held the other. Then Bell started jumping up and down, landing on the man's chest and stomach with her knees while hitting him with the fist of her free hand. Blood started to spurt from his cut lips and nose. Then Rocky started punching too. When the backups got there, they were treated to the spectacle of Peoples and Springfield, both crying, beating the absolute shit out of the car thief, who just lay there, moaning.

Rocky and Bell were pulled off the man and he was handcuffed. A crowd had gathered now, and people were yelling and laughing and whistling. Rocky stood awkwardly and brushed herself off. She noticed that her knees and elbows were scraped. She looked at Bell and saw that she had some lumps and bumps too. Then she watched as Peoples walked over to where the car thief leaned against one of the units. She watched as the black girl put her face real close to the guy and said, 'You ain't *shit,* big man, you ain't *shit!* I see you again out here on my streets and I'll have a piece of your ass like you've never seen! You *hear* me?'

The crowd loved it, laughing and calling, but Rocky pulled Bell by her arm and said, 'C'mon, Bell. Let's get into the station and do some paperwork.'

The stolen car was being towed in. The search continued for the passenger. The driver was transported to the emergency room for his injuries, then to the booking desk. Springfield and Peoples had to fill out an arrest sheet, use-of-force forms, personal injury forms, and the stolen car report.

Rocky parked her car a few paces from Peoples, and they both slowly got out and collected their gear. They stood there a moment looking toward the back door, as if contemplating all the paperwork to be done before they went home. Then they started walking toward each other, torn, bloody, beaten, and tired. They looked at each other a moment, started to laugh, started to cry, and then just held on to each other and did both.

McShaun had heard about it from upstairs. He was waiting in the write-up room when they came in. He helped them with the paperwork. He was good and fast, and it wasn't long before they were out of there. McShaun called Bell's husband at home and told him about what had happened, about the little boy and the fight in the street. Bell's husband thanked him and told him he'd be waiting for her when she got home.

McShaun watched as Rocky said good night to Bell and they promised to do it all again sometime. He followed Rocky to her apartment.

He waited, reading magazines and lounging, while she took a long hot bath. When she came out to him finally, wearing a full-length cotton sleeping dress, he saw the fatigue and the stress in her eyes. He bumbled around in her kitchen but managed to make her some hot cocoa, and he talked softly with her while she drank it and told him about the night.

He held her while she cried, and he held her while she slept in his arms. Finally, early in the morning, he covered her with a blanket he found in a closet, looked at her lying there, so small on the big couch, touched her lips gently with his fingers, and let himself quietly out the door.

He went home, knowing her pain.

119

Chapter Eleven

'Listen, T.S., I'm tellin' ya, this place is a real zoo. I mean, it's like an adult fantasy land over here.'

McShaun grinned as he held the phone and listened to Chick Hummel calling him from the Narc Division offices.

'I'm still the new guy here, Tim, so I'm not working my own cases yet. So far I've just been going out with the other guys and watching and helping. Man, it's *very* different from working in uniform. Sometimes I feel kinda naked, if you know what I mean.'

'So what are they gonna have you doing, Chick – narcotics or vice or what?'

'I guess a little of both. They're telling me that a lot of this stuff is tied together. Dope money feeding organised crime ventures, and pimps and hookers working for dopers, and everybody buying from everybody else. What a fuckin' mess. When I get home at night, I want to take a bath in Lysol.'

McShaun laughed and said, 'Hell, Chick, that would probably do you good.'

'Yeah, you're right. Anyway, listen, I know you have to head on into the station pretty soon. I just wanted to call and say hey. Needless to say, you won't see much of me around the station for a while . . . . Hey, I'm growing a beard now too. And they told us we have to get used to the idea of not popping in and visiting our uniform buddies – if you know what I mean.'

McShaun said innocently, 'Oh, you mean if I see you sitting in Ernie's place with a couple of dirtbags I shouldn't

120

yell across the room, 'Hey, Chick, how do you like working undercover'?'

'Aw, c'mon, T.S., gimme a break, will ya?'

'Okay, I know what you're saying. And listen, you be careful over there, huh? Remember what Scott Kelly said?'

'Yeah, I hear you . . . Scott was a hell of a narc. Like I said, I hope he makes it back all right. In the meantime, buddy, I'll be careful out here – and you be careful up there in the Comm Center. Hell, I don't want you to strain your ass from sitting in that dispatch chair all night.'

They were both laughing as McShaun hung up the phone. He had been told by Janie Majors the night before that she had heard he might be going back out into the street sooner than expected. They were short on manpower, as usual, and he had been quiet and a good worker and had not pestered them, so it looked as if he might get out of there soon. He was elated, not because he didn't like dispatching but because he needed that street.

He gathered his things and went out to his car. He was wearing jeans and a T-shirt and jogging shoes. He had a clean uniform hanging in his locker at the station and would change into it before he went upstairs. He had talked with Springfield on the phone earlier in the morning; she sounded all right, though still a little tired. She told him she was going to work that afternoon and would try to stop up and see him during the shift. She told him she had talked with Bell, and she was okay too. Rocky had laughed and said yes when he asked her out to dinner on their day off, which was coming up, and she promised to do everything she could to hide the scrapes on her knees and elbows so people wouldn't think he had been beating her. He said something about kissing it and making it better, and she had said, 'Hmm.'

McShaun was five minutes from the station, sitting at a traffic light, when he saw it about to happen.

Walking down a side street, away from him, was an old lady in a faded blue dress. Walking slightly behind her was a guy in his early twenties, scraggly-looking and dirty. The guy was watching the woman, and McShaun could almost feel his eyes swinging back and forth with the rhythm of the purse on her arm. McShaun could tell by looking at the woman that if she had anything at all in the purse, it would be a social security check, and he could tell by looking at the man that he was a hunter, getting ready to make his move.

Just as the mugger started running up on the old lady, McShaun accelerated through the intersection and started to make a turn to get around the block. He watched through his side window as the guy came up behind her at a dead run, hit her in the shoulder with one hand, grabbed the purse with the other, and took off down the street. McShaun had time to see the old lady stumble into some bushes before he lost sight of her as he turned the corner.

Up the street, a wild right turn, slide to a stop, jump out, and – here it comes! McShaun timed it as the mugger was starting to pick up speed, occasionally looking back over his shoulder. When the guy was about fifty feet away, still coming strong, McShaun started running also – right at him.

They were both running at full speed when the guy turned his sweaty face and saw McShaun, just as McShaun's right arm impacted his throat. There was a loud gagging noise, the mugger's feet flew out and straight up, and he fell with a slap against the pavement of the street.

As he fell, McShaun grabbed the purse from him with one hand, then he knelt down and punched him as hard as he could, once, twice, three times, in the face and in the throat. The mugger gagged and moaned. Spattered blood from his broken nose speckled McShaun's right wrist.

McShaun stood up and looked around. The neighborhood was quiet; there was no one around. He looked down the street and saw the old lady walking toward him slowly, rubbing her shoulder. He was glad she was up and walking; so many times their hips were broken when they fell. He jogged up to her and, without saying anything, handed her the purse. She cocked her head and looked at him in surprise and said, 'Thank you.' She turned and walked into a yard. He watched her until she was safely inside one of the small wooden houses that lined the street, then he turned and jogged back to his car.

As he passed the purse snatcher he saw that he was trying to sit up, rubbing his face with his hands. For a moment McShaun considered kicking him in the back of the head. Instead he leaned down as he went by and hissed, 'So long . . . asshole.'

He got into his car and drove to work, where he washed up, put on his uniform, and went upstairs to begin the shift in the Comm Center.

His fellow workers enjoyed his unusually good spirits during the entire shift.

Bobby Nails eased his car slowly down the road, looking, looking. He was looking for a house to hit, a nice middle-class place with some decent jewelry and a color TV and stereo. He had a couple of places in mind, in different areas of the city, and he just kept looking to make sure they were cool. He wanted to make his break-ins when there was nobody at home, so he was looking for places where the parents worked and kids went to school. He also included those homes occupied by old people, because even though they didn't go to work, they still had to go out shopping – the drugstore and all that stuff.

Nails took it real easy nowadays. The tag on his car was legit, his driver's licence was current, and he had a bunch of paint cans and rollers and brushes in the backseat, in case he was stopped cruising through one of the neighborhoods.

His crazy days were over. He had been on that thing for a while there with his partner. They had done a lot of coke and a bunch of crazy stuff, and it was fun for a while, especially when they tied up the old ladies and made 'em cry and scared the hell outta' em with his gun, and maybe knocked 'em around a little, too, just for a good measure. Yeah, fun. Fun until that night when the cops just *wasted* his partner with a shotgun, and he had tried to shoot that lady cop and all. Man, that was too much. Of course, he got lucky then.

Well, maybe his luck had to do with his attorney. He still owed the bastard a pile of money. Anyway, he skated on all the crummy charges the cops came up with. They did a 'let's make a deal', he copped a plea, and here he was, out on a suspended sentence, being a good boy and looking for a nice simple hit.

Yeah, a nice simple hit, and then who knows? Maybe another one. Maybe he'd find one that didn't look like much but would turn out to be one of those old ladies that kept all her money in cash under her bed in a shoebox. Who knows? Maybe then he could get himself into a nice sweet ride, instead of this shitbox he was driving, and maybe he could shut that big-mouthed attorney up, all the time cryin' for money. And maybe he could score some more cocaine and feel fine and buy some sweet lady for the night and . . . who knows?

McShaun tore off the shirt he was wearing, went into the closet, selected the one he had picked out in the first place, hung up the one he had just taken off, and put the new one on. He looked at himself in the mirror as he laboriously tucked the shirt in. Stupid hair, sticking up all over the place. You comb it when you get out of the shower and it looks fine. Then it dries out and it looks like an explosion in a silo.

He looked again at the clock beside his bed. Almost six. Damn, she was gonna be here before he could get his act together.

McShaun was taking Springfield out to dinner. He had made reservations at one of the nicer places in the city, on the water. She was supposed to meet him at his place and they would go from there, since his apartment was not that far from the restaurant.

He thought his collar was crooked and was trying to smooth it when he heard the knock on the door. Radar slid out as he opened it, and there she stood.

'Hello, lady. You're looking fine.'

She looked at him. 'Why, thank you, sir. You look nice too.'

She was wearing a lavender blouse with a frilly collar and puffy sleeves, a dark purple straight skirt with a thin silver belt, pale stockings, and shoes that were just straps that matched the belt. Her brown curly hair was pulled back over her ears. Her makeup was subtle, highlighting her face and eyes. He thought she looked great. He stood there, enjoying what he saw and taking in her perfume that played with him as it drifted into the room.

She walked up to him and took his hands. Her nose almost touched his as she said, 'We've got reservations for seven, seven-thirty? Tell me about the place.'

She stood close to him, and the way she looked and smelled and her nearness made him feel as if he were actually a little dizzy. He said, 'It's supposed to be one of the top ten restaurants in the country – high Italine cuisine, super service, and all that. I was there once a while back. I think you'll enjoy it. We can have a drink over at the Marriott first if you want.'

She looked into his eyes. She had dressed slowly, thinking of him, of them. She had bathed and done her nails and her hair and had chosen her outfit and readied herself, thinking about them. She had driven over to his place slowly, listening to the stereo and checking her face in the mirror. *What a night I picked*, she thought, *to have a major skin breakout on my chin.* She had forced herself to leave the little red spot alone and had thought about him, and them.

'Are you hungry?' he asked, squeezing her hands.

'Yes . . . I'm hungry.'

'Do you want . . .?'

'Yes . . . I want.'

Without bending down she used one foot and then the other to step out of her shoes. Her eyes looked into his from a little lower as she pulled his hands and turned toward his bedroom. He let her lead him, his heart starting to pound.

She stopped beside his bed and ran her fingers softly across his chest and up to his collar. She let her fingers play with the bottom of his ears as she said, 'Tim, let's not worry about dinner right now.'

She trembled slightly as he reached up and slowly started to unbutton her blouse, his fingers unsure but steady. When the blouse was open all the way, he leaned forward and kissed the top of each breast softly. She rubbed his arms as he fumbled slightly with the belt and then unhooked the skirt, which fell with a slight rustle to the floor. She stood in her panty hose and bra and slip and held him to her tightly. Then she pushed him away from her, and he sat on the bed and watched as she pulled the rest of her things off.

She stood naked before him, and he took her around the waist and kissed her on the belly. She felt his hard hands cup the shape of her bottom, and she pushed herself against him. He looked up and turned her and sat her on the edge of the bed. Then he leaned forward and kissed her, a very long kiss, full on the lips as he let her lie back.

She watched as he stood and undressed. His clothes fell on top of hers in a soft pile. His body was tanned and smooth and tough, muscled and scarred and lean. His stomach was flat, and the hair on his chest smoothed the sharp edges of his pectoral muscles.

As he climbed into bed beside her she saw that he was already aroused, and she took him in her hand and felt the pulsating warmth. He slid smoothly on top of her and kissed her again, on the lips, on the cheeks, the ears, the neck. He explored her and she moved against him, opening herself to him.

But he wouldn't hurry.

He let his fingers glide over every part of her body, and then his warm lips and his wet tongue. He tasted, he explored, he searched slowly for the places that would please her, and he found them. The apartment was quiet except for their breathing. It grew shadow-dark in the bedroom as evening came.

Her need for him was urgent and strong when he finally entered her. She felt his hardness and his weight and his strength, and she moved herself against him in a satiny-hot rhythm that carried them both into themselves and each other and away from the world.

126

She held him as he loved her, and she let herself be swept away by his passion and soothed by his gentleness and controlled by his strength and pleased by his caring for her.

The night was long and silk-soft, and many times she buried her mouth against his warm shoulder and called out his name, over and over again.

Chick Hummel was feeling pretty good as he drove his plain rental car along A-1A, the beach road on the eastern edge of Fort Lauderdale. It was close to midnight, and he had had a busy and productive night. He drove along and looked at the street people and thought that he might really like working undercover narcotics. Earlier he had gone with one of the other narcs into a hotel room up on Galt Ocean Mile. He had worn the wire, uncomfortable at first with the tape and the small receiver on his chest, and feeling stiff because he was afraid to move his shirt too much against the damn thing, since the movement of the cloth against it drowned out all the other sounds. Two other teams had waited outside in the dark while he and his partner met with a couple of Latino types from New York. They very much wanted to buy some cocaine.

He and his partner had met the men the day before in a gas station parking lot and had acted properly skittish. Then they had agreed to meet the men at their hotel with the coke, the Latins would have their money, and it would go down.

Chick wiped his brow and then rubbed his fingers against his pant leg as he thought of the tension he felt standing there talking to those guys. They were hoping to buy a pretty strong kilo of cocaine, one that hadn't already been stepped on after it came into Florida, for twenty-five thousand dollars. Then they would be able to drive back to the Big Apple and break it down, and even if they took it easy, they could triple their money or their financier's money. That was what they'd said, anyway.

The problem was that both Chick and his partner knew that the chances were great that the two guys actually had no money and were planning to stick a gun in their faces and take the cocaine that they had drawn from evidence for their use in this situation.

Chick eased his car around a carful of college girls who had stopped in the right lane and were talking to some boys who were standing on the sidewalk. He shook his head thinking about it; people actually killed each other over cocaine, and even grass. How totally stupid, and how totally scary when you're walking into a hotel room la-dee-da with a couple of greasers from Gnu Yawk who know you have a kilo of cocaine with you. He had been sweating so much, he was afraid the transmitter would stop sticking to his chest, slide off, and fall onto the floor in front of everybody.

It didn't.

Hummel sat at Bayshore Drive, with the darkness that was the beach and the ocean on his left, and the lights that were the hotels on his right. As he waited for the green he went over how it had gone down. He and the more experienced narc had gone to the room on the sixth floor of the hotel. Hummel carried the briefcase. The two men from New York were waiting, relaxed. They talked freely, happy to be making the deal. It all went through the mike on Hummel's chest, out to the receiver in a car in the parking lot, and onto tape. The narcs needed evidence that the two men were conspiring to buy coke in Lauderdale and then take it north and sell it. The narcs needed the men to discuss it, which they did, and they needed them to make an overt act toward actually buying it, which they did when they proudly brought a gym bag out from under the bed and showed it to the narcs. It was full of money. They all stood there smiling as Chick said, 'That's enough money to take us to the moon,' and his partner opened the door and let in the other narcs, who were waiting in the hallway.

The two guys from New York had been distraught.

Back in the narc offices things had gone smoothly, paperwork was done, and Hummel had learned even more about how it all worked. His fellow narcs told him that he would be given some tips, and he could work up some of his own, and soon they would be working *his* deals. They also told him that they didn't all go as easy as this one had.

Hummel had still been fired up after it was all over, so instead of driving home, he had taken a ride out to the beach, just to look and think and wind down a little before he went to his lady. He lit another cigar and laughed to himself, thinking of how the one guy from New York kept begging and pleading to *please* let him to have a good copy of the booking sheet and the mug shots and everything so when he got back to New York, he could prove he had actually been arrested and the money had actually been seized by the cops. Otherwise – 'No kidding, man' – he'd be rubbed out.

Hummel's mind was full of events of the night as he drove along, but still he saw her. He passed her, drove another half block, made a U-turn, and was headed back toward her before he even became consciously aware of what he was doing. The sidewalks and parking areas along A-1A were full of people walking, sitting, hanging out. Young guys drank beer furtively and laughed too loud as the girls walked by. Local street types slid along, looking to score or to sell – anything. Middle-aged tourists tried not to bump into anyone as they walked along on their sunburned legs, Dad's arm protectively across Mom's shoulders.

But that one girl, sitting on a low stone wall that edged one of the parking lots, caught his eye. Something about the way she sat there, looking down at her feet. Something in her shoulders.

Hummel wouldn't be able to explain it, even if he had to.

He was a working street cop, and like many, he was a people person. He was tuned. He was receptive to vibrations.

He pulled his car into the small lot, turned out the lights, sat for a minute looking at the girl's stiff back, got out of the car, and walked over to where she sat. He stood beside her and felt her bunched muscles and white knuckles sending out her message. He saw her dry stare, the shallow breaths, the heels of her sandaled feet bumping rhythmically against the harsh wall. He said softly, 'Hey, lady . . .'

129

If anything, the girl stiffened more. After he said it again she turned her head toward him and looked up with eyes wide with terror and . . . something else. He looked at her – sixteen, maybe; pretty, though disheveled; beaten down. He watched how her eyes changed from the initial shock to fleeting curiosity and then how they clouded over in defence. Her clothes were of good quality but worn. Her feet in the sandals were dirty, as was her hair. Her eyes were red from crying.

'I'm a policeman, honey, really. I saw you sitting here and I got your message.'

She looked at him and tilted her head, puzzled.

'I got your message that said you're a long way from home and you're scared and you need help and—'

And she was hugging his waist and sobbing, big gulping sobs that racked her whole body over and over again. He patted her head with one hand while with the other he reached into his back pocket and pulled out his badge and ID. He lay it down on the wall beside her and waited until she was just snuffling and shaking her head back and forth. He gave her his handkerchief, and she blew her nose into it while she studied his ID card. She stood up slowly and let him lead her to his car. She sat quietly while he pulled the hand-held radio from under the seat, contacted the dispatcher, and told her he was bringing a young white female into the station from the beach. He looked at the girl, gave the dispatcher the mileage on the car's odometer, said he'd be making one stop along the way, and started the car.

The girl sat quietly, hunched against the passenger door, as Hummel drove toward the station. He could see her tears falling along her face in the glow of the streetlights, and he watched as her fingers dug into the backs of her hands and her feet bounced against each other gently. Halfway to the station he stopped at a doughnut shop, smiled at the girl and patted her on the shoulder, ran in, and came back out with two hot chocolates and a box of mixed doughnuts. He parked the car under a tree near a streetlight. He advised the dispatcher of his location and the mileage again and handed the girl one of the hot chocolates. She took it and cried a little more, then looked at him, then out the window, and said 'Thank you' very quietly.

Hummel leaned against the door of the car and waited. The sugar from his glazed doughnut powdered his shirt.

'I'm from Indiana.'

He nodded.

'I'm from Indiana, and I . . . my parents don't . . . I had to go because they were on me all the time and my friend Muriel and I talked about it and then we just left and we came down here. First we went to Daytona because we talked with some kids who said things here were . . . really . . .' Then she cried some more.

He burned his upper lip on the chocolate.

'I mean, I love my parents . . . my dad is . . . but my mom is always *on* me. I don't know. We hitchhiked, Muriel and I. We got some good rides and had fun and . . . I've been gone about two weeks, I guess.'

She looked at him and brushed her hair out of her eyes. She took one of the doughnuts and ate it in three bites.

'We met some kids in Daytona and they said we could ride down here to Fort Lauderdale with them, but in the morning we couldn't find Muriel *anywhere,* and we looked and she was just *gone.* Muriel was acting bitchy then, anyway. We'd been fighting. So I left and came here with those other kids. And then you know what? They took my money and my knapsack! How could they do that?'

Hummel broke one of the plain doughnuts in half.

'Anyway, I didn't know what to do. This was just the other day. I . . . I tried to call my home . . . but . . . there was no answer, and I got mad and just left it then.' She stared out the window for a long time. He sat quietly.

She turned and looked at him, really looked at him, for the first time. 'Are you like a . . . detective?'

He nodded.

'I mean, you don't wear a uniform. You like, investigate things, right?'

He nodded again and took the other half of the doughnut.

'If a person gave you some information on some people who did . . . bad things, you would go after them, right? I mean, you would arrest them, right?'

'Tell me your name.'

'Sherry. My name is Sherry Ann Stover.'

'Sherry. That's a really nice name. My name is Chick. No, it really is. You're sitting here eating doughnuts with Officer Chick Hummel, FLPD.'

'Chick—'

'And, yes, I'd try to arrest the people doing the bad things if I had enough information. Most of the time cops like me can't get anything done, though, unless we get some help from a person who knows what's going on – like you.'

She sat very still, looking out the window.

He swirled the chocolate around in the cup and said, 'And Muriel, how old is she?'

'She's fifteen – like me.'

She looked at him again, and at the radio.

'Mister, um, Officer Hummel, what if I told you some things I knew about some people? I've seen in the movies where someone, like an informant, gives stuff to the police and then they get killed and all. I mean, I *want* to tell you some things, but I . . . I don't want to stay . . . I don't want to be here . . .'

Hummel wiped his mouth with a paper napkin and said, 'A lot of the time what we do is get all the information we can – say, from someone who's from out of town – and then we send them home.' He saw that she was crying softly. 'We send them home and they are never contacted again. We just use the info they gave us to start the case, to work on it until we can get the people who are bad, without involving the person who helped us in the first place.'

She blew her nose again. Then she took another doughnut. He waited. Then she sat up straight. 'I'm not a virgin.'

He looked at her.

'I mean, I wasn't a virgin already when I left Indiana. I mean, I had this boyfriend there and we . . . we . . . but he was so *childish* about it. Anyway, I'm telling you this

132

because of what happened after I met this guy on the strip the other night.'

Hummel waited, listening.

'I mean, it's not like I don't know what's going on, you know? So I'm stuck here with no money and I meet this guy who was real nice to me, and not bad-looking, in a rough way. He had some grass and we got high and I liked him, and he said I could stay with him and I did.' She stuck her chin out defiantly. 'I stayed the night with him in a motel room.'

Hummel nodded.

'His name is Harv. He has tattoos on his arms. One says, "Who Me?" '

Hummel watched as her fingers picked at each other.

She bit her lip. 'Harv bought me breakfast and talked to me about making some money. He was a photographer, or he had some friends that were or something. He kept me stoned, so I don't remember what it was, but it sounded like fun and exciting and all. Like being a model. So I did it.'

Hummel turned to look at her. 'What did you do, Sherry?'

She looked away. 'I made a movie. There were other men there. We went to a house . . . a big house near a canal. They had a bedroom all set up with lights and cameras. And action – that was me.'

She tried to laugh. She tried to make it a very upstate laugh, a very with-it laugh. It came out like a little girl crying.

Hummel waited.

'At first it wasn't too bad. I mean, I felt funny taking my clothes off, but I was high and all, and I don't know. And then me and Harv were supposed to . . . do it . . . while they took pictures. And we did.' She ran her fingers through her hair. 'Harv was different, rough, and he did things to me and I didn't like it and I wanted to stop, but he grabbed me . . . he grabbed me here' – she pointed shyly with her finger – 'and he pinched me so hard, I thought I would die. I was afraid then. And then she . . . this girl . . . they called

133

her Lindy or Lydie or something like that. She . . . she had her clothes off, too, and she was on the bed and she and Harv . . . and they told me to . . . and then she . . . did things to me.' She cried a little then, hunched up against the window of the car, the doughnut forgotten. She sat up and wiped her eyes. 'She did things, and then they told me to do it but I said no, and then they hurt me again and then he, finished on me . . . on my face . . . and then that girl . . . she . . . she . . .' Sherry sat rock-still. After a moment she went on in a small voice, 'After that I was in a daze, sort of, but I remember that the other two men – the ones who were playing with the camera – they made me do it to them.' She turned her head then and looked at Hummel with distant eyes as she said, 'And they laughed at me while they did it, and pulled my hair, and called me names. They made me feel so . . . so . . . worthless. Worthless.'

Hummel held her while she sobbed, longer and harder than before. He held her and rocked her and waited. He freed one hand to answer the dispatcher, asking if he was all right. He held her while she said over and over again, 'I just want to find Muriel and go home.'

On the way to the station the girl directed Hummel up to the north end of the city, looking for the house. She got lost and they didn't find it, but they got to the area, which Hummel knew as Bayview Drive. The girl said that Harv drove a black Porsche.

She told him how, when they finished with the movie, Harv had driven her back out to the beach. He had parked on a side street and grabbed her by the neck and hurt her. He told her if she ever told anyone what had happened, no matter where she went, he would find her, and when he found her, he would cut her, he would burn her, he would make her ugly. And then he threw her out of the car and drove away.

The night-shift detectives were tired and cranky and swamped with paperwork that the day-shift detectives always managed to slough off on them. They looked at

Hummel and his young runaway with irritation at first. But they liked Chick, and they could see his concern when he told them a little about what he was working with the girl, and they helped him. One detective went off to his phone and the teletype to see what he could do about finding Muriel. He would contact Daytona and see what they had, or at least let them know about the girl.

Hummel waited until Sherry came back from the ladies' room, looking fresher but still drawn and tired; then he helped her call home. He stood by while she cried into the phone, and he talked to the father and then the mother and then the father again, being firm, being reassuring, being sympathetic, being helpful. Hummel hung up, saying he'd call back after they checked airline schedules. Finally they called the girl's parents back, and after more crying, they were able to tell them what flight Sherry would be on. Hummel told the father they didn't have any info on Muriel yet, and the father told him that Muriel's parents – good friends of theirs – were frantic about their daughter, and if he got any news, they'd sure like to know. And thank God Sherry was all right and coming home, and they'd work it out. Whatever it was that made her take off like that in the first place, they'd work it out.

The girl sat and watched Hummel as he spoke into the phone. He said to the father, 'Mr Stover, Sherry's coming home and she's okay, but she's had some rough experiences along the way. She'll need support. She'll need love. She'll need to know you and her mother still want her around.'

One of the new female patrol officers on the midnight shift was called in and told about the situation. She took Sherry with her to her locker where the girl was able to take a shower and get herself together a little. While she was gone, the detective who had been on the phone walked over to where Hummel was sitting, making notes. He sighed. Hummel looked up and saw what was in the detective's eyes.

'Spoke with the shift commander up at Daytona. They found the girl . . . Muriel. Two days ago. Hell, Chick, they found her in a dumpster. Said she was in about six pieces. They ID'd her with the purse that was with her and a school ID card with a photo. They were going to call the kid's parents later today to see about making some positive ID. Said they were glad to hear from me, actually.'

Hummel looked at the floor and nodded. Sherry's schedule would have to change now. She would have to go to Daytona before she went home. Her father, or both parents, could meet her there and take her home after the Daytona PD finished with her. He sighed, a long, tired sigh. First he had to tell her.

The sun had been up two hours when Hummel drove home from the airport and found his lady waiting for him at the front door of his house.

She watched him as he climbed slowly out of his car, and she watched his eyes as he walked slowly toward the door. He stopped in front of her and tried to smile and then just shook his head, and she took him by the hand and led him into his home where it was quiet and cool.

Chapter Twelve

The prosecutor, a young attorney in a new gray suit, looked at McShaun and rubbed his forehead. He spoke as if he were at the end of his patience, speaking to a child.

'Look, McShaun, you know the burglary laws as well as I do. So you've got this clown on an in-progress break-in of a house. You get there, you find him inside and arrest him. Good. Very good. And you charge him with a felony burglary. And you want me to take him all the way through a trial.'

McShaun just looked at him. They were standing in the third-floor hallway of the courthouse, early in the afternoon. The young attorney nodded at a couple of friends who walked past him and continued, 'So you caught the guy inside the house, but you didn't give him time to take what he was going to take, right? I mean, he had no jewelry in his pockets, nothing stacked up by the door, like the stereo or TV, right? So what do I have to prove to the court, McShaun? I have to prove that the defendant *intended* to steal something, and that what he intended to steal had a certain value. As it is, we do have the man breaking into the house, but did he break in to steal? Or did he break in to sleep on the floor or leave a donation or what?'

McShaun looked at the prosecutor, then at his watch. He had another case going on in a few minutes on the fourth floor, and he was tired of this, anyway. He patted the prosecutor on the arm and said, 'Yeah. You're right, sir. I hear you and I understand. So if the guy's defence attorney wants to play Let's Make a Deal, it would probably be better if you went ahead and pleaded him out on something.'

The prosecutor, relieved that he didn't have to really argue over the case with McShaun, saw something in the cop's eyes that made him nervous. He smiled uncertainly and said, 'Listen, McShaun, you know how it is. My boss is screaming about the backup of cases . . . damn burglary case going in front of a jury is considered unnecessary. And we're supposed to get all the convictions we can. Just get those convictions. Really, no big thing. You did good, you got the guy off the street for a while, you saved the victim's property. If this same jerk gets caught again, we'll really get him next time. Okay?' He couldn't help saying again, 'You know how it is.'

McShaun nodded and said, 'No problem.'

As McShaun waited for the elevator he thought about his reaction to that conversation. Maybe he was mellowing out. Or maybe spending time with Rocky was making him relax a little bit. He smiled to himself and didn't see the others in the elevator as he rode to the fourth floor. He had been seeing Rocky almost every day for two weeks now, and it was good. It was very good. Their time together was spent in easy conversation, gentle kidding, very little police talk, and a lot of physical sharing of each other. Yeah, the time they spent together making love . . .

The elevator doors opened. As he stepped into the hall he heard his name, 'McShaun! Officer McShaun! Over here!' He looked to see another prosecutor, this one a little older and fat, wearing a double-knit three-piece suit that looked wrinkled and probably always would. The attorney was waving a thick file and pushing his glasses up on his nose. He was sweaty and agitated, and he stood too close to McShaun as he talked.

'Well, McShaun! I'm glad you could make it. We've got a good thing going here on this robbery case of yours. Looks like we can clear it up today. You know this case is almost a year old? Anyway, the defence told me they'll plead guilty to robbery. You hear me? To *robbery,* man, the actual charge!

138

They'll plead guilty if we'll go along with the judge putting this kid on probation. We're all ready to finalize the deal, but I told them to wait a minute until I could talk to you – as a courtesy.'

McShaun remembered that time almost a year ago, seeing the 'kid' with his shiny 38-caliber revolver and ski mask. He remembered how the kid had hit the drugstore clerk, a woman, across the mouth with the gun before running out into the parking lot. He remembered how he felt his finger tightening on the trigger as he stood and yelled for the kid to stop. He remembered seeing how the kid brought his gun around – almost far enough – before he hesitated and then dropped it to the pavement. He remembered the kid telling him later how he could have killed him, McShaun, but that he had nothing against cops; they were just doing their job. He wanted McShaun to know he was very tough and that he had *let* McShaun live. McShaun remembered wanting to stuff the kid's shiny gun up where the sun doesn't shine, but the circumstances didn't allow it. He remembered the girl behind the counter trying to talk . . . trying to talk with her broken jaw and smashed teeth. He looked at the fat prosecutor and said, 'Two questions.'

The fat guy looked perplexed but nodded his head.

'One. What about the assault charges we laid on him for pistol-whipping the girl?'

The prosecutor looked hurt. 'Well, of course, it will all be part of it. He'll be pleading guilty to that, too, and the probation will be a part of that also.'

'Two. Correct me if I'm wrong, but I read in this asshole's file that he's *already* on probation for robbery. And, if you can believe this, he was put on *that* probation after being given a suspended sentence for a robbery down in another town. Explain to me, please, how a guy riding a suspended sentence can be put on probation, and then explain to me how in the hell he can be put on probation *again* on top of *that!*'

The prosecutor looked at his watch and pulled at his collar with one pudgy finger. He was thanking his stars that

McShaun wasn't aware of the fact that the defendant was actually on probation on a north Florida robbery case on top of everything else. He looked just to the side of McShaun's burning eyes and said, 'Look, McShaun. You know how it is. I have a chance for a conviction here. No fuss, no muss. The judge is badgering me about this case, anyway, because you're the only police witness. I mean, the girl's here and all. But hell, this is a conviction. I think it's a good deal, I'm the prosecutor, and I really don't have to get your permission to do what I have to do, anyway. I was just trying to extend some professional courtesy, that's all.' He stepped back, away from McShaun as he spoke. Now he turned back toward the courtroom and said over his shoulder, 'Hey . . . with a guy like this it's only a matter of time, anyway, right? You'll get him again and we'll *really* put him away next time, right?'

McShaun rode the elevator down to the lobby with the clerk from the small drugstore who had been the only civilian witness to the robbery. With her was a hard-looking man wearing jeans, a shirt and tie, and construction boots. He looked uncomfortable and upset. McShaun figured him to be the girl's husband. He didn't know McShaun, and the girl did not recognize him. McShaun looked at her as they stood silently in the elevator, each in his own space. He could see that the doctors had worked hard to get her face back into shape after it was impacted by the gun.

They came pretty close.

McShaun found himself walking out to his car with one of the men who worked out in the Marine Patrol Unit. He knew the other cop only casually; the Marine Patrol officers kept to themselves most of the time. The Marine Patrol cop, a big man, a little older than McShaun, shook his head and laughed as he said, 'Well, another busy day here in Bullshit Land.' He jerked a sunburned thumb over his shoulder at the courthouse building behind them. 'Yep. I can see by your face that you had almost as much fun in there as I did.'

McShaun grinned and said, 'Yeah. Monty Hall all over

140

the place. I'm not even sure why I showed up. What did you have?'

The Marine Patrol officer rubbed one hand over his face, hard, and said, 'Two guys on the fly bridge of a sports-fisherman. No registration numbers; windows and ports all painted and taped over. Bumper marks along the hull. Stopped 'em for the numbers. Had a Custom's man with me. He boarded and found about eight hundred pounds of marijuana in bales inside the cabin. I wrote 'em a citation for not displaying the numbers, and we arrested 'em for the grass and seized the boat. Had a motion-to-suppress hearing today, you know, where the lawyers argue over whether the evidence was properly seized and all.'

The officer grinned as he stopped beside an old pickup truck and unlocked the door. 'Judge threw the whole thing out. I mean, if we were toilets, we would have been *flushed*, man. Seems that those two guys up on that bridge of that yacht had no knowledge of that grass in their cabin. The judge didn't think I had probable cause to stop them and board them in the first place, and he said we couldn't prove that they *intended* to smuggle anything; we couldn't even prove that the guys knew they were sitting on the grass. I swear, this place could piss off the Pope.'

McShaun nodded in agreement, they waved, and he got into his car and headed for the station. He still felt pretty good; this would be his first day out on the road again since being sent up to the Comm Center, and he was ready. To make it even more interesting, he would be working with Springfield as his partner, for a little while, anyway. She had told him that it looked as if she was going to get that slot in the Detective Division soon, but in the meantime they would work the street – together.

Riding in a patrol car, on the street, in the northwest part of Fort Lauderdale with a woman you're having an intense personal relationship with is a tricky thing. McShaun said this to himself within the first ten minutes of their hitting the road to begin the shift. He was glad to be in the unit, out of the Comm Center, and back out in the world, and he was glad to be working with a partner who was a cop who had won respect by doing a good job on the street, but he was almost completely disoriented by her nearness.

They had sat stiffly through the briefing, ignoring the looks and whispers. They had been quiet and extremely polite to each other while they prepared their car for the shift, careful not to bump into each other, careful not to let their hands touch, careful not to let their eyes meet. She had offered to drive, and he sat now in the passenger seat, trying to get comfortable, trying to relax. They both turned and started to speak, then stopped. Finally he laughed and said, 'I hate to admit it, but this feels weird.'

She kept her eyes on the road and nodded and said, 'I know.'

He watched the sights along Sistrunk Boulevard for a few minutes and then said, 'Here we are in uniform, working, on duty, and I see you sitting there and I have the almost uncontrollable urge to reach over and touch you.'

She nodded again, looked at him, and said very softly, 'I know, Tim.'

They got a call. The wife was going to cut her husband because he was no good and didn't bring home a paycheck. They stood on the dirty sidewalk, and McShaun talked with the husband while Springfield calmed down the wife. The woman had had a knife in her hand when they pulled up but had tossed it into her apartment as they got out of the unit. A small crowd had gathered, watching the show.

McShaun managed to talk the husband into going for a walk. He would go see a man about a job in the morning. Springfield had the woman laughing a little as McShaun walked up and told her what her husband had said. The woman pulled on the hem of her dress and told them that she really didn't want to cut him; she was just upset. And he really wasn't a bad man; he just needed a job, that's all. Springfield and McShaun nodded and turned to walk back to the unit. As they passed through the crowd one of the young men standing there said softly as Springfield passed by, 'Uh-huh, yes, yes, yes.' He was looking at Rocky's bottom as she turned to get into the unit. McShaun saw him and heard him.

'Watchu lookin' at, my man?' asked McShaun. 'You see somethin' you need to be lookin' at . . . *huh?*'

The young man pulled a toothpick out of his mouth, looked at McShaun, and shook his head from side to side. McShaun hesitated for a moment, then got into the unit, and they drove away, the crowd silent.

Rocky wanted to say something to him about what had just happened, but before she could, they got another call. McShaun got the address from the dispatcher and they headed that way.

The big black woman had pink rubber curlers in her hair and a huge flower-patterned dress on. Her face was wet from her tears as she led McShaun and Springfield from her front yard, around the side of her old wooden house and to the back, where a storage shed backed up against the white-washed walls of an old church. A noisy gaggle of little boys ran along at her side, pulling on her dress and looking at the police officers with wide eyes.

'Lord, I just don't know about this chile. I swear, I don't. She goin' to be the death of this ol' woman someday. She be the daughter of my youngest daughter. My youngest ain't had no husband, and now she's up to Clewiston doin' somethin'. And here I am watchin' and raisin' her girl for her. These old bones will rest someday.'

They came around to the back and saw what the problem was. The girl, six years old, had seen a cat climb up on the old shed roof up against the church, and she thought the cat must have become stuck up there because it didn't come down. So she had climbed up a drainpipe to rescue the cat. The drainpipe had pulled away and fallen in a heap just as the little girl got to the shed roof, so she jumped. When she did, one of her legs went right through the rusty sheet-iron roof, and now she sat there in her ragged cotton dress with one leg folded under her, both small hands flat on the metal of the roof, and one leg dangling in the darkness of the shed.

143

Her hair was in two springy pigtails, tied with one yellow and one blue ribbon, and her big eyes were full of tears as she stared down at her grandmother and the two police officers.

'Lord knows I didn't want to bother you po-leeses with this,' said the old woman, 'but I don't have a man no more, and the ones that live around here won't get home from work for another hour at most. It was just me and these boys here, and we couldn't get that chile down by ourselves.'

McShaun looked at the girl, then at the old woman. He nodded and said, 'You did the right thing. We'll get her down.'

McShaun had the boys get out of the way as Springfield slowly drove the police unit alongside the house and across the sparse grass and dirt until the front bumper rested against the shed wall. Then he let the boys help him as he carried a large wooden crate over from the backyard and set it up on the hood of the car. While the boys laughed and yelled at the girl to hold on, the old woman explained that her neighbor had the box because they were supposed to build a chicken coop. 'But nothin' ever come of it.'

Rocky climbed up on the hood of the car with McShaun and held the box steady as he stood on it and then leaned over the shed roof. The frightened girl reached out for him, and he wanted to just pull her out but saw that if he did, he would drag her leg across the jagged side of the metal roofing. He looked at Springfield, grimaced, and then slowly, carefully, climbed up on the very edge of the shed roof. The little girl, crying softly, hugged his neck as he pulled her up and out of the hole in the roof. Then he carefully worked himself down until he sat on the rim of the roof with his feet dangling over the box. He pried the girl from his neck and handed her down to Springfield, who stood on the hood of the car with her legs spread, waiting. Once the girl was in her grandmother's arms, Rocky held the box as McShaun turned, pulled away from the metal roof, and lowered himself.

They moved the box back to where it had been, and

144

McShaun shooed the boys away again as Rocky backed the unit out of the yard, almost getting stuck in the sand along the way. When the unit was back on the street, McShaun looked at the little girl and said softly, 'Honey, if I were you, I'd stay away from that nasty ol' roof from now on. Those silly cats can take care of themselves. Right?' The girl buried her face in her grandmother's neck and then peeked out again and nodded. Then she reached out and pulled his collar and kissed him on the forehead while the boys laughed and Springfield watched. She wondered again at his gentleness, at his caring, at the way the little girl and her grandmother reacted to him.

The old woman looked embarrassed and said, 'All I can offer you-all is some cold water – if you're thirsty.'

McShaun said, 'No. Thank you muchly, though. We'll have to be going along. More work to do here and there.'

The old woman looked at them both, one, and then the other, and said, 'Well, then all I can say is, thank you for helpin' us . . . and I hope you two take good care of each other out there.'

As they turned to get back into the unit one of the little boys, pushed forward by the others, said, 'Hey, Mr Poleese. You gonna be out here all night with your pants torn out like that?' And they laughed while McShaun reached behind himself slowly and felt the ripped cloth of his trousers. He sat down in the car and looked at them and said, 'Why, sure. That way I'll have air conditioning wherever I go.' They were still laughing and waving as the police car drove off and headed back to the station for another pair of trousers for a slightly embarrassed McShaun, accompanied by a smiling Springfield.

They hit the road again after McShaun got a pair of trousers from the supply room. He drove; she handled the radio. They were sent to another disturbance, two more break-ins, and a minor traffic accident. At the end of the shift, on the way into the station, McShaun looked at his partner and said, 'Uh . . . I've never asked my road partner to come

145

home with me after a shift before, but would you? We can have some eggs or something and go for a walk.'

She finished writing out an incident card, smiled, and said, 'What a coincidence. I happen to have brought an overnight bag with me to work this evening.'

During the next week both McShaun and Springfield learned more about their partners and themselves. Some days were hectic to the point of crazy, and some days were slow and easy. This never-ending tension of the roller coaster that was the street kept them in an ever-changing emotional posture the whole time.

McShaun watched with pride and admiration as Springfield let a towering drunk's own strength and anger drive him headfirst into the side of the police car before she bent down and handcuffed him, nice as you please. He hung on grimly and watched as she drove the unit in pursuit of two kids on a stolen motorcycle, staying with them yet managing to avoid killing them when they finally went down right in front of the skidding patrol car. He saw how she handled two angry women dueling with broken beer bottles and how she gently bandaged the cut foot of a little boy in an alley. He watched her pale and turn away after finding a late-stage fetus in a toilet. He watched her give CPR to an electrical shock victim, long after the man was beyond any help. He had to pull her away gently, to tell her to stop. He watched her as she fought not to cry. He heard her curse in the dark of the patrol car as they were told to handle a late call after they were already on their way into the station and heard her laugh at the wild stories that the squad told around Styrofoam cups of bitter coffee and stale doughnuts.

He liked what he saw of her as a cop.

There were still differences, of course. They had argued in the hallways of the courthouse after he watched her deal with a young prosecutor. McShaun thought she should have insisted on a stronger deal against the defendant; Rocky was comfortable with whatever the court did with the case. She waited for him while he gave a deposition at an

146

attorney's office and then argued with him in the car about how he felt as if the lawyer were his enemy.

In the car, on the street, he was the senior man, he was the leader, although they worked as a team. She understood this, but she clearly did not agree with some of his methods. She stood by while he roughed up and intimidated a burglar, saying nothing until they were driving away from the man, who was on his hands and knees in the bushes, searching for the car keys McShaun had thrown over his shoulder. Then she questioned the reasoning behind it, and they argued; she staying with the theme that everything should be handled within the parameters of the judicial system, and he insisting that some things were handled better, and got better results, if they were done on the street level.

Matters were not helped by the news that during the arraignment of the auto thief who had fought with Springfield and Peoples, the presiding judge commented that he was seriously considering throwing the case out because the defendant had been beaten during the arrest. He stated that a trial would be superfluous, since so much 'street justice' had already been meted out by two arresting officers. After Bell Peoples passed this on to them, Springfield sat fuming while McShaun just drove slowly through the streets, saying nothing, but thinking, *See*?

Their arguments did not end as much as they were just called off. Neither would yield; neither could honestly accept the other's reasoning. The job they did was the same, but the way they approached the job was in frequent conflict. They did what they could to keep the work-related conflict out of their private personal relationship.

The time they spent together off duty continued in peace and fulfillment for both, as if they called a truce every night after work, both determined that the personal time they shared with each other should not be spoiled by the conflict from the street.

Rocky's feelings of respect and disagreement, of affection and impatience toward McShaun were magnified and

147

defined during one busy shift toward the end of their time together as a team in a patrol unit.

Early in the shift they were driving through a 'fringe' neighborhood, one that bordered the white and black areas. Springfield was driving and stopped and pulled over near a group of teenagers hanging around the back of a schoolyard when McShaun motioned for her to do so. She got out with him and walked behind him as he approached the group of boys. She saw that they had tensed at the arrival of the police, making moves as if to run, and then waited uncomfortably after covertly dropping a couple of bags behind a low wall. McShaun had seen the bags fall, too, and he bent over and retrieved them as he looked at the teen-agers and said, 'Well, well, looks like someone just threw away a bag of what looks like some pretty crummy grass. And what's this? A bag of Quaaludes mixed with black beauties? My, my. What a ride that would be.'

No one said anything.

'All right, troops. Everybody into the position against the wall there. C'mon. You know the routine – especially you, Dorey.'

Springfield watched as the boys leaned against the wall in the spread-eagle position to be searched by McShaun. She noted that the one named Dorey sneered and was slow but got into position, anyway. McShaun found nothing else on them and let them turn around to face him as he spoke again.

'If I was you guys, I'd get the hell outta here as soon as I tell you you can leave. See this grass? I'm dumping it out. There it goes, into the wind. And see this other shit – these ludes and uppers? Here we go, onto the sidewalk. Now we see if they can stand up to the weight of the law as my size nine steps on them, once, twice . . . oops . . . now they're just dust. As shall we all be someday. Here it is, guys. We got the word somebody is selling shit like this to the little middle-schoolers around here. And, of course, there's the usual house burglaries going on. I think it's you guys. I really do. Of course, we all know that our boy Dorey here has already been arrested a couple of times for breaking and entering. Yeah.'

He walked up to each of the boys as he spoke.

'I'm gonna be lookin' for each of you. I'm gonna hope to find you one at a time. And when I do, I'm gonna check you real good. And if I find some shit on you like I just did, am I gonna arrest you and do all that evidence stuff and paperwork and all? Nope. I'm gonna just take whatever I find, ludes, grass, uppers, whatever . . . and I'm gonna make you eat it, assholes! I'll cram every bit of it down your scumbag throats and watch you swallow, and then I'll drive away and let you figure out for yourself how to get to an emergency room to have your fucking stomachs pumped. *Hear me?*'

He was on the balls of his feet now, his eyes tight, his face stretched. The boys did not move.

'And even better . . . hear this, Dorey. I'm gonna work this area break-in thing real good. People out at work, tryin' to make a living, and some scumbag like you guys breakin' into their houses and taking their things. No . . . no. That won't do at all. I'll tell you this to your faces. Look at my name tag now in case you want to complain to your mommy or your parole officer later; it's *McShaun*. Here it is, scumbags: If I catch any of you' – he looked at Dorey – '*any of you*, inside a house that you've broken into, I'll beat you to death with my bare hands.' He was breathing hard now, looking at each boy, his hands making fists and then opening again, rocking back and forth on his toes. Then he said very quietly, 'I'll fucking beat you to death.'

The boys stood there watching as he and Rocky drove off.

They were quiet in the patrol car for almost fifteen minutes, McShaun tensed like a fist and Springfield knowing that to start a conversation about what he had just done with the boys would be to open up an intense and bitter argument. The possibility of that was curtailed by a call.

They were to make it code three, lights and siren, to a sick person: baby not breathing.

Rocky sped through traffic as fast she dared, taking

149

chances, stretching it, driven by that thing about kids that drives most police officers. They slid to a stop at the address, a tired collection of old prefab apartment buildings with no grass over the dirt lawns and no screens over the windows. Parts of cars with dubious ownership sat and rusted, along with ancient washing machines and broken toys. McShaun was out and running toward the open apartment before the car stopped, yelling over his shoulder, 'Bring the oxygen, Rocky – and find out how far away the ambulance is!' She could see that a small crowd had gathered, women crying and men standing uncertainly, all looking at the open apartment that McShaun ran into.

Rocky opened the trunk and grabbed the oxygen resuscitator while she learned from the dispatcher that the closest ambulance was still ten minutes away.

She ran to the apartment, into a wall of closely packed bodies. Women wailed and hugged each other, and men craned their necks to see into the bedroom. Springfield felt her feet slide on the floor and was afraid to look down; she had a glimpse of a pot of rice on a small table, covered with roaches, and then she shouldered her way past a fat woman in a blue terry-cloth housedress and looked into the bedroom.

'Poor little chile done stopped breathin' . . .'

'Been too long now . . . too long . . .'

'Hasn't been too long . . . been five minutes . . .'

'That baby girl done gone from this earth now.'

'That's her momma there. Says she just looked away for a *minute.*'

'Uh-huh.'

'Yeah, a minute. And then the little girl done stopped breathin' and all.'

Springfield put the oxygen bottle down at McShaun's feet and looked at him. He was sitting on an umade bed with his back against the peeling wall, holding a baby girl in his hands and arms. She could see the sweat on his forehead as he bent over the baby, his face covering hers. He paid no attention to anything else going on around him in the room.

Springfield turned to the people and said, 'Could we have some room please? Could we get some air in here?'

The people turned and pushed each other and yelled at one another, but there was no relief; the bodies were packed as tightly as before.

Springfield watched as McShaun worked. She knew he would be breathing softly, steadily into the baby's nose and mouth at the same time. She heard him say softly, 'C'mon, honey . . . c'mon now,' as he lifted his head and used his little finger to wipe out the baby's mouth and nose. Then he bent over her again.

Springfield felt the press of the bodies and heard their murmuring and was enveloped by the heat and the filth and the hopelessness of it all. The desolate picture of McShaun sitting on a dirty bed, trying to breathe into a baby that had stopped breathing too long ago made her feel an awesome sense of futility. She was sinking lower and lower when she was snapped out of it by a quick gagging sound, and then the baby threw up all over McShaun, who shouted, 'Yeah! All right, little darlin' . . . c'mon now.!'

Some of the people laughed nervously, but most stood silent, holding their breath.

McShaun ignored the mess on his shirt and bent over the baby again, who suddenly choked, gagged, and then started crying loudly.

Primal pandemonium.

Emotional chaos.

Women screamed and one of them fainted. Women shouted, 'Lord! Lord Jesus!' Men laughed and smacked their hands together and danced around the living room. The woman who fainted was ignored while people hugged one another and slapped one another on the back and cried, 'She's all right! The chile's back again!'

Springfield grabbed the oxygen bottle and backed up against the crowd, opening a way for McShaun, who stood exhausted with the baby in his arms, his face still bent over her. They moved slowly through the people, out of the bedroom, through the living room, and out toward the police car. As they moved, Springfield saw McShaun's strong hands cradling the baby, and she saw how his tanned fingers gently stroked one of her little curled ears, and she heard him whisper, 'Hello, baby. Welcome back. That's it, keep crying. Keep crying and breathing.'

The ambulance pulled in, and the attendants jumped out and opened the rear doors. Springfield told them what they had, and the crowd was silent as McShaun stood with the baby for a few more moments before climbing carefully up into the back of the wagon. The crying grandmother and the tight-faced young mother were led up and in, and they sat along the right side while McShaun lay the baby on the bed on the left side and helped while the ambulance attendants adjusted the oxygen mask over her face. She was breathing on her own now; the oxygen would be just a continuous gentle flow across her mouth and nose. The driver waited for the signal to pull out.

McShaun stood bent over in the back of the ambulance as he reached out with one hand and lifted the young mother's face to look at him. When their eyes met, he nodded and smiled at her, as if to say, 'She'll be all right . . . we were here in time. She never really stopped breathing.' But he said nothing, only turned to touch the baby once more. Then he jumped out of the ambulance and closed the doors as the ambulance started for the hospital.

Springfield opened the trunk of the car and put the resuscitator away and got a four-inch compress out for McShaun to wipe himself off with. The crowd was quiet and started to break up and go back inside their apartments.

McShaun wiped the front of his shirt, his neck, and his face. He looked at Springfield and said, 'Ready to go?'

Before Rocky could answer, a young girl, about ten years old, wearing a faded flowered dress and old tennis shoes, tapped McShaun on the hip and said, 'Mister Po-leese.'

McShaun turned and looked down at her.

'Mister Po-leese, the people sayin' that you saved my little niece. They sayin' that you is the reason she still alive.'

McShaun fidgeted, then said quietly, 'Well, I guess you

could say I helped. But you know, it was someone bigger than me that let that baby live.'

The girl looked up at him in silence for a few seconds, thinking about what he had said. Then she nodded her head in acceptance and said, 'Well, thank you for helpin', then.' She turned and ran off across the dirt yard of the apartment building.

Springfield drove slowly out over the bumpy dirt road, the only one left in Fort Lauderdale. When she got to the pavement, she asked McShaun, 'You all right, Tim?'

McShaun told the dispatcher they were ten-eight and shook his head and smiled a little. Then the dispatcher sent them to back up another unit heading to a man-with-a-gun call. Springfield's hands tightened on the wheel, and she stomped on the gas pedal as she muttered, 'God, what kind of shift is this anyway? Isn't it *ever* gonna slack off?'

They slid to a stop in the east, or side, parking lot of Big Joe's Pool Hall Emporium and Dance Club. At the same time the other double unit stopped at the front entrance, on the north. The dispatcher had said there was a man 'dressed like a pimp' who was 'waving a gun around and acting bad.' Springfield and McShaun saw him at the same time, quickly turning the front corner of the building and walking away from the unit that had parked there. They saw his eyes widen at the sight of them and then watched as he walked 'cool', but still rapidly, to the side entrance to the club.

McShaun climbed out of the unit and said, 'Hold it, brother. We need to talk to you.' The man ran the last three steps to the door and darted inside.

Springfield could see that he was probably the one they wanted; he was over six feet tall, and he wore a light blue suit with a pink shirt. He had a neat straw hat pulled over one eye, and he kept his hand in his coat pocket as he moved.

McShaun took off after him and disappeared into the club as Rocky ran around the back of the car, tried to wave at the other officers out front, and then followed McShaun into the side door.

153

As McShaun went from the bright afternoon light to the dark gloom of the interior of the bar, he momentarily lost sight of the pimp. The swinging of the wooden bathroom doors caught his eye and he ran that way. There were a few men sitting at the bar and at rickety wooden tables on the concrete floor, but they ignored him. He pushed his way into the men's room and found the pimp bent over, sticking something behind the urinal.

'So, my man, what we hidin' there, huh?'

'Ain't hidin' nothin'. Get outta my way, po-leese. I'm all through in here. I'm leavin'.'

'Leavin'? Wrong, Buckwheat. You're talking to me first.'

'Lookee, here, paddy motherfucker po-leese. I's leavin'!'

The man put his hand on McShaun's chest and pushed him back against the bathroom door. McShaun hit him in the face and kicked him in the groin. The pimp swung both his arms hard, and caught McShaun on the side of the head and in the stomach.

McShaun cursed and hit the man again, and as the man fell back, McShaun kicked and hit him three more times, until the pimp was saying, 'Okay, okay, man.' But McShaun was screaming now.

'Motherfucker! You *challenging* me, man?'

When Springfield and the other officers burst into the men's room, they found the black man crammed against the urinal with McShaun on top of him, smashing his fists into the pimp's face and screaming at him. The pimp was almost unconscious, and his head rocked back and forth with each punch.

Springfield and the other two cops had to pull McShaun off, yelling at him to cool it. Finally McShaun nodded and stood aside while they pulled the black pimp up and half carried him out of the washroom. Then McShaun reached behind the urinal and pulled out the gun, which turned out to be a .44 Magnum Bulldog.

Springfield looked at him standing there in the stench and shadows of the bathroom. His shirt was torn, and he was cut over one eye. His hands and wrists were speckled with blood. He stood breathing deeply, jaws clenched, his eyes bulging and blinking. He stuck the Magnum in his belt, rubbed his face with his bloody hands, and said, 'Motherfucker'.

Almost two hours later they went ten-eight from the station again. McShaun had cleaned up, and they had done the booking and evidence and paperwork on the gun. The pimp had been taken to the emergency room and released with bruises and abrasions and two missing teeth; then he was brought in and booked for felony, possession of a firearm, resisting arrest with violence, and assault on a police officer. The old booking sergeant had looked at the beaten black man and then at McShaun. He had already been told how they had had to pull McShaun off the man. He motioned McShaun to one side and said quietly, 'Tim . . . uh . . . charge him with everything you can, right? And you better load up on the paperwork. Make it right. Attaboy.'

When they returned to the car, Springfield drove. She was quiet. Her mind was in a jumble. She still wanted to address Tim's handling of the teenage boys at the beginning of the shift, and then the thing with the baby girl, and then the fight in the men's room at Big Joe's. She rubbed her temple hard and thought, Where are you, Tim McShaun? She drove through the early-evening traffic trying to sort it all out.

At the end of the shift they stood in the darkness of the back parking lot, near their patrol car.

'Listen, Rocky. You comin' over my place tonight? Wanna go for a walk?'

She looked at him and then at her feet. 'No. Not tonight, Tim. Tonight I have to go home and be by myself for a while. I have to be by myself.'

He shrugged and said, 'Okay. I'll give you a call in the morning. Maybe we can get together before we come to work.'

155

He kissed her lightly and started to turn away, and she took his hand.

'Tim, about today. Tonight, I mean. I have questions.'

He waited.

'That little black girl, I *saw,* Tim. I *know* how hard you worked. Oh, I know we got lucky with that one, but still, you *wanted* to save her. And yet . . . and yet ten minutes later you tried to *kill* that jerk in the bathroom with the gun. I . . . think you would have beaten him until he was dead if we hadn't stopped you. Do you hear what I'm saying, Tim?'

'He challenged me. It was a combat situation. Just like a burglary: combat . . . challenge.'

'Tim, it's like you have this special code of yours . . . McShaun's rules of conduct.'

He looked at her and shrugged.

She stood on her toes and kissed him on the forehead while she ran one finger softly over his left eyebrow.

'You scare me, Tim. I'm not sure I'll ever figure you out.' She sighed. 'Good night, Tim.'

Chapter Thirteen

A week later Rocky Springfield stepped out of the office of Internal Affairs on the third floor of the police department building and closed the door quietly behind her. She was in turmoil, her stomach in knots and her head pounding.

She had just lied for Tim McShaun.

She bent down and sipped the cold water from a fountain in the hallway and thought, *Well, maybe it wasn't really lying. Maybe it was just something I know not to be entirely true. Or is it*?

The attorney representing the pimp with the gun at Big Joe's had advised the city that he planned to bring suit against McShaun and the city for the beating of his client. He disputed the criminal charges, demanded an internal investigation, and had advised the NAACP and ACLU. The Lauderdale PD would always investigate one of its own on any citizen complaint to try to keep things 'clean'. The Internal Affairs office was open to any citizen or attorney who thought an officer had acted improperly, and those members of the department assigned to the office took their jobs very seriously. It was a high-profile office, directly related to public input and reaction, and so came under the ever political eye of the chief. The men in the office who investigated their peers did so with the basic police attitude: seek out the truth. They did not recommend action on any case, they simply advised the chief on the validity of the charges. Even so, some cases were more difficult for them than others. Some cases, such as those that involved racial undertones and the monitoring by agencies such as the NAACP and the ACLU, had to be worked with the thought of finding the truth – and at the same time finding a politically palatable recommendation for the chief.

The summons to the office had filled Springfield with dread. McShaun had told her angrily about the investigation the day before. She wished she'd had no part in it, she wished she hadn't been there, she wished she hadn't seen McShaun in the washroom with the pimp.

But she had.

And she dreaded their questions because she knew that the technical, procedural, action-witness truth would conflict with the truth she knew in her heart. Things were made a little easier for her by the black man's attorney. The attorney's complaint was based on the fact that his client was 'simply using the men's room when attacked for no reason' by McShaun. He complained that McShaun actually planted the gun behind the urinal to cover himself and that his client was the victim of a racially motivated beating by an officer who had a long reputation for violence.

Springfield knew McShaun had not planted the gun. She knew in her heart that the pimp had the gun on him when they arrived, and she knew that he had to have resisted McShaun initially to make McShaun react. She knew McShaun would not feel 'challenged' by a passive suspect.

She also knew that it was a racial incident only because the suspect was black, not because McShaun was racist.

The two officers from the original unit dispatched to the scene testified to the investigators that they entered the men's room to back up McShaun. They entered behind Springfield. They saw no struggle, only McShaun preparing to handcuff the suspect. They did not see McShaun 'plant' a gun, but they did see him find one behind the urinal. They testified that the suspect was antagonistic toward them after the arrest, and they were stopped then by the investigators, who were only interested in what happened before the arrest. Before they finished testifying, the two officers did mention that they saw bruises, a small cut, and other evidence of injury on McShaun's person.

Then they were dismissed.

Springfield testified that she was positive McShaun did not plant the gun. She had been working with him and knew he did not ever carry any kind of a 'throw-down' weapon. She also reminded the investigators that a .44 Magnum Bulldog revolver would be very hard for a uniformed police officer to conceal on his person. She asked them where they thought McShaun could have carried the weapon before running into the men's room. In his belt? In his pocket? They reminded her that they would ask the questions.

She testified that she saw McShaun and the suspect 'struggling' when she came into the room and stated that she saw that McShaun had been injured, as if hit with fists, while they handcuffed the suspect. She testified that she did not see the actual conflict, that is was really over before she and the others pushed their way into the washroom.

She was told that she might be recalled to take a lie detector test, as might the others, and then she was released.

Springfield straightened out from the drinking fountain and stared at the wall, her emotions in conflict. McShaun was stretched like a humming wire, working a thin line between caring too much for the victims of this world and hating too much those he saw as the predators. He was beautiful to watch with a victim: gentle, caring, genuine in the giving of himself to their well-being. And he was frightening to watch with those that 'challenged' him and the proper order of things, those that preyed on the others.

She knew McShaun gave the citizens of his city everything he had. She knew he worked hard at making their streets a safe place to be. She knew he cared for 'them'. And she was also well aware of commitment to destroy those who would hurt the others.

How could a simple investigative board, looking into the 'facts' of a men's room arrest, be made to comprehend what was in fact a multifaceted, complicated, emotionally motivated, and totally complex truth?

'Hey, Rocky! I've been looking for you.'

Springfield turned from the water fountain to see

Lieutenant James Track standing at the end of the hallway. He was smiling and waving some papers at her. She walked toward him.

'Your orders came through today, Rocky. You're coming up to the division. Ah, I can see you're surprised. Well, you deserve it, you know. Of course, I, ah, well, I had to convince some people along the way that you were the one we wanted for the slot.' He held up one manicured hand, as if stopping traffic, and smiled. 'Don't even try to thank me now, though. Plenty of time for things like that.'

Rocky just looked at him, not as excited as she thought she would be. The Detective Division . . . plainclothes . . . a gold badge. Real investigative police work. A promotion, even if the pay grade stayed the same as patrolman. A detective wasn't just a flatfoot cop. No, a detective was a cop who had something on the ball, a cop who could . . . investigate.

Track smiled at her and went on. 'If you have time, you should slide down to the division and introduce yourself to Calabrini. Ah, that's Lieutenant Calabrini. He's the homicide man. Not like me; I'm not restricted to any one branch of the division. They have me come in and help out wherever I'm needed. Never a dull moment.' He actually patted himself lightly on the chest before going on. 'Anyway, Calabrini works with the new people when they first come into the unit. Then he'll eventually assign you. He's a very competent detective and administrator, but you'll probably see pretty quick that he lacks . . . flair. But don't get me wrong,' he added quickly, 'we need the "plodders", too, right?'

Springfield sat across from Lieutenant John Calabrini and waited while he made some notes on a pad on his desk. She saw that he was neat and trim; his clothes were sharp and well fitted to his lean body. He was a little over six feet, she guessed, and in his middle thirties. His black hair was worn very short, and it framed a hawklike face with a sharp, angled nose that should have hurt his looks but somehow

160

managed to add to his air of quiet dignity. She felt a calm in him. His hand was dry and firm when he had introduced himself and asked her to sit down. She liked him.

'Okay. Rocky Springfield. At work here do you go by Rocky? Good. Sorry I had to make you wait. Stupid paperwork around here could sink a ship. Make that a whole fleet of ships.' He leaned back in his chair. 'I'm sure Lieutenant Track has already briefed you on your orders, who to report to, and when?'

She nodded.

'Good. When you first come up, you'll work for me and with me for a while, and then you'll be assigned to one of the different units within the division. There's auto theft, fraud, larceny, burglary, and so on. And we also keep a general pool of people to fill in where necessary. You'll find that the work here is different from that of the street – and I don't mean better or more important. What goes on out on the street with those uniformed guys is *very* important, believe me. But up here you'll find yourself working with reports, information pertaining to what happened out on the street, and then the subsequent follow-up of that action. It requires patience, brains, and street knowledge.'

He leaned forward and looked at her. 'I think you'll like it, Springfield.'

She nodded again and smiled.

He looked away for a minute, then back at her. 'Also, you know and I know that there are senior men down in patrol who have been waiting to be assigned up here longer than you. You'll find the usual resentment. To be totally honest with you, I was one of the administrators up here who voted for a more senior guy against you for the job. Not that I have anything against you as a person or as a cop – I've seen a lot of your work come through here and you're good. It's just that . . . politics bother me.' He saw the look on her face, waved one of his hands, and said, 'Hey, I know you didn't play politics. You just worked hard and waited for the assignment. I know that. I would have asked for you sooner or later, but I expected the assignment of a couple of guys

161

who have been on the street about two years longer than you.'

They sat there on opposite sides of the desk, both uncomfortable. She didn't know what she was supposed to say. He rubbed his face with his hand and said, 'Listen, I'm not telling you this to hurt you or make you feel bad or anything like that. I can't stand word games and inter-departmental hallway battles. I like the people who work for me to know how things are. You're going to feel some flack here and there. You'll hear about how you were assigned up here because you're a female. You'll hear about how hard Track pushed for you during the staff meetings – and some of it will be true.'

Their eyes met.

'But hear this, too, Springfield. I have the power to veto any potential assignment if I don't think the person can do the job. I've seen your reports. I've watched you testify in court. I've talked to your supervisors and read over your evaluations. You're good, Rocky. You're as good as most of the guys up here. You just lack experience. And I'll see that you get it. Right?'

She looked at him and nodded. 'I hear what you said, Lieutenant, and I appreciate it. I really do. I want the job and I'll do the job. I know how good I am, and I know how green I am. But I can do the job and I intend to.'

They stood up, facing each other. He shook her hand and then released it, nodding as if he had heard what he expected to hear.

She turned to go and he said, 'Excuse me, Rocky. One more thing. You've been working the street for a while now with Tim McShaun. How did you like it?'

She looked at him, searching his eyes for something that wasn't in his voice. She saw that he was uncomfortable with the question as she answered, 'It's been very good for me – in many ways. I've learned a lot working with him and being with him. He's very much a man and very much a cop.'

She was surprised by his reaction.

162

His face brightened, and he smiled as he rubbed his crooked nose with one finger. He had a boyish look of mischief as he said, 'Yes. Tim McShaun. What a piece of work he is. He and I go back a ways. We worked the same section of town years ago. He is beautiful, and I mean that. What a maniac! But his paperwork is just about flawless . . . and he *knows*, know what I mean? He *knows* what he's doing and why he's doing it.'

He looked at her slowly, not like a lieutenant looking at a young cop, but as a man looking at a woman, and said, 'And he's still lucky in life too. You tell him I said hello, Rocky. Okay?'

After that same day had turned into a muggy, cloudy, rain-threatening Lauderdale evening, Chick Hummel took one of the rental cars and went out cruising the town. The Narc Unit had nothing really cooking; the cop he was supposed to work with had called in sick, and he was told just to go out and 'nose around, make some contacts'. He planned to go to a few of the waterfront places and hang around, listening and looking, maybe pick up a couple of tag numbers of guys who looked like 'players'. It would be fun.

Lydia Taylor was out that evening too. She had planned to have fun also, but so far things hadn't been that great. She had gone to Harv Jensen's place to score a little cocaine and maybe party with him. He had sold her half an ounce of coke but had some other girl there with him and was really almost rude to Lydia. She didn't like it, but she took the coke and drove off in her Austin Healey, determined to find someone else with whom to share the coke.

She made it about five blocks when her right rear tyre blew out. She wobbled over to the side of Oakland Park Boulevard, got out, and stood there with her arms folded across her chest, tapping her foot angrily.

To be fair about it, Chick Hummel did not miss the fact that the girl leaning against the Austin Healey with the flat tyre was definitely a good-looking young thing. But in any

163

event, Hummel was the type of person who had a hard time just driving past someone who needed help. He always asked himself, *What if it was my wife?*

Hummel parked his rental behind the young woman's small car, walked up, and offered to help. She was radiant in her joy and showed him where the spare was kept in the 'boot', under that little 'cover thing'. She leaned close while she helped him find the 'jack-up thing and those other tools and stuff'. Chick went to work on the lugs while she told him her name was Lydia Taylor and made small talk. What did he do, how did he ever see her standing there, where was he going, was that a rental car, and isn't Fort Lauderdale sometimes a *lonely* town?

Chick tried to keep his answers short while he worked. He was in insurance, the company gave him the rental car, he was just out for a ride, and yeah, Lauderdale *could* be a lonely town. Then, as he finished, because of something about her, he took a wild shot.

'You know,' he said while putting her flat tyre and jack in the back of the car, 'a lot of people think us insurance types are pretty dull people, but I can tell you that we like to party like anyone else.'

Lydia smiled and nodded.

'The problem is, a guy like me, well, I look straight and all. In fact, I'm growing this beard to kind of be a little more "with it." Anyway, it's hard for me to make the right connection, you know. Find someone who could get me . . . something. Some stuff, uh, to party with.'

She leaned into her car, almost causing an accident out in the center lane as she did so, and pulled out her purse. She walked very close to Hummel, opened the purse, and said, 'You mean something like this?' She laughed as Chick's eyes widened at the sight of the white powder in the baggie.

Hummel nodded his head. 'Yes . . . yeah . . . that's what I mean, all right.'

She rubbed his arm as she said, 'I can get it whenever I need it. And I don't mind sharing what I've got.' She smiled. 'You were very nice to help me with my car. Since

164

you're not doing anything now, why don't you come with me to my place and we'll share this and see if we can have some fun.'

Hummel's face reddened and he almost panicked. Finally he said, 'Uh, that would really be swell. I mean, great. But, uh, actually, I lied before because you seemed so nice that I wanted to not have to hurry while I changed the tyre. Uh, actually I *do* have to be somewhere in just a little while. I would like to maybe buy some of that stuff from you if I could. You wouldn't be offended?'

She stepped back and laughed.

'Listen, guy. I wouldn't be offended. I like you, you're a gentleman. I mean, you can't be with me tonight, okay, I'm not mad. I'd let you buy this right here, but it's all I've got. Maybe we could meet tomorrow or something.'

Hummel couldn't believe what he was hearing. He looked around quickly and said, 'Yes. I'd like that. Do you think it would be all right? Like, you're not a cop or anything, are you?'

She laughed again and shook out her hair and stuck out her tongue.

He said, 'Well, do you think you could get me an ounce? We could meet wherever you want tomorrow night.'

She closed her purse, ran her fingers through her hair, and said with a smile, 'An ounce it is, Sir Galahad. And I'll meet you in the front parking lot across from Dirty Nellie's Bar – over there on the other side of the bridge, at like . . . eight o'clock?'

Hummel nodded, and they smiled at each other. As she turned to get into her car Lydia cocked her head to one side and asked, 'Say, Sir Galahad, what's your name, anyway?'

'Fred Friendly,' he answered with a smile.

She laughed and pulled away.

165

Chapter Fourteen

Rocky lay on her side in the gray-pink of early morning, watching Tim as he slept. She remembered the lovemaking of the night before and smiled to herself, knowing the last thing she was aware of was Tim gently rubbing her back as she fell asleep. She stretched carefully and almost purred. She put her head on his shoulder and looked at him. When they came together physically, it was almost totally consuming, she thought. He was an intense, passionate lover, deriving much of his own pleasure by pleasing her. He was unselfish and caring, and he pleased her as no man ever had.

They lay naked under the sheet, and as she slowly sat up, hugging her legs, she could see where the dark tan of his back ended just below the waist and became a creamy smooth curve. She wanted to reach out and run her fingers along his spine, but she waited. She hugged herself and brushed her lips across the tops of her knees, thinking of how he made her want to give herself to him. In his bed she had no inhibitions; there was no way in which she hadn't given herself to him. She surprised herself in her own reckless carnality. But . . . she listened as he took a deep breath and turned his head toward her, still asleep, but, somehow, with him, no matter how intense she became physically, it was still lovemaking, it was still gentle, there was still that whisper of tenderness that made their coming together a sharing.

She looked at his long eyelashes and thought, Definitely the physical male animal. He jogged between six and ten miles every other day, complaining when his court schedule interfered. He worked out with weights. He said 'lightly', but his arm muscles were incredibly strong and hard to her touch, and she always told him she had a 'thing' for his thighs, which she thought were just big enough and shaped just right. He was tough and tight, he worked hard to stay that way . . . he was male, he was scarred, he was strong, and he took her to bed with his physical maleness and it made her feel totally female. He came to her in fiery passion, his whole body aimed at her, and she let herself be taken.

She watched as he turned his head again, his back to her, and she gently lay her body against his. She touched the back of his neck with her lips, feeling her nipples harden against his back, and waited for him to wake up.

Later that morning, after the lovemaking, after the playing, after the shower, she stood in his kitchen waiting for the water to boil for tea. She stared out the window into the brightening day, but her wide eyes looked only inside herself. She reminded herself that she still had not discussed the Internal Affairs Investigation with Tim. And there were other things. She blinked and took a deep breath, knowing how easy it was to just bask in the warm sunshine that was him, to enjoy just being near him. She needed to talk with him; there were conflicts that needed to be resolved. She heard him in the bedroom, laughing at Radar, and she went over things in her mind.

Despite the fact that she didn't understand him on the job, couldn't figure out what made him tick, was unable to reconcile his ends-versus-means procedures, she found herself admiring his quixotic, noble causes that she was pretty sure motivated him. Being with him on the street was at the same time marvelous and terrifying. He was like some runaway comet, a ball of fire flashing through the streets, driven by his 'code,' hindered but not defeated by the rules of the system.

Being around him while he worked was to burn energy, it

was to feel purpose. To stay with him through a shift was to be part of a righteous stampede, strength driven headlong toward some faraway, undefined goal. Sometimes she felt as if she actually needed to hang on. She had to maintain the same level of intensity or she would be swept back into the world of the ordinary. It all reminded her of the wild rides she went on as a child, the giant roller coaster where you screamed and hung on, frightened and swearing that when it was over, you would never do it again – but when it slowed to a stop you found yourself grinning like a fool, chest pounding, knowing you wanted to go again.

He came out of the bedroom, kissed her on the forehead, then on her left eye, then on her nose, then quickly on her lips, then on her chin, then on the side of her neck, her ear, her shoulder. She laughed and wiggled away from him. She watched him as he took the cup of tea she handed him and walked to the window and looked out at the world. Yes, she thought, he was a difficult man to be around at work, but when he was away from the job, it was easy. Oh, he still burned energy like the sun, and he still took your breath away with his intensity, but he was fun and alive and loving and warm.

She hugged herself and shook her head slightly, looking down at her bare feet. She was in conflict but would resolve it.

McShaun sipped his tea without tasting it and looked out the window without seeing. He, too, was in conflict. Yin and Yang, sweet and sour, positive and negative. His whole being told him he was happy with Rocky, told him he could shape his life around her, told him she pleased him as had no woman. She was special, and she was his for the asking, he knew it. But what? Why the hesitation, why the stutter? Afraid, McShaun? Afraid to give yourself totally to a woman? Afraid, after all is said and done, that you're really not man enough, not mature enough, not confident enough to share life with a real woman . . . a woman who will demand and deserve total commitment?

168

He felt her standing behind him. Her warmth and the smell of her aroused him. Damn, she was strong and silky and smooth, and when she held him, he felt in harmony with himself and with her. There was no denying the physiological magnetism that drew them together. They fit. They fit completely.

But – what?

He hugged her arms as they came across his waist from behind and said to himself, Give us the lofty reasons, McShaun. C'mon, tell us how you know in your heart that you're no good for her, that you actually have *her* well-being in mind. Tell us how you know you can never really commit to her and how you know in your heart that she needs someone who can do that. Tell us how, in the long run, she would be better off without you. Tell us how you wish you could make her see that she should run, not walk, away from you. Sure, she'll be hurt, but won't a sharp, immediate pain now be better for her than one continuous hurt? And how do you know, McShaun, that loving you will only cause her pain in the long run? Because you sense, deep inside you, a drive that will take you over the edge? That to commit to her would be to compromise your mission in life, your special reason for existence?

He felt her nuzzle the back of his neck. 'Hey . . . hello . . . are you in there, McShaun?'

He turned and saw her eyes laughing at him. 'I'm sorry. What did you say? I was . . . thinking.'

'I said, oh great thinker, that you – in a weak moment of foolish desire to help this poor little girl manage a terrible chore – promised this would be the day we . . . that's you, and me, McShaun . . . we would throw a coat of wax on that cute little car of mine and while we're at it, we might even hose off that macho machine of yours, right?'

He looked at her and had to smile. He put down his tea cup and held her. He looked long into her eyes and saw the warmth, and the always-question. He brushed his lips against hers and then kissed her gently, long and warm while he held her tightly against him.

Finally she pulled back, breathless, and said softly, 'Well, I mean, we don't have to just rush right out there . . .'

Those who enjoyed the beautiful sunny and clear Fort Lauderdale day were further rewarded when it turned into a crystal, starry, and clear Lauderdale night. While McShaun and Springfield listened as Knute, their waiter at the Casa Vecchia, suggested an interesting white wine and watched the lights shining from the boats on the Intracoastal Waterway, Chick Hummel sat in Lydia's small car and smiled as she showed him what she had brought.

The guys in the narc office had been skeptical when they heard Hummel tell of how he had met Lydia Taylor in the first place, but the lieutenant had authorized him to take twenty-five hundred dollars from the 'work' fund to try to make the cocaine deal. Hummel's partner still wasn't feeling great, fighting the flu, but he said he'd go along, anyway, to cover Chick's back as he made the deal. It was to be a simple buy-bust: She would see his money, he would see her coke, and then he would bust her. Since it was Hummel's first case, they decided to keep it simple. If things went well, he could talk to her about learning where her supply came from.

Chick's partner dropped him off on the east side of the Oakland Park Bridge and then drove slowly into the parking lot to wait. As Hummel walked through the middle of the big lot that bordered three waterfront lounges, Lydia called out to him, waving and smiling from her car. He climbed in.

They made small talk and then talked price, but Lydia wasn't really into the money end of it as much as she just liked doing it. To her the profit was in the fun, not in the money. Oh, she would earn enough to make it worth her while, but that wasn't the main point.

Lydia held out a little bit of the white powder for him to sample. He handed her the money they had agreed on and then stretched both arms over his head, the signal for his partner to move in. He shrugged at Lydia, reached into his

170

back pocket, and pulled out his badge and ID card. He held it up for her to see.

She said, 'Oh, shit! Fred Friendly, indeed.'

Hummel sat in the dark parking lot behind the narc office with Lydia. After the arrest they had gone to the office to do the paperwork and secure the evidence. The night sergeant had congratulated Hummel, and his partner had gone home to go back to bed. Chick finished up all the formalities and then prepared to take Lydia over to the station for booking. Lydia had been quiet and subdued, and now she sat in his rental car with her hands cuffed in front of her, her head down.

Hummel actually felt bad, seeing her sitting there like that. He wished he could make things better for her. But he had to scare her first. He had discussed what he intended to do with the sergeant and his partner, and they both agreed that it was worth a shot.

He started gently, telling her he knew she really wasn't a bad person. She wasn't really a criminal, not like a real dope pusher or anything like that. In fact, he told her, he felt angry that it was she he had arrested and not some real bad guy. He knew, he said, that she was just a nice person trying to make it through life, and it was a shame she had to go to jail instead of people who really deserved it.

He told her what really bothered him was that jail was such a dead place. You know, dismal. No color, no energy, no fun. Stupid gray clothes and washed-out-looking people all over the place. No partying, no action, nothing but hard, gray women and concrete floors.

He was just starting to get into it when she smiled at him and said, 'Hey, Chick, I've seen the movies, okay? I don't want to go to jail. We'll trade, right? I'll tell you some things about some people that will make it possible for you to investigate them – and you'll let me off on this coke charge. Yes?'

While she talked, she mentally counted off the things she would need when she took off. She was thankful that she had kept that emergency fund stashed away. She would give him good information, and he could do with it what he wanted, but she sure as hell wasn't going to stick around to see it all go down.

She told Hummel about Harv Jensen, a guy with a black Porsche and a tattoo that said 'Who Me?' If she saw how Hummel had stiffened, had become just a fraction more alert, she gave no sign. She told him about Harv's small marijuana smuggling operation, and about how Harv was doing it underneath a real cocaine thing run by a guy named Tom Odom. Harv had the coke because he worked for Odom, and that's where she got it.

She stopped and waited. He looked at her and said, 'What else?'

She told him about Odom and Jensen and their movies. She told him she did it because it was a kick. No, she didn't know any of the other girls involved, and no, she didn't know what happened to them later.

Hummel wanted more names.

Lydia told him about an attorney named Beachwood and about some creepy guy with busy hands that worked for the city – Giles? She hesitated, then said that Harv had also bragged about a big shot, a congressman.

Hummel sat up straight and wished he had a recorder or a partner or *something*.

She told him about the congressman and the radar maps. Then she stopped.

Hummel didn't want to, but he pulled out a small notebook and wrote it all down. Then he smiled at her and said quietly, 'Lydia, if even part of this stuff is good, you won't have to worry about going to jail on account of me.'

She chewed the edge of one thumbnail as she thought, *oh, Hummel, I don't want to go to jail for sure. But now I feel like I'm gonna throw up. You, Hummel, you're a gentleman. And a nice guy and a cop. You'll threaten me with jail, you'll throw the book at me, but you'll still open the door for me when we get there. Fine. And there's Odom and Harv. Which is worse? Jail or having them furious with me?*

172

While Hummel, incredulous, heard the revelations from a Lydia who was just beginning to understand the implications of 'trading off' her charges, Tim and Rocky held each other on the couch in his apartment.

Springfield felt a glowing contentment. The night had been lovely and fun, they had been close and quiet, and she was happy. She lay with her head on his chest and listened to him breathe, wondering about his thoughts. She was comfortable and was tempted just to stay that way, comfortable and warm and relaxed.

But she couldn't let herself.

The night had been very fine, and she felt they were closer than ever. She raised her head and found that his brown eyes were open, watching her. She hitched herself up onto one elbow and smiled at him. 'It was a nice night, Tim. Thank you for that dinner. It was really special.'

He nodded and smiled.

'Tim, I . . . I want to tell you some things.'

He watched her.

'Tim, you have to know how special you are to me. I know you feel it too. We're very special together. You're good for me, and my life is so much better since we . . . came together.'

She kissed him on the chin and said softly, 'I love you, Tim McShaun. There. I said it. Oh, don't get me wrong. I've come close to saying it many times, especially when we're making love. But I don't like to just throw that word around. Like, "Hcy, we've been to bed, so I guess it's love." Know what I mean? No, don't answer, just listen.'

She sat up on the couch and rubbed one finger along his lips.

'Tim, I love you. I want to spend time with you . . . as man and woman. Oh, I know we're together a lot – the job and all – but that's going to change now with me going to be a detective and changing shifts here and there and all that. What I mean is, you're *the* man in my life. I want to learn about you, I want to share things with you. I want to see what it would be like to live with you.'

McShaun looked into her eyes and sighed. He brushed her hair away from her right ear with his fingers as he thought about his conflict. He should tell her he loved her. He felt it, it was real, and he should say it. She had said it to him, and he knew it came from her heart and it warmed him – warmed him and saddened him at the same time. She took his hand and kissed it, and he thought about how he loved her and how great the chances were that his loving her would, he felt inevitably, hurt her.

He put his hands on her shoulders and looked hard into her eyes. She tilted her head, puzzled. He looked across the room for a moment, his eyes far away. He started to speak, stopped, and then said, 'Rocky, you're *the* woman in my life too. And I want to share things and learn about you too.'

She waited, sensing his hesitation but not alarmed by it. She heard him carefully selecting his words, and she understood that he was trying to sort out his thoughts in his own mind as he communicated them.

'I like the way we've come together,' he said at last, 'the way we seem to be growing as a couple. It . . . it has a kind of natural flow to it. It feels good and it's comfortable.' He rubbed his forehead, let his hand drop into his lap, and went on. 'But I'm not sure if we should try to make it more than it is right now.'

He saw her nod her head in agreement but observed how she cooled at the same time. She tilted her head and waited with a guarded look in her eyes.

'Hey, don't take it wrong. The feelings you feel and the feelings I feel are strong and warm and real. We both know it. I just . . . maybe I'm not . . . I'd just like things to flow at their own pace.'

He saw the questions in her eyes, he felt the conflict in his heart, he heard the silence in the room.

Rocky looked down at her feet, struggling with a strange interweaving of emotions. Radar came out of the bedroom, stretched, went to the door, and sat, waiting to be let out. Tim stood quickly and went to the door and bent down and rubbed his knuckles across the furry top of the cat's head.

Then he opened and closed the door and stood there for a moment with his hands in his pockets. Suddenly he grinned and said loudly, '*Hey, Lady*!' startling Rocky. Then he walked over to her, took her hands, pulled her to her feet, and hugged her to him, hard. He held her like that – tight, warm – and rocked slightly back and forth. He nuzzled her neck and kissed her ear. He pulled back so she could see his eyes, bright, dancing, and said, 'I think we might be letting words do funny things to us here.' He kissed her on the nose. 'I'm with you, Rocky, because you're the only person in the world I want to be with. We look into each other's eyes and we know. We hold each other and we know. All we have to do is let things happen as they happen.'

He bent slightly and locked his arms under her bottom. Then he straightened and stood with her and moved in a slow circle around the room, staring into her eyes as he said playfully, 'Hell, woman, you for sure don't know if you can handle me in large doses. I think you have enough trouble as it is.' He nuzzled his face against her blouse, from one breast to the other, and she felt a warm rush. He stopped moving, looked up at her, and then let her slide slowly down until her toes reached the floor, their bodies close together. He kissed her, softly, for a long time, and when her breathing was deep and her hands held him tight across his back, he whispered, 'We'll be fine, Rocky, it'll just happen. Just give it time and we'll be fine.'

Their lovemaking was very gentle and tender, and she sensed his need to please her, and she allowed it to happen without really thinking about it. They stayed close, touching, for a long time, and they both should have slipped into blissful sleep, but they did not. She kissed him on the nose and slid out of bed and dressed silently in the dark.

She came to him before she left, he held her arm, and she saw the question in his eyes and said quietly, 'Too many thoughts tonight, Tim. I'll go roll around in my own bed and let you at least get some sleep. I know I promised I'd go with you to visit your friend. We'll see about that in the morning.'

175

He nodded.

'Okay, then I'll call you, or you call me, Tim, and we'll get together and go see her. And . . . and . . . too many thoughts, Tim.'

He let her go. And later, in the very quiet of his solitude, he thought of all the things he hadn't told her.

Chapter Fifteen

The morning was warm, breezy, and sunny, the traffic was surprisingly light, and it had all the makings of a beautiful day. Fort Lauderdale was at work, alive with energy and bustle. East, toward the beaches, people worked hard to make sure that those who came to play hard spent lots of money in the process. West, toward the glades, people worked hard to build more houses and condos for the people who had already worked hard all their lives to buy when they retired. On the water people worked hard to maintain the shiny toys of those who never had to work hard, and on the streets most people worked hard just to make it through the day.

Tim drove while Rocky sat beside him, quiet. She had been ready when Tim had picked her up at her place, relaxed but subdued. They had kissed lightly, and he smiled at her until she hugged him, and then they were off.

As they made their way through the easy traffic Tim told Rocky about Gina and Ted Molino, about how Ted was a quiet, friendly cop that nobody could remember not liking, and about how Gina was his wife who had borne him two children and worked once in a while with the Ladies' Auxiliary at Christmastime. He told her about how Ted had walked into a jewelry store in response to a silent alarm and how he had been shot in the back and left to die by the robbers, who were eventually captured, tried, and sentenced to death, but who were still alive on death row. He told her about the magnificent funeral, with all the brass and motorcycles and cops from all over the state and a procession that lasted for miles and miles. He told her about the cries in the media from the local and state politicians, calling for stiffer sentences for criminals and the need for a tougher system, and he told her how they soon faded from print . . . just as rapidly as the crowds and well-wishers faded from Gina Molino's door.

He told her how soon Ted Molino had been forgotten.

As they pulled into the driveway of the small house with its once neatly trimmed lawn and its peeling paint and slightly tilted mailbox, Rocky looked at him and asked, 'So why do you come here, then? Didn't you tell me that you and Ted Molino weren't really that close?'

Tim turned off the motor and pulled the keys. He held them in his palm and made a fist as he said quietly, 'Hell, Rocky, I'm not an official representative or anything. I don't really even do anything for Gina. I just feel we . . . uh, the department, should keep contact, you know, check in, let her know that we still remember.'

Gino Molino was a spare, dark woman full of nervous energy and quick mannerisms. Her shiny black hair was cut short, almost severely, and she wore inexpensive loose jeans and a baggy sweatshirt. She gave Tim a quick smile and Rocky a firm handshake and a nod. Gina had coffee ready, and Rocky poured after she and Tim were seated on the worn couch in the excruciatingly neat living room. Gina smoked while Tim and Rocky sipped the coffee. Basic pleasantries and small gossipy bits of news were exchanged. While Gina talked, Rocky was struck with the feeling that the woman was somehow incomplete – and knew it and was desperate with that knowledge.

Rocky listened as Gina, through Tim's gentle prompting, told of the time after the funeral, after the newspaper headlines. She told of how she had been visited and called on by civic groups and the city administration, of how they had told her all the things she was entitled to, all the money she had coming to her because of her husband's death. She told how the weeks went by and the visitors stopped coming and the silence began. She told how, finally, she had to start calling, asking, reminding, fighting.

She lit another cigarette and blew the smoke in a burst toward the ceiling and said to Rocky, 'Tim can tell you. He was one of the ones that still called me and helped me during those . . . the bad times. I just sat there and trusted . . . at first. Then, when nothing happened, I realized that if I was going to see any of those "benefits" that Ted had earned by . . . his death . . . then I was going to have to light some fires under some bureaucratic butts. I had to actually argue and call back and threaten and argue some more, and it was so hard because all I wanted to do then was sit and stare at the wall. But I had my kids . . . .'

A door opened somewhere in the house and was slammed shut. The refrigerator door was opened and then slammed shut, and then a teenage boy, his face creased from sleep and his hair sticking up here and there, came into the living room. He wore jogging shoes and jeans and a T-shirt that said 'Eat Shit and Die.' He ignored Rocky and Tim, went to his mother's purse by the door, took the car keys, and started out.

Gina Molina, finding it both hard and warming to look at a young version of her late husband, said loudly, 'T.J., are you going out? Where are you going? Didn't I tell you I don't want you wearing that awful shirt? Aren't you going to say hello to Tim McShaun . . . and his friend Rocky? T.J.?'

The boy said, 'Yeah, Mom,' and walked out.

Gina Molino stared at the closed door, and the three of them sat in awkward silence while the sound of the car starting and then driving off down the street filled the room.

Finally Gina said quietly, 'My daughter, Terry, she was younger than T.J. when her father was killed. She's in school now and seems to be all right, although raising her by myself scares me to death sometimes. But T.J., I don't know. He's . . . so sullen all the time, and he's so hard for me to talk to. Like he's always angry. He's not in school now because he got suspended for a week for having pot on him and fighting with the school security guard.' She stubbed out her cigarette and gave them a bleak smile. 'It seems so easy to say he needs a man around in his life.'

She looked at Tim and tilted her head and said, 'Did you hear about that man being granted a stay of execution? He was supposed to be electrocuted for shooting Ted. He was supposed to die last week.'

Tim nodded grimly, 'Yeah, I heard. They say it's an indefinite stay.'

Gina's lips tightened as she said dryly, 'The night before he was supposed to die, some woman from the *Fort Lauderdale Herald* called me on the phone. She wanted me to tell her how I felt about him being executed, and she wanted to know if I would be watching the news or listening to the radio, or even if I wanted to actually *be* there when they did it.' She shook her head. 'Then the next day, after the stay was granted, the same woman called – she was really pushy and I didn't like her even a little bit – and wanted to know how I felt about *that*!' She banged a small fist against her knee. 'She kept insisting that I give her a *statement*. Wanted my *feelings* on the whole thing.' She looked at Rocky and said, 'Shit.'

The coffee grew cold, and the conversation started to dry up, so everyone made the right comment and nodded their heads and shared quick, cold hugs, and then they left as Gina Molino stood in the doorway of her empty home and said, 'You two, take care.'

She gave a quick wave . . . a sad woman standing in front of a sad house as they drove away.

They had lunch together before Rocky went in to report to the Detective Division. Tim took her to a French crepe restaurant on Las Olas Boulevard, and they had wine and chicken and broccoli crepes and talked quietly while they held hands. Somehow, seeing Gina Molino so alone made them want to draw together. They touched each other and smiled at each other and looked long into each other's eyes. They felt warm and comfortable and glad to be together.

They took their time, the lunch was a pleasant interlude,

and it wasn't until Tim dropped Rocky off at her place and gave her a quick kiss and left her standing in the bright sunshine that she remembered her faint uneasiness and conflict from the night before. She went in to get ready for work, concentrating on thoughts of the lunch and not the morning or the night before.

Rocky walked into the Detective Division offices for her first assigned shift, a little nervous and emotionally tired. She told herself that she and Tim were fine, that the visit with Gina Molino was just a slice of reality, and that she had to be sharp. She had talked on the phone with Bell Peoples before she headed for the station, and as usual Bell listened and talked, and before long Bell had her laughing. They carried on, and as usual she felt better after she hung up. Bell had told her not to be so quick to read something bad into what Tim had said to her, and Rocky vowed to try to take her advice. She paused just outside the door to the Detective Division, straightened her back, took a deep breath, pulled open the door, and walked in.

'Hey, Springfield!'

A small group of detectives stood around the coffee machine near the rear door of the Detective Division on the second floor of the building. One, a big man with an unruly thatch of sandy hair, wearing bright green double-knit trousers and an orange button-down short-sleeved shirt with a wide brown tie, was waving at her as he yelled. She knew him as one of the 'characters' in the department, a cop who had spent years on the street in uniform before moving up to the investigative role, a cop that other cops told great stories about, a cop who was liked and respected. She knew him as a minor legend but not as a friend.

The group smiled and laughed at little as Stillwater called again, 'Hey, Springfield! Welcome to the dicks! Now we can all call you our own Dickless Tracy!'

She stood there awkwardly, looking for Track or Calabrini.

'Springfield . . . Springfield. Sounds like a rifle. Are you

181

bolt-action single-shot or gas-operated semiautomatic?'
Stillwater asked. The others waited, and when she turned
away without saying anything, one of them said, 'Aw, it's
her first day up here with us amazingly wonderful detective-
type individuals. She's probably nervous.'

Calabrini came in then and took her to his desk. He
briefed her on her schedule again and showed her the cases
they were currently working on. She forced herself to
concentrate after he stopped once and asked, 'Are you all
right, Rocky? You seem a little subdued. Is it the guys?
Hell, don't let them bother you. They're no worse than the
guys in patrol.'

She nodded, glad that he had found something to blame it
on, and said quietly, 'I'm surprised that I'm to be working
with you here in homicide right off the bat. I would have
thought a new detective would start out somewhere else and
work their way up to homicide.'

He leaned back in his chair and looked at her evenly.
Then he said, 'That's true, to some extent. A lot of people
coming up here go right to whatever section they'll work in.
With you I wanted to see personally how it would go. If I
reassign you, it doesn't mean you weren't good enough to
work in homicide, it just means that I think you need some
experience in some other branch. Like I told you before, I
checked you out before you came up. I think you'll work out
fine.'

He sent her to a desk she would share with another detective who worked the day shift, handing her a list of numbers
to call in an effort to locate a man they were looking for. As
she got up he said to her, 'You're sure you're okay? I'll tell
you now: You'll find that more than half of what you do up
here will be on the telephone, so go to it.'

She was getting settled when she felt a tap on her shoulder
and turned to see Lieutenant James Track smiling down at
her.

'Well, I see he's putting you to work already. Good,
good. Now listen, Rocky, I've been up here for a while, and
of course I'm more experienced than you, so if you run into

a problem and don't feel comfortable asking one of these loud-mouths around here for help, please don't hesitate to come to me. Okay? I'll try to watch over you, and I'll be here if you need me.' He looked around and lowered his voice a little as he said, 'And later on, when it's dinnertime, I mean, you being new here and all . . . I'll take you to dinner, okay? I know where there's this cute little café over off Progresso Drive, and since you'll be with me, it won't matter if we take a little longer than normal . . . know what I mean?' He winked as he walked away.

Rocky rubbed her temples with her fingers and thought, You've got to be kidding me. Already it starts? She got up to get a drink of water and saw the group of detectives, including the big detective with the sandy hair, watching her. She smiled at him and said, 'Hey, big detective, how long has it been since someone told you you were a thirty-caliber bore?'

Stillwater looked surprised, then his face split into a grin, and while the others laughed he said, 'Springfield! You're gonna fit right in with the rest of us wackos around here! Now, when do we get to inspect your receiver group?'

Chapter Sixteen

Sam Beachwood stood behind the lights and the camera and watched Harv Jensen with the two young girls on the beds. His curiosity had finally overcome his caution, and he had told Odom he would like to watch a filming. He still felt he was a very careful attorney; it was just that, hell, he just wanted to have a little fun, that's all. What he couldn't recognize in himself, of course, was his personality change when he used cocaine, which he was doing with increasing frequency. When he did coke, he felt he could accomplish almost anything. Everything was easy and fun.

He was excited by what he had seen so far this afternoon.

Harv had brought two girls in. One was a little chunky, but the other one was a real cutie. A real lollipop. Where in the hell did Harv find them, anyway?

The girls had been impressed by the cars and the house and the boat and the older men, and they had been caught up in their own efforts to act like grown-up women. They had also been under the influence of whatever Harv had given them on the way over, which Beachwood guessed was probably half a Quaalude each.

They had all kidded around a little bit, and then Harv went into his modeling scam and started taking pictures of the chunky one, and then, reluctantly, the cute one posed too. The chunky one went nude first, and she actually helped Harv pull down the cute one's bikini bottom. After the 35mm and the Polaroids, Harv was ready to move things to the bed for the real action on the video. Again the chunky one was ready, but the cute one got a case of the bashfuls and said she wanted to go home.

That's when Harv got tough for the first time.

Beachwood surprised himself again by enjoying the way Harv scared the little girl into the film. He and Odom watched as Harv grabbed the girl by the neck and held the nude photos up to her face as he hissed in her ear that he would find out where she lived – he knew she wasn't out of school yet – and make sure copies of the photos got to her living room, to her school, maybe in the boys' locker room, or in the library maybe. How about this one where you're spreading yourself open with your fingers while you grin into the camera? The girl had cried and hesitated, and then Harv soothed her and told her that it was all just for fun, and when they were finished, she could have all of the pictures and the film and everything, and she could sell them to magazines and become a famous model, or she could burn them if she wanted. It was just for fun – that's all.

The cute girl climbed onto the bed, and Beachwood touched himself with his hand, aroused.

Maybe it was the coke they were all doing, maybe it was because the one girl had to be almost coerced, but Harv was wild with the two girls in the bed. He was very physical with them, grabbing them by the hair and turning their heads when Odom said he wanted a face shot, pulling one to the other when Odom said he wanted one girl's face between the other's legs, manipulating a two-headed dildo between the two girls while they sat staring blankly into the camera. Odom and Beachwood were both further aroused when the cute girl actually struggled with Harv before submitting to him, forcing his way into her from behind while she knelt with her face buried in the other girl's crotch. Odom had the whole thing on film, and he thought it was great. Once he turned to Beachwood and said quietly, 'Hell, this is almost as neat as what a snuff film would be. I mean, we're not gonna kill the girls, but I think all this makes the film more realistic, don't you?'

Beachwood nodded and licked his lips. He was high and

excited, and he suggested something now to Odom that had crossed his mind before. He wanted to be in the film. Well, not *him* actually – just part of him.

Odom laughed, and they worked it out.

Beachwood stood by the edge of the bed while the chunky girl straddled Jensen. Odom moved the focus of the camera in close, to where it only filmed the cute girl's face and Beachwood's erect penis. Beachwood stood with his pants around his ankles, holding the tails of his shirt up out of the way, while the young girl felated him. He thought it was wild, and the thought of being able to watch the whole thing later drove him to a frenzied climax, which ruined the quality of the film from a porno man's viewpoint, because in his excitement he had dropped the tails of his shirt and grabbed the young girl's ears, allowing the shirt to fall over her face, thus preventing the film from capturing the image of his semen dripping down across her lips and chin.

Then the filming was over, but Odom wasn't through yet. He had Jensen hold the chunky girl's shoulders while he bent her over the bed and entered her. He told Beachwood to bring the other girl out of the bathroom where she was washing her face, and they made her kneel beside the bed. Beachwood held her hair and laughed while Odom moved against the chunky girl as he smacked his hand, hard, against the cute girl's bottom, making her squirm and cry and her white, tender skin turn red. The girl was crying softly, and the chunky one was saying, 'You don't have to do this . . .' when Odom suddenly pulled out of the chunky girl, turned, and ejaculated onto the other girl's back, laughing all the while.

Beachwood and Harv laughed, too, and pushed the girls down onto the floor and left them there.

Odom and Beachwood fixed themselves new drinks, still laughing, while Jensen hurried the girls into their clothes. The chunky one actually wanted to stay, and when she pulled at Jensen's shirt in an attempt to get some of the cocaine he was holding, he slapped her hard across the face. He just wanted to get them out of there and back out to the strip where he had picked them up in the first place. While Odom and Beachwood stood by, Jensen sat the two girls on the couch in the living room, grabbed each one by one nipple, squeezed just a little, and talked.

He told them, with Beachwood and Odom grunting and nodding, how he would hurt them if they even thought about telling anyone what had happened at the house. He went into clinical detail about what parts of their bodies he would cut into first, and while he did so, he increased the pressure in his fingers. He went on to tell them, with Odom and Beachwood snickering in the background, about how the film would be a very private thing, no one would see it, and soon it would be destroyed . . . unless the girls talked. If that happened, then they could bet that the film would go public, in one form or another. He smiled at the cute one and asked her what she thought her father would say if he sat through the feature presentation of his sweet little daughter doing her own version of *Deep Throat*. When he was finished, he squeezed and twisted both his hands just enough to bring both girls up off the couch, gasping in pain. Then he led them out to his car and headed back out to the beach.

Harv couldn't know it then, but when he had first met the girls on the beach and had gone into his little bag of lies about what he had planned for them, they had lied to him too. They weren't runaways. They weren't from some little town far away up north. They both lived and went to school right in sunny Fort Lauderdale and had only gone out to the strip along A-1A for the excitement. Maybe it wouldn't have made any difference to him, anyway, though he usually stayed away from local talent.

Beachwood and Odom were sprawled in the living room, coming down, trying to relax. Jensen wasn't back from the beach yet, and the house was quiet. The quiet was shattered by the insistent ringing of the door bell, which caused Odom to jump up angrily and head for the door while he yelled, 'Jesus Christ! Ring the fucking thing off the wall!'

He opened the door to see an extremely agitated Alan

187

Giles standing there, actually wringing his hands. Odom let him come in. Giles went right into the living room, looking at Odom and Beachwood, and blurted, 'Lydia got busted. She got busted for coke. The narcs had her last night, and they got a good charge on her, and she knows just about everything we're doing, and I think it's a real problem, and—'

Odom grabbed Giles by the shoulder and shook him, saying, 'Hold it, Alan. Take it easy. Just tell us about it.'

Beachwood sat up on the couch, rubbed his face with his hands, and said, 'Yeah. And how do you know this, anyway, Giles?'

The man from the City Manager's office turned and looked out the sliding glass doors, across the pool, past the dock, and into the brown water of the canal where Beachwood's boat sat. He frowned in concentration as he said, 'Well, as you know, the City Manager is almost like the Chief of Police's boss. He's the one the chief reports to. You also know how sensitive *this* chief is to public and city administrative reactions to police matters. He'll sacrifice police effectiveness for public relations.'

Beachwood applauded.

Giles looked hurt, then went on. 'Anyway, that Organized Crime Office of theirs, the Narcotics Unit and all that, well, that's a sensitive thing there. A lot of money is handled, a lot of chances for police officers to go dirty, if you know what I mean. So, the chief has it set up where we, the City Manager's office, we monitor what they do. Their lieutenant briefs us on big cases. They have to show us what they're doing with cash for drug buys and all that. Hell, you guys know this.'

Odom and Beachwood were quiet, waiting.

'Anyway, the lieutenant over here is so used to us looking over his shoulder all the time that now we can check on even the routine things, like arrests. In this case they had drawn over two thousand dollars. As it turned out, they returned it, but it caught my eye . . . they had it on a nightly summary thing I saw this morning. I checked further and came up with Lydia.' He stopped, pained and puzzled. 'They arrested her, got an ounce of cocaine, did a lot of paperwork – but she wasn't booked.'

Beachwood and Odom looked at each other.

Jensen walked in the door, saw the grim faces, and said, 'Now what? Did we lose another plane? I'm tellin' ya, I think that fucking congressman and his funny little maps are a waste of money. We lost that first plane in Colombia, well, so they crashed and burned. Then the other one was "seized" by the Bahamians, although, of course, we'll eventually get it back if we pay enough. And now what? Another one? We should go back to the old way of doing things.'

He was still pumped up from the drugs, the girls, and the threats, and he knew he had run off at the mouth but didn't care. He saw how they stared at him, and turned to make himself a drink.

Odom said quietly, 'Make us all one, Harv. Lydia got herself busted for nose candy.'

They sat around in a huddle, talking in low murmurs with Jensen saying over and over again, 'That stupid bitch.'

Lydia pulled her car up into Odom's driveway and saw that Harv was there. The other car she guessed belonged to some friend of Odom's. She didn't feel hurried yet. Oh, she knew it was time to go, time to leave Lauderdale, and she was making her plans. She didn't want to be anywhere around when the cops started working on these guys – no, no. She had no faith at all in the ability of the cops to protect her from the hard guys. She hated to have to leave Lauderdale; she thought it was a fun town, but it was time. She had a friend in Vegas who had told her he could get her a job anytime, so that's where she would go.

She got out of her car and walked toward the door of the house. She wanted to talk to Harv about scoring some more coke before she left, and she thought Odom owed her some money from a while back. She wasn't worried about them knowing about the night before. Hell, it had just happened.

She hadn't been booked, anyway; the cop had explained that they would hold the charge against her while they checked her story. If her info was good, her paperwork would go into the shredder. If she had lied, they would come looking for her. She rang the door bell and grinned. She would do her business with these guys, and then they would see her cute little ass as it wiggled its way right on out of there.

The door opened, Harv looked at her, grabbed her by the hair, and dragged her on her knees into the living room.

The two girls whom Harv Jensen dropped off at the beach made their way to their homes. The chunky one had been bitchy and the other one sullen and sulky. They had fought bitterly and blamed each other for what had happened. When the cute one became quiet and just cried softly, the chunky one stopped yelling and made sure her friend got home all right. Then she went home, too, but not for long.

When the cute one got to her home, she went quietly into her room and closed the door. Both her parents were at work.

When the chunky one got home, she found her father sitting drunk at the kitchen table, her mother asleep on the couch in front of a blaring TV. She went into her room and began packing her knapsack. She looked at her face in the bathroom mirror and was surprised by the anger she saw in her own eyes. She got herself all ready and then waited for the night. She was through with this silly town. She was going to New York where things happened. She could make it.

Lydia pulled her head back and turned her face to the side as she felt the cold steel of the pliers against the skin of her breast. She watched the pliers with her eyes, not moving, like she would watch a snake on her chest. The teeth of the tool surrounded the nipple and closed, just a little.

Jensen, holding the pliers, said quietly, 'Look, Lydia, we've had some fun times together . . . we all have here. We

190

know each other, right? And we know how things are with the pigs. You got busted. You tried to sell that ounce I sold you so cheap, and your boy turned out to be a cop. Okay. It was a mistake. We all make mistakes, Lydia. But what bothers Mr Beachwood and Mr Odom and me is, well, you got busted – but you didn't. Know what I mean?'

He bounced the steel tool lightly on her chest.

Beachwood watched, fascinated. He knew he shouldn't be here for this kind of thing, but he couldn't leave. It excited him to watch it. The girl had tried to fight Jensen at first, and he had hit her across the mouth and then punched her in the stomach twice. She didn't fight again.

Lydia watched Harv as he went on. 'You weren't booked, Lydia. That tells us something. Right? It tells us that the cops are holding the charges against you. For what? Because they're trying to win the "Pig of the Month" award? No. No, Lydia. It's because you gave them something.'

Lydia felt the pliers tighten on her nipple and winced from the pain. She was too smart to die for this or to be mutilated for life. The cop was a nice guy and all, but hell, she was a survivor.

She took a deep breath and said, 'I gave them a little bit, not enough to hurt anybody.'

Jensen screamed, 'Liar! Fucking bitch liar!' He slapped her with his left hand.

Her face reddened and she cried, 'No – don't!'

Odom said evenly, 'Hold it, Harv. Just hold it a minute. Let's hear what she told them.'

She lied.

She lied knowing that somehow they would eventually find out the truth. She knew Giles was there, the guy from the city, and she guessed he had some kind of access to the police files. She knew she had to give them enough to validate her story but not enough to make them kill her.

She told them that the cop wanted to know where she got the coke. He wanted to bust her source, he had said, and that's what he was working toward. He was pushy and threatening and wouldn't let her get away with being evasive or lying too much. She had been scared and confused, not knowing what to do, and he kept telling her that she was going to jail for a long time and it made her cry.

She cried for them now.

They waited.

She told them that finally she had to give them a name. He wouldn't believe her when she told him she bought coke from a guy whose name she didn't know. She told them she gave the cop Harv.

Jensen stood up, knocking his chair over, and yelled, 'You gave me away? I can't believe it! You gave *me* away?' He stood over her with his jaws clenced and his fists bunched. She cowered in front of him.

Again Odom calmed him. He made her go over it again, and then once more. Then she sat there while they huddled.

Beachwood said, 'If they work on Harv, you know, step by step, they'll eventually get to us.'

'Well,' Odom said, 'they might not get to the movie thing, but they'll be able to look into the cocaine thing for sure – and whatever Harv has going on the side that he doesn't tell me about.'

'They won't get anything from me.' Jensen said. 'No way!'

Beachwood shook his head. 'Well,' he said, 'even with just a little info a good cop can just start chipping away, you know, a bit at a time. Then he can call in the feds. And if he isn't making any progress criminally, he can always call in the IRS.'

'Shit!' said Jensen.

'You got that right,' said Odom.

Beachwood held up a hand. 'Well, let me make a suggestion. I think in this case it might be better to get offensive. Instead of waiting for them to come to us, let's go to them.'

'Are you crazy?' said Jensen.

'Look, as far as we can see, we've got only one narc working on this. It's in the formative stages. He says he bought an ounce from Lydia here. Suppose Lydia goes to their Internal Affairs – and it wouldn't hurt if the *Herald* got wind of it – suppose she goes there with an attorney, not me, of course, but there are plenty of young counselors out there who would love to take a client on my covert recommendation. Anyway, Lydia goes in, all pissed off. This narc, this cop, owes her money. She tells how she's been selling him coke and taking him to bed, of course, and now he's holding out on her. In fact, last night she actually brought him half a kilo, and yet when he took it to evidence, it was only an ounce. Are you with me?'

'Yeah. I like it,' said Odom.

'But won't it stir up a bunch of shit?' Jensen asked.

'Exactly. It will stir up everything and everybody. A smoke screen. Oh, don't get me wrong, you guys are out of business – at least for now. But if you get the cops looking cross-eyed at one of their own, it will take the pressure off you long enough to cover your tails.'

'*Our* tails?' said Odom.

'All of our tails. Hell, that chief over there has a history of letting his guys go down the tubes when it comes to a choice between one of his cops and any kind of bad publicity. He'll take one look at this situation, if we play it right, and he'll throw that narc away like a piece of spoiled pork.'

'Yeah,' said Odom, 'I think it might work. Of course, Lydia, here, has to cooperate. Right, honey?'

Lydia looked at them sitting there. She thought about the cop, she thought about herself, she thought about what she saw in the eyes staring at her now, and she said with a smile, 'Hey, I'll play it any way you guys want. You can kiss that cop good-bye. Believe me. I understand how important this is, and I know how serious you are about it. I don't want you to hurt me. I really don't. I'll do whatever you ask.'

Odom smiled without warmth, and Beachwood turned to Giles and said, 'You can get the home numbers for these cops, right? Okay, let's start this game rolling with Lydia phoning the cop's home and talking to his wife. That should tense things up.'

Chapter Seventeen

Early in the afternoon shift of the next day, McShaun, riding alone, heard the dispatcher send Hammer, the young black cop, to a reported suicide call. The call wasn't in McShaun's zone, but it was in the area. Hammer was sharp but pretty new, so McShaun headed that way to see if he could help out.

He arrived at the house in an upper-middle-class white neighborhood to find a hysterical woman standing in the open door to her home, looking in and sobbing. Hammer's car was in the driveway, the door open. When McShaun called, Hammer's voice responded, 'I'm here – inside the house.'

McShaun turned to the woman, and she looked at him wild-eyed before sobbing, 'She acted funny last night. Withdrawn, quiet. We asked her what was wrong, but she just shook her head and smiled. I kidded her about taking the world's longest shower, and she just turned away and went into her room. Then later she . . . she told me she loved me before we went to bed.' The woman had one hand on McShaun's arm, and she looked around and said, 'Where's my husband?' Then she sobbed.

McShaun started to go into the house and was stopped by the woman, who said quietly, 'This morning seemed all right. I mean, the usual Chinese fire drill trying to get everybody off to work and school and all. Then this afternoon, after lunch, the school called. They wanted to know where she was. I thought, I thought she was there.

McShaun looked over his shoulder to see a detective unit

pull up. He saw Springfield and recognized Lieutenant John Calabrini.

The woman started crying again. 'I came home to see if she was sick. She's in her room. She found . . . she got some of my Valium, I think. The doctor prescribed them for me a couple of months ago. I . . . I had forgotten about them.' She looked into the house again, then back at McShaun; then, very seriously, she said, 'Officer, this must be some kind of mistake. She's only sixteen years old.'

McShaun walked slowly through the house and entered the girl's room. Hammer stood there shaking his head. The girl lay on her back on the bed. Her hair was brushed out, framing her beautiful face, and she wore a white cotton nightdress. Her face and hands were scrubbed clean, and everything in her room was neat and in place. Her bed was hardly disturbed by the form of her small body. Her eyes were closed, and her hands were folded across her stomach. She was very cold to his touch. Balanced along the head-board were several stuffed toys, and one, a silly green frog, rested by her left shoulder.

He turned and walked from the room.

McShaun watched while Springfield both comforted and interviewed the mother and Calabrini and a couple of other detectives worked in the girl's room.

Calabrini motioned McShaun aside and said, 'Tim, we found a note . . . a note she wrote for her parents. I want you to see it. Tell me if it means anything to you.' He held a lined piece of notebook paper up to the hallway light. McShaun could see the painfully neat longhand in green ink.

'Most of it,' Calabrini said, 'just apologizes to her mom and dad for what she is about to do . . . doesn't mean to hurt them . . . wanted them to be proud of her always . . . didn't mean to do anything that would make them ashamed.' Calabrini tilted his head. 'Do you think she means the suicide itself or something she already did?'

McShaun just shrugged, so Calabrini went on, 'Here, take a look at this. Near the end of her paragraph she's writen a short poem. Take a look at the poem and tell me if you see anything there that we should work.'

McShaun took the paper. He read:

The silly flower really wasn't ready
To be picked and framed for the world to see;
But he in his black chariot just vomited a laugh
And grinned as she read: Who Me?

McShaun shook his head and handed the note back to Calabrini. Something in his mind told him he knew what the poem meant – the alarms were sounding – but he looked at the lieutenant and said, 'Search me, Lieutenant. She's just a schoolgirl. Could mean almost anything.'

Calabrini nodded, 'Yeah. Well, we'll keep working on it, anyway. And listen, Tim, you can clear the scene here. We'll wrap it up.'

McShaun nodded and began to leave. He stopped in the living room, hoping Rocky would look up from her conversation with the mother, but she didn't, and he walked out the door.

McShaun met the young cop, Hammer, for coffee the next day during his shift. It had been quiet so far, and although McShaun wanted to be alone, he liked the young cop and had agreed to meet him by the side of the Davie Boulevard Bridge. They made small talk for a moment, and then Hammer said, 'Listen, McShaun, I don't think it's supposed to be going around yet, but I heard something earlier today and I really feel I should tell you about it.'

McShaun waited.

'I heard Chick Hummel's got his tit in the wringer for somethin' over there at the narc office. Heard it from a girl I speak to who works next to the chief's office there. I don't have any details, but according to this girl, ol' Chick is really in some shit.' He looked at McShaun evenly and said, 'I just thought you should know. Right?'

Later that day McShaun received a call from Scott Kelly.

Scott was in good spirits, excited about going to work after being shot. It had been several months, he had worked hard, and now he was going back.

'I'll tell you, McShaun, I feel like I'm ready. I really do.'

Tim scratched Radar under the chin as he said, 'Well, that's great, Scott. It really is. Only go easy at first. Know what I mean? I know you've been working out and you feel good and all, but you're still walking with that cane, and I know you're a little out of touch with what's been going on over in the narc office lately, so just take it easy and keep your eyes peeled, right?'

Scott's good mood couldn't be dampened. 'Yeah, I hear you, Tim, and I appreciate what you're saying, but hell, I'll be all right. Remember, the chief promised me that when I was ready to come back, he'd have my job waiting for me. Now all I want to do is go back and do it.'

McShaun nodded at the phone and said, 'Okay, Scott. Good luck – and be careful, will ya?'

'Okay. Thanks. Talk to you later.'

'Right.'

McShaun hung up and then lifted the receiver and immediately dialed Hummel's home number. He wanted to check out Hammer's story. There was no answer. He swore under his breath and hung up.

Later, after McShaun had gone out for a while and returned, he was lying on his back, on a towel, doing stomach exercises. He had already done his stretching, and next would come a light workout with a curlbar. Then he looked forward to a long run out to the beach and back. He was in a jumble over Rocky, his mind in constant conflict, his stomach churning, and his whole body restless and edgy. He hoped a long, hard run would calm him down a little before he started climbing the walls.

He heard footsteps coming up the walk, and then the knock on the door, and he jumped up to open it, hoping it was Rocky, even though he knew she was planning to go to a movie with Bell Peoples.

It was Chick Hummel and his lady.

McShaun looked at his friend and saw that whatever was happening was deadly serious. Hummel's wife had a determined, pale look, and Chick looked ready to explode.

Hummel looked at McShaun and said quietly, 'You wouldn't believe it, T. S.! You just wouldn't believe it.'

McShaun stood aside while they came into the apartment. Hummel's wife sat on the couch, staring at her husband while he paced back and forth in front of the window. McShaun grabbed the towel off the floor and went into the bedroom to put on a shirt. He came out and said, 'Anybody want some tea or anything? Something cold?'

Chick's wife said, 'Yes. A cup of tea with a little sugar would be nice, Tim. Chick? Some coffee or something?' She looked at McShaun. 'He hasn't eaten since this mess started two days ago.'

McShaun started the water, and then Hummel turned and said, 'I'm suspended. The chief suspended me. Made me give my badge and ID card for chrissakes. Do you believe it?' He turned his face away, and McShaun could see that he was fighting to keep himself from breaking down.

'Chick, you have to tell me what's going on, man.'

Hummel looked over at his wife, then at his friend, and started.

'There was that girl I busted. My first real narcotics bust – for cocaine. Then I flipped her and she gave me some info and some heavy names. Fine. Looks good. I'm really fired up. Gonna bust the bad guys and all.' He began pacing again.

'Then it started. First we get the calls at my home. It's the girl. Tells Donna here that she's lookin' for Chick – to continue the good times she's been havin' with me. Says things to Donna about what we've done together in bed – all kinds of shit.' He kept his back to them. 'This, needless to say, causes some concern in the home camp.'

Hummel's wife stared at the floor.

'The next call I get, first thing this morning, is from the brass: Get my butt over to the chief's office. *Now*. I go there.

They tell me I'm suspended pending internal investigation and probably criminal charges. *They read me my rights!*'

The room was quiet for a moment.

'They tell me to get a lawyer. I . . . I just can't believe it.'

McShaun prepared the tea, carried a cup to Dee, and said, 'Charges?'

Hummel began punching his right fist into the palm of his left hand.

'It's beautiful when you think about it. It really is. I mean, they used their heads – and I think it's going to work.'

Chick's wife, blowing across the tea to cool it, said, 'Tell him, Chick.'

Hummel frowned. 'I busted the girl, Lydia Taylor. She told me about Jensen, the guy with the "Who Me?" tattoo.' Dee saw McShaun's expression harden for a moment. 'She told me about Odom and Beachwood, and Giles and the congressman. Somehow, probably through Giles in the Manager's Office they found out she was flipped. They must have threatened her with much worse than anything we could threaten her with. Okay. She's got to try to survive. I can understand that. They force her to call my house. Then she shows up at the station with a young attorney, a guy named Jeff Bottle . . . don't know if you know him or not. Anyway, they march into Internal Affairs, and Lydia puts on record that she's been dealing coke to me for a couple of weeks, and sleeping with me, of course. She says she came in to complain because now I've ripped her off, threatened her, and busted her, and that I lied about the amount of cocaine she had with her – and all this other shit. The lawyer tells them that the *Herald* is doing a thing on it in tonight's paper. Can't wait to see that. And he says he's going to sue and protect his client from the dirty cop and on and on and on.'

He looked at McShaun and frowned again. 'They done a good job, T.S., really. I don't have to tell you the brass reaction, right? Zoom . . . I'm in the chief's office. Zap, I'm suspended pending the investigation.'

He walked over and took a sip of Dee's tea. He rubbed his face with his hands. He went on.

'The part that's just killing me about this whole thing is how the chief is taking it. I mean, the bad guys are scumbags, and you expect them to act like scumbags. But the chief . . . the chief . . . Tim, he's gonna throw me away, man. He's gonna throw me away.'

McShaun just listened, seething.

'I'm sitting there with the chief and several other assorted pieces of brass, and he says, "Hummel, you know I'm behind you in everything you do, but I have to look after the best interests of the entire department, not just one cop who screwed up." He goes on to tell me that just the trial-by-media is going to hurt us all terribly. He says, correctly, that I'll be found guilty by the news and the reading public. He says sometimes sacrifices have to be made for the good of all. He says that if he takes quick preventive action, he can lessen the damage. He says he can't let this blow up into a huge internal investigation that would have committees and boards and all that shit looking into everything the department does.'

McShaun said, 'But hell, Chick, there really even hasn't been an investigation yet, right? I mean, the dirtball attorney just made the allegations, right? How could the chief know it was already time to sacrifice someone?'

Hummel's wife spoke quietly. 'Oh, Tim, that man is so politically gun-shy, it's pathetic. You've heard the rumors about him wanting to run for sheriff or governor, or whatever. Tell him the rest, Chick.'

Hummel started hitting his palm again. 'He gets all finished with his speech. Then he has all the other brass clear out of the office so it's just him and me. Then he looks at me like I was his son and tells me he thinks it would be best, best for everyone, if I just resign. He must have been reading my mind then, because before I could bring it up, he tells me that the attorney refused the polygraph for his client at this time but might consider it for later. And he goes on to say that even if I *volunteered* to take the lie box, and *even if I passed*, he would still want my resignation. Said the public doesn't trust the lie detector when applied to public officials and said for my benefit that guilt or innocence isn't really a factor in the situation. I looked at him like he was crazy. ''Won't that make me look guilty as hell?'' I say. He looks me in the eye and says, ''Maybe. But it still doesn't make any difference to the big picture.'' Then he tells me that one resignation and a quick blow-over are better than weeks of investigation and trial and media coverage. He goes on to tell me that even if I clear my name – *even if* – things will never be the same for me here ever again. My career will always have a ''dark cloud of doubt'' hanging over it.'

He sat on the couch beside his wife and said, 'Nice, huh?' He put his face in his hands.

McShaun stared at the floor and thought about it. It was so terribly wrong that it made him actually want to scream out loud. He felt his muscles tightening, and he looked down to see his hands clenched into fists. He looked out the window and said evenly, 'Well, you'll fight it, of course.'

He did not see how Chick and Dee looked at each other.

'You'll fight it all the way and you'll beat it. And in the meantime we'll take care of the crudballs. Oh, I know any investigation of them now – the porno, the coke, the grass – that wouldn't work. Hell, we wouldn't be allowed to work it, anyhow. No, but we can take care of the shitheads in other ways. We can take care of them, all right.'

He saw that Hummel and his wife were just looking at him, sadness in their eyes. He said again, 'You'll fight this all the way. Right?'

Hummel stared at the floor. Finally Dee nudged him and said, 'Tell him what we decided, Chick.'

McShaun waited, tense.

Hummel stood up, looked at his friend, then walked over and stared out the window. His voice sounded raw as he said, 'We've talked it over. Our daughter is almost two years old. We've been talking about getting out of this insane Lauderdale area for her sake, anyhow. We've been thinking about moving up to the middle of the state, maybe

201

where there still are some of the old values. You know, a smaller town, better people. No more police work.'

He turned and looked at McShaun.

'Tim, I'm not going to fight it. It will take weeks, months maybe. It will be hard on Dee and the baby. It will be hard on us all. And in the end will there be a clear-cut victory? Will I start clean? No. Even if I win, I lose. I'm not going to fight it, Tim. I'm going to resign and we're going to move away from here as soon as I can get it together.'

McShaun looked at Hummel, and then at his wife, and then back. 'Chick! You can't just lay down, man! It's too easy for them this way! It's too easy! They just can't do this! You can't let it happen.'

Hummel looked at his friend and shook his head slowly. 'You're right, Tim. It *is* easy for them. But hard for me. Hard for me all the way. Listen, man' – his eyes misted – 'a whole lot of things I've believed in for a long time died in a few minutes. They died just like that, and I don't think I want to be around here anymore. The way I see it is, they're all crudballs – especially the chief – and it will hurt my family to fight them, and I won't do that. They can have it, they can have the whole goddamn city for all I care. They can take the cocaine and the movies and Lydia and the congressman and ''Who Me?'' and the newspapers and the department's reputation – and they can stick it up their ass.'

Hummel took his wife's hand and walked her to the door. He rested his other hand on McShaun's shoulder and said quietly, 'I'm finished with it, Tim. Finished with it. I've got some loose ends I have to take care of before I go – and then I'm gone.'

They left.

McShaun stood quietly for a long time, breathing slowly. Then he did more stretches, put on his running shoes, and ran twelve hard miles, pushing himself, chasing demons.

Chapter Eighteen

McShaun came back from the run sweating and breathing hard but still stretched tight. He took a long, long, hot shower, put on some jeans and a T-shirt, looked through the refrigerator and cupboards, made a list, and headed for the Winn-Dixie.

He parked and walked toward the front doors. He was stopped by a three-column headline under the main headline of the evening paper. People moved past him pushing shopping carts and pulling children while he stood there and read how another stay of execution had been granted to Alvin Buford.

So Buford would live on death row for at least another year. He had already been there almost ten years and had tried every appeal known to the judicial system, and each time they had been denied. This time the governor had signed the death warrant, and it looked as if Alvin Buford was finally going to die in the electric chair. But no. Alvin's eyes blinked now, and his hands twisted nervously, and he talked of dealing with extraterrestrials . . . and God. Alvin's attorneys suggested to the court that Alvin was now insane and it would be wrong to execute an insane man. The court agreed, so a year's stay was granted so that Alvin could be examined to see if he really was insane.

McShaun leaned against the newspaper machine and rubbed his eyes with his fingers. Alvin's eyes blinked and he spoke of extraterrestrials . . . and the police officer he shot down in cold blood had been buried for almost ten years. McShaun remembered the murder of the officer. He remembered that the officer had already been shot several times and probably would have died, anyway, but still Alvin had to take the officer's own service revolver and shoot him once more in the head, execution-style, and Alvin had been sentenced to die for his crime, but now he wouldn't die . . . because his eyes blinked. And Ted Molino's murderer would not die, either, on some other bullshit technicality.

McShaun had to step aside so that an old man could buy a paper from the machine. He looked once more at the article, sighed, and went inside the market.

When McShaun got back to his apartment, he parked his car, grabbed his two bags of groceries, and walked toward his door. As he did so, he saw a young girl sitting on his front step. He slowed but kept walking. As he got closer she stood suddenly and stared at him. He looked into the feverish eyes of a young girl, in her late teens, early twenties. She stood with her head cocked, looking at him while her hands rubbed slowly up and down her forearms. Her face seemed familiar, and he stared, trying to remember how or why or when.

The girl's tongue darted out and licked her dry lips. She said, 'He's out, you know. He's out. I *saw* him.'

McShaun wrinkled his brow and started to say, 'Who's out?' when it hit him.

Lorenzo Walker. Rape. She was a rape victim. More than a year ago he had made a highly applauded arrest of Walker, a carnival worker who had raped a nineteen-year-old girl after beating her. He remembered that the trial had been almost more brutal for the girl than the rape itself. The defendant's attorney – Jeff Bottle! – had been a young counselor in the public defender's office, and he had worked very hard at making the victim in the case look like a wanton, teasing little girl who had coerced his hapless client into sex and then had cried rape. Bottle's strategem hadn't worked, and the rapist was convicted and given a long jail sentence, but not before the girl was traumatized on the stand.

McShaun looked at the girl and said, 'I thought you moved out of town after the trial.'

She looked at him with a smile and those burning eyes.

'Yes, I did. For over a year. I've been getting myself together, you know? And now I've come home – because I felt better.'

She ran one finger lightly around the edge of one of the glass jalousies in his front door and gave him a lopsided grin.

'So I felt better and I came home. And this morning I saw him. That . . . man. I was in my car at a traffic light and he was there, on the sidewalk. He looked at me. *He saw me*!'

She looked around wildly for a moment and then smiled again. McShaun felt a shiver in the small of his back as he looked into her tortured eyes and listened to her questioning, childlike voice.

'So guess what, Officer McShaun. Guess where I'm going? I'm going back – back to that quiet place where I've been. You know why? I'm going back because *he's* here, and he's seen me, and I can't live here anymore!'

He felt her pain and her fear, and he was helpless.

'I can't live here anymore, Officer McShaun. You said he was being sent to jail for a long time. What was the sentence? Over eighty years or something, right? You said I should work hard to put my life back together because he was gone and would stay gone and I'd never see him again.'

She started crying then, and she raised both small fists up in front of her face and moved toward McShaun. He thought she would strike him, but instead she cried out, covered her eyes with her hands, and brushed past him on the sidewalk, moving toward the small parking lot. She stopped, her back rigid, and turned and screamed, 'I *did* see him . . . I *did* see him!' Then she turned and ran down the sidewalk, away from him.

He stood there, stunned, and could hear her sobbing while a car door was opened and shut, an engine was started, and then a compact rental car sped out of the lot and down the street.

He stood there watching . . . until it was quiet again.

McShaun went inside and tried to call Rocky before he unpacked the groceries. Then he tried once again after everything was put away. Then still once more after sitting and staring at the wall for a while. There was no answer.

He wanted to talk with her very badly.

He was sitting there, watching the evening turn into night when the phone rang. He grabbed it. It was Scott Kelly's wife.

'Tim? Tim . . . listen, can you come over here right away? Please?'

He heard the panic in her voice, and he said quickly 'What's wrong? What's the matter?'

'Oh, Tim, it's Scott. He's – he acting crazy, I'm afraid. Something happened when he went back to work. I don't know what it is because he won't tell me.' She started crying then. 'Oh, Tim, please come over here.'

It took him twenty minutes, driving like a madman, his head pounding. He got to the small duplex and hurried to the door. Scott's wife answered the door and said quietly, 'He's in there.'

McShaun walked slowly into the bedroom and found Scott sitting on the floor, his back against the bed. He was surrounded by newspaper clippings, letters of commendation, some photos, and a couple of guns. His eyes were red.

McShaun stepped quietly into the room, over the pieces of Scott's cane, which had been smashed against the door-jamb.

'Scott, what's going on, man?'

Scott looked up at him, stared, and shook his head. He rubbed his eyes, hard, with the knuckles of his fists, and said, 'You know what you're looking at here, T.S.? Huh? You know what you're looking at?'

McShaun waited.

'You're looking at a *liability* and a *cripple* and an *embarrassment*.'

Scott looked down at the papers scattered around him.

'I went into the narc offices this morning, feeling good, like I told you on the phone. I got in there ready to straighten out my desk and get my act together, and the first thing I see is that my desk now belongs to somebody else.

Okay, no problem, we've always been short on room over there. So I try to find out from the lieutenant where I should work, you know, where I should put my things. He wouldn't even look me in the eye. He just fidgeted around and finally said I was to drive over to the main station and see the captain. I didn't like the sound of it, but I figured, you know, more administrative bullshit. So I went.'

McShaun sat on the edge of the bed.

'Went upstairs there to see Captain Fronseca – you know, the one with the stupid toupee? Wears those shiny three-piece suits and slides into the chapel during lunch hour with that little secretary from records.'

McShaun nodded.

'Yeah. Well, he sits me down, puts on a real fatherly voice, and tells me I'm not going back to the narcs. I'm going to work either in Records or in the Comm Center. I started to argue with him. I reminded him of what the chief had said about my old job waiting for me. He cut me off. Told me that even though I felt good, and the doctors said I could come back to work, there was just no way they were going to put me back out on the street. I was a *liability*. I had to work light duty. I mentioned the lawsuits about cloistered employment, and he puffed himself up and told me I should feel lucky that they'd even let me come back at all.'

Scott shook his head. 'It gets better, I told him I wanted to talk with the chief about it, and he got mad as hell. Told me the chief didn't have time for it. Of course, now you and I know he was too busy because he was covering his ass after sending Chick Hummel down the tubes. What a travesty that is. Anyway, then Fronseca told me it had been decided that they couldn't have a *cripple* out on the streets for the public to see. That I would be an *embarrassment* to the whole department! Said I could take the job in admin or I could *hobble* out of there and find another job. He even let me know that they had considered the possibility that I might try to get a lawyer and fight them in court. Said they were ready to go all the way. The decision had been made and that was that.'

He lay his head back on the bed and closed his eyes.

'I'm a cripple and a liability and an embarrassment, after almost ten years on the job, almost eight of them in undercover narcotics. I'm the only federally trained narc in the area. My track record is hot, I gave them over a hundred percent, I love the job and fought hard to get back to doing it. And now I can either answer the phone in the Comm Center or shuffle papers in Records.'

He pulled himself up onto the edge of the bed with his muscular arms. He called softly, 'Honey?' and his wife came slowly to the bedroom doorway, tears in her eyes. He looked at McShaun, and then at his wife, and he said to her, 'I'm sorry, honey. I really am.' His wife knelt and then sat on the floor, her head against his legs.

He looked at McShaun. 'Came home berserk. Said a bunch of stupid things. Was gonna kill them all over there, kill some maggots, kill myself. Go crazy.'

He rubbed his face with his hands. 'I'm glad you came over, Tim, I really am. Listen, I'm not gonna do anything stupid, okay? I'm gonna think it over. Maybe I *will* get a lawyer and fight them all the way. I'd like to hurt *somebody*. But then again, maybe if that's the way they think of me over there, then I'm kidding myself, anyhow. All the damn good work I've done for the city means nothing . . . the whole thing means nothing. Maybe it's time to throw in the towel and get the hell out of here for good.'

McShaun stayed with Scott and his wife for several hours, his head reeling with feelings of déjà vu. He left depressed and angered. He drove home in a steady drizzle that turned into a downpour as he parked his car and ran for his apartment.

He stood there dripping and dialed the number.

She answered.

He heard her voice and started to speak.

He couldn't.

She said, 'Hello?'

He hung up. First Hummel, then the stays of execution, then the rape victim, then Scott . . . it was all so depressing, so down, and he didn't feel right about dumping it on her.

He fed Radar, put on his jungle boots, got out an old raincoat, and went for a long, long walk through the rainy night.

The man running the supply room of the Fort Lauderdale Police Department in the midmorning of the middle of the week was a police aide, a civilian who had retired from a fire department in the north. He was an older man of Italian descent with a hook nose and curly gray-and-black hair. He smiled a lot and kidded with the officers who came by for various pieces of equipment, or uniforms to replace those that had been broken or worn.

He was busy sorting out a recent delivery of radio batteries when the cop walked into the supply room. The normal procedure was for the officers to come to a window that opened to the main hallway. From there they would lean in and yell at the aide for whatever they needed, and he would bring it. It was not a rigid procedure, however. Senior officers who felt relaxed about it all would sometimes walk into the room through the rear door and have coffee and chat with the aide or try, usually with success, to badger him out of another flashlight or a new raincoat.

The cop walked in and grinned at the aide, who grinned back and waved. The cop hesitated and then held up some flashlight parts and asked the aide if there were any spares lying around. The cop didn't need the whole light, just the reflector part from around the bulb and a new lens. The aide looked at the parts, rubbed his chin, nodded, and walked into a side room where there were boxes of miscellaneous parts and supplies, leaving the cop standing alone in the main supply room for several minutes.

During those minutes the cop's eyes scanned the shelves and cupboards, looking for the right box of items. Once the cop saw what he was searching for, a handful went from box to pocket.

The aide returned from his search triumphantly and presented the cop with the flashlight parts with a flourish. The cop thanked him and made small talk for a few minutes and then left. The aide went back to what he was doing. He had no idea that anything had been taken.

The body bag was actually much too big for her. She was only five years old, and small for her age. Her tiny feet pointed in toward each other, and her hands rested on her stomach. The cruel marks on her neck and throat were dark blue and purple and greenish. She wore a Peanuts T-shirt and pink-and-gray jogging shoes. They had not found her shorts or underpants.

McShaun stood looking down into the body bag, his face grim. He was on duty, riding alone again in the south end of the city. He had been dispatched to a report of a 'hurt little girl', whom an old woman had found under a big hibiscus bush in the backyard. The old woman now sat crying in her kitchen, talking to the sergeant, and McShaun stood and watched as the Medical Examiner prepared to take the body away.

Lieutenant Calabrini was there with Springfield. McShaun had nodded to them both when they arrived at the scene, but he had not spoken directly to Rocky. He felt a coldness inside, full of anger and hard things, and Rocky was so warm and soft.

Calabrini stood beside McShaun as the body bag was closed and lifted into the wagon. He said quietly, 'Medical Examiner says there was sexual battery involved. She was raped and strangled, not necessarily in that order.'

Rocky came over and stood beside the lieutenant. She looked at McShaun, and he could see the pain in her eyes. 'This is awful,' she said, 'Do we have any recent rape-murders of children like this, Lieutenant? I don't remember seeing anything in any of the files.'

Calabrini shook his head. 'Not really. We had a problem a year or so ago. Can't remember the guy's name. Some sicko. But he was sent up. Crime scene ready to do their thing? Good. What do we have from the mother? Anything yet?'

Rocky looked at her notebook. She brushed the hair off her forehead and said quietly, 'Devastated, of course. Not much help at this point. All she knows is that her daughter was supposed to be one house away, playing with another little girl. When she was late, the mother went looking. Found the other child home with no knowledge of her daughter's whereabouts.' She turned the page. 'One suspect – sort of. The victim's friend says a ''nice fat man'' played with them for a couple of minutes and then went away. She says he was not as tall as her daddy – the father's about five-eight according to her mother – and was not good-looking. She said he was nice though and made her and her friend laugh. None of the neighbors saw anything at all.'

Calabrini nodded and scowled.

McShaun listened to her speak, watched her move, and wished they were somewhere else, talking about anything else. He walked away from them and stood on the curb watching as the wagon with the little girl's body slowly drove away.

The shift ended, and McShaun left the first-floor locker room where he had changed out of his uniform and into a pair of jeans and an old, long-sleeved work shirt and loafers. He hurried, hoping to catch Rocky before she left the Detective Division offices on the second floor. He made the turn at the bottom of the stairs and started up two at a time.

He met Rocky, who was on her way down, at the first level. She was wearing the same skirt and blouse she had worn during the shift, her hair brushed out and shining. He looked at her and smiled.

'Great minds think alike,' said McShaun. 'I was just coming up to get you. Thought you might want to spend some time helping a semi-burned-out street cop shake off the effects of the last few days.'

She tilted her head, reached out, touched the end of his nose with one finger, and said quietly, 'You're right on the money, Officer McShaun. The only problem will be deciding which one of us is really the burned-out cop . . . and who, exactly, will be helping who, uh, whom.'

McShaun followed Springfield to her apartment and waited while she took a quick shower and changed into a pair of sailcloth slacks and a sleeveless pullover with a hood and simple leather sandals. They took his car and went for a late dinner at a rib restaurant on the Seventeenth Street Causeway.

Their order was taken, and they sipped their drinks, she a Blackjack and ginger, he a Bushmill's, as they waited.

McShaun reached across the table and took Rocky's hand in his. He searched her face a moment and then said, 'You look tired, girl. Oh, don't get me wrong, you're for *sure* beautiful, you just look a little beat. I think you need to ease up a bit.'

She sighed and nodded. Her fingers played in his palm as she said, 'You're right, Tim. But it's hard, you know, to back off. I guess I never really knew how much the day-to-day stuff you see on this job can start to wear at you.' She sipped her drink and ran her tongue around her lips before she continued. 'It was nice seeing you heading up those stairs. I'm glad we're here . . . together, and I'm glad you can understand how I need to be with you right now.'

He swirled the ice cubes around in his glass and said, 'Hey, it takes two, lady. And to tell you the truth, I'm a little frayed around the edges right now, too.' He looked into her eyes and smiled. 'I feel better already, just being near you.'

The dinner was served and eaten with more enthusiasm than either of them thought possible. The conversation was light and easy, and they were relaxed and sleepy when he paid the check and they walked out holding hands.

He drove east from the restaurant, over the Causeway Bridge, and north on A-1A. Just north of Sunrise Boulevard he parked the car at the edge of the beach; they took their shoes off and walked down to the water's edge.

The night sky was clear and sparkled with the stars. The wet beach sand looked like dark gold as they walked hip-to-hip along the waterline, their footprints being washed away

212

behind them by the gently rushing waves. They stopped often and held each other sharing the warmth. They spoke very little, touched often, and enjoyed a steadily building desire.

Before they walked through the soft, cool beach sand to his car he held her tightly at the water's edge and kissed her gently, a long, intimate kiss that took her breath away and made her heart pound.

He took her home, and their lovemaking was unhurried and tender. They gave and they received; they pleased each other without having to think about it. The warm crescendos they reached left them breathless, and they held each other tightly each time until their breathing was easy again.

They slept entwined, silk-soft and safe, all the fears and pressures and conflicts and pain banished for the night.

The next day McShaun was stopped in the hallway by Stillwater, the big detective. McShaun was on his way to check out some equipment before he hit the road. He could see that the detective was upset and wanted to talk. He and Stillwater had worked together in the same part of town a couple of years ago, and they respected each other.

Stillwater ran a hand through his always disheveled hair and said, 'Hey, Tim, how's it goin', man? Listen, I wanted to tell you I'm really sorry to hear about Chick Hummel getting jammed up like that. Everybody knows it's a frame. Can't understand why the hell they would give him away like that. Of course, I'm sure you saw that newspaper article, too – what a bitch that was.'

McShaun nodded. He had seen it, and it was just as bad as they had feared. Phyllis Green had worked herself into a journalistic frenzy over the situation. Most of the time negative articles about the police were made up of sly innuendos and calculated misleading remarks. Not this time. This time the article flat ate Hummel up. He was indicted, tried, found guilty, and his blood was then screamed for. The article attacked him as a cop and as a husband and as a man. He was displayed as a perfect example of any cop who had

213

ever gone bad. He wasn't just the bad apple, he was the whole corrupted tree.

McShaun remembered the feeling he had while reading the article. He knew that Green must have worked herself into some kind of orgasmic lather, carrying her typeset torch of righteousness and pointing her ink-stained finger at them all while she force-fed her readers her version of the truth. And he knew how bad it must have hurt Hummel to see it.

Stillwater grabbed his arm. 'And another thing, Tim, just between you and me. How are you and Springfield doing?'

McShaun stared at him hard.

'Listen, Tim, everybody upstairs was taking bets on who was gonna get to Springfield first, you know? I mean, Track's obviously trying to hit on her, and those that know say Calabrini treats her a little special too. Between you and me, if it had to come to that, I hope she goes with Calabrini. That Track is a real asshole. He's my boss now, by the way. Anyway, I told them all to put their money away because I knew she was seeing you, right? I mean, if she's with you, she sure as hell isn't going to go out with Track or Calabrini.'

McShaun's throat was dry as he said, 'So what's the problem, Stillwater?'

'Hey, easy, Tim. No problem . . . just thought you'd want to know who your competition is.'

McShaun looked at the big detective. He felt him tightening. He was on the balls of his feet as he said in a low voice, 'I ought to break your big face for not minding your own business.'

Stillwater put his hands up in front of him and stepped back, saying, 'Whoa. Easy there, Tim.' He liked McShaun and knew Tim liked him, and he knew he had gone too far. 'I'm sorry, guy . . . didn't know it was an off-limits subject.'

McShaun took a deep breath and tried to relax. He waved one hand and started to turn away. As he did,

Stillwater touched his arm and said, 'Hey, Tim. One more thing, man. I'll change the subject. You were down there on the scene where that little girl was found murdered yesterday, right? Right. Well, do you remember a name like Ronnie Toreen or Ronald Toreen, back about a year ago?'

McShaun was still rocking from the earlier conversation, but he was a cop. 'Toreen? Yeah, he got sent up for child rape and assault and all that. Why? You think the guy that killed that little girl falls into the same category?'

'No, Tim. I think it's the *same* guy. Where it happened is down there close to where that guy's mother used to live. I worked one of those cases back then. Anyway, I started doing some checking into where Toreen was now, and guess what? Can't get a clear answer. He was judged mentally incompetent and sent away, but no one can tell me where or for how long. I'll bet he's out again. I tried to talk with Track about it, and he gave me a bunch of shit about how I should be doing more work on a *new* suspect instead of trying to blame it on an old one. What a pile of crap. Just between you and me I'm going to keep my eyes peeled, anyway. And while you're working that south-end area, why don't you see if you come across some pervert named Toreen . . . right?'

McShaun nodded, his mind elsewhere, and turned and walked away.

McShaun hit the road. He heard the babble of the radio without listening; he saw the street activities without watching. He was a uniformed police officer on duty, seemingly functioning as he should. But if he had come in contact with someone who really knew him, they would have seen that he was very much detached from what he was doing. There was a great distance behind his eyes. He was aware of it and studied himself with wonder as he went through the day, doing the job. He couldn't really define what was going on inside him. He knew his mind was in conflict and in pain, and he knew jumbled parts were trying to settle down into some order. He felt disassociated, unstable, drifting.

It was a hot day, but he felt very cold inside.

During the afternoon he was dispatched to a dilapidated wood frame house in one of the older neighbourhoods in the south part of town. Someone had called in to report sounds of a struggle and a woman moaning and calling out for help.

He found the address. The front door was locked. As he moved around the side of the house he heard gagging noises coming from inside. He hurried.

The rear of the house was a screened-in Florida room. The door stood open. The back door leading into the interior of the house had glass panels. They were smashed out and the door was ajar. He crunched across the glass on the floor and moved toward the gagging sounds.

He was too late.

The elderly woman had come from the drugstore, her purse filled with a couple of prescriptions and some toilet articles. Her Social Security check had just come in, and she had gone out to stock up. She had unlocked the front door, relocked it as she always did, and turned around to face the burglar.

The burglar hit her very hard in the stomach.

She curled to the floor, gasping, and lay there.

The burglar rifled her purse, took the few dollars left, and went back to ransacking the house.

She struggled to her knees and crawled to the telephone. As she lifted it off the cradle he hit her again, in the head. When she went down, he sat on her chest and choked her with his hands. She tried to push him away, tried to claw his face. He laughed horribly and hit her again, knocking her dentures out.

Finally he left her, and she lay there gagging, trying to breathe through the pain and feeling the wet tears fall along her cheeks.

She died as McShaun knelt beside her and held her hand.

McShaun left the house and walked towards his unit. He saw a couple of TAC officers standing with the patrol sergeant and walked over to them. The sergeant looked at him and asked, 'Lab guys getting anything in there, Tim?'

He shook his head, 'Doesn't look like it yet. They told me they're not picking up any prints, only cloth marks, like the guy was wearing gloves or socks on his hands. They said they got one good tennis-shoe print near the back door, though.'

There was a grim silence for a moment. Then one of the officers said, 'There's one witness down the street, in that dirt alley that runs parallel to the regular streets here. He saw a thin, greasy-looking guy moving around behind the houses. Had an old beat-up car. Didn't get a tag, of course, but we might be able to get a tyre impression from the dirt back there. Who knows.'

McShaun just nodded.

The big TAC officer named Al spoke up then. 'Know what I heard the other day? Heard that guy who took a shot at your partner a while back is still out and about. Remember who I'm talking about? Little squirmy shithead. We had him booked and everything after you blew his buddy away with the shotgun. Then he skated on the charges. Remember?'

McShaun remembered.

'Couple of our guys stopped him last week in the north end,' said Al, drawing a half-moon in the dirt with the toe of his cowboy boot. 'He was driving this clunker full of paint cans and brushes and stuff, but they stopped him because he was doing the residential area nice and slow, looking . . . right? Of course, he was Mr Polite and Mr Innocence for our guys, but they thought he smelled. Had to let him ride, though. 'Course, here we are down in the south end and we've got a B and E with a homicide, and that crudball came close to killing a couple of old ladies when he and his buddy were doing their things regularly until you ruined their day. Remember? Remember who I'm talking about, McShaun?'

McShaun remembered. Bobby Nails.

When he got home that night, McShaun's phone started ringing. McShaun grabbed it.

It was Scott Kelly.

'Hey, Tim . . . how's it goin' with you, man?'

'Okay, I guess. How about you, Scott?'

'Made a couple of decisions . . . wanted to brief you.'

McShaun sat on the floor, his back to the wall.

'Listen, Tim, I'm not going to fight them. I'm . . . I'm pretty torn about it, but the way I see it, it will just hurt my family more in the long run. I know they pissed all over me . . . but, but there's my family, you know?'

McShaun said, 'Uh-huh.'

'Yeah. Well, I'm going to just keep my mouth shut, keep my head down, and keep my job.' He gave a funny, choking laugh. 'I mean, you worked in Communications for a while. No big deal, right? I mean, I can handle it, I keep my pension, my insurance, and my paycheck.'

McShaun said nothing.

'Tim, I wish I could explain how I feel. You know how hard I tried . . . when I was on the job, after I was hurt, working to get back. All I ever wanted to do was be a hard-working cop for them. That's all. Now . . . now I feel like telling them to jam it, but I . . . I *can't*. I've got my family, I've got a high school diploma and a handful of police-related certificates worth nothing out in the real world. I've got my family, Tim.'

He paused, and there was just the sound of their breathing.

'Anyway, Tim, I wanted to let you know. If you hear it said around that I gave in to the brass, that I . . . I puked out, that I decided to do what I had to for that lousy paycheck – well, it's true.' He paused again, and McShaun could feel his pain through the phone. Again, the choked laugh. 'Tell ya, Tim, the way I feel about all of this inside will probably make me a pretty fucked-up and dangerous guy to be around for a while. Hope nobody gives me any shit.'

McShaun sighed. He said quietly, 'Look, Scott. After all is said and done, you're the one who knows what he has to do. You have a reponsibility to your family, and if you feel like you can't break away from the department now – over this – then nobody is going to badmouth you. Hell, ride it out, man. Other guys have been sent to the Comm Center ''forever'', and they're back out on the streets again. Just ride it out and stay cool. Don't get pissed and do something crazy.'

'Yeah, I guess I hear you, Tim. And thanks for saying it. But you know and I know that it sucks, the whole thing. And, God, I wish I had enough balls to tell them to go to hell.'

He hung up. McShaun held the phone to his ear for a moment, then gently put it down. He sat on the floor, tense and scowling. It was too much. Chick Hummel gone. Scott Kelly destroyed. He was going to explode. Again he debated calling Rocky and sharing his pain. Again he decided against it.

He changed into a workout outfit and did a furious set of stretching exercises. The he went through a basic kata, striking and kicking and jumping, hissing out the 'Ki' through clenched teeth. He put on his running shoes, fed Radar, and went out into the dark streets. He rarely ran at night, but he knew there was no way he would be able to sit in his apartment this night. He stayed away from the busy streets, and he ran, hard, through the night-darkened neighborhoods, the sweat flying off his extended fingertips and his breath strong and steady.

His mind was filled with images of blinking eyes and maniacal grins, of sweet little sleeping girls and silly green frogs, of smashed walking canes, T-shirts that screamed 'Eat Shit And Die!' and frightened eyes that accused him of broken promises, of too big body bags, and of the sad-angry eyes of a dying old woman.

He ran hard, and sometimes his deepest breaths sounded like a sob.

Chapter Nineteen

Lorenzo Walker left his aunt's house in northwest Lauderdale and made his purposeful way through the dark streets. He moved with an easy confidence that most very big, well-muscled men have. He was a physical, aggressive predator, and he feared little in this world, especially from his fellow-man. Since his youth others had always made way for him, avoiding any conflict with him because of his size and demeanor.

He sweated, excited about his hunt. He had been out of prison only a short while and he had already come across an easy way to find and 'take' more girls.

In the last week he had taken two.

He slept most of the day and then got up and ate as much food as his old aunt had around the kitchen. He would stare at the TV and amble around, waiting for the dark. He felt comfortable with the dark. He belonged there.

He found, through just hanging around, that if he stood on the corner of a reasonably big intersection, on one of the main roadways through Lauderdale, he would eventually see a possible girl to take. She would pull up in her car, alone, and sit waiting for the light to change. Her mind would be on work, or her date, or her hair, or whatever – he didn't know. He did know that he could just walk up to the car, open the driver's door, shove her across the seat, and drive away. It didn't even make any difference if there were other cars in the intersection at the time. The other people either didn't see what happened, or they didn't care, or they were frightened.

Once he was in the car he had to scare the girl, maybe hit her with his big fist a couple of times, and then she would just sit there and cry until he found a dark place to park.

Then he would take her.

It was very easy, and he liked it. He had no way of knowing that it was also very effective as far as avoiding being arrested was concerned. He had no way of knowing the problems that he caused by overlapping jurisdictions. He would grab the girl in the car in the western fringes of Lauderdale and then drive them farther west, out into the unincorporated areas. The abduction took place in the city; the actual rape took place in the country. The girls weren't sure about anything after the attack, and police agencies involved didn't always work together smoothly.

Lorenzo Walker had no way of knowing this, but he felt secure in his methods, anyway.

On this night he decided he would hang around off West Broward Boulevard, on the west of I-95. He could walk south along the railroad tracks there, in the dark, get to Broward at the I-95 overpass, and maybe find the right girl sitting at a light there. If not, he could walk down a couple of blocks.

He wiped one big hand across his sweaty brow and headed that way. He paid no attention to the sound of the car engine that started up as he reached the end of the street where his aunt's house was, and he was so attuned to his own hunt that he failed to pick up the intense energy transmitted at his back from the burning eyes that watched him patiently.

Lorenzo Walker moved slowly under the I-95 overpass at Broward Boulevard. He wanted to relieve himself before he climbed up the incline and stood at the intersection up there. He moved through the dirt and litter into the shadows, up close to the huge concrete abutments, unzipped his fly, and stood there holding himself. He heard a horn far away, and he heard the rush of cars going by on the interstate, but he did not hear the soft tread of feet coming up behind him.

He looked down to watch as he shook himself and zipped up, and then he felt the thin loop of steel fall past his ears and hit against his shoulders before being drawn impossibly tight around his neck.

He gagged and lunged forward, digging his fingers into the sweaty flesh of his throat, using all of his enormous power to pull himself away from the terrible choking wire.

But he was too late, and the power that had served him so well his whole life now helped his attacker kill him.

The killer hung on to the wooden toggles fixed at each end of the piano wire and pulled very hard. He did not use the Korean method of turning under his own arms to put his back against that of his victim and then bending forward. No, he just put his booted foot hard into the small of the big man's back and pulled down. As the big man struggled to pull free, the killer just hung on grimly, waiting. As his victim's huge legs gave out, the killer backed up rapidly, still pulling tightly on the steel wire. He pulled Walker until he was flat on his back in the dirt. Then he knelt by his head, waiting.

Lorenzo Walker soiled himself as he died, his feet pounding raggedly in the dirt. After he was still the killer stayed frozen in place for a moment. Then he quickly unlooped the wire from around the bloody neck, put it in a plastic bag, and reached into his pocket, pulling out something small and soft to the touch.

He looked down at the body of Lorenzo Walker, bent over the agonized, twisted face for a moment, made sure it was in place, and then walked steadily and evenly away into the shadows.

Lieutenant John Calabrini bent over the dead face of the big man that had been found by the wino under the I–95 overpass. He stared, incredulous, at what he saw stuffed into the open mouth.

It was the shoulder patch from a Fort Lauderdale Police Department uniform.

He looked up at the assembled uniformed men and detectives and said angrily, 'Is this some kind of sick joke? One of you sleazy bastards cram this thing in this stiff's mouth?' The other cops just stared at him, shaking their heads.

Up until now it had been just another homicide. The wino, scared, had flagged down a patrol car and managed to talk the skeptical young officer into going with him to look at what he had found. Once the officer had determined that the wino had indeed discovered a body, and obviously the body of a murdered man, things had been set into motion. Supervisors and the Detective Division had been notified, the area roped off, and the investigation initiated.

Calabrini had arrived with Springfield. Surprisingly, a wallet had been found in the dead man's trousers, with an ID card. The name didn't mean anything to any of them until Rocky told Calabrini that Records had one Lorenzo Walker on file for a whole list of things, primarily rape. The last thing they had was that he had been convicted and sentenced and sent up to Raiford prison.

'Well, he's sure as hell out now,' Calabrini said to the others. 'Will you look at the size of the bastard? The guy who did this definitely had his act together. Garrote, right? Some kind of heavy-gauge wire maybe. Man, that took some strength.'

He looked around at the scene. They had a bunch of footprints in the dirt, but with the wino and the cops and everybody else that wandered through here, he knew that would be a very long shot. He ordered photos of everything, anyway.

Now, he thought, to address the problem of the patch. 'None of you wise guys put this patch here, huh?'

Heads shook, shoulders shrugged.

Calabrini thought about it. If none of the men here did it, then maybe the killer did it. But if the killer did it – why? And why a Fort Lauderdale Police patch for cryin' out loud? Unless . . . He shook his head.

He motioned everyone there to circle around him as he knelt several feet away from the body, Springfield standing beside him. He looked up into the faces of the uniformed men and the detectives and Medical Examiner. They looked at him and waited.

'Look, you guys,' he began, 'use your heads for a minute and think about what you're looking at here. If this isn't a joke, and if it is, I'd rather know about it now and we can all laugh and forget it . . . if this isn't a joke, then it has extreme significance in this homicide. I don't have to spell it out for you. If the killer left it there, why? And where would the killer get one of those patches? And who is the killer? Are you with me? This is going to have to be treated with the utmost sensitivity for now. Let's do a good job out here, get what we can, let the Medical Examiner do his thing, and then I can go to the brass and give it to them. But . . . but we really need to keep a lid on it for now, right? You guys know how fast stories spread around this damn department. Somehow we're gonna have to keep this thing to ourselves, *especially away from the news types*. Yes? Know where I'm coming from, troops?'

Nods all around.

'Okay. Let's finish up and get outta here.'

He looked down into Walker's mouth again, grunted, and walked over to his car to make some notes. Springfield followed. She stood beside him and asked quietly. 'Do you really think we can keep something like this from getting out before we're ready, Lieutenant?'

Calabrini closed his eyes, pinched his nose, and said evenly, 'First of all, when in the hell are we going to be ready? And second, no way.'

The next day, as McShaun walked into the rear door of the station, the first thing he heard about was the body of the murdered man that had been found under I-95. The locker room was buzzing with what had been found in the open mouth of the corpse. McShaun was curious. He was standing among a group of other officers when he was advised to see the shift captain.

He walked into the captain's office to find his lieutenant and Sergeant Chris Dryesdale already there. He took a seat and waited. The captain looked up from some paperwork on his desk and said, 'Well, McShaun, looks like you've done it again!'

McShaun just looked at him.

'After all the chief has done for you around here you'd think you would make an effort to do a good job for him out on the road, but I guess that's just not your style, huh, McShaun?'

The lieutenant looked at the ceiling, and Dryesdale sighed audibly. The captain went on, 'Let me tell you what I'm talking about here. The city has settled – out of court – with that black citizen that you beat up in the men's room of Big Joe's. The city offered them ten thousand, and that attorney snapped it up.'

McShaun looked at him, relaxed, and said, 'So what's the big deal, Captain? Goes on all the time. Hell, that black guy will be lucky to see half of that money.'

The captain bridled. 'That's not the point, McShaun. The point is the chief gave you another chance. He showed faith in you, and you let him down. He's hurt over this. Upset.'

McShaun grunted, and the captain looked at him hard while Dryesdale said, 'What about Internal Affairs, Captain? What did they come up with?'

The captain, irritated with the question, shuffled some papers before answering. 'Their investigation was "inconclusive". They recommended nothing. Probably because those other patrol officers covered for McShaun.'

McShaun sat up straight, ready to argue, but Dryesdale went on, 'So we got nothing from Internal Affairs, there are no criminal charges against Tim here, all the charges against the black guy are dropped as part of the deal, and the *city* decided to pay him and his lawyer ten grand. Like Tim said, Captain, it happens all the time.'

There was a small smile on the lieutenant's face, but he remained silent.

The captain, flustered, busied himself by aligning several pens and pencils on his desk blotter, then he looked up and said to them all, 'Before this it was that Cuban that McShaun put into the hospital. We got real lucky on that one. Anyway, listen, McShaun, the chief is so upset over this that he told me he didn't even want to see you – besides the fact that there

225

are even *bigger* problems going on today that you don't need to know about. He wanted to pass this along to you, though. He says that the next time you do *anything* that gets complained about by a citizen or attorney, you're *gone*. That's it. He says he can't fool with you anymore. Either straighten up and fly right, or pack your kit and get the hell away from this police department. Got it, McShaun?'

McShaun stood, stretched, and surprised everyone in the room when he said quietly, 'Yes, sir, I understand. And I very much appreciate another chance. I won't do anything to let you, or the chief, down in the future.'

Then he turned and walked out, watched in stunned silence by the other three.

While the hallways and locker rooms and parking lots full of police officers coming and going from their shifts buzzed and rumbled about the murdered man with the patch in his mouth, there was a gathering held in the chief's office to discuss the same subject.

The chief looked at the others in the office, then at Calabrini and said, 'Do you think it's *real*, Lieutenant? I mean, do you think it's authentic?'

Calabrini, not knowing for sure what the chief meant, said, 'Well, sir, I think that it's not a joke. I think that whoever killed Walker stuffed that patch in his mouth. I really grilled the guys on the scene, and I guess we could put them all on the lie detector if you want, but I think they were being truthful with me. None of them did it. Okay, so then, to be really sick, we can say maybe one of the midnight-shift guys, on patrol, found the body early in the morning, then he, or she, not only did not call it in, but also they stuck a patch in the mouth as a sort of joke.'

The room full of majors and captains and lieutenants was silent as they thought that over.

Calabrini collected the black-and-white glossy photographs of the corpse and said, 'Maybe – and again, we could use the lie box on the whole southwest midnight patrol shift – but I don't think that's where the problem is. Maybe I'm

226

sticking my neck out – too soon in the investigation and all that – but I've got a sinking feeling that it was the killer who left the sign.'

The silence that followed was finally broken by the chief, who said to them all, 'But why? I mean, for what?' He lit a cigarette, forgetting about the one already burning in the ashtray on his desk. 'And even worse, who?'

He looked around at the faces of his administrators and said in a low voice, 'First of all we need a lid on this until we can put something together. It's got to be tight. I don't want this out in the media, especially so soon after that Hummel deal. And, of course, tonight they're doing a thing on McShaun's latest fuck-up. The city felt they had to settle, and the Manager's Office wants to know why they have to keep shelling out ten grand every time one of our officers makes an arrest.'

All of the men in the room fidgeted and looked piously outraged, except for Calabrini, who hid a small smile behind his hand. The chief went on. 'Anyway, we don't *need* this shit at this time, so keep a lid on it. Calabrini will be working with utmost haste to get a handle on this. The patch itself is going to forensic, yes? And if we can't get enough locally, we'll send it to the FBI labs, right? Match the thread ends and all that. In the meantime, if questions come up, we're working this homicide with our usual professionalism. And if the part about the patch gets out, God forbid, then our official posture will be that whoever the killer is, he's trying to bring discredit down on the department. We've been hurting the bad guys, and now one of them is trying to mess us up with this macabre prank. The dead man, Walker? He was no angel, long rap sheet and all. And I'll bet if we look hard enough, we'll find he had a drug involvement of some kind. It will be another ''drug-related incident''.'

The administrators in the room all relaxed a little. This was the kind of game they understood. The chief looked around at them and went on. 'So, a drug-involved murder where the killer has made a clumsy attempt to put us in a bad light – to throw us off the scent or whatever. But remember, this stuff goes out *only* if the media gets the word on this patch thing. Let me make myself clear – it would be much better for now if we keep a lid on it. Right?'

McShaun worked a fairly normal shift, comfortable on the street. He handled a stolen bicycle report in front of a drugstore, the ten-year-old boy crying and scuffing his feet and saying he didn't lock the bike because he had only gone inside 'for a minute.' He helped a traffic unit at the scene of an accident involving two men who were both so old that they could hardly hear or see, but both of whom knew beyond any shadow of doubt that the *other* guy was the one who caused the whole thing. He sat with his doors open under a huge old tree behind a church and had a tangerine and some cranberry juice. He checked some tag numbers on cars he had seen sitting for several days in different parking lots – none were reported stolen. He was sent code three, lights and siren, to a 'heart attack' call, only to find, along with the medical unit, an old lady whose chest pains were apparently intensified by her loneliness. He backed up another unit on the edge of his zone at the scene of a domestic argument, the other officer dealing with a wife while he tried to calm the husband. He spent some time in one of the fire stations, doing his paperwork and joking with the fire fighters on duty. He made a traffic stop on a car with Canadian tags that was weaving from lane to lane, slowing and speeding up. There were seven people in the car, and the driver explained that he was having difficulty finding an address – and was surprised to learn that he wasn't in Miami. McShaun tried to give the man simple directions and sent him on his way. Two winos stumbled through the motions of a fight in front of a fast-food place. McShaun talked them out of the horrible things they insisted they would do to each other, and they walked off, patting each other on the back and sharing their sad bottle.

The shift ended.

When McShaun got home from work, he found Rocky sitting on the front step of his apartment waiting for him. He looked into her eyes and she looked back, and then they held each other, tightly, for a long, soft moment in the dark.

They went inside, touching each other, and he put some water on the stove while she got out two teacups. He put his gear away quickly, kissed her lightly on the forehead, and hurried into his bedroom and got out of his uniform, took a fast shower, and threw on a pair of shorts and a T-shirt. He came out to find a cup of tea waiting for him and saw that Rocky had already fed Radar, who now lay on the small kitchen table, licking Rocky's hand.

They were quiet for a few moments, sipping their tea. Finally, she said, 'I . . . I felt very alone tonight. I didn't want to be alone.'

He nodded.

She drew her fingers through the curly hair above her ears. 'I was supposed to go for a drink with John . . . Lieutenant Calabrini. He's nice.'

McShaun smiled and nodded again.

'But I couldn't. I don't know. It's probably the job. Working in homicide is so . . . intense. You know, hard. Every other day this last week it seemed I was standing over some dead body. And then today we had that guy out there and he had that . . . that thing in his mouth. And all the brass are going crazy and . . . oh, I don't know, Tim, I just feel like . . . like . . . '

'Like you need to be held,' he said quietly, and he stood in front of her, took her hand, and pulled her to her feet. She stood in front of him, looking into his unusally calm eyes, and he put his arms around her and pulled her to him.

They stayed that way, Radar watching, for a long time.

He pulled back from her a little, looked at her face, brushed his fingers against her lips, and led her by the hand toward his bedroom.

Their lovemaking was long and warm and comfortable. He was gentle and sensitive to her every desire. They stayed a long time coupled, he looking down into her eyes, she looking up into his. She felt warm and safe wrapped up with him, in his strong arms, under his gentle weight. She felt herself warmly shudder and release, once, again, and then again, and then she felt him tighten, and then call her name softly while she felt his hot wetness pour from him into her. He held her still, kissing her breasts and rubbing her shoulders and running his fingers across her nose and forehead.

She hugged him tightly, put her face against his, and said gently, 'I just want to be with you, Tim.'

They fell asleep holding each other.

That same night, what started out as a strategy meeting at Tom Odom's house had degenerated into a fairly wild party. Oh, Beachwood and Odom and Giles and Jensen had gloated over how they had screwed up the narcotics cops, and they talked about how they would try to get an airplane-load of cocaine though the radar, based on one of Lavon's new charts, and they talked about how Odom's porno connection was still badgering them for more new videos, and they quietly talked about what would have to be done with Lydia once the police thing died down. They had let her go back to her own place, after making sure she understood that to try to leave them would be painfully fatal. Sure, they talked about all these things, but when Odom saw Jensen looking at his watch constantly, he asked him why. Harv admitted he was anxious to get back to his place because one of the chicks he hung around with was coming over with another girl to do some of his toot. So Odom suggested that Harv go get the girls and bring them back to his place. Why should he hog all that sweet stuff for himself? Harv had hesitated. He didn't like other guys tapping his chicks. But he hesitated for only a few seconds, realizing that Odom had much more cocaine available for them all.

So they had all partied through the night and slept very late.

A little after noon the girls got up, washed up a little, went for a quick swim in the pool, and left in their rental car. Giles had staggered out in the middle of the night, and both Beachwood and Odom were still crashed out in the back bedrooms. Jensen sat smoking on the couch, feeling fuzzy and off-balance. His head hurt and he was depressed. He thought about fixing some breakfast, but he just sat there, staring out through the glass doors into the pool.

He was getting ready to go when he saw that some of Odom's coke was still lying around – several ounces, in fact. He thought about it. They had done a lot of the powder during the night. There was no way Odom would know how much. He grabbed three of the one-ounce bags, stuffed them into his pants pocket, and left. It was early afternoon by this time, and he headed for the south end of the city, knowing he had to stop by the small marina where one of his marijuana hauling boats was moored before he could finally go home. He was tired and cranky and depressed as he jumped into his black Porsche and eased out of Odom's driveway.

Springfield and McShaun were up early, making love, then showering, then having a big breakfast together. They talked little, touching occasionally. And when she had the courage to look deep into his eyes, she saw there was a quiet calm and a peaceful sadness, but also an expression of distance. She pulled herself back to the surface, just letting herself bask in the warmth of his smile and relax in the soft sound of his voice.

She left him in the early afternoon. They both had to go to work. They held each other and kissed each other and laughed a little, and when she left him, she felt mostly at peace and unafraid but a little puzzled.

Harv Jensen was only three or four blocks from his town house, in a residential neighborhood, when he found himself stuck behind a three-car caravan of people who were apparently lost, or part of a funeral or something. They were moving at a maddeningly slow pace, and Jensen was in no mood for it. He looked down the street, saw no oncoming traffic, downshifted the Porsche, and punched it. The black car jumped ahead and into the left lane, easily roaring past the first two cars and doing over sixty by the time he came even with the last car. He shifted again, swerved back into the right lane, and continued up the street, right past a Fort

231

Lauderdale patrol unit sitting under a tree. He glanced in his mirror and said, 'Shit' as he saw the flashing lights come on. For a second he considered fleeing but then watched, angry, as the police unit came up behind him and honked its horn. He pulled over, put on the parking brake, and jumped out. He found himself looking into the smiling eyes of Tim McShaun, who stood there with his ticket book in his hand.

McShaun had been working on a report when the Porsche had gone flying by. He hadn't started to smile until after the black car stopped and the driver jumped out wearing a sleeveless T-shirt. McShaun started to smile when he saw the 'Who Me?' tattoo on the man's upper arm.

He took a deep breath, felt his own determined calm, and said, 'I'll need your driver's license and the registration for the vehicle, sir.'

Jensen nodded, started to speak, then just shook his head and reached into his back pocket for his wallet. It wasn't there. He thought for a moment. Oh, no. The damn thing must be still at Odom's place! He turned and stuck his head in the side window of the Porsche, looked around, came back out, and said, 'I, uh, I don't have it with me, Officer. I must have left it with a friend last night. My whole wallet, in fact.'

McShaun nodded and said, 'I see. Well, what about the registration, then?'

Jensen, walking around to the other side of the car, said, 'Sure thing, Officer. I always keep it in the glove compartment here.'

McShaun followed behind him and stood with his hand on the butt of his revolver while Jensen leaned in, popped open the glove compartment, and pulled his hand back quickly from the 38-caliber revolver that was lying there. He turned and saw that McShaun was standing back a little, one hand on his service revolver, a curiously intense expression on his face.

Jensen stammered, 'L-look, Officer, I . . . I can explain that gun there. I mean, it's legally owned and all. I'm a businessman and sometimes I carry cash with me so I . . . I take the gun along. I honestly forgot the damn thing was in there.'

McShaun stood on his toes, looked past Jensen into the car, and said, 'And the registration for the car? All I see in that glove compartment is the gun and one pack of rolling papers . . . sir.'

Jensen racked his brain. Where in hell was that damn registration?

McShaun started talking. Quietly.

'Look, here's what we have, sir. You were speeding – residential area, twenty-five unless otherwise posted – you were doing over fifty even after you were trying to slow down. I have to write you a citation for that. I also have to write you a citation for having no registration—'

Jensen interrupted. 'But, Officer, I have all that stuff. I just don't have it with me.'

'Right, sir. Then there's the ticket for no driver's license. Now, all of this is going to take a few minutes. During that time I have to decide whether or not I even believe you – about whether or not this is really your car, know what I mean? And I also have to decide whether or not to arrest you for carrying that gun in your car. As far as Florida law is concerned, you are in manual possession of that weapon, which is a misdemeanor.'

Jensen felt the blood rushing to his head.

McShaun, still smiling, said, 'So, since all this is going on, and we're going to be here for a few minutes, I'm going to have you sit in the back of my unit. And the awkward thing about that is that I have to pat you down. You know, frisk you. Not only is it departmental policy, but it's also something the Supreme Court allows me to do – for my protection and yours.'

Jensen said, 'Hey, do what you think you have to do, man. I'll just have my attorney take care of it for me, anyway. Here, you want me to get into the position against my car so you can search me? Well, go ahead.'

He didn't remember what he had stuffed into his pants pocket until he felt McShaun's hand stop at the bulge. He started to pull away from the car and then felt hard fingers against the side of his neck, under his ear. He felt McShaun's breath as the cop whispered, 'Go ahead, sir. Push back. Resist my legal search. Fight me and I'll be forced to . . . subdue you.'

Something in the cop's voice made Jensen hesitate. Then he felt himself being handcuffed. He stood there with his head down, swearing softly.

McShaun called for a backup and just stood there waiting until Hammer pulled up and walked over beside him. He pointed silently into the car and Hammer looked in, saw the gun, and nodded. Then McShaun pointed at Jensen's pocket, reached in, and pulled out three one-ounce bags of cocaine, two from the right pocket and one from the left. Hammer's eyes widened. McShaun placed the three bags on the roof of the car near Jensen's fuming face, went to his unit, came back with a small Polaroid camera, and then took photos of the gun in the glove compartment and the bags of coke on the roof of the car alongside a handcuffed Jensen. He did not speak while he did this. Then he called for a wrecker, searched the car, took the gun, and gave Hammer instructions to make sure the wrecker driver took extra care with the car, it being an expensive one and everything. Hammer smiled.

Before he drove off to book Jensen, but after the tattooed man was stuffed into the back of the unit, McShaun took out his little Valtox kit and, with Hammer watching, tested the powder for cocaine. It showed positive.

He got into the patrol unit, advised the dispatcher he was 15-19, coming in with a prisoner, and then turned and looked over his shoulder at Jensen.

McShaun smiled as he looked in Jensen's sweating face said, 'Who . . . you?'

Chapter Twenty

McShaun took his time doing the arrest and evidence paperwork on Jensen. He felt calm and in control of what he was doing, and he worked with deadly efficiency. He organized the report step by step, from the telling of the reason for the original traffic stop, through the legal citation, through the sighting of the weapon, through the legal pat-down, and finally to the cocaine. Step by step, from probable cause to arrest, he nailed it down. He knew Hammer would do a supplement to his report, and the young officer's paperwork was known to be good. He included copies of his photographs from the scene of arrest, weighed the cocaine with a witness from the sergeant's office, and filed everything. He walked away from it only after he knew it was tight.

He was walking down the hallway, heading for the back parking lot and then back out on the street, when he was stopped by Lieutenant James Track and Captain Fronseca. Both of them appeared agitated, and both wanted to speak first, so they spoke together.

'McShaun! We need to talk to you about the arrest you just made!'

McShaun looked at them and nodded politely. Then he said, 'Actually, Captain, Lieutenant, I made the arrest almost two hours ago.'

Track straightened up and said sternly, 'Look, McShaun, no smartass remarks. You've got a big problem here.' Fronseca nodded and glared. Track went on, 'That Jensen character is part of that Hummel deal, and the word came from the chief's office that anyone or anything connected with that was to be left alone until the investigation is over.'

McShaun shrugged. 'Gee, Lieutenant, I thought the investigation was over after Hummel resigned. That's what we heard down in patrol, anyway. And, also, the general feeling in patrol was that the hands-off order was for the narc troops.'

Fronseca scowled, and Track looked bewildered for a moment. Then he leaned toward McShaun and said, 'Never mind all that, McShaun. You knew what you were doing and who you were doing it with. You know what attorney just came down and bailed Jensen out of jail? Bottle. The same guy who came in here with that girl that Hummel was buying cocaine from. What does that tell you?'

McShaun's eyes gleamed as he said quietly, 'It tells me that Bottle is a very busy greaseball attorney. And it tells me that you've already found Hummel guilty of something he didn't do.'

Before Track could sputter a reply, Captain Fronseca spoke up in his full administrative tone. 'Forget that for now, McShaun, and tell us what you plan to do about this arrest of yours.'

'I intend to go back on the road, Captain,' McShaun said evenly. 'I'm finished with that arrest, and it now lies in the capable hands of the rest of the wonderful judicial system. Before you get too upset, why don't you and the lieutenant here have a look at my report. Read it. See what happened. And *then* tell me what other action I could have taken in this case. I stopped a car for traffic violation. It turned out to be this crudball, who was armed and packing a nice load of coke. So what should I have done? Called the chief? Are you telling me that the chief and his staff are *protecting* the people involved in the Hummel accusations? I mean, is there some kind of fix here or what?'

Both staff officers recoiled as if in the presence of a terrible reptile that hissed at them from the hallway floor. Fronseca

236

looked at McShaun, and Track looked up and down the hall wildly. Then he turned and sputtered, 'Go easy with that kind of talk. We – the Captain and I – we just wanted to make sure you didn't get yourself into a jam. We were just looking out for you. That's all.'

McShaun nodded politely.

Captain Fronseca straightened his tie, looked at the lieutenant, and said coldly, 'Yes, McShaun. Go back on the road. But hear this – we *will* look over your arrest paperwork, and it had better be right.'

McShaun nodded again and walked off. He hit the road and had a relatively quiet shift. He felt wired as tight as a trip flare but somehow settled into a solid, comfortable groove that kept his direction straight and his mind at peace.

The captain and the lieutenant spent most of the night going over the arrest report and evidence paperwork on Jensen with the legal adviser for the department. They could find no flaw. McShaun's simple, straightforward possession case against Jensen was a beauty.

When the shift ended, McShaun changed into jeans and a pullover and drove to Springfield's apartment. She opened the door to his quiet knocking, and they stood there looking at each other. 'I'm sorry,' he said, 'that I didn't get a chance to talk to you during the shift. Thought I'd come by and see if you were still up and about.'

Springfield smiled and stood back while he walked into the apartment. She felt his warmth as he passed by her and kissed her lightly on the forehead. 'Tim, I just tried to call you. To say good night.'

'Well, now at least I can look at your eyes while you say good night. Yes?'

They stood looking at each other. She had tried to call him to hear his voice, and tell him she was thinking about him. But she had not made plans to be with him because she did not want to push him, and because she knew she loved him and she feared what that love would eventually do to her. She was particularly vulnerable now, being torn emotionally by the things she was seeing on the job and by her own internal conflict about McShaun. A distance was growing between them, and she didn't know if he was pushing her away or if she was the one who was backing off, doing so to protect herself against his hurting her.

She had been thinking of having a drink with Calabrini on this night also. John was still politely and gently insistent, explaining to her that he wasn't trying to 'put any moves' on her. He wanted to have a drink and share some time with her in a nonwork mode. But when the shift ended, she found that she couldn't do it, and yet she also felt she needed to spend another night away from Tim . . . to catch her breath. And now he stood there, with an easy grin, those dancing eyes, and that new and somehow ominous calm about him.

She looked down at her feet and said quietly, 'Want to take a walk around the golf course with me? It looks like a nice night.'

He smiled and nodded.

They held hands while they walked, and talked quietly, a little at a time. She found herself talking more than she wanted to about the job; homicide was bothering her, and she found herself dumping it on him. He didn't say much, just the right things, and once or twice he stopped and held her for a while. When she mentioned the murdered man with the patch in his mouth, she missed the stillness that came over him, but she did hear the edge in his voice when he said coldly, 'He who dances . . .'

They walked in silence for a few minutes, and then she told him about John Calabrini, about how he was obviously attracted to her and about how she felt very comfortable with him. She surprised herself to be talking to him about another man, yet she was comfortable with it, and so was he. He listened intently as she told him how she respected Calabrini and how she found him to be an attractive man, a man who treated her like a lady and like a fellow professional.

She couldn't see Tim's gentle smile in the dark as he said,

238

'Rocky, in my opinion, if you had to get yourself into a serious relationship with a man, he would be one of the top candidates.' He stopped and lifted her chin up with his fingers. She searched his darkened face as he said, 'He's a good man, the kind of man you need, the kind of man who'll take care of you – always.'

They stood quietly like that, on the soft edge of the smooth grass on the golf course, under the pine trees. She listened to his words and tried to understand how a man who she knew loved her could tell her that another man was the one she needed. She stored his words, wanting to examine them, each one, closely, knowing he was telling her many things – but she stored them now because now she didn't want to search for his other meanings. Now she just wanted to hear his voice, to feel his touch, and to walk beside him in peace. His whole bearing and aura was one of poignant caring and warmth and some underlying, undefinable . . . something.

By the time they got back to her apartment she was drowsy and relaxed, and she felt very safe as he undressed her slowly and held her gently in the darkness. She chased persistent doubts and troubling speculations out of her mind and let his nearness become a peaceful hiding place.

She fell asleep, knowing there were answers, but too relaxed and content to puzzle over the questions.

The next day, actually in the very early evening at the end of the day, Ronald Toreen decided it was time to go for a walk around the neighborhood. He felt deliciously naughty but at the same time pompously self-righteous. He had spent the last week or so in his mother's house, rarely coming out of his room. At first he had been terrified of what he had done and of what would eventually happen to him. But as the days went by and he watched the news and read the papers and waited for the knock at the door, his confidence increased. As it did, his reasoning worked overtime to help him feel better.

They made it seem so . . . so *ghastly* somehow. The little

girl found dead under a hibiscus bush, strangled and raped. He shrugged as he walked down the alley between all the small old houses in the area. He gripped the cotton under-pants in his pockets with a sweaty fist and shook his head. Why couldn't they understand? Why couldn't they see that what he had done was actually an act of love? The little girl had been promiscuous, teasing him, leading him on, but he knew what she really wanted. And then, because she had fought him – because he wanted to help her – *then* he had held her tightly until she stopped crying.

He remembered standing back in his room after he had left her, standing there shaking and finding the little cotton panties in his hand. He had slept with them against him that night, and now he carried them with him always. He felt good this evening: he would look around and find another pretty young girl or delicate young boy, and after he loved them he would make them be still, and then he would take from them something sweet that he could remember them by.

He was musing about this when he first saw the killer.

The killer was a fluid, compact figure, dressed in dark clothes and walking toward him with a grace and certainty that both aroused him and frightened him. He glanced around at the fringes of the shadow-dark alley, into the backyards of the warm little homes where friendly pools of yellow and white light spilled from dining room windows. He felt chilled and stopped, his feet spread, his lips dry. He felt rooted to the ground and watched with his bulging eyes as the dark figure approached him. He decided not to run. There was no reason to. He would just stand there, the figure would pass him in the alley, a voice would say, 'Good evening,' and that would be all. But there was something about the way the figure's eyes shone at him . . .

The killer walked at a steady pace in the quiet of the alley. His senses seemed tuned to all the sounds and movements, his muscles coiled and ready. He felt no other eyes, heard no other breathing; he smelled only the fear of his target.

The killer stared at Ronald Toreen as he walked to within

240

one step of the fat little man. He saw how Toreen started to turn away, how the troll-like form hesitated, then brought his hands out of his pockets, holding his balled fists in front of his chest.

The killer launched himself.

His right hand was a claw as it impacted the soft throat of Ronald Toreen. It hit, dug, squeezed, and tore, in one impossibly fast combination. Even before the claw left Toreen's throat, the killer brought his right foot up in a front snap-kick, into his victim's groin.

Toreen could only gasp, and then hiss the air out of his clenched teeth. He started to bend forward, curling his pudgy arms around his stomach. His face was lifted to his attacker, and his frightened, bulging eyes looked with terror into a face set into an expression of deep loathing. He knew his attacker was going to kill him, and he hated being so helpless, so totally unable to do anything to stop him.

His mind screamed about how unfair it was as the killer began beating him, backing him up against a telephone pole in the dirt alley. He could not believe the pain he felt, and he longed for the power to stop what was happening to him.

But he had none. He was like a worthless child in the hands of the demonic figure. He could only reel away from the rain of blows and watch with fascination as his blood spattererd out from his shattered face. He could only stumble there in the alley, being beaten to death.

The man was on the balls of his feet, using leverage and power to make each punch and kick have terrible effects on his target's body. What he was doing took only seconds; it was perfectly choreographed and timed. And it had a deadly effect. He smashed his gloved fists and booted feet into Toreen's groin and body and face and head with precision and crushing force, and the fat man's body twisted and jerked and rocked as if caught in machine-gun crossfire.

As Toreen slumped to the dirt of the alley the killer stood over him, stepped back, and then kicked him, hard against the side of the head, just behind the ear. Once, twice, then again the booted foot impacted the head with a heavy, solid sound.

The killer stopped and stood there, breathing easily while his bright eyes surveyed the alley. Satisfied, he knelt beside the motionless body, pulled something from the palm of his left glove, and curled it slightly before pushing it down into Toreen's bloody, smashed mouth. Then he stood, looked down at his victim, turned, and walked slowly out of the alley.

Rocky Springfield spent most of the day with Bell Peoples. Tim had left in the morning after breakfast, saying he had a court case and some other things to do. Rocky told him she had a day of shopping and just messing around with Bell, and they kissed before he left. Her day with Bell had been fun, and good for her. They had gone to the Galeria Mall on East Sunrise Boulevard, near the beach. They tried on clothes, looked at jewelry, and watched people, They had lunch, and then ice cream, and they were both happily tired when she took Bell home. She ate a light dinner and then fell asleep on the couch watching the news. She woke up around nine in the evening, feeling fuzzy but all right. She called Tim.

He sounded tired but glad to hear from her. They talked for a long time, and he made her laugh. There was something in his voice, a sad determination, that made her ask if he was okay. He told her he was just tired. He had a lot on his mind. He had been feeling down about Hummel leaving and Scott being transferred to Records. All the shitty things seemed to be getting to him just now. Then he laughed and told her he was fine – really. He was going to go for a walk and then go to bed.

She said good night, took a long bath, and took a book to bed with her. She read for less than an hour before she fell asleep.

The killer looked at the night sky and pondered what he was feeling. Was he supposed to feel an overwhelming guilt? Was he supposed to be experiencing a self-destructuve conflict? He felt warm and at peace, though tight and still combat-ready. He examined himself and the things he had done so far, and he found them to be correct. He reminded himself that reason became more flexible as those things you believed in became more unreasonable. Was he actually taking the law into his own hands? Yes. No. He took the law into his hands every day. That was his job. He was the one who made the law *work*. But not for himself. He didn't make the law work for himself, he made it work for . . . them.

Was it the old argument that said when the judicial system failed, then some visionary hero had to do *something*? Was it because he had a responsibility to the people that was greater than his responsibility to the system? He could tell himself he was just helping out, just helping the crippled system cope with overload and judicial hamstringing and endless technicalities. He could ponder those words about the rights of the accused meaning more to the system than the rights of the victims. He could bring out that incredibly complex word: *justice*. And he could dissect it and cross-examine it and try to define it. Or he could just *apply* it. He shrugged his shoulders and flexed his arms.

He was mission-oriented, that's all. Through the years his mission as a cop had become clearly defined for him. He now knew more clearly than ever what that mission was, and he was now completely dedicated to fulfilling that mission in one way or the other by hook or by crook, by fair means or foul.

Simple.

He walked through the night, feeling profoundly that it mattered not that others would not understand. He had a job to do. Things had to be done, and he would do what was necessary. Those who led him, and those who thought they controlled him, had lost sight of the mission. But that was all right. The job he did for them would only be a part of the cosmetic framework of the real job he did for the people.

Doubt was nowhere in his mind as he walked through the darkened streets.

During that same night the group met again at Odom's place off Bayview Drive: Lydia, Beachwood, Odom, and Jensen.

Giles from the City Manager's Office had been called by Beachwood, but he was nervous about the way things were going, so he said he couldn't make the meeting because his wife wasn't feeling well. The others didn't like it and agreed that it would be good to keep a close eye on good old Alan Giles in the future, because it would not do to start getting nervous at this stage of the game.

Lydia was at the meeting so that the others could make sure she understood her precarious position. She did. She said the right things, acted sorry for whatever troubles she had caused so stupidly, and was teary-eyed grateful when Beachwood told her that he had gotten the word through Bottle that the charges the Lauderdale PD had pending on her had been thrown out after the cop, Hummel, resigned. She acted very relieved and eager to please them all. She did not discuss with them her plans to leave town and move to Las Vegas. She did not discuss with them the connection she had made in that fast town or the promises of protection her future employer had already made to her. She just made the right sounds and faces and saw how they now seemed relaxed about her.

Beachwood attended the meeting with money on his mind. He had some coming, both for legal services and for his share of some of the recent cocaine passages. He found the porno part of it exciting and fun, but the coke was the real money part, and that was why he was there.

Beachwood reviewed how Lydia's charges were dropped, and he went over Jensen's arrest for them. He had spoken with Jeff Bottle and learned that the cop who had nailed Harv had done a sweet job of it. It looked very tight, and some finesse would be required to straighten it out. He recoiled at Jensen's anger and frustration. He didn't think it was necessary for Harv to pace up and down the room, yelling that he had been set up and pointing a menacing finger at Lydia. No, and he also didn't think Harv's arrest had anything to do with Lydia's arrest or any ongoing investigation of them as a group. It was just one of those things, and Bottle could handle it as any good attorney

244

would – using the system to delay, delay, delay. The more continuances, the better. If the case could be delayed for months, the greater were the chances that things could change, evidence get lost, the cop fired – anything. He advised Jensen to let it ride and to be more careful in the future.

Beachwood closed his eyes and shook his head while Harv ranted about how Lydia had started the whole thing in the first place, and he mentally agreed that something would have to be done about her, eventually – for the good of them all. In the meantime he had to get more money out of Odom. There was that ranch up in North Carolina he wanted, and he had a beautiful picture of himself living up there, keeping his office in downtown Lauderdale and only flying into this crazy town when he had to be with a client.

Jensen fidgeted and fought his way through the meeting, knowing only that he was very angry at having been busted and knowing that somewhere along the line that slut Lydia had to pay the price for giving him away. He was sour about the whole thing. After he had been busted, he had shut down his little marijuana runners and, in doing so, learned that the group he had formed had been very close to breaking off from him and working on their own, anyway. They told him they felt he was getting too hot, and they gave him a line about how they, the grass people, really didn't like working with anyone who messed with cocaine. Could you believe it? That, and of course Odom looking at him cross-eyed about the coke that the cop found on him. Crap. For now he would do as Beachwood suggested; he would leave the arrest in the hands of Bottle. Fine. But very soon he would get the money Odom owed him from the last coke run, he would take care of Lydia for good, and he would get the hell out of Lauderdale and go someplace fun.

Odom sat through the meeting trying to gauge the others and feel out where he stood. He didn't like what he felt. He already knew there was a problem with Giles: The guy was a squirrel and although he liked the money and the girls that Odom provided him, he was just the type to turn to jelly if

245

some serious cops ever started leaning on him. There was no doubt that Giles would give them all away before he took a fall himself. Odom was glad he had videotapes of Giles taking money and of Giles in bed with teenagers. Of course, Giles didn't know he had the tapes, but when the time was right, he'd find out.

Then there was the congressman, Lavon. He had to admit that the charts Lavon brought him had appeared to be accurate so far. And even though they had lost a couple of planes due to other problems along the way, they did have one that had made it through recently. Odom smiled. One load was a very big pile of money, indeed, even after it got spread all over the place. He stopped smiling when he thought of Lavon again. The guy was young and on his way up. He was a political player, and he would rather be in office than have piles of money, although at this time he was gathering all the money he could. Odom understood that Lavon was another one who would turn on him in a flash – and he would be much better at it than Giles. Odom knew Lavon was more capable of surviving a big bust than any of them. He would have the right answers, he would have a cover story for everything, and he would stand by piously, waving the flag, while the rest of them were carried off to the pen. Odom decided he must either compromise Lavon totally or break away from him while there was still time.

Actually, it was probably time to pull the strings right now. Hell, he had the accounts in the Cayman Islands, certainly enough to let him live in comfort anywhere in the world for the rest of his life. He could shut the whole coke thing down and get out. But then there was the porno thing. Now he was very, very glad he had not used any money from the boys who had helped him fit into the distribution end of things. Those guys that were into the porno setup were indeed *connected* – the big machine and all that. Odom swallowed hard, knowing it was extremely difficult to break away from the syndicate in business matters. They leave *you*; you don't leave them. He was good with them because he didn't owe them any money, and he had a nice little stack of films, raw, that he could give them as a going-away present – for go away he must. Soon.

Odom listened to the meeting with one ear while he thought about getting rid of Lydia, forever, getting rid of the syndicate and a pile of raw film at the same time, and getting himself far out of here before the roof fell in on the whole thing.

The meeting ended quietly, no film, no sex, no cocaine. Many things were agreed on verbally, but only two were agreed on mentally: It was time to get out – and it was time to make Lydia disappear from the face of the earth.

Moses Johnson stopped the big garbage truck in the alley and carefully opened the driver's door of the cab. His two footmen were behind him, grabbing the cans along the edge of the alley and throwing the garbage into the back of the truck. The alley was narrow, actually rubbing against the sides of the truck in some places; this area of Fort Lauderdale was one of the few left that did not use the automatic truck that came along with a big hydraulic arm and grabbed the can and emptied it. That was all right with Moses Johnson. He had been picking up garbage for the city for over twenty years. Made no difference to him whether he had footmen or a hydraulic arm.

This alley bothered him, though. It was too narrow, and the folks who lived along it didn't always keep their cans up far enough on their back lawns so he could get by. When that happened, he had to stop the truck, squeeze his large body out, and move the can. It slowed him down, and that was what he didn't like. He wanted to finish his route, clean the truck, and hurry home to his one-man furniture refinishing business.

This morning he had been edging his way along the alley when he came across the drunk guy – or it looked like a drunk, anyway – lying in the bushes and garbage cans, his feet out in the dirt. Moses Johnson didn't like to swear, knowing it wasn't the way of the Lord, but this morning he did mutter some things as he squeezed past the front of the truck to get a better look at the drunk. He leaned forward, ready to grab the guy by the seat of his pants and move him out of the way.

He stopped, his eyes wide.

'Oh, Lawd! Oh, Lawd!' he mumbled under his breath.

One of his footmen behind the truck yelled. 'What's the matter, Moses! What's that you got up there, anyhow?'

Moses Johnson looked down at the savaged body of Ronald Toreen, backed up a little, and called back, 'Go over to one of those houses there and knock on the door and tell the peoples there to call the police. There's a poor man here done been run over by a truck or somethin'. Oh, Lawd!'

The footman had to go to three houses before he found one where an old man would call the police.

Lieutenant John Calabrini had no trouble swearing. He rarely did in the course of a normal conversation, but when he felt it was warranted, he could blister the paint off a battleship – like any good cop. He stood in the alley now, looking down at Ronald Toreen's body, and he swore with such elegance and perfection that Springfield, who stood beside him, couldn't help smiling to herself. She was not amused, however, by the body, which did indeed look as if it had been hit by a truck.

The first officer on the scene, a day-shift man, had called it in as an accident victim – hit and run. When his sergeant got there, they began to have doubts. And when they looked much closer and saw what was stuck in the dead man's mouth, they looked at each other and the sergeant had started the homicide ball rolling. Calabrini had been called at home, and he had phoned for Rocky to meet him at the scene. Rocky had been up, having her second cup of tea, but Calabrini had been out late, and the call had dragged him out of a sound sleep. He hadn't had his coffee and he was grouchy.

'Will you look at this guy, Rocky? He's been beaten to an absolute pulp. Where's the guy from the M.E.'s office, anyway? What are we supposed to do? Stand here all day? Both ends of the alley are sealed, right? I don't want any gawkers – and *no news types*. Damn, this is bad. This is the pits.' He rubbed his face with his hands and knelt beside the body. 'Same type of patch in his mouth. And there's something in his fist here, see it? A rag or a piece of cloth or something. Where's that patrolman with my coffee, anyway? I didn't ask him to grind the beans, for chrissake.'

Rocky hugged herself and stood back a little. She looked at the body and felt her stomach turn. Calabrini had said he was sure the victim had been beaten to death. Beaten to death. She could see that the victim hadn't been a big man, but still, how many guys would it take to *beat* someone to death? And why? Robbery? They could see the wallet in the victim's back pocket, but they were waiting for the crime-scene guys and the Medical Examiner to do their thing before they got into it. She looked up and down the alley, at the backyards of all the houses, and remembered being there just a short while ago, looking at another body, just a short distance from where she actually stood now. She sighed; at least this body would fit into the bag a little better that the last one.

Calabrini was intent on keeping the lid on it. He spoke personally with every cop on the scene. He cautioned those looking for witnesses not to mention what had been found in the corpse's mouth. He warned them all about giving away information, and he forced himself to search again, in vain, for a practical joker among them. He knew in his heart that finding this second patch changed the whole investigation. Now they *really* had a problem.

Detectives combed the neighborhood door to door, looking for witnesses, and patrolmen manned the entrances to the alley, keeping the inquisitive away. Everything was done to keep the lid screwed on tight. The problem was that news types have noses, too, and they learn to smell out any case that is different. They learn to sense when the cops get uptight about something.

Phyllis Green from the *Herald* stood in the kitchen of a friend's house and looked out the window into the alley at all of the activity. She could see a small part of the body, the legs, and she could see Calabrini from Homicide with that female cop – what was her name? She had heard the first

249

call come across her scanner, and then she'd heard the first
units on the scene calling for the detectives. She drove to the
area to see what was up, couldn't get near the alley, and had
to park her car and walk to her friend's place where she
hoped she might be able to get a look at the scene. She could
see that they were tense out there, and her news nose told
her the body was somehow special. She would definitely
have to get to work and find out what was happening here.
The cops were tense about this murder – and she was going
to find out why.

Chapter Twenty-One

Calabrini made a few notes on a legal pad in preparation for his staff meeting with the chief regarding the latest murder. While he did so he grinned at the handsome FBI agent sitting across the desk from him. The agent, Stan Matthews, was about the same age as Calabrini and cut from the same professional mold. Matthews had worked cases with the sharp lieutenant from Lauderdale PD before, and they respected each other.

Calabrini looked up from his notes and said quietly, 'So you're telling me some of the info that Hummel had matches stuff you've got? His informant had the names right?'

'Yeah. Well, you know, John, we consider this *very* sensitive right now, so we've been keeping it to ourselves. The funny thing is, Hummel worked his way up through a list of names, the cocaine guys, the attorney and all, and got to our young congressman last. We started with the congressman and sort of worked our way down from there.'

Calabrini nodded and said thoughtfully, 'Tell you the truth, Stan, I'm surprised you're even discussing it with me. You guys could keep working on it with us never needing to know or becoming involved.'

The FBI agent shrugged in agreement. Then he went on. 'Yeah, I know, John. But this is just you and me, right? You know they've got us working with the Drug Enforcement Agency now. There's some talk that we'll be taking over their stuff or integrating them into us. Drugs aren't our bag, you know. But here's a young up-and-coming congressman, and he's on the take, uh, unofficially, and one of your good people went down the tubes indirectly because of it, and – oh, hell – I guess I just wanted to talk to someone about it cop-to-cop, if you know what I mean.'

Calabrini nodded and started gathering his things for his meeting with the chief. The FBI agent stood up and put out his hand. 'Just wanted you to know, John, that Hummel was right, that's all. Not that it'll do him any good at this point.'

Calabrini shook the offered hand and said evenly, 'Tell you something, Stan. I think ol' Chick Hummel may turn out to be the lucky one around here. Hell, I really believe he's better off away from this nuthouse.'

Matthews smiled, knowing Calabrini didn't mean it, and said, 'And you've got another one of those "funny" homicides now, too, huh, John?'

Calabrini shook his head and made a face. 'How'd you hear about it so soon?'

The FBI agent patted Calabrini lightly on the arm and said, smiling, 'Big Brother – he's everywhere.'

The meeting in the chief's office went very much like the first one, except things were slightly more tense. The tension caused agitation among the administrators, who really didn't know what to do about the situation but felt they should suggest *something*. One suggested that every officer on the department be made to bring in all his uniforms so a 'patch check' could be made. Another suggested the lie detector for the entire department, making an aside to the effect that of course this would not include the administrators. This only started a rambling discussion about the Police Officers' Bill of Rights and other legal hassles that would crop up. The chief was still concerned about publicity, and most of the meeting was taken up with preparatory statements covering the department in case the worst happened and the public found out the facts.

Sitting through all this hubbub and bickering were the

only two cops in the room, Lieutenant Calabrini and Springfield. The lieutenant had brought Springfield along because she was working closely with him on the case. Springfield was still green enough to be genuinely surprised at the quality of ineptness in leadership she saw. She felt as if she were witnessing something on the level of a quilting-bee gossip shop.

Being the only two cops in the room, they were the only ones present who knew what had to be done and how to do it: they had a couple of murders that appeared to be related, or at least committed by the same individual. They had to find out what the motive was and, at the same time, come up with a common denominator linking the two dead men. Then it could be worked like any other homicide case. They sat there thinking about it, neither one wanting to say to themselves the one terrible and very real possibility: They might end up arresting a cop when it was all over.

When the minor hysterics calmed down, the chief asked Calabrini what he was doing at this point. Calabrini briefed him on the extensive records check that was going on in reference to the dead man. The victim had a name: Ronald Toreen. The chief might remember the name as that of a man sent away over a year ago for child molestation. No, there never was a clear criminal trial outcome. All charges had been pending until the man underwent psychiatric testing and counseling. No, there was no answer as to why he was out of custody.

The room got very quiet when he told of the crumpled panties found in the dead man's fist. They belonged, as far as could be determined at this time, to the little girl who had been raped and strangled a week ago in the same area. The dead man fit a couple of witness descriptions. If he was alive, he would be worked as a prime suspect in the rape-murder of the child. As it was, who knows? Did Toreen's killer place the panties in Toreen's hand? Was Toreen's killer the little girl's killer? Possibly. But it somehow didn't fit. And the panties were being processed to see if there was any evidence, hair, body fluids, anything, that would point

253

to anyone other than Toreen. Calabrini told them he thought Toreen killed the little girl and then was killed by someone who beat him to death and left a police patch in his mouth. Then he sighed and waited.

The chief lit another cigarette and pointed it around the room while he asked about the first dead guy with the patch in his mouth. Didn't it turn out that he had just been released from doing hard time for rape? And didn't we learn since then that he probably had already done a couple more since he got out? Wasn't the County Sheriff's Office working a couple of rape cases where he would be the main suspect – if he was still alive?

Calabrini had to say yes. The first guy was probably good for a couple of rapes, and the short fat guy in the alley looked real good for the murder of the five-year-old girl.

And our killer? What of him?

Calabrini looked at Springfield, who cleared her throat and told them of the one witness they had so far. An old man, bothered by his arthritis, who stood by his darkened kitchen window and watched a dark figure move silently through the alley. The old man said there was something about the way the figure moved – in a sure way – that made the old man consider calling the police so they could check the guy to see if he was a prowler. But the old man had thought about it too long, he said, and a short while later he watched as the dark figure walked past the back of his house again, out of the alley. The figure did not hurry, said the old man, and he remembered what it was about the way the figure moved; it was something from his proud past. The figure moved through the night like a soldier – sure, silent, and with a purpose.

But the patch? The patch in the mouth? The staff all talked and questioned at once, reminding the chief that they still knew so very little.

The chief held his head in his hands and said to them all, 'So . . . what? We got some kind of goddamn Don Quixote running around out there killing people? This . . . this can't be happening.'

254

Rocky worked all day with Calabrini, checking reports, making calls, harassing forensics and the Medical Examiner, and trying to get as much done as they could under the tight lid the chief was still trying to keep on the case. Day turned to afternoon, and then to evening, and still they worked. Rocky thought of trying to have the dispatcher advise Tim to give her a call, but it didn't work out. Late in the shift she went to dinner with Calabrini, and they talked about the case. She told herself she would call Tim after work.

She enjoyed having dinner with the lieutenant. There was something very stable about John Calabrini, and she liked it. She felt comfortable with him, and relaxed. She felt his quiet strength and was aware of him as a man, but she recognized that he did not operate at all times on the razor edge of an intense emotional and physical volcanic eruption, as did Tim McShaun. She felt herself warm to the dangerous and impossible thought of sharing time with both men, and she cautioned herself. It was thinking like that that got brave little girls hurt. She would try to call Tim later.

The killer prepared himself. It was after eleven at night, hot and muggy. He put on old jeans, soft and worn. He pulled on a dark blue long-sleeved 'surfer' pullover. He sat down and slid his feet into a worn but highly polished pair of boots, comfortable old friends. He laced them tightly, stood, and wrapped a camouflaged scarf as a headband around his head. He took the Remington 870 pump 12-gauge shotgun from behind the closet door, loaded the tube with three #1 buckshot rounds, racked one into the chamber, put the weapon on 'safe', and slid one more round into the tube. He hung a raincoat over his shoulder and carried the shotgun alongside his leg as he walked out into the night, watched by a pair of unblinking yellow eyes.

The killer drove slowly, relaxed, to the area of town he knew so well, the shotgun under the raincoat on the seat beside him. He found the run-down apartment building and pulled into the parking lot filled with old cars, pickups, and motorcycles. He parked at the north end of the lot, between a large green dumpster and an old gray sedan with broken windows and no rear wheels. He saw with satisfaction that the nearby streetlight still hadn't been fixed.

He waited.

Bobby Nails turned onto the street where his apartment was located and swerved his car just enough to hit a garbage can sitting in someone's front yard, near the road. He laughed out loud as the can tumbled, crushed, into the owner's driveway. He was in a rowdy mood, not drunk but feeling hyped up. He had been out to a topless bar, drinking and spending his money and making like a big man. True, that blond-haired bitch wouldn't go home with him – even after taking most of his money and sticking all of his coke up her nose. But she did squeeze his leg and say that she hoped he would come back real soon. Yeah.

Nails slowed his car, ready to turn into the apartment parking lot, and scowled. Of course, he needed more money. That's all there was to it. Damn, money just wouldn't last. Raisin' hell with the ladies and buyin' all that toot was getting to be a regular thing, so there was a regular *need* for the money. He drove slowly through the lot, to the south end, near the part of the building where he lived, and he thought about the last one. That stupid old lady had to come in – had to come in and he had to kill her.

Oh, well.

Actually – he smiled – actually he had kind of liked it.

So maybe in the morning he'd go out looking. And who knows? Maybe he could find another one.

He parked his car, turned off the motor, pulled out the keys, and stepped out, shutting the door with his shoulder as he stood between his car and another. He turned toward the back of his car to walk behind it and then to the sidewalk leading to the apartment. He came face-to-face with the killer.

The killer stood six feet away from him, holding a pump

shotgun and looking at him with a curious smile on his tight face.

Bobby Nails felt himself covered with sweat instantly, his face, his brow, the small of his back. He felt his knees go weak and his throat dry out. His stomach fluttered and churned, and he thought he would lose control of his bowels.

Bobby Nails looked at the killer and said, 'What . . .?'

The first load of #1 buckshot hit him in the stomach, picking him up off his feet and hurling him backward onto the trunk of his car, arms spread wide. As he rebounded off the car and back toward the killer, he started to scream, but it turned to a wet gasp as the next shot took him in the groin and legs. He made a mad, twirling circle in the air, like an insane, berserk puppet, and found himself looking into the killer's bright eyes again as the third load of shot hit him full in the chest, ripping him open and killing him.

He fell in a bloodied heap at the killer's feet.

The neighborhood fell silent, as if shocked by the roaring of the shotgun, and there was a pause in the night before the dogs started howling and the babies started crying and the people started asking themselves, 'What *was* that?'

During the pause the killer knelt down and picked up the three spent shotgun casings. Then he used his boot to turn the grimacing face of Bobby Nails, stuck the small piece of cloth across the pink tongue and yellow teeth, and stood up and looked around.

Then he walked through the lot, got to his car, got in, and drove away slowly.

Several minutes went by before a tenant of the apartment building, armed with a flashlight, hesitantly walked out into the parking lot. When he saw the bloody lump behind the car, he ran back to his own apartment to call the police. That done, he went back out, and soon a little crowd gathered: old ladies, pregnant girls, working men, and schoolboys, all looking into the twisted face of Bobby Nails, all staring in the light of the flashlight at the patch stuck in his mouth.

This time Phyllis Green was ready. She had been listening to her radio scanner, covering all the police channels, as frequently as she could lately. Her plan was simply to go to every reported homicide that came in, to see for herself what was going on. Maybe it was nothing. Maybe it was something.

She had gone to an all-night store for more cigarettes and had been on her way home when the call went out on the radio: 'Apparent shooting death, one man down, ambulance and squad cars moving.' She heard the address and drove there as fast as she could.

She got there before the cops had a chance to block off the area. Patrolmen were there, and they were already trying to make the small crowd move out of the way, but they had not yet had time to really control the scene. She could see the body. She walked closer, carrying her camera. She stood three feet away and looked down at the incredible devastation wrought by the impact of the shotgun rounds.

She looked into the face of the dead man, saw what lay against his teeth, and nodded. Now she knew. She was absolutely right to follow her hunch.

That was all the congratulations she allowed herself. She got busy taking photos of everything she could before a young patrolman chased her away.

John Calabrini and Rocky Springfield had a long dinner, followed by coffee and dessert. They talked easily and a lot. There were only a few busy tables by the time they decided to have a liqueur, and she excused herself to go to the ladies' room. In the hallway she used a pay phone, feeling a little guilty and arguing with herself about it, to try to call McShaun at his place. There was still no answer.

The evening had gone well. She enjoyed being with John, but he wasn't Tim. And Tim was the man she wanted, the man on her mind, and the man in her heart.

They were taking their first sip of Grand Marnier when the maître d' politely informed Calabrini that he had an urgent phone call at the desk.

It just got worse, it didn't get any better.

Rocky stood in the glare of lights looking down at the twisted and torn body of Bobby Nails and frowned. Calabrini stood beside her, silent. They both stared with awe and dread at the cause of their evening's interruption, amazed at the amount of destruction wreaked by the weapon used.

The area was roped off now, and they were alone with the body, waiting for the Medical Examiner. Outside of the lines there were many patrol officers and sergeants, monitoring the crowd and searching for any evidence that might turn up in the lot. Phyllis Green stood in the shadows, watching and making notes.

Calabrini spoke without turning his head. 'Shotgun, I believe, and it looks like three rounds hit him. I'd say fired from less than ten feet away.' He rubbed his face with his hands, looked around, and said, 'The first officer on the scene, luckily one of the older ones, told me there were no shells on the ground. He says he looked around, hands and knees, under the cars, everywhere. What does that tell you?'

Rocky was silent for a moment, staring, then she said, 'The person who killed him fired at least three times and, after he was finished, had the presence of mind to retrieve the shell casings before he left.'

Calabrini nodded and sighed.

'Let's go through it real carefully, okay? We'll need more people out here. I want to interview every person in this apartment complex before the sun comes up. Somebody had to have seen or heard something. A car leaving. . . *something*.'

He started to turn away, and Springfield grabbed his arm.

'John, I . . . I know this one, or I mean I know who he is.'

Calabrini waited, watching her eyes.

Rocky stared at the dead face with the cloth patch in its mouth and remembered the night, so long ago, when she followed Tim through the alley and waited until this evil

259

man came out of the dark and tried to kill her. She remembered that he had shot at her, had tried to kill her, and she remembered hesitating too long with her gun pointed at the small of his back. She licked her dry lips and said, 'It's Bobby Nails. He's a burglar. In fact, I'm pretty sure B and E squad has him as a suspect on several house burglaries right now. And he was mentioned as a suspect in that murder of the old woman in her house – remember? She apparently surprised him? It's Bobby Nails, all right. He tried to kill me once.'

Calabrini remembered.

Chapter Twenty-Two

The next morning, while Rocky slept at her apartment and Calabrini sat up brooding over coffee at his house and McShaun moved with easy fluidity along the beach road, jogging his eight miles, Lieutenant James Track met with Phyllis Green.

Track had been a source for Green for several years now, both being served by the liaison. He was political and liked being the man in the know with the lady reporter – and he liked being able to count on good print when his name was involved in the news. She liked having a piece of the police brass tell her what was going on inside the cop shop.

He told her that there had been other killings where the killer had left a cloth patch in the victim's mouth. He told her that an intense investigation was under way and that all of the department's resources were being used to find the killer. He told her of what they knew about the victims: who they were and how they'd died. He stressed that he was only telling her all of it in the strictest confidence, off the record, because he was sure there would be confusion in the media, and he wanted at least one reporter to have the story right.

Green smiled and assured him that she understood perfectly. She didn't tell him that she already knew who the other victims were, where they had been found, and when. She also knew about their past histories, but she didn't tell him that, either. She didn't want him to know she had other sources.

They shook hands at the end of their little meeting, and both went their self-serving ways.

Phyllis Green couldn't know for sure, but she could correctly guess that Track would also talk to radio and television reporters on an off-the-record basis before the day was out, and she knew she would have to spend the day working very hard to make her story in the evening edition of the paper *the* big story on the 'patch killer.' Her editor had already given her the green light on the direction she wanted to take, and she felt sure that when it came out, her story would be a blockbuster.

It was a strange day around the Fort Lauderdale Police Department. A kind of quiet, expectant peace fell over the building and over those who worked there. The word was out in the open about the latest killing, and everyone, from the chief down to the newest rookie, knew that great globs of sticky stuff were going to hit the fan real soon. Patrol officers rode the streets, answering calls, detectives did their follow-up work, lab technicians did their photos and prints, juvenile officers struggled with their unbelievable case loads, the TAC squad prepared itself for night felony work, and the narcs shifted around, trying to get comfortable in their temporary street skins. All the different sections and units went about their jobs like a man working under a loose ceiling fan. Even the voices of the dispatchers sounded hushed on the radio.

The chief and his staff made phone calls to the editors and station managers, trying to lay some groundwork for the direction they would take when the storm came. The Public Information Officers prepared statements and rehearsed possible reactions, and everyone in any position of command tried to make sure that when the storm hit, *their* particular area of responsibility would be all right. It was a good day for smoking too many cigarettes, for wishing you hadn't stopped drinking, for sucking on antacid tablets, and for being on vacation.

John Calabrini had come in early, his stomach in knots, his brow furrowed. By mid-morning Springfield was with him, and they went over and over the evidence and information they had, which wasn't much.

Instinctively Calabrini knew that what they were dealing with was genuine: the person or persons doing the killings were deliberately selecting their victims, and they were deliberately leaving the patch as a sign. The criminal personalities of the victims had a great deal of meaning. He knew, although he would have trouble explaining it, that each victim had been carefully selected for death by the killer or killers, and because of that, he directed the detectives working on the case, including Springfield, to research victims of crimes that the dead men had committed. Was there someone out there, some citizen, who had been attacked, assaulted, vandalized, or ripped off by all three of the dead men? And, if so, then why the patch?

The patch.

The patch told Calabrini what he didn't want to hear.

It told him, whispered to him, that the killer was a cop.

In the early afternoon, after the third meeting with the chief, Calabrini called a meeting of all the detectives working on the patch homicide cases. They gathered in the captain's office, serious, quiet men and women who spoke in worried tones and listened with bowed heads. Everyone felt as if they were sitting on a hand grenade.

Calabrini wanted to do some scenarios.

If the killer is a citizen, how does he select his victims? How does he have access to information that will tell him where they are and what they are up to? And if the killer is a citizen, where does he get the patches that he stuffs into people's mouths?

How about a reserve officer, one of those men who are not full-time cops but come in once or twice a month to ride a shift just to help out? Wouldn't they have access?

How about the husband – or wife – of one of the department's employees?

Aren't police uniform patches collected by police admirers all over the country? Doesn't the training division have an aide who does almost nothing but answer letters from all over the place, sending patches upon request?

Calabrini took three aspirin, two men unwrapped Di-Gel tablets, and one of the women detectives excused herself to get a drink of water.

Calabrini asked them if they didn't agree that it looked more and more as if there was only one individual involved? The first killing was with a garrote; no evidence that two people would have been involved. The second one was still up for debate, with many of those who had seen Toreen's body or photos of it, feeling strongly that it would have taken at least two men to beat someone that badly so quickly. Calabrini reminded them that the Medical Examiner concluded that the beating was the act of just one man, a man who knew exactly what he was doing and had the power to do it. This last one, Nails – that, too, looked as if only one killer was needed. It has been determined that he had been hit by three shots, all #1 buck. This stirred some low whistles and *oohs* and *aahs*. And the angles of the shots indicated that the killer stood in front of the victim as he fired, spacing each shot so that the body was responding to the impact of the first before proceeding with the next.

How about some evidence?

No garrote left on the scene. We can only guess that it was something like piano wire.

One thing at the site of the beating, we'll get to that in a minute.

No shotgun shells to later match to a weapon if one is ever recovered.

One witness from the second murder who says that a 'dark figure' moved 'slowly . . . not hurried' through the alley. Same witness says the figure moved 'like a soldier'. Two witnesses from last night, both of whom looked out of their apartment windows after the blasts, only to see nothing in one case, except for a car leaving at moderate speed, and in the other, 'a solitary man dressed in dark clothes and walking as if in no hurry.'

And now, troops, the one thing we have that might make us feel just a little lucky: Because extensive photos were taken at all three crime scenes and then checked over very carefully, the guys in the lab have been able to say that they have one boot print that was photographed in the dirt under the I-95 overpass – and also in the dirt of the alley where Toreen was beaten to death.

Hurrah.

The lab guys say they have a definite match, cuts in the sole and wear on the toe. They're now working to determine what kind of boots they are.

So, did we have a working patrol officer who wears boots and was at both scenes *after* the murders as part of the investigation? Unlikely. It was the same shift, day shift, but one was on the west side of town, the other on the east side.

And none of you detective types would think of wearing boots with those nice clothes you all wear here to work every day, right? Everyone in the room looked at their feet.

Another scenario. Let's say the killer is a cop, male, working alone.

Motive?

Who do we know around here that's had the shaft real bad lately?

Silence for a moment. Uncomfortable silence.

Uh, there's the thing with Hummel. He got it pretty bad. He's gone. He was fried in the papers, and now we're all hearing whispers that he might have been right. Even if he wasn't, the chief gave him away and everyone knows it.

The captain made a disapproving face.

Yeah, Hummel was definitely bitter about the whole thing, but hadn't he left the area?

There's Scott Kelly. When he finally got back here, they told him he could sit on his ass – like it or lump it. He made some noise about quitting and then said he would accept the assignment. He's pretty bitter about it.

The clock on the captain's desk ticked away, the only sound in the room.

Calabrini looked at them. He rubbed one finger around the neck of his shirt. He pinched his nose. He cleared his throat.

The key question is this: Who is bitter enough to start killing people?

Rocky was on her way out the back door of the station with the big detective, Stillwater, to pick up some takeout chicken for the troops at dinnertime when she got a chance to speak with Tim for a few minutes. He was on duty and had come into the station with a stolen lawn mower that some citizen had found in a canal behind his house.

They stood and talked quietly and made plans to try to get together as soon as they could. He looked at her and said gently, 'Hey, Rocky, you worked last night, all day today, and now into this evening. I've got a feeling when you leave here tonight you're going to be one very tired detective.'

Springfield nodded and looked furtively at Stillwater standing a few feet away, trying not to listen. She smiled a little and said, 'Well, I might also be a detective who needs a little TLC.'

He nodded.

'This case is getting to me, Tim. Somehow there's this incredible amount of tension wrapped up in the whole thing. Guess you heard all about the latest killing? And you know the media is going to go public with it tonight?'

He nodded again.

'Tim, it's just that . . . this case is scary somehow.'

He lifted her chin with his fingertips and looked deep into her eyes. He smiled a little smile and said softly, 'There's no need to be afraid, Rocky. Everything will be all right.'

They parted.

She was quiet as she rode to the chicken takeout place with Stillwater. What she had seen in Tim bothered her. Three murders had taken place, three dead men with Lauderdale police patches in their death-grin faces, and the whole town would soon be in an uproar. Every cop on the force knew what was happening; everyone was tense and edgy and excited. Emotions were running high, and a quivering tightness quickened the actions of even the slothful types.

But there was Tim McShaun, calm and composed as ever. Almost serene.

It really bothered her.

IS KILLER COP LOOSE ON THE STREETS?

Phyllis Green's article in the *Herald* was a sensation. It was well researched and well written. She had the facts, and she was clever enough to draw a lot of conclusions for the reader. Her story considered a nonpolice murderer only long enough to discount it. She went into great detail explaining how the chief of police had purposely kept information on the first two patch murders from reporters. How, in fact, a cover-up had taken place in order to keep the people from knowing the truth. She included enough of the chief's quotes to show that he was indeed uncomfortable with the situation and had in fact held information back.

She pooh-poohed the press release about narcotics-related murders and supposed efforts by some criminal organization to discredit the police department. She showed the reader how all three of the victims were local men who had run afoul of the law. She showed how all three men had been arrested by the Fort Lauderdale Police in the past. She reported that all three of the dead men were currently suspects in rapes and murders, but she put enough of a slant on it to make the reader suspect that this, too, was part of a scam on the part of the police brass, as if by somehow making the victims look like undesirable citizens, this would lessen the impact of the killings.

The most sensational part of the article was about police suspects. She mentioned an unnamed ex-narc who had become embroiled with the administration and resigned, reportedly bitter and angry. She went over the Hummel case again, reporting his bitterness and anger and pointing toward his resignation as a clear indication of guilt. She even quoted an unnamed 'highly placed source' from within the department who said that the investigators were looking closely for any connection between the girl that had brought the charges against Hummel and any of the dead men.

She saved her best for last.

Being very careful to supply only the facts, gingerly leading the reader to the only possible conclusion without really saying it, the article told about the latest victim, Bobby Nails. Nails, who had been killed by three close-range shotgun blasts. Nails, who had, a year ago, survived a police shoot-out in which another man was killed, by shotgun: Nails, who had been charged with attempted murder against a female officer, Rocky Springfield, and who later was allowed to go free by the court because the charges were invalid. Nails had allegedly fired two shots at rookie Springfield, and she had allegedly attempted to shoot him at that time but had failed for some reason. Nails, who had walked away from the charges of trying to kill Springfield and who now was an alleged suspect in another murder that had occurred during a burglary.

Did the killer have to be male? asked the article.

Weren't *all* officers of the department, male and female, qualified with the 12-gauge shotgun?

Phyllis Green ended the article by saying that Springfield, now a detective reportedly working on the patch murder cases, was unavailable for comment.

There were copies of the paper all over the Detective Division on the second floor of the station. They were all over the department, in fact: up in Communications, down in the patrol locker room, over in Records, and up in the chief's office. Television sets were going too. The six o'clock news was full of the story, with some scanty film coverage of the Nails scene, and then a lot of shots of windblown reporters standing in front of the Lauderdale Police station, talking into their microphones, asking damning questions without answers.

Calabrini sat with his tie loosened, reading and listening and shaking his head while he waited for Rocky to finish reading Green's article for the third time. Finally she looked up at him, and he noticed that her eyes, which he thought were gray, were an intense green.

'Actually, what she says here makes sense when you think

268

about it. I guess I really could be considered a suspect.' Springfield said it with a dry voice, her face hot.

Calabrini waved his hand. 'Yeah, you have access to the info on the bad guys, you could get the patches, and you're shotgun-qualified. There's just two problems.' He looked at her and smiled, the first smile she had seen from him all day. 'First, you don't have any motive that I know of on the first two dirtballs – and I don't think revenge on Nails is a good enough motive for you.' He rubbed his eyes. 'And second, although I'm sure Green could have a field day with this, too, if she wanted, second, you were with me, enjoying a fine slice of chocolate cheesecake in that restaurant at the time that Nails was turned into shark bait.'

The phone rang. He made a face at her as he straightened his tie and said into the phone, 'Yes, sir. Be there in a minute.'

She sat alone in the middle of the Detective Division, surrounded by bustle and hubbub. She was worried, not about the allegations by Green but by wraithlike feelings that drifted through her heart and mind. She felt a heavy unease, a nervous fear, a fluttering uncertainty. Something about this case of the patch murders worried her greatly, not when she worked the small sections of it one at a time, but when she forced herself to sit back and examine it as a whole. Her heart was permeated by an undefined dread, a sure sadness, a knowing anguish. She felt pulled along by it, an unwilling witness, a coerced participant in some macabre, terrifying drama – a victim herself.

There was something deep down inside her that she didn't want to know. But it wouldn't leave her alone.

Chapter Twenty–Three

That night Tim McShaun stayed with Rocky at her apartment. He had showered and changed after work, and when he got to her place, he waited while she took a fast shower and fixed them both some tea. She was tired but fidgety; he was relaxed. Then they went for a walk around the golf course.

She was still caught up in work and the case, and she needed to talk about it all. He listened and asked a few questions . . . letting her go on, knowing she needed it. He acted curious and interested, and she did not see that he stayed with the conversation only because she wanted it. Finally they got to the point where they started: her frustration at trying to understand the killer, especially if the killer was a cop.

'Tim, don't you see what I'm saying? If the killer *is* a cop, then he – or she, for that matter – has just absolutely *lost* it. You know what I mean. What can he be thinking? That by killing these bad guys he's going to actually *change* things? By going beyond what the system allows he's going to make things *better*? Oh, don't get me wrong, the three that have been killed so far were definitely prime candidates. I mean, if they were alive tonight, they'd probably be out there hurting people, but . . . but, oh, hell.'

McShaun was silent as he walked beside her.

'Remember some of the talks you and I had, Tim . . . about the system and all . . . about how it seems like it just doesn't work, and when that happens, a good cop – a cop who cares about the people – is justified if he bends the rules a little to get the job done? Okay, so I'll go along that there are working things a street cop can do to get a little better results here and there. But picking people out and killing them?' She stopped and turned to face McShaun as she went on. 'I mean, even you, Tim, even though you've argued for bending the rules, even you would agree that this is going over the line. Right?'

McShaun looked at her for a moment, then he said quietly, 'I don't know, Rocky. Seems like it would be a very personal decision to me . . . if it actually is a cop that's doing the killings.'

'What do you mean?'

'Well, I'm just not sure anyone would be able to fit their own standards of conduct into this person's decision. Obviously, whoever he is, he has made a great personal decision to do some things that go way beyond any acceptable law we have. Also, even if he was a cop, when he made the decision – once he stepped over the line, decided, and then actually *acted* on the decision – then he became something else, something beyond a cop.'

She stood in the darkness, looking into his shadow-covered face. The wind whispering through the tall pines was the only sound. She turned and started walking again. 'So, all right, what about the fact that what he's doing really has no long-term effect on the lives of all of the people that live in the city? What's he going to do? Keep an active list of felony suspects and go around killing the worst ones? This sounds silly, I know, but that's not even logistically feasible. Still assuming that it's a cop – and I really don't have any other feeling, and neither does John . . . uh, Lieutenant Calabrini – he's killed three bad guys. So what does that really accomplish? What has he really done for the people or for the system . . . or for himself?'

McShaun walked beside her, his face to the night sky. Without looking at her he said, 'Maybe the long-term results are not that important to him. Maybe he just feels like he has to do *something*. And maybe, to him, getting immediate results is good enough for now.'

'What immediate results, besides bodies lying all over the place?'

'Well, he is now very sure, whoever he is, that the three that he's killed will never again hurt anyone in this world.'

Rocky heard Tim speak; she heard his words, she understood, and they scared her.

'Look, Rocky, let's go with an argument I've given you before. You're walking along the street, you see someone that needs help, they've fallen, or something is about to hurt them. You can see it clearly; you can recognize their pain and potential loss . . . and more importantly, you have the power and the capability to *help* them, to *do* something that will change things for them, for the better. If that's the case, don't you have a *duty* to act? Can you just pass by, or stand there watching and doing nothing?'

'Sounds like you're hitting me with the parable of the Good Samaritan. And, boy, are you stretching it, Tim.'

'Am I? Am I stretching it because we're talking about helping someone who has fallen down on the one hand while I'm talking about killing people on the other? Who is my neighbor? And what should I do – or what *can* I do – to help my neighbor? This cop, if that's who he is, this cop just may have made a very personal decision to help his neighbor. Oh, it's a radical one, all right, and he'll eventually pay the price for it, but is he really so hard to understand, Rocky?'

She felt him walking beside her, felt his strength and his warmth, and she heard his words and felt saddened by the conversation. And she knew what bothered her most.

'All right, Tim,' she said. 'I hear you. What you're saying makes some sense, at least in the context of this talk we're having. But let me ask you this: What about him? What does he, the killer, get out of this – besides some perverse kicks or a power trip? Even if, for the sake of argument, I'm his advocate, let me ask you a question: Isn't he then sacrificing himself for no reason? Surely he'll be caught. Let's face it, he's not exactly being covert about all this, is he? Sticking police department uniform patches in his victims' mouths? It's like he's not content just to do the job. He has to leave a sign, to justify it or something.'

McShaun said nothing.

'Anyway, so what happens to him finally? Jail? The death sentence? His life ruined – wasted, actually – just to rid this city of some scumbags who would eventually, even with all of the system's shortcomings, be sent away, anyway? He's sacrificing himself, Tim. If he's motivated by some of your lofty arguments, he might even be a compassionate man, a man who actually cares and thinks he's doing the right thing . . . and he's sacrificing himself. And if he *is* a cop, he'll eventually put himself in a position where he'll never be able to help anyone again.' She stopped to look at him again, saying, 'Oh, Tim, this whole case is just so close to us all. If the killer is a cop, then we'll all know him when he's caught, and he may be someone we all respect and like. I just feel as if it's going to hurt us all so bad.'

He held her shoulders and kissed her lightly on the end of her nose. He rubbed his fingertips softly across her lips, and he looked into her eyes as he said, 'Many good things in this world hurt us in one way or another, Rocky. We just have to be able to accept the pain and recognize the sacrifices for the qualities they possess. Like I said, this whole thing seems like a very, very personal matter to me. Whoever it is, he has his reasons. They're good enough for him, and that's all he needs. You can try to understand them, even if you know you'll never be able to accept them. You're still a cop, and you're working a case, and all you have to do is keep believing what you believe in and do what you can to serve the people and the system while you do your job.'

She took his hand and they started walking back to her apartment.

They talked themselves into taking a long hot bath together. They laughed and snuggled and played, and after he toweled her off he carried her to her bed and massaged her all over. He kneaded her muscles and rubbed her and cracked her back. He started with her fingertips, went all the way to her toes, and ended at the small of her back. He listened as her breathing softened and deepened, and he trailed his fingers gently over her skin.

He held her while she slept.

The media coverage of the patch killings caused a sensation among the citizens of Fort Lauderdale. City Hall and the Tourist Board had headaches and upset stomachs. The chief's phone was ringing off the hook even before he could take his coat off when he walked into his office an hour earlier than usual. City administrators applied great pressure on the police department, and the chief and his staff were forced to promise that they would have the killer, whoever he or she was, in custody soon, very soon. They promised, and then they went back to work and screamed at any cop working on any part of the case to get results.

The Public Information Office of the police department had a hysterical day trying to put out as much accurate and less damning information as they could. Matters were not helped when Communications called down to say that during the morning they had received four phone calls from unidentified citizens who were phoning in their requests for people the killer cop should hit next. The black businessmen's association leaders called the chief's office to let him know that they were going to monitor the case closely, to make sure that if the killings were in any way racially motivated, the police department would not just stand by and let it happen. The chief responded by saying all the right things. After he hung up the phone he cursed loudly and threw his cigarette lighter against the wall.

Reaction from the greater part of the public seemed to be 'wait and see', or mixed at best. Even though most of the media coverage had downplayed the criminal histories of the three victims, the people who read between the lines felt that they really had nothing to fear from the 'killer cop', if that's what it was. The only people killed were those the community was better off without, anyway.

Patrol officers out on the street were stopped by citizens asking questions and giving opinions. The officers had been briefed to say only that every effort was being made to catch the killer and that the official stand was that the killer was probably not a cop . . . just some maniac who was trying to make the police department look bad. Most of the cops kept what they really thought to themselves, because most had mixed emotions about the whole thing.

Morning briefing had been fairly quiet, but by the time the afternoon shift straggled into the briefing room, the news had been going all day, and the administrators had been working all day, and orders were flying, and the brass was tense. Consequently, when in the briefing, the shift captain came in and tried to caution the officers about saying too much out on the street and then, when he threw in a couple of his personal opinions about how the killer was making them all look bad, he was greeted with mumblings and undertones of disagreement. One hard old veteran sitting in the very back row stated loudly that he thought the killer should get a medal, and he was backed up by several yeahs and all rights. The captain was flustered and the briefing ended.

The captain in charge of the Traffic Division was hauled onto the carpet in front of the chief and chewed to little bits after a weeping mother of a known teenaged car thief came in carrying a patch in her hand. The chief, almost vibrating, advised the captain that two of his motorcycle officers, two of those crème-de-la-crème types, had pulled over the kid, and even though he was actually in a car that he legally owned for once, wrote him a couple of citations and then clipped an FLPD patch to the tickets before handing them to the kid. The mother told the chief that her son was still trying to figure out if they were playing a joke on him or if he should leave town. The chief told the captain that he felt the two officers should get at least two days off without pay. The captain actually clicked his heels before he walked humbly out of the office.

After the traffic captain left his office the chief closed the door and called the Detective Division to speak with Calabrini. When the Detective Lieutenant was on the

275

phone, the chief told him about the motor cops and gave him their names. He suggested that Calabrini check them both out carefully, to see where they were when the murders were committed and if either one had a possible motive.

Calabrini hung up the phone and held his head in his hands until Springfield, who was sitting at his desk, asked him what was wrong. He told her. She got up to get him a cup of coffee, patting him on the arm as she walked by.

When she came back with the coffee, he was hanging up the phone again. He looked at her and said, 'Just got confirmation from the lab on those patches. They're still waiting for the report from the FBI, but they're telling me now that all three of the patches found in the dead guy's mouths were new. In other words, they had never been sewn onto a shirt. When uniform shirts are issued, the patch is already sewn on. Both shoulders.'

Rocky nodded her head. Calabrini went on, 'But they keep extra patches down in the supply room, in case somebody gets a new jacket or an old patch gets torn off or something.'

Rocky nodded again.

Calabrini sipped some of the coffee. Then he pinched his nose. 'So this afternoon, how about you going down there and checking with whoever is in charge – and all the people who work there, all the shifts. Find out where the new patches are kept, how accessible they are, how many are missing, the whole thing. Someone got a bunch of new patches, and that's probably where they came from. I doubt it they keep an actual piece-by-piece count of an item like that, but ask them, anyway.'

Springfield stood up, her notebook in hand. Calabrini said, 'I guess it would have been too easy for us if the killer had actually ripped a patch off his uniform shirt, huh? Then we could at least match the thread ends. It would have been too easy.'

Rocky nodded, gave him a small smile, and walked away.

That same afternoon it was business as usual in the Internal Investigation Unit. They had a visit from attorney Jeff Bottle. He came in representing his client, one Harvey Jensen, who had been arrested recently by a patrolman named McShaun. Bottle told the officers in the unit that Jensen was contesting the criminal charges, of course, and that he, Bottle, was there to file a formal complaint against McShaun and the police department on behalf of his client. The complaint stated that McShaun had stopped Jensen only to harass him, that McShaun had violated Jensen's rights in several places, that McShuan actually planted the alleged cocaine on Jensen before the backup officer, Hammer, got there, and that McShaun physically 'roughed up' his client before he took him to jail. Bottle also told the investigators that it was his opinion, and one that he would include for the benefit of the chief, or a judge if it came to that, that McShaun did all of this to Jensen because McShaun was good friends with ex-officer Hummel, and because Jensen was one of those falsely accused by Hummel after he arrested that girl, Lydia Taylor. The whole thing was bad, said Bottle, and now McShaun had planted dope on his client to further the harassment. A lawsuit was being seriously considered.

The Internal Affairs officers sighed, took down the complaint, and assured Mr Bottle that the matter would be investigated diligently and that the chief would be notified.

After the attorney walked out of the office and down the hallway, the lieutenant in charge of the Internal Affairs Unit, a good man trying to do a hard job, swore tightly and swept all the papers and pens, memos, and in and out boxes off his desk and onto the floor. Then he sat there for a long time, breathing deeply and staring at the wall.

Lydia Taylor waited in her sports car, sipping a diet cola. She was parked in the shade of a huge oak tree in a well-groomed, historically rich, and pleasantly quaint cemetery near South Miami Road, in the southeast part of the city. She thought of what had happened yesterday evening and of what she was ready to do.

Lydia's life-style precluded trappings of permanence wherever she lived, but still there were some things that she wanted to pack in preparation for her move. She had been sorting shoes and clothes, cleaning hanger bags, and straightening out makeup kits when Harv Jensen pushed his way into her apartment, a little high and a lot agitated.

He told her that he and the attorney, Bottle, had decided to use the same attack against the police that she had when she so stupidly got busted. They hadn't talked it over with Odom or Beachwood; they were going ahead on their own. They felt that if it worked so well for her, it would work as well for him. She had listened, not really caring.

She had started caring, however, when Jensen grabbed her by the hair and threw her down on her bed, telling her that he wanted her to follow up on her good performance of before. He and Bottle wanted her to go into the Internal Investigation Unit and 'muddy up the waters' again. She could say she knew that cop, McShaun, was good buddies with the other one, Hummel. She could say she knew the cops were going to set up Jensen. She could say all these things and help old Harv out, or he could take the pair of pliers he held in front of her nose and he could rip her nipples off.

She had promised to help him in any way she could, talking to him as if he were a friend, laughing with him, assuring him that she was on his side all the way.

After he left, she had continued to pack, but while she did, she thought about the whole thing. She decided she didn't like the part she played in it at all. She decided the people she felt the best about in the whole thing were the cops. That Officer Hummel was really sweet, and truly, *hadn't* he just been doing his job? They had forced her to hurt him, it had worked, and she didn't like the way she felt inside about it.

And now there was another one, another cop who was just doing his job, and they were getting ready to mess him up and they wanted her to help. Hell, she had been secretly laughing her head off when she learned that the tough and mighty Harv Jensen had been arrested and taken to jail in broad daylight by a uniformed cop for possessing cocaine. What a dumb ass. She decided she liked the cop even though

278

she had never met him. She decided, even though she was still getting the hell out of Lauderdale, that she would help the cop – or at least warn him.

McShaun had been irritated by the dispatcher's call. He was to meet a subject on the old Everglades Cemetery. No reference, no description other than female. Typical. Send you off somewhere in your squad car with just enough info to get you killed. He had swung by the cemetery once, seen the sport car, saw no one else around, and drove in slowly and parked under the same tree.

Lydia smiled and said, 'Thank you for coming, Officer McShaun.'

McShaun looked her over carefully, pulled off his sunglasses, and said, 'Lydia . . . right?'

'Right. And I wouldn't blame you if you took your night-stick or baton or whatever you call it and hit me right in the kisser. I know you're good friends with Chick Hummel – he told me.'

He waited.

'Look, I know I hurt him. I know I lied. I know I did bad things.' She ran her fingers through her hair. 'Did I cause him trouble with his wife? I really hated them for making me call her at her home like that.'

McShaun sighed and said, 'Things were a little tense for a while for them, I guess, until he explained to her just who – and what – you are. They have a strong relationship, though, so you didn't hurt them that much. On the home front, anyway.'

Lydia looked down at her legs and asked, 'And what am I, Officer McShaun?'

McShaun's eyes shone brightly as he looked into hers and said, 'You're a whore.'

Lydia just watched him.

'You're a whore, Lydia. Not in the standard sense of sex for money, although I guess I can't really say about that. I mean, you're a whore because you sold yourself to save yourself. They said they'd hurt you or disfigure you or kill you maybe, and you gave Chick away.'

She was silent, digesting what he said. Finally she said, 'Guilty. Harv Jensen likes to play with pliers, know what I mean? Those tool things – like pincers. He grabs parts of your body and he squeezes until you cry, and he'll rip pieces of you away if you don't agree to what he wants. I like myself, McShaun. I like how I look and how I attract men. It's important to me. I don't want parts of my body ripped off by a pair of pliers. So I'm guilty. I'm a whore. I tried to save myself and I had to hurt your friend in order to do it.'

They sat looking at each other, neither one saying anything. The cemetery became very quiet, almost still, as if the permanent residents there were poised, waiting to hear what was said next.

Lydia sighed and said quietly, 'And now I'm doing it again – or I'm supposed to, anyway. Let me ask you something: Tom Odom and Sam Beachwood. Those names mean anything to you? Okay. Them and Jensen and that city creep, Giles. I know they're going to kill me . . . soon. I'm going to disappear forever. Before it happens, though, I'm supposed to do one more thing. I'm supposed to come in and back up Jensen's complaint against you. I'm supposed to say that you and Hummel bought that cocaine from me and then planted it on poor Harv.'

She smiled then, and even though he was consumed by the conversation, he understood immediately that she was very female and capable of reminding him of it easily.

'But guess what, Tim McShaun? This little whore isn't going to do what they want this time. Pliers or no pliers, I'm not going in with that attorney to complain against you, and I'm not going to let them kill me, either. Today, right after this meeting with you, in fact, I'm outta here. I'm gone. I'm going to a real fun town out West. I've been promised a job and all the protection I'll need. I'll be working for a group of very serious guys – a lot of long Italian names, know what I mean? I'll do what they want, have some fun, and they'll take care of me.' She made a small face at him. ' 'Course, you could say I'm just jumping out of the frying pan and into the fire and all, but hey, any port in a storm. And please, McShaun, don't try to tell me about police protection and all that. We both know that's not good enough, right?'

McShaun wasn't going to tell her about police protection, but he nodded, anyway.

'So, anyway, Officer McShaun, there it is. Hummel was very right about Odom and Beachwood and the others and the cocaine and the movies with those young girls and all of it. They forced me to hurt Hummel, and now they want me to do the same to you. And I'm leaving here forever, I don't like myself for what I did to Chick, and I just wanted you to see my face as I said it.'

He stared at her for a moment and said, 'Be careful, Lydia.' He got into his car. She watched as he backed out from under the tree and slowly drove away. Then she shrugged, started her own car, and drove off into her future.

As McShaun hit the streets again he remembered that he had almost said 'Good luck' to Lydia before he drove off. He shook his head. Lydia would take care of herself; her kind did. And she would survive – probably.

Chapter Twenty-Four

FBI Agent Stan Matthews sat at his desk in the Miami office and read over his reports on the Lavon situation. He had made a decision, his bosses had approved it, and he was preparing to implement it. He sat back and thought to himself, Wonder what old Calabrini would think of this one?

They had good 'work' information on Congressman Lavon being involved with a drug and porno ring. This meant they had enough to work the case but probably not enough at this time to do any prosecuting. Time was needed to build a case against Lavon that would stand up in court. Time, and more investigation and paperwork, and that was the problem. He knew time was running out. Things up in Lauderdale were starting to get crazy. They had those killings going on, that jerk Jensen had been busted, Tom Odom had flown down to Grand Cayman twice in the last week, and that attorney, Beachwood, hadn't been in his office for days.

He checked his watch, straightened his tie, and looked out the window onto the bustling Miami River. There were inhouse pressures too. Cocaine smuggling was a hot item, and if a bust could be made, then the bosses wanted it made. Porno was always a good one, of course. The syndicate would be involved and there was a lot of noise nowadays about child abuse and child porn, so it was definitely an agency target.

So, which would be more profitable? To work long and hard to nail a junior congressman on a shaky case and risk charges of entrapment and a big media hassle and in the process lose touch with the actual porn and drug dealings? Or maybe approach the young congressman with the info about how he was selling updated radar interdiction charts to the bad guys, shake him up, and get him to see that it would be infinitely better to work *with* the good guys – better legally and better career-wise. Matthews knew a guy like Lavon would take one look at the FBI proposal and instantly admit that he was, in fact, on his own initiative, investigating a drug smuggling ring. He knew Lavon would stand proudly and describe for the cameras and judges how he, at great personal risk, decided to covertly infiltrate a drug ring and pass the information he learned from them to the FBI, which, of course, had monitored the entire operation. Lavon could be a hero, get reelected, and someday be Speaker of the House or something. And the FBI could nail the crap out of a nice little group of scumbags – with good, sticky charges.

Matthew's expression was composed as he put all the papers into his expensive briefcase. And, he told himself, young Congressman Lavon would join the long list of elected officials who would always support the efforts of the good old FBI.

Lieutenant John Calabrini called a meeting of his detectives on the patch murders. After everyone was in the captain's office and settled down, he began. 'Okay, I want to form three teams. Each team will have four detectives assigned, one team per victim, right? Bill Morris, your people will concentrate on Lorenzo Walker's unplanned departure.'

The smallish veteran detective with the friendly, beat-up face nodded. Calabrini went on. 'Stillwater, your team will work the child molester, Toreen. Incidentally, I know you had the creep figured for the murder of that five-year-old girl before anyone else.'

Stillwater shrugged, and Calabrini continued, 'And, Deavers, you get your people working on the Nails case.' He paused, cleared his throat, and said evenly, 'And listen, people . . . each team will be working their own homicide but with the thought in mind that there is a common killer, so info learned should be passed back and forth. Also remember that there is no clear picture yet of the suspect. We're still considering the possibility that he may be a cop.'

The big detective, Stillwater, ran one scarred hand through his disheveled hair and said quietly, 'Lieutenant, I wouldn't want to work this case if I really thought the killer was a cop.'

There were nods all around and mumblings of agreement.

Calabrini spoke harshly. 'We're considering *both*. The teams will work their victims, and all of the gathered info and observations will then be passed to me and to Springfield, here, for evaluation and consolidation. That way we'll cover the entire spectrum. But get this: This is a *homicide* case; three, actually. There's a killer out there. How many of you swinging dicks thinks we've seen the last body, huh? And how many of you have considered the fact that whoever this person is, they've stepped over a line that will be impossible for them to step back across? *Now* the killer is justified because he's killing documented scumbags . . . hurrah. So how far is it for him to take the next step and kill *suspected* bad guys or maybe just people *he* thinks need to be killed? Hear what I'm saying? Sure, it's exciting to think that this guy is some homicidal Robin Hood, ridding our town of the baddies, but he's *still* a killer, and he's trashing our laws, and he's taunting us all with his goddamn patches, and if any of you don't think you can work this case like any other and bust this guy when you put it together, then let me know now and you can get your asses back down to patrol.'

Silence.

Calabrini looked at the faces watching him, a good team of people and he knew it. 'Look, I'm tense about this damn case, too, and I don't like it any more than you people. But we've got to work it like professionals.' He nodded at Springfield.

Rocky checked her notes and said, 'You all know by now that the patches left at the scenes are new, never attached to clothing. So far none of us has been able to link the three victims in any way other than the fact that they all had records and all were actively being considered as suspects in murder and rape cases. We have a sketchy description of a dark vehicle – period. And of a "figure", probably male, wearing dark clothing and "moving like a soldier".' She looked up from her notes. 'Witness statements and the scenes themselves indicate a killer who is very much in control of himself; there's no panic, no hurry. He leaves no evidence other than the patch and footprints, which I'll get to in a minute. He took with him whatever he strangled Walker with, he wore gloves when he did Toreen, and he took the time to bend down and collect the shotgun shells off the ground after shooting Nails. This is not some hyper wacko running around killing people. This guy knows exactly what he's doing, and he does it well.'

She wiped a film of perspiration off her brow, then rubbed her fingers together. 'The ME says there were traces of black shoe polish on the side of Toreen's skull. We've got photos of matching boot prints from the first and second scenes. The lab tells us now that the pattern on the boots suggests they're a military type, possibly those "jungle boots" from the Vietnam era.' She looked up again and blew a stray lock of hair from her eyes. ' 'Course, every army-navy and sporting-goods store in the world sells that type of boot to the general public, so trying to trace them through a purchaser would be next to impossible, especially since the lab guys say the soles are worn, indicating that the boots are old. The only good thing about it is, if we get a suspect and find those boots on him and the pattern on the soles matches those at the scenes, at least we can put him there.' Rocky nodded to Calabrini.

Calabrini said, 'Thanks, Rocky. All right, people. You've got it. Organize your teams and go to work. Needless to say, this is an around-the-clock deal now. My desk is the command post, and I'll take any pertinent info there or at home anytime.'

Everyone stood to leave. Stillwater said, 'Did you guys

hear about the fracas down in briefing earlier today?'

They all waited.

The big detective wore a sly grin as he said, 'Seems like about a dozen of the patrol people came to work today wearing only one shoulder patch on their uniform shirts. The brass didn't notice it at first, but when they finally did and started collaring guys and asking them what was going on, all the patrol types had the same answer: "Gee, is there a patch missing? Wonder where I left it?" '

The killer stood in the quiet room and looked at himself in the mirror. He met the reflection of his own eyes, and he challenged himself: leave the immediate, physical, judicial arguments aside for a moment and talk about the big picture. Or do you believe in the big picture?

Yes.

Okay, then, if there is a big picture, then there are the laws of God. What about them? What about that one big commandment that you learned as a child? What about the killing?

Never mind the sin part. That's no problem, there are a lot of sins committed in this lifetime. What makes killing a special sin is that it's one of those sins that means death – real death, forever death. So what about the justice thing, then? Same old argument. Everything happens in this world for a reason; even though we see unfairness and a terrible lack of justice, we must believe that justice does prevail somewhere down the line.

So, I'm just not waiting. I see what must be done and I'm doing it.

And so, in the end, somewhere down the line, you will suffer real death, forever death, because during this lifetime you have knowingly and purposely taken the lives of others . . . the lives of your brothers. Who are you to make such a decision?

I am me . . . I am right . . . I know what must be done.

Where's your faith? Where's your belief in the One that has a reason for everything? Where's your knowledge that

286

all of the world's injustices will someday be made right by Him?

The killer again looked at himself in the mirror. He was not afraid, and he had no doubts.

I believe in Him and what He does.

And I believe in me and what I am doing.

The evening shift for the Fort Lauderdale Police Department came and went, pretty much like any evening shift. There were some traffic accidents, one bad one; several disturbances, all of them involving at least one person who was drunk; and many reports of thefts. The Patrol Division did its thing out on the streets, and a skeleton detective crew did the follow-ups on the regular backlog of cases. Most of the detectives were assigned to the patch murders. They spent the shift compiling and comparing information and looking for the hidden witnesses they knew had to be out there, or maybe hoped would be out there. The evening shift ended at midnight without any real progress being made by any of the divisions.

It was a little after midnight when Harvey Jensen came back to his town house apartment in the southeast section of Lauderdale. He was in a foul mood. He had been called earlier by an overbearing Odom, who had insisted it was time to watch Lydia every minute; they couldn't be certain their threats would keep her in line any longer. Odom had told Jensen to go over to Lydia's place, get her, take her back to his town house, and keep her there. Then they'd decide whether to go ahead and get rid of her permanently. Jensen had hung up the phone without telling Odom that he didn't mind keeping Lydia at his place until they were finished with her, but he *did* mind getting rid of her before she went in and did her thing with the Internal Affairs guys. Harv Jensen was very much worried about the charges against him and he wanted them gone.

He had driven his Porsche to Lydia's place and knocked on the door. After a few minutes of silence he got a funny

287

feeling in his gut, broke in, and saw that she was gone. He had left there, cursing, and had driven around Lauderdale to all the places she liked to hang out, to apartment buildings where he knew she had friends – every place he thought she might be. He didn't find her, and as the night wore on, he knew she had taken off. She was gone from the area. He had shrugged his shoulders; that was all right. It would be a little harder to find her, that's all. And when they did find her, and they would, he would make her cry a lot before she died.

He tried to call Odom from a pay phone, got no answer, and went home.

Harv Jensen unlocked his front door and walked into the living room of his split-level town house apartment. The place seemed cold, even to him. He turned on the lights and went into the kitchen for a beer. He opened the can and took a long pull and headed to the upper level to go to the bathroom and change into a pair of shorts. He set the can of beer down on an end table in his bedroom, took off his shoes, shirt, and pants, and went into the bathroom. He was sitting on the toilet, thinking about Lydia, when the killer appeared, standing in the bathroom doorway, looking down at him.

Jensen tensed, said, 'You!' and got ready to stand up. He was tough, he was in shape, he knew how to fight and liked to fight, and he was now fueled by fear and anger. His antagonism was fueled by a burning desire to destroy his target.

As Jensen's leg muscles drove him up, the killer kicked him, hard, in the chest. Jensen grunted, and his back hit the ceramic toilet, but he started up again, his hands reaching out for the killer. He was almost to his feet when the killer hit him twice, from the left and from the right, with his gloved hands, striking him hard on the edges of the throat.

Jensen felt himself going down again, and he felt acute fear.

He struggled to clear his head and get his footing. He grunted as he managed to grab the killer's left hip with his right hand. His fingers dug into his assailant's side as the killer stepped back, reached behind him, and, with his right hand, pulled out a large pair of shining metal pliers.

Jensen's eyes widened, and he felt his mouth go dry.

The man swung his arm, gripping the heavy tool, and hit Jensen in the left side of the head. Jensen twisted and fell onto the tile floor, beside the toilet. He lay there, breathing hard, trying to figure out what to do.

The killer jumped into the air and came down onto Jensen's left ankle, breaking it with a bone-crunching noise. Jensen gasped and tried to sit up. When he did, he felt his assailant's gloved hand grab him by the hair and pull him out from beside the toilet. He felt his attacker's full strength, saw the glint of the pliers in front of his eyes, and felt terror.

He looked up at the killer and pleaded, 'Please . . .'

His assailant looked down at him, held the pliers in his gloved fist with the pincers closed, and swung them at Jensen's head with all of his might. The tool made a sickening sound as it impacted against the side of Jensen's skull, cutting skin and cracking bone. Jensen reeled, stunned, and the killer hit him again, and then again, harder each time, until finally the pliers hit the bloodied side of the head and penetrated through the shattered bone, deep into the skull, and into the core of Jensen's brain.

Jensen screamed, a long scream, a terrified, horrible, dying scream of helplessness and fury, but it came out as a sickening, dry rasping gasp. His body stiffened; his heels pounded on the tile floor. And then he was dead.

The assailant stood bending over the body for a moment, holding up the head with his left hand while he pried his gloved fingers off the handles of the pliers. He left the tool buried in the dead man's skull.

The killer stood for a few seconds, breathing steadily. Then he reached into his pocket, pulled out a patch, bent down, and stuck it into Jensen's grimacing mouth.

Then he went through the apartment, taking his time, looking, searching, finding what he was after here and there, hidden away in all the usual places. When he had an armload, he went back upstairs to the body and emptied his arms.

Before he left, the assailant took one last look at the body of Harvey Jensen, lying twisted on the tile floor of the bathroom, in between the toilet and the wall, jockey shorts down around the ankles, the pliers sticking out of the skull, the patch in the mouth, the rest of the body covered with money, several ounces of cocaine, and dozens of photos of him with young girls. The photos were all pornographic. Many of them showed his 'Who Me?' tattoo clearly.

The killer walked out of the apartment and let himself be swept back into Fort Lauderdale's night. He had one more thing to do before he went home.

Chapter Twenty-Five

Early the next morning Jeff Bottle threw the sheet and summer blanket off his pudgy body with a grunt and swung his feet until they hit the carpeted bedroom floor. He sat there for a moment, rubbing his face and running his fingers through his hair. Then he reached for his glasses lying on the nightstand, stood up scratching himself, and walked into the bathroom stretching. His mind was already starting to go over the things he had scheduled for the day; his small law practice was busier than ever, and he felt good about it.

His bare feet hit the cold of the tile on the bathroom floor, and he bent over to lift the lid on the toilet – and then stopped and stared. Suddenly he no longer felt the need to relieve himself. He reached slowly with one outstretched hand to touch what was lying on the toilet lid and then pulled it back after determining that it was real. He felt the sweat break out on his forehead, his stomach tightened, and his breath grew short. He straightened and looked around, his eyes wide. He went back into the bedroom, over to the glass sliding doors leading out to the patio and pool, saw that they were locked, and hurried downstairs. Nothing was disturbed; both the rear kitchen door and the front door were shut and locked. He stood in his living room, puzzled – and scared.

Whoever left those things on his toilet had to have been in his house during the night, and whoever he was, he had walked right past him, as he slept in his bed, at least twice. He felt panic as he hurried back up the stairs and returned to the bathroom to look at what had been left there—and to try to understand their meaning.

He leaned against the sink and forced himself to look very closely. There were two objects there. One was a color Polaroid photo of a naked Harvey Jensen kneeling behind what appeared to be a young girl, also naked. The girl's face was turned away from the camera, but it was obvious that Jensen had entered her, and he was holding a can of beer and grinning. Bottle was slightly repelled by the photo; it looked so . . . so stark. His hand trembled slightly as he picked up the other object lying beside the photo and examined it closely.

It was a Fort Lauderdale Police Department uniform patch.

Lieutenant John Calabrini hung up the phone and looked again at Rocky Springfield. She sat at another desk, going through a large file, her head propped up on one hand while the other slowly turned over the papers. He was busy, but he permitted himself to enjoy watching her for a moment. He had to admit to himself that he took pleasure in being around her. She excited him and challenged him, and he knew he was becoming attracted to her in a way that would eventually have to lead either to a serious effort to win her or a serious effort to keep it strictly business. That damn Tim McShaun . . . Oh, he could never feel genuine anger at Tim, but he could feel jealousy.

Calabrini shook his head as Rocky stood up and walked toward him. He knew that if he had the chance, he would make damn sure that she knew he wanted her around. If ol' Timmy McShaun relaxed his hold on her, even for one minute . . .

'Excuse me, John. I wanted to suggest something.'

He forced himself back to reality, motioned to the chair in front of his desk, and said with a grin, 'Sure, Rocky. What do you have?'

She ran her fingers through her hair and looked up at the ceiling. 'I've been going over what we have, and if we go with the possibility that the killer is a cop, I have a direction we might want to think about.'

He straightened up and looked at her, all business now.

'Maybe getting up early and coming in here with the day shift has my brain going a little better.' She smiled. 'But here's what I thought: So far, the only witnesses we have say our killer looks like a male, acts calm, and moves like a soldier. We have some boot prints that appear to have been made with a military-type boot. We have a killer who stalks his victim, makes his hit, and leaves almost nothing behind. We have a killer who's strong and apparently fast, and who seems to have some knowledge of personal combat, like martial arts. All of this suggests to me some type of military background.'

Calabrini watched her closely, his brow creased.

'So, John, what I'm thinking is that we could go back to all of the personnel records for all of the men working here and check to see which ones have a military background. When they're hired by the city, they have to provide copies of their discharge papers and medical records, right?'

He leaned forward and made a note, saying, 'Right. It wouldn't be all-conclusive, but it sure as hell would be a place to start. Who knows? Maybe we can go through the records and see which men are better candidates, which ones have special combat training or experience or whatever . . .'

He looked at her with approval. 'Good idea for a new kid. How'd you come up with it?'

She hesitated, and he could see a cloud of mixed emotions cover her expression fleetingly. She bit her lip and then said quietly, 'I don't know. I've just been thinking about the whole thing. What the killer is doing is so radically different from anything we normally see here – know what I mean? I started thinking that the killer is repeating something he must have learned while he was a soldier doing things as if he's a military person involved in a war environment. Only now he's doing them here, in our city.'

Calabrini watched her as she continued, 'He could be deadly. He learned how to wage war and how to soldier and how to play for keeps, then he comes home with that in him and he becomes a cop, learning street combat and surveillance and all the rest. Now he's combining the two. He knows how to move through our streets as a cop, and he knows how to kill as a soldier.' She stopped and looked into Calabrini's eyes.

Calabrini was silent for a long time, leaning back in his chair, thinking about what she had said. She could be right on the money, and he was respectful of the way she had thought it out. Finally he said, 'Okay, we'll get started on it. I'll get some of the men to help. Maybe it won't be so difficult. Over half of the Records Division is computerized now. Oh, and since I very much agree with what you say about the war and combat experience, we can tell them that we especially want to look over those files of guys who served in Korea and Vietnam.'

Rocky went back to her desk, leaving Calabrini making phone calls down to the Records Division. She sat down and, staring at the papers on her desk without seeing them, thought about it all.

Was it possible that she already knew who the killer was, and all of her work and bright investigatory ideas were but a sad charade?

Was it possible that she would be instrumental in bringing the net down on the killer, only to confirm those chilling whispers in her heart?

Could she do it?

Calabrini was the only one who noticed how pale Springfield was when she suddenly stood up from her desk and hurried out of the Detective Division. He lost sight of her as she went out into the hallway, and he couldn't know that she had run into the ladies' room at the end of the hall.

She was very much alone as she stood over the toilet, waiting to vomit, feeling the bile rise in her throat. She stood there for a long time, shaking slightly, until her stomach finally settled. She washed her face with cold water and then stood looking into the mirror, seeing the questions in her eyes.

She was still there, staring, when she heard Calabrini's voice calling her name. She went out into the hallway to find the lieutenant, holding her purse and notebook, a grim look on his face.

'We've got another one, Rocky' was all he said.

The woman from the realtor's office was waiting for them outside the town house. With her was a uniformed police officer and a road sergeant. They both nodded when Calabrini and Springfield arrived. Before they went into the town house, Calabrini asked the woman, who appeared very upset, to tell him why she was there and how her discovery had come about.

She looked at him, wiped her nose with a tissue, and began, 'Well, these town houses are all leased, this whole section of them. At the same time they're for sale, and our office represents the owner in those sales. So we have the keys and we have permission – goes with the lease, actually – to use the keys to enter and show the town houses when we have a customer.' She stopped and held her chest for a moment, then continued. 'This . . . this particular town house had a little note with the key, see here? It was because the man who rented it said that he would only let us show it when we gave him advance notice, and when he was there. It's not that unusual, really. When people lease property, they still like to have some control over it. Anyway, this morning when I opened my office – I'm the early girl – there was this attorney there waiting for me. I'm pretty sure I've seen him with the man that lives here, uh, lived here—.' She stopped again. They waited. She took a deep breath. 'He showed me his card. His name was Bottle. He seemed very agitated, almost rude, actually. Said he *had* to check inside the town house. I told him I wasn't sure I could do that since he wasn't looking to buy and I hadn't made previous arrangements with the tenant, uh, Mr . . . Jenner?'

The patrolman shrugged, but the road sergeant said, 'Jensen, ma'am.'

Calabrini and Springfield looked at each other.

The woman said, 'Yes, that's it. Jensen. We have so many people in and out of here during the year, you see. Well, he, the lawyer, he became very insistent. Said it could be a matter of life or death. So I said, then we should call the police, but he just got more excited and said there was no time for that. Finally I gave in, and he followed me over here, and we knocked real loud several times and rang the bell, but there was no answer, so I . . . I used the key. And we went in.'

She blew her nose, said, 'Excuse me,' took off her glasses and wiped her eyes, and then looked at Rocky. 'I'm sorry I'm not doing too well here this morning. It's just so – terrible. I'm not used to it.'

They waited, Calabrini unconsciously tapping one foot on the pavement.

'So we went inside, the attorney calling out the man's name. It was very quiet. I waited downstairs while this Bottle person went upstairs to where the bedroom and bath are. After a few seconds I heard him gasp, and then he came flying down the stairs with a wild look on his face, sweating and puffing and terribly upset. I tried to make him tell me what was wrong, but he just stood there – like whining. He looked terrified, and I guess it scared me because all I wanted to do was leave and call you, the police. But when I said that's what I was going to do, he grabbed me and told me he was leaving – he said "*really* leaving" – and then he shoved these into my hands and ran out the door. I could hear his car motor roaring as he left.'

She handed the Polaroid photo and the patch to Springfield, saying, 'The picture is filthy, and that other thing is one of those patches that the news has been full of lately, isn't it?'

The police officers surrounding her all nodded.

'After he was gone, I went upstairs. I don't know why. I . . . I wish I hadn't now. Anyway, I did, and I saw that man laying up there like that – naked and dead – and I got sick, then ran out, finally called your headquarters, and here we are. And I think I'm going to be sick again if I can't get some cold water or something.'

Calabrini patted her arm and said, 'You've done great so

far. Try to relax now. We'll call your office and have someone come over here to be with you. We're going to have you spend some time with us, but you won't need to go back inside. Can you tell me if the attorney, this Bottle, told you anything about the patch and photo he handed you?'

She looked at him blankly, then brightened and said, 'Yes, yes, he did. I'm sorry, I forgot. He handed them to me and said he found them this morning when he awoke. He found them in *his* bathroom. And then he said he was leaving.'

Springfield sat in the passenger seat of Calabrini's unmarked car while the lieutenant drove through the midday traffic. They were on their way to Jeff Bottle's home address. They had called his office and had learned from his secretary that Mr Bottle wouldn't be in today. After some coaxing, the secretary admitted that something strange was going on. Mr Bottle had called in, had been almost irrational, and had told her to cancel all of his appointments and tell anyone looking for him that he was out of town.

Springfield was quiet, still getting over the shock of what she had seen at the town house. The body looked so . . . without dignity . . . lying there with the underwear crumpled around the ankles. The skin looked like wax, making the 'Who Me?' tattoo stand out starkly, while parts of the skin had already turned dark blue and purple. The powdery cocaine and Polaroid pictures scattered over the body had an almost artistic effect, setting off the spatters of blood, the tile floor, and the ceramic toilet bowl. The worst part had been that thing sticking out of the skull. And the expression on the face of the dead man – anger, terror, helplessness, agony – all stretching the skin and baring the teeth.

And, of course, the patch.

She was sickened by what she had seen. It was the end product, she knew, of what had been an incredibly violent encounter. She had no trouble imagining the terrible, physical, raw power that had been required to kill him that way, but she did have trouble understanding what it

297

would take mentally for someone to go through with it.

She pictured Jensen's violated body lying on that tile floor, and she knew in her heart that the person who killed him was like a monster, an aberration. Someone who inhabited a form like other men but who, inside, was really like no other man she knew.

Then she questioned what she had just thought, and it scared her even more.

They pulled into the driveway of Jeff Bottle's home and saw him carrying two suitcases out the front door, heading for his car. He stopped when they got out of their car, dropped the bags, and ran back into his house, slamming the door. They looked at each other and then approached the door and knocked. First there was no answer, and then the door opened a little and Bottle said, 'Go away.'

Calabrini said, 'Just a couple of questions, Mr Bottle. Then we'll leave you alone.'

'Leave me alone now. Please, just leave me alone.'

The door started to close, and Rocky said gently, 'Let us help you, Mr Bottle. Let us help you, and maybe you can help us and eventually help everyone.'

The door closed, then swung open, and they walked in.

They left an hour later, after going over the entire incident with Bottle and after having a crime-scene team go over his house. They came up with nothing: no footprints, no glove prints, nothing. Bottle wasn't even sure he had locked all the doors before he went to bed, although they were all locked in the morning. He could tell them very little about Jensen's schedule the night before, because in truth he knew very little about Jensen. The murdered man had been referred by another attorney, Sam Beachwood, and he was trying to represent his client, that's all. He was just trying to do his job. He didn't notice how Calabrini and Springfield looked at each other when he mentioned the referring attorney's name.

Bottle became insistent then, demanding to know what was being done about this murder and demanding to know if he was on some police 'hit list'. He would take them to court, he would file suit, he would do a lot of legal things to make them leave him alone. He stopped when he saw how they looked at him, and then he started sobbing.

He was terrorized.

He wanted to be able to reach into his briefcase, into his trusty bag of legal tricks, and defend himself. He wanted to be able to take some action – some writ, perhaps – or an order to show cause. He wanted there to be some orderly, defined, intellectual legal action to be taken.

Calabrini and Springfield remained silent, and Bottle understood that what he feared was something that all of his training and schooling and experience and professionalism could not defend him from. He understood, with utter clarity, that the person who left the patch for him operated in an environment that was totally alien to him and one in which he was totally helpless.

Before they left, he informed them that he was leaving the city, the state – immediately. It was irrational, it was not well thought out, it was a knee-jerk reaction to his terror, and he knew it. But he was leaving.

Calabrini and Springfield drove back to the station in silence, each one caught up in their own private thoughts.

Phyllis Green of the *Herald* was waiting for them when they parked their car in the rear lot. Calabrini preferred not to avoid reporters; he felt it was better to give them what you could, as long as it was accurate. He introduced her to Rocky, who nodded coolly.

Green opened her notebook and said, 'A pair of pliers? Dope and porno pictures scattered all over the body? What kind of maniac are we dealing with here? A real sicko, I guess.'

Calabrini started to say something but was cut off by Rocky, who surprised him by blurting out, 'Did you stop to think, Miss Green, that whoever killed Jensen may have scattered those things on his body as a message, a sign to others who deal in dope and pornography?'

Green's eyes were bright. 'And the patch, Officer Spring-field? The patch was there too. That's a sign too. Right?'

Rocky was silent.

Green continued. 'I understand that your investigation is leaning toward the probability that the killer is a male, isn't that right? And you're still considering the possibility that he's not a cop, although all of the evidence so far points to it? And how about the pliers?'

Calabrini spoke up. 'As far as we can tell, the killer used a pair of pliers that he found in the victim's toolbox. As for the other things you mentioned, we're still open to various possibilities.'

'What about the fact that this man, Jensen, was one of the names involved in that Hummel affair? And isn't it a fact that an officer named McShaun – an officer who has killed before several times, on duty – recently arrested the victim on narcotics charges? And hasn't the victim's attorney already been in to your Internal Affairs Unit claiming that the dope was planted on his client and threatened to bring charges against McShaun and the city? Wouldn't that make McShaun and Hummel suspects in this murder?'

Where does this woman get her info? thought Calabrini as he said, 'Listen, you're coming up with some wild probabilities there, but to calm your doubts, hear this: We're working this homicide like we work all other homicides. Any and all suspects we come up with will be worked, and we will keep working until we find the killer, and at that time – whoever he is – we will stop him and prosecute him.'

He started to walk away and Springfield followed. They stopped as Green, loath to let it go, said with a smile, 'But isn't it true that the killer is sick? After what he did to Jensen, isn't it obvious to you that he's a mad dog, a twisted, per-verted maniac and, at the same time, could very well be a working police officer out on the streets of our town?'

Calabrini refused to acknowledge the question and abandoned the conversation by turning away. He was surprised again by Rocky's reaction.

Springfield's eyes were bright green as she pointed her

finger under Green's nose and said tightly, 'Consider this with all your "maniac and pervert", Green. Consider the possibility that the killer, whoever he is, has his own reasons for doing what he's doing and the way he's doing it. Consider the possibility that he is doing something that you – and maybe us, too – can't understand. You don't know if he's a cop, you don't know if it's a "he," you don't know if there's just one, and you don't know *why*. So why don't you wait, learn the truth, as we do, and print some facts for a change?'

Rocky turned and walked away, past Calabrini and into the rear of the station.

Phyllis Green just stood in the parking lot, smiling.

McShaun was 10-8, on the road, on duty. He was alert and aware of the feeling of the street and the tones over the radio. He felt the energy of the city and was comfortable in his role as a working cop. He had cleared a vandalism call and was back on patrol. The vandalism had been to the beautifully manicured front lawn of an elderly man's house south of State Road 84, near Little Yankee Stadium. McShaun had listened and shook his head as the man pointed out where someone had driven a car across the lawn, stopping in the middle to 'peel out', uprooting the sod and ripping out much of the sprinkler system. The man was aware that there wasn't much the police could do about it, but he was angry and wanted to make a report. As McShaun was leaving, the man told him that the next time he had to call the police it would be to show off all the pieces of car that would be in his yard, as he was going to bury strong steel rods, just long enough to do some real damage, in a nice grid all over his lawn. McShaun let the man get it off his chest, gave him the report number, and drove away.

As he cruised down a side street behind a large shopping center, McShaun saw two young teenage boys pushing a shopping cart full of household items. The two boys turned their heads as the patrol unit came alongside. Then, as McShaun looked at them, they both looked forward again, acting very cool.

McShaun called out the window, 'Hey, boys, hold up a minute, please.'

The boys stopped and stood very still, the smaller of the two holding onto the push-bar of the shopping cart. McShaun walked up and looked closely at the items in the cart. He saw a toaster, a small radio, an umbrella, two china vases, a wooden jewelry box, a framed picture of a sailboat, an adding machine, and a pair of reading glasses.

He looked at the boys and said, 'First of all, that shopping cart is valued at almost one hundred dollars, believe it or not, and you should not have taken it away from the shopping center.'

The larger of the two boys scuffed his shoe on the pavement and said, 'Uh, yeah, but we had all this stuff to carry.' The other boy nodded in agreement.

'So where did this stuff come from?' asked McShaun, folding his arms across his chest.

'My grandmother's,' said the older boy.

'The church's charity yard sale,' said the other.

McShaun sighed, unclipped the radio speaker from his shoulder, and held it close to his mouth. He did not press the transmit button as he said, 'Dispatcher, this is Alpha Five-One, cancel that lookout message for the two burglars from the South End. I've got them here. I'll bring them in for the detectives shortly.' He restuck the speaker to the Velcro patch on his shirt and waited.

The older boy spoke up first. 'It was *his* idea,' he said, pointing to his partner.

'Was not.'

'Was too.'

Fifteen minutes later McShaun had the stolen goods in his trunk, the shopping cart back in front of the grocery store, and the two kids in his backseat. He followed their directions back to the house they had broken into and arrived there just as the resident, a middle-aged working housewife, hung up the phone after calling the police.

McShaun was at the house for almost an hour. The woman decided not to press charges against the boys once they promised they would never do it again and once she knew that the Juvenile Division officers, who arrived at McShaun's request, would counsel the boys and notify the boys' parents of the situation.

McShaun made sure the boys observed him carefully writing their identifying information in his notebook, then he leaned into the backseat of the Juvenile Unit's car and said to them both, in a serious tone, 'You were lucky this time because this lady, who works hard for her living just like your parents, is a nice person and doesn't want you two to end up in Juvenile Detention Hall. But I'll remember who you are, and if I see you doing anything fishy in the future, your feet will never touch the ground. Got it?'

Both boys nodded vigorously. They did not see McShaun smile and wink at the Juvenile officers as he straightened and closed the car door.

He hit the road again and was dispatched to a 'suspicious incident'. An elderly woman wanted to report to him that someone had stolen all of her lawn furniture. McShaun had been there before. He carefully walked the woman around her house to the backyard and showed her that the furniture was still there. She was very pleased. He walked her back to her front door where they chatted for a few minutes, then he left her, promising to keep a close watch on her house every day.

The old woman smiled and waved as McShaun drove off, already responding to the next call that had come through on his radio.

The next day Springfield showed up at McShaun's apartment just as he came back, sweating and breathing hard, from a long run along the beach. They had spoken on the phone the evening before and had made plans to meet for breakfast, hoping to be able to spend some time together before they both went back to work and things got crazy again.

'Hey, lady. Perfect timing – except that I probably smell like the inside of an old shoe.'

She wrinkled her nose, kissed him lightly on the end of his, and said, 'I'll just stay upwind.'

He grinned as they went inside. He headed for his bedroom, saying over his shoulder, 'I'm gonna go ahead and get cleaned up. I'll take a good long shower so you don't have to worry about the wind at breakfast. Help yourself to anything you want.'

She smiled and said, 'If I helped myself to anything I want, you'd have help in the shower and we'd never get to breakfast.'

He was grinning as he disappeared into the bathroom.

Rocky played with Radar for a few minutes, then put hot water on for tea. She was a little angry with herself; she was here to have a nice breakfast with Tim, because their work schedules were so hectic lately that they might not be able to get together during the next couple of days. She was here to relax and enjoy herself. But there was something on her mind.

Something from her past with McShaun.

Something she had seen that bothered her then and nagged at her now. It wouldn't let her go. She had to pursue it, and she was afraid – afraid of breaking his trust by going uninvited into his memories, afraid of what she might find.

She heard the water in the bathroom sink stop running, and then the shower started up. She stepped through his bedroom door and stood next to the only closet in the apartment. It was a walk-in and served as a place for him to hang his clothes, store his tools and miscellaneous gear, and stack things when there wasn't room in the rest of the apartment.

She opened the door and looked inside. Hanging with the civilian clothes and police uniforms were parts of military fatigue uniforms, jungle blouses and pants, camouflage jackets. She knew that most men who had served in any of the military branches still had some parts of their old uniforms around and would wear them occasionally: navy pea coats, Marine running shorts, air force flight suits, army camouflage jackets.

On the floor, near the door, were Tim's boots. Jungle

boots with the green-cloth ankle parts and the lightweight, comfortable boot part. She knew he wore them all the time, shopping, walking, whatever, and she remembered him telling her once that they were probably the most comfortable pair of boots he had ever owned.

He had owned them for a long time.

She let her eyes move up to the shelves, looking for the box. She saw it, listened to the shower still running strongly, reached up on her toes, and pulled the box down. Inside were the albums. Quickly she pulled out of the box the one album she sought, put the box on the floor, and started going through the album, page by page.

She felt her breath get short, felt her face muscles tighten, saw that her fingers were shaking slightly as she let her eyes follow a young Tim McShaun through the ugliness and adventure, the violence and the camaraderie that was Vietnam. The photos were as she remembered them, stark and somehow cold. She knew it was ridiculous but couldn't rid herself of the feeling that the photos didn't like her staring at them, as if they knew why she was there and that she had no right to let her eyes see what the pictures had to show without Tim by her side. She tried to hurry.

Then she stopped.

She stopped and stood there holding the album, not looking at it. She struggled with herself, wanting to confirm what her memory told her was there, wanting to plunge on – on into Tim's past and the pictures he had skipped by so rapidly when he showed her the book. She wanted to force herself to look, to know the truth, *if* it could, in fact, be found there. The police officer in her told her that important answers could be found reflected in those old and angry photographs, that she needed to look, to see, to learn.

The lover in her told her to close the book, told her that the now was important, that the now was reality, not some faded images from another world, another lifetime. The lover won out over the police officer.

Her hands shook as she gently closed the album.

She heard the shower stop and Tim moving around in the

bathroom. She fumbled the album back into its box, set it up on the shelf, closed the door, and went out into the kitchen to find that her tea water had boiled away. She started some more and then waited for Tim as she stared out of the window.

They had a nice breakfast: quiet, kidding, and relaxed. If he noticed that she was a little more quiet than usual, he gave no sign. He found her looking at him intensely several times and kidded her about it. When he did, she smiled shyly and told him she was thinking of something else besides breakfast.

They parted with a kiss.

Chapter Twenty-Six

Rocky waited until the evening shift was half over, then she could wait no longer. She had the dispatcher set up a meeting between her and McShaun, who was riding solo out in the southwest part of town. It hadn't been that busy, and her hand-held radio was quiet as she drove toward the Mormon church where she and McShaun had met the TAC squad to set up the ambush for the ski-mask burglars, now so long ago.

Calabrini had not asked her any questions when she told him she needed to get away for a while. She had told him she probably wouldn't be gone that long, and she wasn't certain whether or not he knew she would be meeting McShaun.

She pulled in behind the church, under the huge oak trees, shut the motor off, got out, and stood in the shadows, waiting and thinking. She wasn't exactly sure what she wanted to say to McShaun. She just had a great need to see him.

She watched as his patrol car eased into the lot, the lights going out as it stopped in front of her car. She felt her chest tighten and her lips go dry as he jumped out, smiled, and walked toward her. She saw him standing in front of her, a friendly look on his face, and she didn't know whether to be afraid or happy or laugh or cry, or all of it. She stood there, a jumble of mixed emotions, and he stepped closer, took her in his arms, kissed her softly on the side of her neck, squeezed her, and said, 'Hey, lady, you look lovely tonight.'

She said, 'You look good, too, Tim. And it feels nice to be held.'

He let her go, stepped back, and looked at her at arm's length. He seemed relaxed, and he had a slightly amused, patient look on his face, as if he knew why she was there.

She found herself wishing things were simple. She looked into his eyes and wished life could be just the realization of their love.

But no.

She forced herself to stay on the surface, forced herself to pull back from his warmth. She was terrified of the end result, but she was determined, once and for all, to chart some kind of course for them . . . a direction, a definition. She wanted to know what was happening to them, where they were going. Even though she told him and herself that she didn't care about anything else, that she only wanted to be with him, deep inside she knew that wasn't good enough; deep inside she knew she had to have an answer one way or the other.

Her heart told her she already knew the answer, but she didn't want to hear it.

'So . . . what's going on, Tim?'

'Same old stuff. Just out here fighting crime, and vice versa. How about you?'

She sighed. 'That case is my whole life now, it seems. Guess you heard about the latest one, that guy you booked for cocaine, Jensen?'

McShaun nodded.

'His death was bad . . . ugly. It scared me. Even John was shaken by it, I could tell.'

'Any more information on the killer?'

She hesitated, then said, 'We're still considering the possibility that the killer is not a cop, but most of us believe he is. The first three victims were your basic grab bag of felons with no common denominator; at least, we don't have one yet. But Jensen, well, he was part of Hummel's thing, and you did just arrest him, and his lawyer was already threatening to sue the city. Guess you heard that the lawyer received a little greeting card, too, huh?'

McShaun nodded again, then tilted his head and asked her, 'Am I a suspect, Rocky?'

She studied his face closely to see what was behind his

308

smile. She saw no guile and said slowly, 'I guess you are, Tim, because of this Jensen thing. But, really, we *all* are in a way. Right now we're going with the working officers on the department who've had military training, because the killer supposedly moves like a soldier, and for . . . for other reasons.'

They stood silently for a few minutes, looking at each other. He took her hand and they were quiet. He turned and leaned against her car, and she stood close beside him. He slid his arm around her waist and pulled her close to his side. She could feel his warmth.

She thought he would keep asking case-related questions and was startled when he said, quietly, 'You know, Rocky, it will be difficult for anyone to keep up with what the killer is going to do next.'

She turned her head to look at him, but he looked down at his feet.

'What I mean is, unless a person could be, in their head and in their heart, exactly where this killer is, they'll never be able to anticipate what he's doing. They'll never be able to catch up with him.'

She took a breath, held it, and then said, 'But, Tim, don't you think there's a point where the killer will stop? Maybe he felt he had a mission, he did what he had to do . . . and now it's time to end it. Couldn't he end it now – and maybe never get caught?'

He shrugged and started to hit the palm of one hand with the other fist. He looked up into the darkness and seemed troubled. 'I don't know, Rocky. It's like, whoever he is, like he stepped over a line that can't be recrossed. He's made a life-changing decision, he's implemented it, and I'm not sure he can just say, "Okay, that's good enough, guess I'll leave it now." Know what I mean?'

She nodded.

He turned to face her, his face tight, his eyes bright in the darkness. He had an aura of deep sadness about him, coupled with a patient, resigned determination. He touched her face with one finger and said softly, 'In fact, he's probably very much aware, deep inside himself, how alone he must be now.'

A single tear fell from her eye, and it ran down the smooth skin of her face until he wiped it off with his finger. She looked at him and said, 'But can that be fair, Tim?'

He was silent and she knew the answer.

He held her then for a long time, in the quiet of the dark church parking lot. He held her while she buried her face against his chest and cried softly. The cold metal of his badge was warmed by her breath, and the fresh smell of her hair was his to breathe. She cried until she couldn't cry any longer, then she hiccupped lightly a couple of times. She turned her face and lay it against his shirt. She relaxed, and their holding became very soft and warm. She allowed herself to feel safe for a time. She allowed herself to feel loved for a time. She allowed herself to feel close to her man . . . for a time. Then she straightened, kissed him once, long and soft, and stepped away from him.

He touched her lips lightly with his fingertips and looked into her eyes.

She turned and walked away from him. She got into her car, started it, and drove slowly out of the lot, leaving him standing next to his patrol unit.

The next morning the chief called the biggest meeting yet on the patch murders. The entire staff was there, as was the Detective Division captain, Lieutenant Track, and Lieutenant Calabrini. The Public Information lieutenant was there, as was the lab boss. The only person there with no real rank was Rocky Springfield, and she was a little nervous about it. Calabrini wanted her there, however, so that was that. She sat beside him now, her notebook on her lap, and he kept looking at her covertly because he thought she looked pale and shaky.

Track looked at her, too, thinking to himself that he didn't know why he had ever been attracted to her. It was obvious that she had a terribly base sort of taste in her men; first that absolutely low-class McShaun, and if not him, then it was very clear that she liked Calabrini. He grunted slightly as he admitted to himself that the man did know how to dress and he did carry himself well. Track sighed. No problem, he thought. There was that little redhead due to come out of the academy soon. She would be worth looking into for sure. He was thinking of the little redhead when the chief started speaking; he forced himself to put on his most concerned, professional face.

'All right, everybody,' said the chief, who looked tired and subdued. 'We're here to have a little update on this case and to try to see if we can figure out where it's going or what we're gonna do next.'

Chairs creaked and notebook pages rustled.

'You all know pretty much what we have in the way of evidence so far. Not much – just enough to keep us thinking our killer is a cop, although we're still, for the record, looking at the other possibilities. Right, Calabrini?'

Calabrini agreed.

'Because of this latest murder, this Jensen guy, we've decided we should take a close look at Hummel as a suspect. He would have capability and motive. The big problem is, we don't know where he is. He's out of that house he was living in and his mail is to be forwarded up to the center of the state, but I e's not there yet. Another problem is, even though we might say that Hummel has all the ingredients necessary for this last killing, we can't really come up with a motive for the first three.'

He stopped and lit a cigarette, but he did not encourage anyone else to smoke.

'We also have the fact that Tim McShaun arrested this guy Jensen shortly before he was killed. The guy's attorney was gonna bust our balls about it, but from what the legal adviser says, ol' McShaun had a really pretty case on the crudball, and it looks like we really wouldn't have had a problem with it. I've already told Calabrini to work McShaun quietly, as a suspect in the killing, but it's my feeling that although McShaun gives me many headaches and gets his ass into a sling at least once a week . . . I don't know, it just doesn't seem to me he could go that far.'

He paused and did not notice Springfield's grim expression. 'But I've been wrong before, so who knows? Anyway, we've got boot prints we can eventually match; we've learned that the patches are new and all from the same lot, probably all taken from the supply room at the same time. We've got a dark vehicle and a male in good fighting trim who knows what he's doing and moves like a soldier. Calabrini tells me the military records check is going well. We've got about a dozen officers who served in Vietnam and a little less than that from the Korean thing. Out of these we've got some helicopter pilots, some support types, one medic, and some regular riflemen, or grunts – Marines and army types. Out of these almost all saw some type of combat, and a couple were actually in the thick of things, doing special work.'

Track spoke up then. The chief seemed irritated but did not stop him. 'Excuse me, Chief, but could you tell us what Lieutenant Calabrini expects to do once he gets that list down to where he wants it? I mean, will we follow those officers that have the type of military background we're looking for? Or will we ask them to come in so we can speak to them about this? Or will we try to determine where they were when the murders were committed? Seems to me that this might not be the right way to go about things, respecting John's difficult assignment and all. We've had suggestions of putting the entire police department on the lie detector. Then we were going to check all the uniforms to see who was missing a patch. Now we're going over old military files. Like I said, I understand the difficulty of Lieutenant Calabrini's assignment here, but it seems to me that there should be other ways to go about it.'

Everyone in the room started fidgeting. Springfield stared at Track, Calabrini looked at the ceiling, and the chief smiled. He was not surprised by Track's comments, but he was surprised at the ambitious lieutenant's timing. He knew Track saw this case as a chance for a dramatic climb up the ranks, and he knew Track wasn't the only one.

312

He looked at Track and said, 'What suggestions can you give us, Lieutenant Track?'

Track sat up straighter and said, 'I feel that what is needed is someone who is clearly in charge of the investigation. As it stands now, John, uh, Lieutenant Calabrini, is running the show, but he's also working the case like a street detective, being on the scene and talking to witnesses and all that. I feel we need someone who controls things from here, at the station, someone who is in overall control, someone who can take all the work, organize it, and present it to you directly. Someone who is not so close to the case that they lose touch with the fact that this thing is *very* big and that it is hurting us all the longer it goes on.'

The chief put out his cigarette and lit another one. He nodded and said, 'I'll think it over, Track.' Then he looked at Calabrini and said, 'John, can you give us some idea of where we're going from here?'

Calabrini shrugged off his irritation at Track's political meddling, pinched his nose, and said, 'Besides working with what we have now, we've decided to try to predict the future – in the sense that so far, all we've been doing is going around looking at the bodies this guy leaves behind. We feel now that he is motivated in a certain direction. Something specific has him hitting these people. We want to project likely targets he might go for, and, if practical, watch those targets for a while.'

Track spoke up again. 'You mean, determine who's the biggest felon out there on the street and then baby-sit him twenty-four hours a day? Do we have enough people to do that?'

Calabrini looked at Track, and the chief looked at Calabrini and motioned for him to go on.

'We do have a short list of three men we feel would qualify for this guy's hit list – *if* he knew they were out there. One is a white guy who's built like a football player and wears nothing but a mask when he breaks into homes and rapes the single women living there. The other two are blacks who've been hitting the drugstores. They like to shoot the clerk after they've taken what they want. There may be more, of course, and we're trying to connect this Jensen with others. Maybe he's part of a ring like Hummel suggested to us.'

He looked at the chief, who looked down at his desk, then continued. 'The problem is that with all the damn publicity going on about this, it could be that Jensen was part of a dope or porno ring, and was killed by his own people for any number of reasons, and they left the patch to throw us off. So we're going slow – maybe too slow for some. If we can connect Jensen to other suspects, like Hummel said, we'll try to watch over them as much as possible. Our killer has his reasons for what he does. We have to keep looking at it all and see if we can figure out what those reasons are. Then maybe we can be there when he goes for it again.'

The room was silent for a moment, everyone digesting what had been said.

The chief looked pained as he asked, 'And what about police officer suspects, John? How will you handle that?'

Calabrini rubbed his face hard and scratched one ear. 'With kid gloves, Chief. If we can narrow it down to a couple of possibilities, we can try to learn where they were when the murders occurred, as Lieutenant Track mentioned. We have to be careful, of course, because cops will know all the games we play. They'll be hard to watch, and they'll be hard to question. Everyone around here knows everything, so it will be a real hard thing to keep a suspect from knowing he is one – and when that happens and I confront him, I don't know what I'll tell him. If we suspect someone, we have to give him the rights routine before we ask him *anything*, and I think that will spook him, guilty or not.'

Captain Fronseca straightened his tie and said, 'Well, what about suspending any officer we feel is – or could be – a suspect. I mean, we can't have these men out there representing our force, can we. If they're murder suspects?'

The chief sighed and looked at Calabrini, who said, 'I'm not sure that's practical at this point, Captain. Hell, to be honest, there could be a hundred suspects in our ranks. And even if we whittled it down to three or four, if we told these guys that they were being suspended from their jobs because they were suspects in a murder case, hell, even I would want a piece of their lawsuits against the city when it was all over. Plus, believe it or not, I think that a working cop will be easier to watch than one who's on his own time. Once he's cut away from us he might be real hard to find and to watch.'

Calabrini paused, waiting for any comments. The room was completely silent. He went on. 'This brings me to my final point: secrecy. We have to keep this case from being like every other case we work around here; we're brothers and all that, and anything the detectives are doing is common knowledge down in the patrol locker room. We've really got to start watching what info goes out of here. The way it stands now, the killer only needs to come to work, and he can learn how close we are to making him.'

The room fell silent again.

Finally the chief said, 'Okay. That's it for now. Keep me posted, troops.'

After everyone had filed out, the chief sat there thinking, *Yeah, Track, I know you want to head the investigation, and you're right in a way, but I'm surprised you made your move so soon. It would have been better to wait until the case is a little more developed. Then you could come in and ride Calabrini's work to glory.* He smiled grimly. *And because of your media appeal, Track, I just might let you do it.*

Chapter Twenty–Seven

There was another meeting taking place across town, at Tom Odom's house. It consisted of two men: Odom and Beachwood. Both were angry, edgy, nervous, and more than a little scared.

Odom handed Beachwood a drink and said disgustedly, 'Look, I told you you'd get your money. It's just that I don't have it here. You know that. Why don't you fly down to Grand Cayman with me?'

Beachwood took the drink, sipped it, and said, 'Because the word is that the feds are there photographing anyone who steps off a private plane carrying a briefcase. I just don't need that kind of publicity – and neither do you.' He took a long pull on the drink, grimaced, and went on. 'Listen, you have to feel it too. Things are starting to stink. Lydia is gone – she's outta here. We didn't get to shut her up, and I guess I'm supposed to feel a little better because you don't think she's under some kind of witness-protection program, spilling her guts. I'm supposed to feel better because you think she's just run off to some town where she thinks she can hide from you. Then there's Giles, who's acting real squirmy. I'm glad we're supposed to meet him after he gets off work. I want to make sure he isn't thinking about giving us away. Then there's the thing with the congressman, Lavon. Now he calls *you*, and *he* wants to set up a meet. I don't know. I just don't know.'

He rubbed one hand over his sweaty brow, then took his Rolex watch off and massaged his wrist. He looked at Odom and said, 'And then there's our original bad boy, our tough guy, our enforcer. What happened to him, hmm? I thought that sniveling Bottle was going to have a coronary right in front of me, describing what he'd seen. He's spooked. Says he's leaving town, and I believe him. But Harv? He's very dead – with a pair of his famous pliers sticking out of his skull and a Lauderdale police patch in his mouth. It all adds up to this: time to get the hell out of here.'

Odom swirled the ice in his drink and nodded. Beachwood was right, but they had a couple of things they had to do yet. 'Listen, Sam, here's where we're at. I have to get you some money. You don't want to go down to Cayman with me, so I'll have to get it here. We have to meet with Giles tonight to see what he can tell us about the police investigation to this point. I'm going to talk with Lavon, but I doubt if I'll meet with him. I'm going to talk to my friends in the movie business. I'm in good shape with them, and I think I can deal with them. I have a batch of raw film for them. I've been selling it piecemeal, but now I'll offer it to them in a lump. If they go for it, I'll have your money, or most of it, right there. Then you can split – and so can I.' He looked out the glass sliding doors at the rear of his house. 'Maybe I can set it up for tomorrow night. By then we'll have talked to Giles and Lavon, we can make some plans, you'll get your money, and that will be that.'

Beachwood looked at Odom, emptied his drink, and nodded. 'Tomorrow night, then – and good-bye to Fort Lauderdale.'

After the big meeting in the chief's office, and while the meeting between Odom and Beachwood was drawing to a close, Rocky Springfield went to Bell Peoples's house for lunch. They hadn't seen as much of each other since Rocky had been assigned to the Detective Division, and Bell had gone to day shift up in the North End. Rocky had called Bell in the morning, before the meeting, and something in Rocky's voice made her friend invite her over.

Bell's husband was at work, and the house was quiet and cool. They enjoyed a lunch of soup and salad and made light conversation to go with it. After the dishes were cleaned up, they sat in the living room with coffee, and Bell asked her friend what was bothering her.

Rocky started out haltingly, talking about the patch murder case and its horrors, and then talking about her love for Tim and the fact that she felt she was losing him. She kept them separate, as if what bothered her about the case was in no way connected with what bothered her about her affair with McShaun. Once she got into it, it really started to come out, and she was surprised at how much she really needed to talk to someone.

Bell Peoples did more listening than talking. She had a lot of respect for Rocky, and she genuinely liked her. She suggested to Rocky that she work the homicide case like any other. Rocky wanted to be a cop, and she wanted to be a homicide detective, and what she had to do now was work the case – that's all. She had to work the case, applying herself to it professionally. It would not be her last hard-to-take murder case. Sure, it was different this time because the killer might be a cop, but the bottom line was that it was a murder case, she was a cop, and she had to work it.

Bell looked her friend in the eye as she said, 'Rocky, you may learn that being a cop isn't for you, even though you've been at it about two years now and you've proven yourself and you can handle yourself and all that. If you have doubts now because of the terrible things you're seeing in this case, if you're feeling like you've been forced into a corner where it's impossible for you to really do your best, then maybe you need to ask yourself if this is the type of work you want to be doing for the rest of your career. They're not gonna get any better, honey – the murders – in this case or any other case. The end results will always be horrible to see and work with.'

When Rocky talked about McShaun, it was different. Her voice became heavy, her eyes filled. She was hurting, confused, and Bell could see it and feel it. She let Rocky talk about it, she let her tell how much McShaun meant to her, how she wasn't sure she could picture herself going through

318

life without him. And yet deep in her heart Rocky suspected that McShaun had already told her good-bye, for some reason. Bell took Rocky's hand as she sat and cried softly, describing the confusion in her heart, the loss she felt, and the helplessness. Bell could feel the pain as Rocky told her about how she had been struggling with the thought that she might lose him, and how she forced herself to get up every day and go through the motions of her life, when inside she felt like crying. Rocky told Bell how she would fill herself with resolve during the night, telling herself she didn't need him if it came to that – there were other men who wanted her – only to have that resolve melt away to nothing at the sight of him walking across the parking lot, or smiling at her, or touching her hand.

They talked into the afternoon, and somehow Bell made her feel better. They were actually laughing a little before the afternoon ended. But the thing that burned deep inside Rocky's heart, the secret that she knew was there but which she consciously refused to acknowledge, the feeling that both terrified and saddened her, she kept locked up in her breast.

Bell Peoples was a cop and she was a woman, a woman who knew about love. Her life hadn't been easy, but she had been able to find love in the person of a man who cherished her and shared her life. She felt lucky about that. And because she was a cop and a woman and a friend of Rocky's, she knew there was more to it than Rocky was admitting.

She hugged Rocky tightly and laughed with her and sent her on her way back to work with an open invitation to come back for lunch on her day off anytime. She stood at the door and smiled and waved as Rocky drove off. Then she went back inside, sat down, and thought about everything she had heard from Rocky, the entire conversation, the feelings, the expression on her face, everything. She thought about what Rocky had said about the case, and she thought about what Rocky had said about McShaun, and she let it all tumble around in her head.

Finally she sat back, closed her eyes, and said softly to the

319

quiet house, 'Oh, Lord, please stay with that little girl now – and give her the strength she's going to need.'

John Calabrini closed the door to the captain's office and nodded at a chair for the FBI agent, Stan Matthews. Matthews sat down, opened a pack of gum, offered some to Calabrini, and grinned.

'Well, John, remember our last conversation? About Lavon? You'll be happy to know that we did in fact approach the young congressman, and we did show him some info we had about those drug enforcement radar interdiction charts. We also showed him some reports we had about him hobnobbing with some attorneys and other undesirable types here in Lauderdale. It was amazing. We had barely suggested the possibility that he was working some kind of solo undercover operation when he practically knocked us over with a rather humble statement to the effect that we had guessed exactly what he had been up to, and by a great coincidence had been about ready to call us in to help us out. We were all smiles and we all greatly admired each other, but I kind of threw a little damper on the party when I told him that for a while there, we were actually suspecting him of working with the crudballs. And if, in fact, that had been the case, we would have made sure that by the time he went through the trial by media and then the trial in the courts that he would have been stripped, literally, of every square inch of skin on his sanctimonious congressional body.'

The FBI agent chewed his gum contentedly for a while, then continued. 'He did get kind of pale there for a few minutes, but he definitely got the picture. And now he's working with us like a real trooper. I mean, you could't *find* a more patriotic and selfless guy. He's ready to go right in there and *get* those bad guys, yes, sir.'

They sat silent for a few moments, contemplating how nice it was – and how much it stank.

Calabrini broke the silence by saying, 'Guess you've heard about that guy, Jensen, getting it? It doesn't look good around here. The brass and the city management and the press are all over my ass to do something about these damn murders, and I'm not only having trouble making any progress on the ones that have already occurred, I'm positive we haven't seen the last of them.'

Matthews sat up and nodded.

'Listen, John, that's what I wanted to talk with you about. Your boy Hummel was right on the mark. Lavon was tied up with this Odom character, and the lawyer, Beachwood. Jensen was part of it, and that girl too.' He rubbed his eyes with his knuckles. 'By the way, we know where she is if you need her in the future. Seems she went right out and went to work at one of the hotels in Vegas. It just happens that some people we're interested in own it, and we check out all new employees. Anyway, she's there, and I guess she feels pretty secure as far as any problem from the likes of Odom is concerned.'

Calabrini nodded, his face grim.

Matthews said, 'Lavon has already told us that one man from your City Manager's Office, Alan Giles, is working with Odom – for a fee. We took a look at him, and our feeling is that he's not that important to the whole thing. And he's a squirrel – we think we could flip him in about ten minutes, and then we could use him in testimony against the others if we needed it. We'd like to have Lavon make contact while he's wearing a wire for us, maybe pass some radar info, take some money. Then we could work on nailing one of their planes, loaded, and make a nice conspiracy case.'

Matthews stood up and took off his jacket, hanging it on a hook on the door. He said, 'And then there's the porno thing. I'm fired up about that because some of our syndicate-type friends with their alligator shoes and pencil-thin moustaches are involved. It would be sweet if we could not only punch them for the dope but also for the porno stuff, and from there we could go knocking on the doors of the distributors, who are those same guys with the alligator shoes.'

Calabrini smiled, a rare expression on his face these days, and nodded in agreement.

He stopped smiling when the FBI agent asked, 'And what about this patch murderer, John? Is it a cop? Can you get him?'

Calabrini made a steeple out of his outstretched fingers and spoke through it. 'Officially we're still open to all possibilities. In my heart I think it's a cop. He's too close, he's too good. These aren't random killings. They all have to do with something that's happened right here in the city. This last one, Jensen, is the first one that really seems like it could be tied to anything. He's hooked in with Odom, he was part of the Hummel fall, and he was starting to bring some shit down on another of our guys.'

'You mean that McShaun – the ass kicker?'

'Yeah, Tim McShaun. I have to tell you, Stan, I start saying names like that, guys I know and have worked with, and I think I'm going to vomit. I know it's one of our guys, on our department, and that thought sickens me. And to be honest about it, it sickens me not so much that they're doing the killings but that we're all heading for some kind of final showdown. I know it will happen, I'll be there – and that sickens me.'

Matthews was quiet, watching his friend. He could feel the weight on Calabrini's shoulders.

Calabrini shrugged and pinched his nose. 'Jensen might be the arrow that points toward more victims. I talked it over with Rocky – Detective Springfield – and she agrees. Whoever killed Jensen may want to wipe his whole group out. Based on that speculation, we've been thinking about trying to keep an eyeball on Beachwood and Odom as much as possible. I hadn't really thought about Giles that much.' He turned his head. 'The damn City Manager's Office. Boy, does that ever suck!'

Matthews took out his gum, wrapped it in the foil it came from, and dropped it into the wastebasket. He made a face as he said, 'What would you think if I said the case you're working could dovetail with mine? You've got the murders, and I've got the dope and porno conspiracy, and it looks like they're both going in the same direction. We could work together. The only drawback for you would be that the news eventually would get hold of it, and then it would be ''FBI Steps In to Help in Investigation,'' and all that shit, and I know how sensitive you local guys can be about that.'

Calabrini grinned at his friend and said, 'Hell, the brass and the media would probably love it: ''Bringing in the Big Guns.'' ' His face got sober again. 'Actually, Stan, we could use any help you can give us. And if it ties in with your thing, all the better.'

'That's what I thought you'd say. I was thinking we could pick up Mr Giles this evening, after he leaves his office. We'd pick him up, but you'll be with us and you'd sit in on the talks. If we go with the possibility that this Jensen murder will lead you to others, then that leaves only Odom and Beachwood to watch, right? The girl's gone, Jensen's dead, Lavon is sleeping with us for a while, and if we flip Giles, we can offer him a quiet place to stay also. If your killer isn't a cop, or if he decides to go after some other dirtbag out on your streets, then none of this will help, but I think it's worth a shot.'

'I do too,' said Calabrini. 'And listen to this. We picked potential targets for our killer, you know, people that were really trying to make the heavy filth list on our area. We had three that we thought were perfect. We had already put teams on 'em. And wouldn't you know it, two of them decide to rob a convenience store out in the country, and one of those felony squad teams nails them red-handed. Beautiful. As if that's not enough, on the same night my team that's watching the third guy, a rapist, sees him park his car, take off his clothes, and go tiptoeing off through the yards behind the houses up in the northeast section of town. My guys hang back while he finds the house he wants, pulls on his ski mask, and breaks in. My two guys jump him and beat his ass so bad, they had to take him to the hospital. That kind of eliminated any real potential targets for my patch killer. Unless, like you said, he's going after Jensen's buddies.'

The FBI agent stretched and said, 'Ah . . . life. Well,

then, why don't we ride together this evening when we go pick up Giles?'

Calabrini said, 'Fine. We've still got some time, though, right? I want to wait for Rocky to come back in. I told her she could take a long lunch. She went to see a friend.' He looked a little sheepish, hesitated, then went on. 'Truth is, I'm kind of worried about her. She's a good lady, and a good cop, and she's been working hard on this case with me, and I think it's getting to her. She's been looking drawn lately, pale . . . upset. I don't know. Anyway, I'd like to have her with me when we get Giles. All right?'

Matthews stood. 'No problem, John. Glad to have her.'

Calabrini pulled on an earlobe and nodded absently. He didn't tell Matthews what really bothered him about the way Springfield had been acting. What really bothered him about Rocky was the nagging thought that her involvement with McShaun was somehow getting in her way of being a good cop.

When Springfield came in, Calabrini introduced her to Matthews and briefed her on their conversation. They discussed avenues of approach and alternatives. They went over old evidence and prayed for new. They revised their lists of men with military backgrounds and made plans to interview those officers they thought might qualify as suspects.

They meshed their information with that of the FBI, they exchanged descriptions and tag numbers and addresses of potential victims and known criminals. With the way things were falling together it was becoming clear that they had a good shot at making a big, clean dope and porno bust. Whether or not they would be able to solve or stop the patch killings at the same time remained to be seen.

As the late afternoon turned into early evening and they prepared to go after Giles as he left City Hall, Calabrini found himself watching Rocky closely. He could sense her inner turmoil, and he was enveloped by the sadness that she wore like a cloak. She was businesslike and sharp, professional and determined – and sad, torn, and scared.

324

As the pale blue four-door Chrysler driven by Matthews with Calabrini and Springfield as passengers, pulled into the northwest entrance to the City Hall parking lot off Andrews Avenue in downtown Fort Lauderdale, a dark brown older-model car pulled away from the curb space near the southeast entrance to the lot and entered traffic southbound on Third Avenue. The driver of the older car did not see the Chrysler, and the occupants of the Chrysler did not see the brown car.

Matthews slowed as he entered the lot and said over his shoulder to Calabrini, 'It's that white Plymouth over there by itself, isn't it, the one under the oak tree there?'

Calabrini looked past Matthews's shoulder and nodded. 'Yeah, that's it. Guess we got here just at the right time. If he's still in the office, then he won't be there long. We can approach him as he gets to his car.'

Rocky put her hand on the dash, leaned forward, and put the other hand lightly against her throat. She looked through the windshield and said quietly, 'John, I'm not sure, but it looks like there's someone in the car now.'

Both Matthews and Calabrini sat up and stared. Matthews said, 'Yeah, scrunched down there against the side window.'

Calabrini said, 'Son of a bitch.'

Alan Giles looked as if he had been crying when he died. His head was back and his mouth was open. His chin was covered with thick, incredibly red blood that he had gagged up while pleading for his life. The patch stuck in his mouth was soaked with it. It had apparently taken him a few minutes to die; his lower body was covered with blood from the bullet wounds in his groin, stomach, and lower chest. His hands and fingers, entwined, were folded neatly across his slightly bulging belly.

The initial reconstruction of the crime showed that Giles had walked to his car, opened the door, and slid in behind the wheel. At that time the killer, who was either already in the car or, more probably, waiting close by, sat down beside him in the front seat. Giles turned toward the killer, and the killer shot him five times with a large-caliber handgun, quick estimates indicating at least a .357 Magnum. The windows of the vehicle were rolled up, there probably hadn't been very many people around the lot, and the killer may have muffled the shots, either with a fitted silencer or simply by putting a small towel over the barrel of the weapon.

Calabrini watched Springfield closely while they worked the crime scene. He was concerned that the case was getting to her. At first she became very pale and shaky, and he thought she might faint or be sick. She took several deep breaths and wiped her face with a handkerchief. As he watched and as afternoon changed to dusk in the parking lot, he saw a subtle change come over her. He saw her biting her lip, he saw her straighten her back, he saw her face tighten, and he heard her voice take on an edge that he had never heard before. Her indecision was gone, and she now worked with her usual crisp, efficient style. He had the feeling that she had faced some kind of internal barrier and, after balking at it, had pulled herself together and surmounted it through sheer determination.

Chapter Twenty-Eight

The killer thought about what he had done, and what he still had to do, while he walked through the dark streets. He felt a profound sadness and recognized it as the first really disturbing emotional reaction to his actions over the last few weeks.

Maybe it would get to him, after all.

He knew he was not invulnerable to normal human emotions. He was actually surprised at the extent to which he had been strangely emotion-free up to this point. He had done what he had to do, and he had felt neither elation nor joy. He took no pleasure in the killing and felt that that was as it should be. What he was doing was not for his satisfaction. It was an extreme but logical extension of his regular job, to be handled in an impersonal and efficient manner.

He thought about it: Maybe it was some kind of built-in defence mechanism. Since he took no pleasure from the killing, maybe he really wasn't emotionally warped; maybe he was still reasonably normal. He was aware that he had stepped over some kind of line, no sense trying to fool himself about that. He was killing people for reasons that he thought fully justified, but he knew that this was an extreme departure from the norm. He smiled a small smile. Still, one must always try to like themselves, yes? One must not think of oneself as *totally* warped. One must have confidence in the continuing self-integrity, self-honor, and self-respect of his own special persona.

What about the fact that it must end?

Why? Why must it end?

Well, on an immediate basis there are two more who must die. That would be the end, right? There will be no more.

Why not?

After these two a break in the action, to be sure. But then what? Won't there be more? Won't our environment breed more predators, more deviants who will bring pain and suffering to innocent, helpless people? And if so, then what? Can I do whatever I can within the normal limits of my regular job and then let the judicial system make its feeble, diluted attempts to handle the problem?

It will not be enough.

Eventually there will be another one, and another, and by the same logic that guided me in the past I will have to take the same action with them as with the others. No, these next two will not be the end of it.

Are you being truthful with yourself?

You know very well that they're getting close. Eventually they have to come to you or trap you at the scene. They're good and they care, and they're working their jobs to the same capacity that you used to work yours. They can't understand how you've transcended their limits, but they can recognize the results and they'll keep working until they put it together. And then they'll have to act.

Do you want to die?

Is this some form of elaborate, dramatic, self-martyring suicide, contrived at the hand of others?

No.

I'm not trying to die. I'm not ready to die.

What if they try to stop you? Are you blind to a possible deadly confrontation?

I know it can happen, but I'm working very hard to see that it doesn't.

What if you're caught? Handcuffed and charged with breaking their laws? Examined within the parameters of their judicial system? What then? An attorney, a legal battle? Incarceration? Treatment?

I don't want to think about that.

What do you want to think about then – hero?

The job. I want to think about the job I've started, the job that won't be finished until it's finished.

They worked in the Detective Division until almost midnight. They worked at the scene of Giles's murder, and in the station on the initial follow-up and coordination with the Medical Examiner. FBI Agent Matthews helped with his many resources. Calabrini went through the night angry, frustrated, driving his detectives and venting his fury at anything that slowed their work.

Rocky Springfield went through the night maintaining almost complete silence. She still seemed sad, but she worked with a cold, deliberate, determined sureness. When they finished for the night, she went home and went to bed. She did not try to call McShaun.

Phyllis Green's article in the morning edition of the *Herald* was factual and objective. She had been on the scene of Giles's death; she had watched the detectives at work; she had spoken with Calabrini again; and she had recorded it all. Her article did not scream for immediate results; it did not question the efficiency of the police department; it did not try to stir up panic or create fear in the community. It simply reported what had happened and what steps were being taken in the investigation. The article seemed almost subdued.

She had recognized something while she was putting the article together, something she had not felt before.

What she saw happening on the streets of her city in this case intrigued, scared, and challenged her. She realized that she was witnessing some form of expression in the absolute extreme. The bodies were very real. The deaths were very real. She watched the police officers work, saw how they went about their jobs, every one of them knowing the complexities and potential ramifications of the investigation, and to her surprise she felt herself pulling for them.

At the same time she felt she was beginning to understand the incredible decision the killer had made. She felt she was beginning to understand how totally the killer had separated himself from everything that he had been a part of. She understood that the killer had dedicated himself to a mission, one that he had defined in his own way and was striving to fulfill without regard to the consequences, whether to his victims or to himself.

The grim reality of that mission awed her. It forced her to look at her own mission, and somehow she felt deflated. She knew it should not affect her, but somehow it did. She was a reporter, a good one. She cared about getting the information out to the people; she cared about the transmission of the facts. But she merely reported . . . while others acted.

For the first time in her career she was bothered by the fact that her job was only to report what others actually did. She was just a mirror reflecting their actions.

She forced herself to stiffen in the face of her own self-doubts. Certainly the people had a right to know. And it was her job to tell them. Yes, she would observe. Yes, she would report. And maybe, just maybe, she would sell a book based on the story she so diligently pursued.

Tom Odom had been awake only a few minutes and was trying to get some coffee going when Beachwood came pounding on his door. Odom was muttering to himself as he opened it, and the attorney pushed past him, insisting, 'Take a look at this!' He handed Odom the morning paper.

Giles's murder was on the front page, photo and all.

Odom went pale, cursed, and threw the paper across the kitchen. He looked at Beachwood and said, 'What the hell is going on around this town, anyway? Some fucking maniac just runs around murdering people when he wants to? Leaves his "sign"? What the hell are the police doing out there?'

Beachwood sighed, poured some coffee, and said, 'Listen, Tom, what's happening here couldn't be more serious. When Harv got it, I thought it could have been almost anything – maybe one of the people from his grass deal got pissed off and did him, or maybe one of those cops that we fucked with really decided to teach him a lesson. I even thought you might have done it, or had it done, because he was getting a little wild and had the potential of hurting us.' He stopped, and they stared at each other, neither one moving or taking his eyes off the other.

Yeah. Beachwood thought. *I know your history, Tom Odom. I checked. I know you've killed before, and I know you've paid others to kill for you. And I heard the story from Harv about how you tortured and killed that young couple that blundered into one of your early deals down there by Norman's Cay. Yeah, Tom. I know you're capable of it.*

Aloud Beachwood said, 'Now we've got Giles very dead. Giles, after Harv, is no accident. Lydia is gone, we haven't heard from Lavon, Harv is killed, and now Giles.' Beachwood ran manicured fingers through his thinning sandy sand. The skin around his eyes was puffy and pasty-looking. He licked his lips and said, 'I feel a very real sense of dread. This whole thing is about to come crashing down. Either we're gonna get the big knock on the door, with warrants and Miranda rights and all that crap, or some maniac is gonna come over and blow us both away.'

Odom was nodding his head and thinking of what Beachwood had said. *Ah, Sam, Sam, you're right, of course. Things are starting to look desperate. And now you're starting to whine and whimper and get sweaty hands, and I know that if a bust does come, down you'll go into your lawyer act and scamper around and give me away without blinking an eye. And, yes, I do believe I'm gonna have to blow you away, slick guy. Blow you away and slide out of this country and go live like a king somewhere with all my sweet money.*

The phone rang, and Odom went into the living room to answer it, leaving Beachwood standing in the kitchen, sipping his coffee.

When Odom came back, he looked puzzled and a little more nervous. He broke off part of a bagel and, chewing it absently, said, 'That was our young congressman, Lavon. Has new info. All excited and pushy about doing more work for us. Wants a meeting here, or somewhere around town, but he wants it soon.' He chewed the bagel. 'He sounded much too enthusiastic . . .'

Beachwood bent down and tightened the laces on his deck shoes. 'Maybe he's decided he really likes making all that money with you and he wants to keep it going.'

'Maybe, Sam, maybe. But something in my gut tells me that's not it. Something in my gut tells me we won't meet with him soon or ever again. It's time to leave this shit behind.'

The attorney stood. 'Which brings me to my next question—'

'Look, Sam, I told you I'd have the money. Last night I contacted my representative from the film distributors. After a couple of calls back and forth they said they could live with what I was trying to do. They said they'd buy all the remaining raw stock I had, wipe the slate, and I could walk away from it – and them. I told them a little about my business problems in other areas, and they agreed that they didn't need to be standing near any heat generated by me. So they're going to come here and get the film and drop off the final monies to me, and then I can pay you what I owe you and we can both split.'

Sam Beachwood leaned back against a counter and stared at the lights in the ceiling. Then he nodded and asked, 'When are they coming, and when can I get my money and get the hell out of this town?'

Odom felt close to choking as he tried to force down the bagel through his dry throat. He gulped some coffee and said, 'Tonight. They're coming tonight.'

That afternoon Rocky Springfield walked up the steps from the lobby of the station to the second floor where the Detective Division was located. Waiting near the elevators, she noticed a hard-looking man she was sure she had seen before but really didn't know. The man's tough face broke into a gentle smile as he approached her.

'Rocky . . . right?'

Springfield nodded and shook the outstretched hand.

'My name is Scott Kelly. I used to be an active part of what goes on around here. Did narcotics work for a long time. Now, I, uh, I work inside here.'

Rocky looked at him. He looked all right physically, she thought, but he carried an aura of resentment mixed somehow with embarrassment . . . shame? She looked at him and said quietly, 'I remember.'

'Yeah, well, got a minute? I need to talk to you about a friend of ours.'

Not sure what to expect, Rocky let herself be led over to a wooden bench against the wall. They sat down, and Kelly looked into her eyes as he said, 'I'm worried about Tim, but it's not something I can explain very clearly. I've been watching this case like everyone else has, and I know it's getting everyone down.' He rubbed his left leg with the palm of his hand. 'Look, Tim is one of the special ones, you know? One of the few truly dedicated cops around here, or anywhere. This kind of thing can eat away at him. Sometimes he cares too much. Maybe you can help him . . .'

She watched him as he stood, suddenly embarrassed, and turned away from her. He started to walk away, stopped, and said quietly, 'Even if it's just making sure he's not alone too much . . . do it.'

Rocky watched him walk away.

McShaun had been sitting in the quiet of his apartment, his eyes closed, letting his mind drift, when the phone started ringing again. It seemed it had been ringing all day. He had ignored it. What if it was Rocky? What could he say? Did she deserve more of an explanation? *Was* there an explanation?

The phone kept ringing. He finally picked it up.

Chick Hummel said, 'Tim. You there, T.S.? Talk to me, guy.'

'I'm here, Chick. Are you in town?'

'No, man, I'm still up north here. I'm supposed to come down to talk with Calabrini in a day or so – about what's going on. You know?'

'Yeah, I know. Calabrini thinks you're the killer?'

'Tell you the truth, Tim, I don't think so. I think he feels he has to clear me, for the record, that's all – though he might want to ask me questions about someone else.'

Silence.

'You still there, Tim?'

'Still here. Just thinking about what you said.'

'Yeah, well, listen, Tim. You know I'm not shedding any tears for Jensen – or Giles, for that matter. Must have been their karma. But it seems like whoever did it, if it's the same person that did both, seems to me like he could call it quits now, like, walk away from it now.'

McShaun stood holding the phone, waiting.

'Maybe he could see that enough is enough, you know? Those first three were just dangerous garbage and he did them. All well and good. Then he does Jensen and Giles. Okay, but hell, it can't go on forever, right? It's got to stop somewhere. Whatever it was that he was trying to show, I'm sure he's accomplished it. Now, whoever he is, now he needs to start thinking about saving his ass. Know what I mean, Tim? Know what I mean, man?'

McShaun said, 'I hear you, Chick.'

'Yeah. All right. Listen, you working tonight?'

'No, I'm off tonight. Last night too.'

'Good. Why don't you just kick back, man? Ease up a little. I'm trying to get out of here late tonight to head down that way. Should be there some time tomorrow. Our little girl's sick, and I don't want to leave Dee until I see that there's someone who can stay here with her. Anyway, I'm coming down there, and I really want to get together with you, Tim, so we can talk. All right? Think we can do that, man?'

McShaun's voice had a faraway sound as he said, 'Sure thing, Chick. I'll look forward to it.'

'Good . . . good. I'll call you as soon as I'm in town, or if it's in the afternoon, I'll have the dispatcher set up a meet, right?'

'Right, Chick.'

'Okay, I'll see you then. And listen, Tim, be careful, would ya? And . . . and . . . just kick back until I get there, okay?'

Rocky pulled into the small parking lot at McShaun's apartment building just as he was getting out of his car. He stood there smiling, waiting for her as she got out of her car and walked toward him.

She had argued with herself all the way from the station over to his place. The bottom line was this: She simply had to see him, to talk with him.

They were quiet as they walked down the path and into his apartment. They stood awkwardly, looking at each other, until he took her hand and gently pulled her over to the couch. They sat down facing each other.

'I'm glad you came over. I was thinking about you.'

'I was thinking about you, too, Tim.'

She tried to let herself enjoy looking into his eyes and being close to him for a little while. She knew he loved her, and yet somehow he had made a decision to leave her, despite that love. He was already gone; he may as well be living on Mars as far as her actually getting to him went. Something more important to him had made him turn away from her, made him leave her behind.

She sat holding his hand. She felt the tears forming in the corners of her eyes. She promised herself she wouldn't cry. 'Tim, you know how I feel about you, about us.' She stopped, bit her lip, and then went on. 'The case, Tim . . . the case with the patches. Why does it just *seem* to be part of everything because it's so overwhelming? It's hurting me, like feeling I'm losing you is hurting me.' She looked deep into his eyes. 'It's like they're the same, you know? I ask myself, can't there be some solution, can't something be worked out? Does it all have to be so . . . final? Why can't the killings just stop? Isn't it enough? Hasn't the point, whatever the hell it is, been made?'

She turned away from him, brushing a stray curl over one ear with her fingertips. 'I can't help hoping for some kind of last-minute saving of the situation. Why does it all have to be so . . . inevitable?'

She watched him as he looked at her. He didn't answer her but simply took a deep breath, let it out softly, and looked at her with eyes that enveloped her with warmth. He shrugged a long, eloquent shrug.

She stood and turned away from him.

He came up behind her, put his arms around her, and held her gently. She felt herself relaxing, and she knew she couldn't let that happen. But it felt so good to be held by him. She wiped a tear from her eye, turned toward him, and said, 'Tim, I'm . . . I have to go. I just wanted to see you. I just wanted you to know that I'm going to keep going, working – living. I know you'll do what you think you have to do.' She turned in his arms and took a step back. She looked up into his eyes as she said huskily, 'And I guess I'll do what I have to do.'

He stood very still, watching her, then, with a small smile, he nodded, an almost imperceptible nod, and let her go. She turned from him, walked to the door, looked back once, and then walked out, away from him.

She would think back many times about that short meeting with Tim, and one of the things she would ask herself is why she didn't notice that Radar, the cat, was gone. Would that have made any difference somehow? She would think back and ask herself if there was something she should have told him, something she should have said, that might have changed things.

Her heart told her: No.

She had no way of knowing about the young girl who lived on a sailboat a couple of blocks away from his apartment. She had no way of knowing that the girl had admired Radar in the past and that she now had custody of Radar because the cat's owner, a guy the young girl saw jogging all the time, was taking a long trip. Radar had a new home, and the young girl was delighted.

Rocky had no way of knowing about Radar. But she had too many ways of knowing that Tim McShaun was already gone.

Chapter Twenty-Nine

The hot, clear, breezy Fort Lauderdale afternoon turned into a still and clear Fort Lauderdale night, with a sky filled with stars and a sliver of moon. The city paused, as if catching its breath after a long, noisy day, and there was quiet for a little while as the lights started coming on here and there. Sunburns looked more red after showers, and thin-strapped evening dresses slid over tender skin. Rough hands that had worked construction sites or boat yards were washed with strong soap. Spattered jeans were changed into the tight ones with somebody's name on them. Dinner reservations were confirmed, cocktail waitresses and bartenders tried to psyche themselves, and rock bands came dragging in, head fuzzy and eyes still red from the night before.

The city changed from a tropical beach playground to a tropical night bazaar. Every pleasure was catered to, every desire was sated. The traffic, which had paused during the lull, picked up again. The roads heading east toward the beach were the busiest. Along US 1, or Federal Highway, north, and in the northeast section of town, valets were busy running back and forth between the Cadillacs and Lincolns and Mercedes and Jaguars. Along the beach the hotel bars were filling up with tourists, out for some fun in this playfully wicked little city. In the northwest, those who worked the hardest for the least tried to stay cool with electric fans. The bars here filled, too, but they had concrete floors and some hot dice games going on out in the back lot. There were whores on the sidewalk along South Federal Highway, walking slowly, watching for the car that came around the block and then returned cautiously, driven by a nervous man from Duluth or some other distant city. There were whores out on the 'strip', too, that half mile of beachfront sidewalk from Las Olas Boulevard, north. Drifters, runaways, thieves, pimps, cops, dopers and tourists – they all walked along the same mean sidewalk along the strip, watching, watching. A lot of the whores here were young boys who would be taken back to cool hotel rooms by middle-aged men darting furtive glances behind them.

The city seemed forgiving during the day, almost relaxed. The city seemed to welcome one in its sunshine and on its beaches: Come, enjoy the 'Venice of America'. The boats at the dock at Bahia Mar, or Pier 66, or those going by in the Intercoastal Waterway, or out over the second reef, seemed to be bright toys, sparkling pleasure rafts, nice to look at and fun to dream about.

At night, though, it changed. The same boats looked stealthy in the darkness, showing only a couple of small lights and seeming to be going somewhere secret.

At night the city stopped smiling; it laughed instead. It became a cold place, a hard place, a place that let you take your chances and turned its back on you if you fell.

The tropical night lay over a place of hunger, a place of greed, a place of furtive meetings and disappointing liaisons. The people, both locals and visitors, went out into the night to 'have fun', but as they did so, they kept one eye on their purse and the other on their partner, and they went through the night looking over their shoulders.

Much of the conversation that took place around the city in the night had to do with the killer who left a police patch in his victims' mouths. He had struck again, an executive of the city management this time, and it was beginning to take on the feeling of some macabre high drama. Complex intellectual discussions were woven through the theories of right and wrong, of justice and punishment, of courage and sacrifice. Adrenaline pumped, and verbal combat was waged by those who supported what the killer was trying to do and by those who abhorred it. The verbal arguments were intense with no

338

clear winners either way, and in many cases the participants felt a thrill at having actually identified with something so . . . real.

Fort Lauderdale went into its hard plastic nighttime act: the humming of the tyres on the unforgiving asphalt roadways; the pounding of the disco music on the stainless-steel dance floors; the throaty rumbling of powerful engines on the shiny dark waterways; the clink of fine silver; the scuff of dirty tennis shoes; the sustained crashing roar of jet engines; the laughter of the hunter and the hunted; and the smell of expensive perfume and rotting garbage, of sweet cloying jasmine and diesel fumes, of fear and anticipation.

Odom got a couple of beers out of the refrigerator and gave one to the attorney, who seemed more agitated and upset than ever.

Odom grunted as he opened his beer. 'Take it easy, Sam. You look like you're gonna jump right out of your sweaty skin.'

'I don't like the way it went today, Tom. I don't like it at all. And I don't like being here now, waiting.

'I know, it's a pain in the ass, but it will be all right, I'm telling you. I put Lavon off. He called back, and I told him I would be glad to meet with him sometime in the next couple of days, but that I would be out of town until then. He bought it. I told you I made contact with those syndicate guys. They'll he here tonight for the films, we get the money, and that's it.' He took a long pull on the beer, finished it, poured himself a large tumblerful of Scotch, took a big gulp, made a face, and said, 'So relax.'

Beachwood wasn't convinced. He chided himself for still being there. He knew he should have been long gone, maybe making arrangements to get the rest of the money later. Now here he was, at Odom's, waiting for some of those real hard guys to show up and not knowing what the cops were up to. He went into the living room and sat on the couch, his hands folded together.

Odom turned on the television set, and they both stared at

it with distaste. Beachwood got up and started pacing around, stopping now and then to try to look out of the decorative glass panes in the door. Odom watched him and finally said, 'Sam, will you sit down? Relax and stop looking out the window like there's some monster out there. Chrissakes.'

Beachwood sat down again.

Odom had more of his drink, poured one for Beachwood and another for himself, and said, 'Tell you what. I've got all those films in there, and a lot of them are stuff you haven't seen – some good stuff too. Why don't we go into the screening room and watch them? C'mon, it'll do you good. I might even be able to dig up a little toot we can do while we're waiting. No sense in sitting here chewing our nails. When they get there, they'll ring the bell. We'll hear 'em, and then we'll call it a night. Whaddya say?'

Beachwood sighed, and he nodded. This is what it comes down to, he thought, two grown men waiting for people who make them nervous, sticking cocaine up their noses and watching dirty movies together. He felt himself drawn by the pleasure and release he knew the coke would bring, and he felt himself aroused by the thought of those grainy carnal images on the screen. He followed Odom into the den, which was his screening room.

A short while later, from a ten-story office building on Oakland Park Boulevard, one of Calabrini's men checked the area for the first time with his binoculars and spoke into his radio. Two blocks away, parked along the fringes of the Coral Ridge Country Club golf course, Calabrini acknowledged the message and turned to the FBI agent, Matthews. 'Nothing now. Odom's car is gone. Beachwood's Caddy is still at his place, and there's no movement anywhere. Most of my people are getting into position all around the neighborhood.'

Matthews nodded. 'Sorry I couldn't bring in more guys, John. We've got a bunch of people up in Atlanta this week.'

Matthews had arrived that evening with two other agents, one older man who had worked the Miami office for years, and the other a very young kid, just out of college, with less than a year on the job. The older agent sat in the back of Calabrini's car with them, and the young man was with Springfield.

Calabrini allowed himself to smile, thinking about how Rocky had reacted when she was told she would have the kid working with her tonight. She had groused and bitched like any veteran who was told he would have a temporary partner, a new one at that, and an FBI agent on top of it. But that hadn't dampened her spirits over the good news that Bell Peoples would also be riding with her tonight. They had discussed it before, Rocky telling him that Peoples had expressed an interest in coming in and riding a shift with the detectives, on her own time, just to get the feel of it. Calabrini knew that Peoples and Springfield were goods friends, and it would do Springfield good to share some time with Peoples. *Besides*, he thought wryly, *the way this case is shaping up, I'm going to need all the manpower I can get – if that's the right word.*

He stopped smiling, and his face hardened as he thought again of the secret thread he was following in the case. He had not even discussed it with Rocky, and it was unsettling because he wasn't sure why. He drummed his fingers on the steering wheel and thought of it: One cop had arrested Walker the last time he was sent to jail for rape, before he was released in time to be killed. One cop blew up Nails's partner with a shotgun while Nails tried to kill Springfield. One cop was on the scene of the old woman's death and on the scene of the little girl found under the hibiscus bush. One cop read the young girl's poem and said he did not know what the 'Who Me?' meant, although Calabrini was able to come across it later in Hummel's original information report from Lydia. One cop, whose police street record and military record bespoke a professional – a hard, efficient, dedicated achiever. The thread was there, and though the path was circumstantial, Calabrini sensed that it led to his man.

He blew out a short breath of air, not realizing he had been holding it. He knew Rocky and her partner were parked in the shadows under a huge banyan tree at the end of the island that Odom's street was on. She was actually the closest to the house, and it bothered Calabrini a little, but he reminded himself that she was a cop and should be able to handle it.

He turned to Matthews and said, 'Well, we're here, and we'll just hang loose and see what develops, if anything. Too bad Odom put Lavon off, but maybe we'll come up with something, anyway.'

Matthews nodded.

They waited in the darkness.

A short distance away, Rocky Springfield sat in the darkness also, trying to make polite, if inconsistent, conversation with the new young FBI agent. Bell sat in front, on the right side, and the young agent sat in the back. Rocky had decided he was a nice kid, and that term was a little odd because he was actually only a year younger than she was. She could tell that he was uncomfortable. He played his role as government agent awkwardly, trying to appear cool and experienced but not quite knowing where to stand or what to say. She hoped that if the stuff hit the fan, he would just do as he was told and stay out of the way. She looked over at Bell and felt better. The big girl looked confident and relaxed, and Rocky was very glad she was there with her.

Rocky was staring down the street, which was blotched here and there by the streetlights, when the young agent cleared his throat and said quietly, 'Uh, Detective Springfield, I was wondering . . . what do you think about this killer that's leaving the patches in his victims' mouths? Does it bother you, thinking he could be a cop like you, an actual representative of the law-enforcement community?'

Peoples blew out a short breath and rolled her eyes.

Rocky thought, Shit. She said, 'Yes. It bothers me.'

'I've read everything that's come through our files about the case, and I must say I can't even begin to understand what drives the man. And I bet when they catch him, they'll find out he was a cop who never could really do the job, anyway.'

342

Rocky turned her head to look at the kid. He went on, 'What I mean is, he must be one of those cops who never becomes really competent at understanding how our system of laws work.'

She looked at him, then over at Bell, and said softly, 'Maybe he understands it too well.'

He thought about that for a moment and then kept after it. 'I see what you're saying. Still, he's really gone off the deep end here. He's abusing everything the system stands for and is trying to do.'

Both Springfield and Peoples were into the conversation with the young agent, but at the same time both had been on the street long enough to stay tuned to the night, to the radio, and to the reason they were there.

Bell was very still for a moment, her head cocked, then she relaxed a little and said, 'Well, you're right about that one thing.' She looked at Rocky. 'Whoever he is, he's lost touch with *our* reality.' She rubbed her nose with the back of her hand. 'But I don't have to tell you that a person who comes into this job isn't the same person a couple of years later.' She looked at Rocky and wondered if her friend remembered, as she did now, that night so long ago when she had lost self-control and beat the guy driving the stolen car after they had found the dead boy in the camper.

Rocky rubbed her arms, turned toward the young agent again, and said, 'What you said about abusing the system. Just what is the system trying to do?'

'To maintain law and order and disseminate justice.'

She nodded, 'You could argue that the killer is doing the same thing. Right?'

The young agent, fidgeting, looked out the window a moment and then faced her again. 'Yes, but . . . but he's taken the law into his own hands, become the whole system incarnate in one man. He acts like he *is* the system.'

'Maybe he believes he is,' Springfield said.

The FBI agent moved his coat around; he couldn't get comfortable with his gun stuck under his belt at the hip. He

343

sighed and said, 'Maybe when I've been out here longer, I'll be able to understand what motivates someone like that a little better.'

Rocky and Bell sighed at the same time. They both thought it was the most intelligent thing he had said yet.

While Beachwood stared at the movie showing a naked, laughing Harv Jensen roughly pushing a wine bottle between a young girl's open legs, and while Odom sat beside him, furtively eyeing Beachwood and easing the 9-mm Beretta from under his shirt, the killer moved with quick, soft steps across the pool patio behind Odom's home. He reached the large glass sliding doors leading into the living room area and pulled on them one at a time. They were all locked. He moved to his right and tried the kitchen door. It was unlocked. He backed away and crouched in the shadows, waiting, feeling in the night.

He had parked his car one block north and had moved quickly through the darkened yard of a house for sale until he'd reached the seawall of the canal almost directly north of Odom's house. He had been very still there, watching, waiting, listening. Then he had moved along the seawall, jumping over cleats and avoiding lines that held expensive yachts to the private docks. He was dressed in soft jeans, jungle boots, a camouflaged jungle blouse, and black leather gloves. Around his neck, partly covering his face, was a loosely knotted camouflage scarf. In his left hand he carried a Ruger .357 revolver with a four-inch barrel and wooden grips. It was very much a standard police service weapon – accurate, powerful, and reliable. It was very nonstandard in one way. It had been purchased over two years earlier, in another state, by a man using very good false identification. The killer had come across it in the course of his duties, had checked its history, and kept it. The killer carried it now, confident that it was untraceable . . . 'clean'.

He crouched now in the shadows, holding the revolver. The night felt vaguely uneasy to him, and he waited for it to settle.

Calabrini sat up. He had seen the big Lincoln go by on Bayview, and now his lookout reported that the car had turned into Odom's area and appeared to be slowing, possibly to turn into Odom's place. The lookout couldn't tell for sure, but he thought there was only one person in the car.

Matthews said tersely, 'Odom drives a Lincoln, right? What do you think? Wanna go with these cheap warrants or wait for something better?'

Calabrini scowled, thinking. They had used the link between Jensen, Odom, Beachwood, and Lavon's testimony, and the fact that another potential witness, Giles, had been killed, to convince a local judge to issue warrants for the arrest of Odom and Beachwood. They weren't federal warrants, and they really weren't that strong, but they had them if they wanted to use them. Calabrini hesitated because he knew that whatever case was made against the two could eventually be determined because of the questionable causes for the original warrant. Crap, he thought, if nothing else, maybe the warrants will save the two crudball's lives. He was weighing it when the lookout came on the radio and said the Lincoln had pulled into the drive at Odom's place and that one man had climbed out, reached in for a briefcase, and was walking toward the front door.

Calabrini decided to go for it.

Rocky sat tensely at the wheel, her fingers on the ignition key. She was waiting for the word to move, and she didn't want to start the car until she had to, on the chance that it would spook their targets.

Bell Peoples hunched forward a little on the seat. She felt the sweat on the palms of her hands. She took a deep breath.

The young FBI agent checked his flashlight, felt his gun on his hip for the nineteenth time, and asked, his throat dry, 'Is this it? Is this it?'

Rocky heard Calabrini's voice over the radio, steady, even, 'Okay, troops, get ready . . ..'

The man who climbed out of the Lincoln stopped in the

driveway and listened. He was in his early forties, fit and trim and hard. His black hair was cut short and neat, and his dark blue suit fit him as if it had been tailored for the body. It was. He wore beautiful, soft, tight calf-hide gloves and carried an expensive leather briefcase in his left hand. He patted his coat pocket to feel the cloth patches there and stopped in front of the door.

His boss had told him just enough so that he could do the job intelligently. He had heard it through, then smiled approvingly. His boss had told him that there would be two guys. They had films. They wanted money. His boss had told him that, unfortunately, these two guys had become hot . . . so hot, in fact, that it made his boss uneasy. They could bring trouble, right? Nobody needs that. So he went to get the films and then kill the two guys. In the briefcase was a six-inch double-action .22 Magnum revolver with a custom-made silencer. It was his favourite type of weapon . . . and he was very good at what he did.

He had accepted the next part with professional respect. After the two slobs were dead from the Magnum he was to stick one of the little cloth patches into each of their dead mouths, like a joke, except it wasn't a joke. His boss had told him that the cops were going crazy in this town with a maniac running around killing people and doing the same thing with the patch. His boss said it would take the heat off them. Very simple.

He turned his hard eyes toward the doorknob. He didn't want to ring the door bell; he felt better when he could just . . . step in. His gloved hand touched the knob to see if, in anticipation or stupidity, it had been left unlocked.

It had.

Outdoors, the killer felt himself coiling. His whole being tightened and pointed itself toward the target. He moved on the balls of his feet, and in his gloved hand he felt the purposeful weight of the revolver.

He was close, so close.

He felt a ripple in the night, a whisper, and hesitated.

Then he shrugged if off and moved toward his enemy. His eyes quickly scanned the rear yard, the canal, and the hushed night once more before he slowly pulled open the kitchen door.

The man with the hard eyes stood in the living room, frozen, listening. He felt uneasy. He had felt the ripple in the night too. He knelt quickly, opened the briefcase, and took out the revolver. He looked to his left, toward the kitchen, then let his eyes confirm that the living room was empty. To his right, muted, he heard the sound of something running, a machine, and soft voices. He felt an unexplained need to hurry. With the weapon held up in front of him he moved down the hallway toward the source of the sounds. He came to the bedroom door. It was almost closed but not quite. He pushed it open slowly with his foot and stepped inside.

He saw Odom and Beachwood were sitting in big recliners to his right, watching a movie that was being projected on a large screen on the far wall. His eyes flicked across the screen long enough to register the image of a young redheaded girl staring at a wet erection. His eyes returned to the two forms in the recliners.

Tom Odom, feeling magnificently powerful and capable from the effects of the cocaine, slowly brought the 9-mm Beretta up to the level of Beachwood's waist. He didn't look over at the attorney; he just started tightening his finger on the trigger.

The man with the hard eyes saw the weapon in Odom's hand and went into a crouch, his revolver, with its ugly silencer, held out in front of him. His shadow fell across the screen, the stark outline of his arms and weapon breaking up the soft, skin-toned images.

Beachwood, seeing the sinister, lunging shadow on the screen, sat up in his chair, looked at Odom, and saw the Beretta pointed at him, and his eyes went wide with fear and understanding. He started to gasp out, 'What the *hell* . . .' and stiffened as the man with the hard eyes fired a .22 Magnum slug into Odom's forehead, then turned the bulbous nose of the gun to him. It only took an instant, but it was long enough for Beachwood to lock eyes with the man behind the gun and feel the terror of helplessness. Then he felt his head explode, and his world turned red.

The man with the hard eyes flinched as the 9-mm went off in Odom's hand, the bullet tearing a gash under the image of the redheaded girl's right eye on the screen and then imbedding itself in the wall behind it. The roar of the weapon seemed very loud in the small room, and the man with the hard eyes said 'Shit', as he fired one more bullet into Odom's head, whose face was twisted into an angry, silent scream, and then another into Beachwood, who was slumped, crumpled and shrunken, into the corner of the big recliner.

The man with the hard eyes whirled around and moved toward the hallway. He knew he still had to place the patches in the mouths of the two men he had just killed, but the sound of the 9-mm going off bothered him. He wanted to take a real fast look around the house before he finished the job.

The killer had frozen in an almost graceful stance at the other end of the hallway, near the living room. He was on the balls of his feet, his Ruger held with both hands in front of him. The darkened walls and ceiling were to him like the jungle canopy, the soft carpet like the rotting loam beneath his boots. He had become deathly still when he had heard the sharp bark of a gun going off in the room at the end of the hallway, and the other, muted spits. His eyes were bright now, wide-open and unblinking.

The man with the hard eyes stepped quickly into the hallway, his right hand holding his Magnum, his left jammed into his jacket pocket and clutching the two cloth Fort Lauderdale Police Department patches. His hard eyes took in the image of the killer at the end of the hallway, and he instinctively pointed his weapon and squeezed the trigger.

The killer had hesitated.

Still bound by his code, totally aware of his vulnerability because of it. He knew he couldn't kill an innocent . . . or a cop. He hesitated long enough to see the gloves on the hands

348

of the other man, to see the way he moved, the hard eyes, and the ugly shape of the silencer on the weapon that spit at him twice in the narrow confines of the railway.

The killer felt the burning slugs punch into his chest as he fired twice, rapidly, into the body and face of the man with the hard eyes. He watched as the man straightened back, grunting, then fell forward heavily onto the carpet, the blood dark and thick on the back of his head.

The killer took a deep, shuddering breath, felt the fire in his lungs, and leaned against the wall, weakened. His face was turned toward the front door, his eyes wide, as he heard the anxious sounds of cars pulling up outside.

He lurched toward the kitchen.

Rocky and Bell and the FBI agent jumped out of the car and moved forward across the front yard of Odom's house. They had seen Calabrini and Matthews move toward the front door. Rocky saw Calabrini suddenly flinch and crouch down, Matthews beside him on the grass, weapons pointed toward the door. At the same time she heard what sounded like shots, muffled, coming from inside the house.

Everyone in the front yard froze for a few seconds, stunned. Then Calabrini started for the door, yelling, 'Inside! Move! Rocky, you and Bell cover the back!' Matthews followed Calabrini inside the house at a run, gun drawn and ready.

They stepped over the briefcase just inside the door, scanned the living room, and looked down the hallway. They were tense, hot, their weapons pointing where they looked. They saw the body lying on the carpet, the right arm outstretched, holding the silenced revolver in a gloved hand. Matthews stepped over the body, leaned into the room at the end of the hallway, and said, 'Holy shit'.

They did not hear the sighing of the kitchen door as it was opened and closed.

Rocky Springfield was at a dead run as she moved across the wet grass along the side of the house, heading for the pool patio area. Bell Peoples was slightly behind her, to her left, and the FBI agent followed them both. They were all breathing hard, their eyes wide.

Rocky made it to the rear yard, by the pool patio, and looked down toward the seawall and the dark canal. She saw nothing. Then something moved off to her left, and she turned, her small 38-caliber revolver warm in her hand.

Bell whispered, 'Rocky, I'll move right, down the edge of the yard and toward the canal. I'll be able to watch the whole rear yard area from there.'

Rocky nodded, tense. She looked over her shoulder at the sweaty face of the young FBI agent and said quietly, 'Go with her. Do what she says.'

He gave an affirmative shake of his head, and he and Bell moved off.

The killer made it to the seawall, fighting the pain, almost doubled up, limping. He started to move to his left, heard yelling from there, and caught the flicker of movement at the end of the canal in that direction. They were moving in on him. He reminded himself with a grunt that he wasn't the only cop on FLPD who was tough, who was good, who was combat-oriented. They were moving in on him and they were hot. He decided to move to his right, one yard or so, and then slip into the dark waters of the canal. From there he would have a chance.

Then the pain gripped him, and he went down on his knees. The world spun crazily for a moment, and he tasted his own blood in his mouth. It was his life's blood, he realized, and he knew then with that sweet certainty that he would go no farther. He knew one of the slugs in his chest had reached his heart, and he thought. So soon?

He choked back a painful sob and leaned back, his face toward the star-filled night sky. With his right hand he reached into his waist and brought out the two patches he had tucked there earlier. He looked down at them in his gloved hand, each a small piece of cloth that meant so much, and marveled at how fast he could feel his life slipping away.

Rocky moved swiftly through the shadows toward where she had glimpsed the flicker of movement. She felt tight but ready, her breathing quick and shallow but the gun steady in her hand. She moved around a group of bushes in a half crouch, trying to cover as much ground as she could and still not miss anything, and she almost bodily ran into Tim McShaun, kneeling in the grass in the darkness, near the seawall.

She jumped back, still in her crouch, her gun in front of her, startled.

She saw the gun in his hand, and the gloves and the camouflage. And she knew. A storm of realization hit her, and she knew why he was there and what he had done.

Like a fist, she was impacted by the immediate awareness that the nightmare she had tried to chase away had become reality. She knew that all the weeks of speculation and gnawing suspicion and agonizing wonder had become The Now.

She saw the Ruger, tight in his hand, and saw that, still on his knees, he held the weapon comfortably, easily capable of killing with it. She felt the solid weight of her own gun in her hand, the short barrel pointed at him, her finger already tightening on the trigger. In a crashing, whirling vortex, the thoughts that had plagued her for so long seared her mind with breathtaking clarity. He had told her so long ago . . . . She would know in her heart when it was time to shoot, when it was time to kill.

She saw the gun move in his hand and she tensed.

Their eyes locked, and for a timeless second her entire being was consumed by the conflict in her heart and the image of him. Then she recognized pain in his eyes, and the sadness, the inevitability . . . She saw him start to fall, a tiny trickle of dark blood at the corner of his mouth as he smiled.

She whispered, 'No!' ignored the gun in his hand and her own, and moved forward and caught him, kneeling with him and cradling against her. Her eyes filled with tears as she cried softly, 'Oh, Tim . . . Tim . . . why?'

He lifted his eyes to hers; sleepy, peaceful eyes. He gently caressed her face with his gaze, then coughed slightly and said, 'Hey, Rocky. It's all right now. It's . . . all right . . . I . . .'

His eyes closed and he was very still.

Rocky held him tightly to her, swaying back and forth and crying, 'No, Tim, not yet . . . not yet Tim . . .'

The soft night sounds were broken by urgent voices, and she turned her head quickly toward the back of the house. She heard Calabrini call her name, a worried sound. She heard Matthews's harsh voice, saying, 'I'm telling you, John . . . I'm sure it's the same syndicate guy we've had a make on from another hit just a few months ago . . .'

She looked into McShaun's face, his eyes closed, his mouth in a small pout, as if asleep, and she said quietly, in a tone of mild and loving reproach, 'Tim McShaun . . . in the middle of the action again, off duty, but still in the thick of things, still showing up on the job, even when you're not supposed to be there.' She shook her head and wept.

She heard Calabrini then, closer. 'Here comes Peoples, and your young agent. Where the hell is Rocky!' A pause. 'Anyway, that hard-guy in there definitely wasted the other two . . . and wait till I tell Rocky what we found clutching in his coat pocket!'

Rocky looked down at Tim's right hand and saw the FLPD patches in his palm. With a quick look over her shoulder she gently pulled them out of his fist and tucked them into her blouse, warm against her breast, out of sight.

She knelt there then, holding him, and was quietly surrounded by the others. They held their breath and stared in silence at the picture of them, huddled together in the warm night, while she cried softly and said his name over and over again.

THE END